PRIDE

&

Preston
Lin

PRIDE

&

Preston Lin

Christina Hwang Dudley

THIRD
STATE
BOOKS

SAN FRANCISCO

THIRD
STATE
BOOKS

Third State Books
93 Cumberland Street
San Francisco, CA 94110
Visit us at www.thirdstatebooks.com

First edition: March 2024

ISBN 979-8-89013-004-4 (trade paperback original)
979-8-89013-005-1 (e-book)
979-8-89013-006-8 (audiobook)

Library of Congress Control Number: 2023950672

Cover and text design by Kathryn E. Campbell
Printed in Canada by Friesens Corporation

To Scott,

in memory of our days

on the Farm.

CHAPTER 1

I t was a fact of life that if anyone worth looking at came into the restaurant, Auntie Rhoda put him in Jenny's section. Rhoda didn't care if it meant double- or even triple-sitting her oldest niece, and she didn't care if her second niece, Lissie, was just sitting around rolling silverware. Good-looking young men went to Jenny.

There were two reasons for this: first, Jenny had graduated from college, and God knew when Lissie ever would; and second, Jenny Cheng was beautiful and therefore ought to be, as Lissie put it, "the face of the franchise." Not that there was more than one Four Treasures restaurant. Starting this one seven years earlier had taken every penny Auntie Rhoda and Uncle Mason had, and pennies hadn't been plentiful to begin with.

Therefore, giving any and every eligible young man a chance to fall in love with Jenny just made sense, while families with kids who dropped half their food on the floor, picky middle-aged Peninsula women who asked for ingredient substitutions, and tired couples with nothing to say to each other were earmarked for Lissie.

But this Saturday night was an exception. One of the local tech rock-star founders was having a banquet for his board, in celebration of some milestone, and despite the hoodies they loved to wear, you never knew which one might turn out to be an actual billionaire. "Sixteen people, Jenny!" Auntie crowed. "Maybe one of them is single. Maybe two!"

"Is Lissie going to help me?" asked Jenny, as calm as Auntie Rhoda was excited. "Sixteen is a lot."

"No. Jeremy will help you," Auntie replied, frowning as she did lately when she mentioned their cousin.

"You trying to marry him off now, too?" Lissie grinned, glancing up from the booth closest to the kitchen doors, where Auntie always placed diners she hoped wouldn't come back again. All the silverware and chopsticks were rolled neatly in Four Treasures' signature crimson napkins and stacked in a pyramid, leaving Lissie free to tap away on her laptop.

"Someone might need an intern," insisted Auntie, giving the back of Lissie's head a gentle push. "So more tables for you tonight, Lissie, and no smarty pants, okay? And no fake Chinese accent."

"It's smart aleck, Auntie Rhoda, not smarty pants."

When the doors opened at five, Lissie was doing her best Jenny Cheng imitation, trim in a black cheongsam with gold piping, her shining dark hair twirled up and jabbed with a lacquered stick. She didn't have her sister's hourglass figure, but she would do.

The Fongs came at 5:15 sharp—the Fongs came every Saturday at 5:15 sharp.

"Lissie, how are you today? You look so nice. Are you expecting a special young man?"

"There's no special young man, Mrs. Fong." It was easier to take this kind of teasing from the Fongs because they were old enough to be her grandparents.

"Lissie, you did your hair today. Is it my birthday?"

"If it is, I'll bring you a lychee pudding, Mr. Fong, but I don't know if Ray can fit a hundred candles in it."

"Aiya," complained Auntie Rhoda, who passed behind her with a stack of menus she had wiped down with Purell. "What did I say about the smarty pants?" She greeted the old couple in Chinese, which Lissie could follow because they said pretty much the same thing every week. Auntie Rhoda didn't bother seating them anymore. They went, as they always did, to the table just ahead of the rejects' one.

"How is your play coming?" Mrs. Fong asked. "You finish it yet?"

Lissie set down the teapot and slid into the booth with them. "I turned in the first act to my advisor on Thursday. If she hates it, I don't know what I'll do with what I've written since, so cross your fingers."

Mrs. Fong dutifully held up both hands with her fingers crossed, but Mr. Fong shook his head. "You should become a doctor, like your sister. A smart girl like you. Why do you waste your time writing things?"

This, too, was a familiar interchange. "Jenny isn't a doctor yet, Mr. Fong. She's a medical assistant at Stanford Hospital while she studies for her MCATs. And I can't be a doctor because of my overactive gag reflex, remember? No one wants a doctor who barfs on them."

"The world needs English majors, too," Mrs. Fong told her husband. She patted Lissie's hand with her frail, dry one.

"Fifth year of school!" he groused, as if he were footing the bill. "How long can it take to study grammar and punctuation?"

"And literature," Lissie reminded him. "Don't forget the literature part. And be nice, Mr. Fong, or I'll put my finger in your mapo tofu."

"It was good you changed your major," said Mrs. Fong solemnly, now abandoning her supportive position. "Even if it means you take five years or more to graduate. Drama was no good. Drama is for fun, not for spending your aunt and uncle's money."

"I know, I know, Mrs. Fong." Even if they didn't bring it up weekly, it didn't take much for the guilt to operate on Lissie. She knew her Auntie Rhoda and Uncle Mason had never expected to be saddled with the three Cheng girls. They'd put all their chips on their son, Jeremy, and the Four Treasures and called it good. But first Jenny and Lissie's mother died of cancer, and then their father, Auntie Rhoda's older brother, in a car crash, and the next thing the Liangs knew, the three nieces were their responsibility. Jenny was already a freshman at Santa Clara University by that time and Lissie a senior at Milpitas High School with a couple years' worth of tuition savings in her 529, but little JoJo was only eight when it all went down.

"I'm trying not to spend all their money," Lissie said. "This isn't my only job, you know, and Jenny and I have two other roommates to split the rent on our apartment."

Mr. Fong sucked in his breath, and Lissie cursed inwardly for mentioning the roommates. They had no objection to Melanie Espinosa, who was Filipina and—more to the point—a *girl*, but they disapproved of Nelson Nguyen. A boy. Even Lissie's assurances that Nelson was gay didn't help matters, so the less said about the Cheng girls' living situation, the better.

"Where's Jenny tonight?" Mrs. Fong tactfully changed the subject.

"There's a banquet in the Golden Dragon Room, so she and Jeremy are working that, and I get her tables."

"Banquet! Better put our order in, Lissie, before everyone gets here."

"Mr. Fong, Carlos and Ray start cooking your food the second you walk in the door. I bet your soup is already in the window."

"Then go get it. We want to be home in time for *Jeopardy!*"

Lissie obeyed with a grin. The game show wouldn't be on for two hours, so it looked like the Fongs would be doing their usual camping out. Not that she minded, especially tonight, if she was going to have twice as many tables.

By six o'clock, the Four Treasures was full and the walk-in list was forty-five minutes deep.

"Lissie," hissed Auntie after seating a six-top in David's section (David got the Chinese-speaking customers, who were always disgusted by Lissie's broken, preschooler Mandarin), "go tell that person she can't hang her coat on your uncle's terra cotta warrior."

Sighing, Lissie braced herself. She marched over and plucked the light wool jacket from the warrior's concrete spear. "May I hang this up for somebody?" she asked loudly, turning in a circle.

"Oh, excuse me," blurted a young man, darting forward. "That's all right. I'll hold it."

He was a good-looking guy—medium height with a wave to his

jet-black hair and a deprecating smile that hinted at shyness gotten over sometime in adulthood. Definitely Auntie Rhoda would have sat him at a Jenny table, which meant Lissie would get him tonight.

"This belongs to your date?" she asked, knowing Auntie would be affronted if Lissie didn't pump some information out of him.

"It's my sister's. She's in the restroom."

Sister? Even better.

"Are we getting closer to the top of the list?" he asked. "We didn't make reservations. I told my friend and his mom—the rest of our party—that it'd be a long wait without reservations." He nodded in the direction of the leather-upholstered benches. The guy indicated had his head down and was looking at his phone, but he was lean and had the broad shoulders of an endurance athlete who spent time in the weight room. The mom stood nearby on a call. In her heels, knit suit, and silk scarf, she was easily the most elegantly dressed person in the restaurant.

"Just four in your party? Tell me the name and I'll check."

"Bing. Charles Bing."

Auntie Rhoda was one step ahead of her, torn between delight and frustration. "Why tonight? Why does this handsome young man come tonight, when Jenny is busy? I will seat them soon. After the soup is cleared from the Dragon Room, and she and Jeremy deliver the main courses. Then she can at least come by the table. She can refill their water. Or take their drink order. Or deliver their complimentary appetizer. Okay. Go away now. Don't you see table eight wants to pay? We need their spot."

But Auntie Rhoda didn't anticipate the constant demands placed by the banqueters, and when the Bing party was finally seated—prominently, at a table two-thirds of the restaurant-goers would have to pass on the way to their own seats—Jenny was nowhere to be found.

Lissie grabbed the water pitcher.

"Good evening. Welcome to the Four Treasures. My name is Lissie and I will be your server. Is this your first time with us?"

Charles Bing smiled at her, but the others barely glanced up from their menus. "Yes, this is our first time, but I feel like we've already met."

At this, his sister's head jerked up and she looked Lissie over. She was not nearly as attractive as her brother, her hair lank and her eyes too prominent.

"He and I spoke about your coat," Lissie explained. "I think you were in the restroom."

"Oh," Sister Bing responded, losing interest. "What is everyone having to drink? Mrs. Lin, did you want to order a bottle of wine?"

Up close, Lissie thought Mrs. Lin could pass for an older sister to them. She favored Sister Bing with a smile but then touched her son on the shoulder. He stiffened ever so slightly, and she withdrew her hand. "This is my son's night. What would you like, Preston?"

He turned the page of the menu. "No wine for me, but you guys do whatever. I'll be having a beer."

"A beer! What a great idea, at this . . . casual place." Mrs. Lin turned to Lissie. "What beers do you have?"

"Tsingtao and Yanjing."

Preston Lin finally raised his head, and she got a good look at him. He was—well, he was very, very handsome. And really big, Lissie realized, now that he straightened up. Like somewhere in his gene pool were those freakishly tall Chinese basketball players from who-knows-where that turned up at the Olympics every four years and then sank back into the gene pool of their billion compatriots. His size must come from his father's side because his mother was no Amazon. He had longer hair than Charles Bing's, and it was a shade darker, but his eyes were more brown than black. To these features he added a long nose and strong jaw. Make that a strong everything.

Jenny's got to see this one if I have to drag her out of the Golden Dragon Room myself, thought Lissie. *And Auntie Rhoda will kill me if I don't remember the two guys' names so she can Internet stalk them.*

"That's it?" the overly hot Preston demanded in a low voice. "Just Tsingtao and Yanjing?"

It was on the tip of Lissie's tongue to retort, "That's it, apart from the fifty-seven other beers I didn't bother mentioning," but she swallowed it with a practiced smile. "Only Tsingtao and Yanjing, I'm afraid. But they're good."

He grimaced. "Are they at least on tap?"

Oh, yippee. A beer snob. Lissie succeeded in not saying this aloud. Honestly, Auntie Rhoda didn't give her half enough credit.

"In the bottle," she smiled and smiled.

Beer Maestro shrugged. "I guess I'll have a Tsingtao, then."

Just look at you, not sweating the small stuff!

"Perfect. Any beverages for the rest of you?"

"You know, a Tsingtao sounds great," said Charles Bing, and Lissie silently blessed him.

"Make it three," added his sister.

"I, on the other hand, will do a glass of Chardonnay," Mrs. Lin said. Clearly her son's beer nitpickiness did not descend to him *ex nihilo*. "I am sorry about your father's business trip, Preston. He would have insisted we go somewhere a little . . . fancier. Not that you didn't choose a nice place, Charles."

Poor Charles looked uncomfortable. Preston said nothing.

Affecting deafness, Lissie announced, "I'll have those right out." And she meant to. It wasn't like servers could go around punishing every customer who annoyed them, but Lissie did have twice as many tables as usual, which meant Auntie Rhoda couldn't help double-sitting her. It was two cash-outs and one serving and one more drink order before she could pour the wine and grab the Tsingtaos from the refrigerator and make it back to the Bing party.

"Sorry about that! Busy night, and we're a little short-staffed." Lissie set down their glasses and expertly flipped off the bottle caps. "Can I answer any questions about the menu? Are we celebrating a special occasion tonight?"

"Very special," Mrs. Lin answered, with a lift of her chin and a determined glance at her son.

"A birthday?" guessed Lissie.

Preston shook his head and made a dismissive gesture with one hand. "Nah."

But Charles Bing said, "No, come on! This is totally a special occasion." Sister Bing clapped her hands, and Mrs. Lin looked at her son harder, as if willing him to indulge her.

"Let's just be cool about this," said Mr. Man-of-the-Hour.

"Oh, don't spoil their fun," urged Lissie. "I'll get it out of you. Let me see . . . so it's not your birthday. And most people celebrating an anniversary do tend to bring their spouse—"

"Unless they had a bad year," said Preston, the twitch of a grin flitting across his face.

Mrs. Lin's and Sister Bing's brows knit identically, but his friend openly laughed.

"You're completely cold," Charles Bing pronounced. "But keep trying."

"A big promotion, then?"

"Warmer!" Charles struck the table.

"Ooh, I'm warmer," said Lissie. "Gosh, let me see . . . it must mean . . . " She gave a dramatic gasp. "You finally made Eagle Scout?"

"He's clearly too old for that," snapped Sister Bing, losing patience.

"All those merit badges," replied Lissie. "It can be a long wait."

"As *we* are waiting," said Mrs. Lin with a raise of her penciled brows, "to order."

Charles leaped in. "Sorry, Mrs. Lin. Preston here is too modest—Lissie, was it?—but he's starting a microbiology and immunology Ph.D. program at Stanford, and the first article he ever got listed on as an author was just accepted by the journal *Cell!*"

"No way!" cried Lissie. Not for nothing was she an ex-drama major. "That's much harder than being an Eagle Scout. In fact, that's incredible. Congratulations."

"Are you a big fan of the journal?" asked Preston dryly.

"Lifetime subscriber. Okay, maybe not really, but I'm a big celebration fan. After your meal, would you like the lychee pudding we bring

8

out for birthdays?"

"Only if it's the same one you bring out for making Eagle Scout."

"The exact same. And David and I could sing to you." She indicated the other waiter with her pen.

"There's a song?"

"I'd think of something," said Lissie. "Maybe 'Happy Academic Achievement to You?'"

She thought amusement flickered across his face again, but it was gone before she could be sure. "That's a mouthful," he said. "I almost dare you to do it."

"Except I have so many tables tonight," she sighed. "Which means there would only be time for the first ten verses."

"This is all very funny," Mrs. Lin interrupted, "but may we begin our order?"

"Right-o." Lissie flipped open her pad, all business. "Tonight's special is—"

"No special," Mrs. Lin cut her off with a raised hand. "Because it's prawns, and Hazel has a shellfish allergy."

"Glad you mentioned it!" returned Lissie, noting Sister Bing's real name. "Are there any other allergies we should know about? Gluten? Peanuts? No? All right, then, did you want to start with anything?"

As if on cue, Auntie Rhoda sailed up and deposited a dish of cucumber-sesame salad on the table. "Compliments of the house." She laid a casual hand on Lissie's shoulder and pressed down, which meant she'd overheard the smartassery and wanted her to dial it back. "Is our Lissie taking good care of you? May I recommend the special tonight? Sichuan pepper prawns."

"Prawn allergy." Lissie scooted out from her aunt's grip. "And I've got it."

"She's doing a great job," volunteered Charles Bing. "And thanks for the cucumbers."

Auntie Rhoda gave a little bow and zipped away again, but Lissie knew she'd gotten a good look at the young men and was going to slip into the Golden Dragon Room and see if she could pry Jenny loose, even for thirty seconds.

But Lissie wasn't out of the woods yet. Ordering was its own adventure. Mrs. Lin had particular dishes in mind, which she asked for by their Chinese names, whether or not Lissie understood and whether or not they were on the menu. Lissie knew the words for "beef" and "Chinese cabbage" and "fish" and "rice," but that only got her so far, and Mrs. Lin's eyes glinted fiercely when Lissie asked for the second time if she could please point at the requested items on the menu.

"Just ask her in English, Mom," said Preston after this went on a minute, and even Charles Bing got in on the action, barking out at appropriate moments the translations "chili peppers," "braised," and "eggplant" like he was on a game show.

"This is a Chinese restaurant, and this is Chinese food!" Mrs. Lin insisted.

But at last, at last, it was done.

"All good?" asked David, when Lissie was punching the order into the terminal a few minutes later. "I thought I was going to have to come rescue your illiterate ass."

"Could you please, please, please run the food to nine for me? Because six is up too, and I see Auntie giving me the evil eye."

Later, when Lissie tried to recall where everything had gone wrong, she wondered if it was that her attention was divided in too many directions that night, or if it was the bilingual ordering ordeal, or that Preston Lin was so unsettling, or that his mom had decided to hate her. Whatever the cause, the one thing utterly clear was that it was her fault. Because Mrs. Lin, however unpleasant she might have been, had also been utterly clear. Hazel Bing had a shellfish allergy. End of story.

The first thing Lissie knew of her big mistake was an, "Oh! Oh, no! Oh, God!" She looked over—everyone in the Four Treasures looked over—and there was Hazel, her hands to her lips, her fingertips patting frantically at the sudden swelling she found there. Not just swelling, but also spreading redness. Lips, eyelids—she looked like someone with a rashy sunburn who'd done too many filler shots.

"Oh, no—no!" Before Lissie put two and two together and slammed down the little plastic tray with the Amex and payment slip at four, every person in the restaurant was staring, dumbstruck, and Auntie Rhoda and Uncle Mason were weaving and scrambling toward the scene of the crime.

"Hazel!" cried Mrs. Lin, the serving spoon in her hand clattering to the dish. "What is happening?"

"It's her allergy!" Preston Lin accused, rising from his chair and throwing down his napkin. "We told our waitress! One of these dishes must contain shellfish."

"We are so sorry . . . so sorry," Auntie Rhoda and Uncle Mason were floundering. "Should we call an ambulance?"

Hazel shook her head furiously while she groped for her purse.

And then, just as Lissie reached the table, there was Jenny beside her. Calm Jenny. Blessed Jenny. She bent down beside Hazel, handing her some ice in a washcloth and asking her murmured questions.

"Ambulance?"

"No."

"Do you have an EpiPen?"

"No. No need."

"Then Benadryl and ice and time will do the trick. Can I help you to the restroom? I may have Dramamine in my purse because I get carsick easily."

Jenny whisked Hazel off to the Liangs' private bathroom, Hazel pressing the ice to her lips, her head bent toward Jenny's shoulder. But the show wasn't over yet for the rest of the Four Treasures customers. Poor Uncle Mason found himself berated by both Mrs. Lin and her son, while Charles Bing looked on, distressed by the conflict.

"Food allergies are dangerous things—thank God hers isn't so severe, though hives and swelling are bad enough. But you might have killed her!"

"She was very clear with the server, who was too busy flirting and cracking jokes to pay proper attention."

"I've got this, Mom."

"What? It's true!" insisted Mrs. Lin. "She *was* flirting!"

"There was a lot going on, Mrs. Lin," Charles added. "I think Hazel will be okay. Preston, I'm sure they realize the seriousness now."

"Did you or did you not hear us tell you she has a shellfish allergy?" demanded Preston Lin, looming over Lissie as she slunk up to the table. If she'd had a tail it would have been between her legs.

"I did hear. I am so sorry. I can't tell you how sorry I am," said Lissie. Her panicked mind had run through the order again. "It must have been—I mean—I completely forgot there was shrimp paste in the pork belly with ong choy. It's like a teaspoon, but I should have remembered. I own it. I am so sorry. Mr. Liang—" she added to her uncle, not wanting to burden him additionally with acknowledging his relation to her, "I take full ownership of this."

"This is very bad, Elisabeth," her uncle frowned. "Very careless. Very dangerous."

"She's never done it before!" hollered Mrs. Fong across the room. "It's too busy tonight. Too much to ask. Very distracted. We distracted her."

"I noticed when we entered that this restaurant has only received a rating of 'Good' from the health department," Preston Lin continued inexorably, "so carelessness toward food allergies might only be symptomatic of a more general indifference to—"

"It so happens 'Good' is a perfectly acceptable passing grade," Lissie interrupted hotly. Suddenly she was between her uncle and this big, stupid Ph.D. person trying to throw his weight around. His mother apparently was willing to let her son do the heavy lifting—she stood back with arms crossed and lips tight—but Lissie couldn't leave her uncle to take the blame. What if her negligence got the health department on their case? Or what if this self-righteous lordling or his silk-scarfed mother who thought the Four Treasures wasn't fancy enough sued Auntie Rhoda and Uncle Mason?

Auntie put a vise grip on Lissie's elbow, but Lissie was too upset for caution, and she yanked herself free. "I already admitted it was my mistake, so if you want to blame someone, blame me."

"Oh, I do blame you," he answered.

"Oh! Then I'm betting it'd make you feel better if I were fired?"

"Fired?" echoed Uncle Mason and Auntie Rhoda.

"You can't fire her!" called Mrs. Fong, trying to struggle up from her booth, even while Mr. Fong had her by the wrist.

"Surely firing her won't be necessary—" interceded Charles Bing, but his friend turned on him. "Bing, think about it. The next time they let this happen to someone, it might be *fatal.*"

Whirling to face her aunt and uncle, Lissie burst into tears, which wasn't hard to do because she was furious and mortified. Then she snatched up Hazel Bing's napkin to bury her face in it, peeking at Auntie Rhoda beyond the edge of it to give her a significant look.

Auntie Rhoda caught on. She would have made a respectable drama major herself, because the next instant, she pulled herself up coldly. "Yes, Mason, she must be fired. Such sloppiness. Dangerous. And please," her look sliding from the irate Preston Lin to his stone-faced mother, "this dinner will be on the house, as will your next visit to the Four Treasures. As for you, Elisabeth, take your things and go home."

"Yes, Mrs. Liang," Lissie sniffled.

Before she went, however, she addressed the table one final time. "Please excuse me, and if I don't see her again, extend my sincere apologies to the young lady with the allergy."

"You can do it yourself," said Preston Lin, sounding appeased and calmer, now that he had gotten his way and exacted revenge. Jenny and Hazel were returning, and, if Hazel's swelling had not gone down, it was at least not worse, and the hives were less angry. But more important, she was nodding at something Jenny was saying and even managed a half smile with her tightened lips.

"I had antihistamines!" announced Jenny cheerfully. "And the ice is soothing it a little. Once everything kicks in, she should be feeling better."

"Jenny works at Stanford Hospital as a medical assistant," Auntie Rhoda announced proudly, with a touch of defiance. "Thank you, Jenny."

"Amazing," breathed Charles Bing, but he was looking at Jenny, rather than his sister.

"There, Hazel," murmured Mrs. Lin tenderly, coming to put an arm around her. "It will be all right. Preston and I spoke up for you, and the careless girl has been fired."

A tiny gasp escaped Jenny, and she sought her sister's eyes, but Lissie refused to look at her. Heaven knew, if the Lins discovered anyone else related to the villainous waitress, Mr. White Knight might run them through as well.

"Thank you," muttered Hazel, through her thickened lips.

"And that's my cue," whispered Lissie. Hunching into what she hoped was invisibility, she went to gather a few of the dishes, including the murderous one with the teaspoon of shrimp paste, but her aunt hissed, "Leave it, leave it."

Lissie didn't need to be told twice. Spinning on her heel to escape, she ran straight into stupid Preston Lin, standing like the Rock of Gibraltar in her path. His chest being only slightly less rock-like than his presence, Lissie ignominiously bounced off and would have stumbled into the table had his hand not flashed out to steady her.

This only made her angrier, and while she blurted her thanks through gritted teeth, her glare told a different story. And it worked! He must have seen his life flash before his eyes because he released her instantly and backed up a step, lifting apologetic palms. *That's right, mister—you better not meet me down a dark alley.*

Mrs. Fong tried to intercept her on the way back to the kitchen, but Lissie shook her head quickly and vanished through the swinging doors.

She couldn't go home, of course, because Jenny was her ride, but her sister swapped roles, hiding Lissie away in the Golden Dragon Room until closing.

Hours later, when they were headed down El Camino Real in Jenny's old Civic hatchback, and Auntie Rhoda and Uncle Mason had told Lissie not to show up again for a couple weeks, Lissie told her sister the whole sorry tale. "That Preston Lin and his mom didn't have to be such jerks about it! They acted like I tried to kill that girl on purpose! Not that I didn't already think they were jerks, after Tsingtao-gate."

"Charles Bing didn't seem like a jerk," ventured Jenny.

"Well, no, he was nice enough, except for the company he kept."

"And you really could have killed someone, Lissie."

"Am I denying it?" she demanded. "How many times can I say I'm sorry and *it's totally my fault?*"

"Maybe just a few more times than you think you need to," Jenny laughed. "But I have to ask: do you think you subconsciously did it on purpose?"

"Tried to kill Hazel Bing *on purpose?*" squeaked Lissie. "She wasn't even the one who was obnoxious about the beer!"

"No, not because anyone was obnoxious about the beer." Jenny reached over and squeezed her sister's forearm. "Maybe you subconsciously did it because you have a secret fear you'll end up working at the Four Treasures the rest of your life?"

"I don't have that fear," objected Lissie. "Because no way will I work at the Four Treasures the rest of my life."

"It's just my fear, then." Jenny said ruefully. "If I don't get into med school."

"You'll get into med school," insisted Lissie. "Don't think like that. One day we are going to shake the five-spice powder off our feet and never look back. Okay?"

"Okay," but Jenny was smiling now.

"Though the tips aren't bad," Lissie mused. "And every actor and playwright waits tables at some point. It's like a rite of passage."

"Well, you're on hiatus from your rite of passage for a couple weeks," Jenny pointed out. "Do you think you can make it up with more hours at the library?"

"Maybe, if someone needs a shift covered. But it's fine. It'll give me more time to work on my play. And I could drive JoJo's swim carpool for Auntie Rhoda. Guilt-chauffeuring. But really, Jen, do you think I need to sit out two whole weeks? What are the odds my sad little victims come back for that complimentary meal? Wouldn't that be like admitting it wasn't such a big deal after all?"

Jenny bit her lip. "I think they'll come back. At least some of them."

"You do? Which some of them? And why are you trying not to smile?"

That did it. The smile bloomed across her sister's beautiful face, and she elbowed Lissie playfully. "I guess I mean I think Charles Bing will come back, whether or not any of the rest of them do."

Lissie gaped. "Why do you think that?"

"Because after you were gone, when his friends were headed out, I was busing the table, and he came back."

"No."

"Yes. And he asked for my number."

CHAPTER 2

A Doom of One's Own
by Elisabeth Cheng

Act I, Scene 1

Outside the Lu family McMansion, next door to the Bian family tear-down. Present day.

Mrs. Lu enters, emerging from the McMansion, dressed expensively.

Mrs. Lu

Aside to audience

It is a truth universally acknowledged that a boy is something to brag about, but a girl is a blessing. At least, that's what I told Mrs. Bian, when she had her first, second, and third girls. Those Bians! Thrice blessed, I guess, but still nothing to brag about.

Mel pushed her glasses up on her nose. "'A boy is something to brag about'—God, where'd you get that, Lissie?"

"My Auntie Rhoda said it to my mom when she had Jenny."

"That's cold."

"I think she thought she was being comforting."

"That's why it's cold. She thought your mom needed to be comforted for having a healthy baby girl? That's so old school. So one-child policy." Mel's glasses slid down in indignation. They were non-glasses anyhow, the prescription hardly stronger than demo pairs at the optometrist's.

"My mom thought it was funny," said Lissie. She frowned at the sentence she'd just written and then deleted it. "And she would think it was even funnier now because Jeremy is going through a hopeless phase, either sleeping or playing video games when he isn't at the restaurant, and definitely *not* working on his grad school applications. It drives Auntie nuts."

"So if Jeremy isn't anything to brag about, good thing *you're* such a blessing, Lis, almost killing her customers."

"Yeah, all right. Point taken. Keep reading, Espinosa."

Melanie slumped back across the sofa cushions. "I can't. I'm still stuck on this opening speech. If this is supposed to be *Pride and Prejudice*, why are you giving Lady Lucas the famous line—or your spin on the famous line?"

"Mrs. Lu, not Lady Lucas," corrected Lissie. "And this is supposed to be *Pride-and-Prejudice*-y, not straight up. Mrs. Lu opens the play because she's the Greek chorus. You know, she comes onstage from time to time and gossips with the audience about the Bian family. Get it?"

"Hmm." Mel took off her non-glasses and stared up at the water-stained popcorn ceiling. With her fake lashes, her huge eyes looked like sea anemones.

"Okay," she said, "but in the book, Lady Lucas is irritated about her daughter Charlotte getting married first, so you can't have her throwing shade at Mrs. Bennet—Mrs. Bian, I mean—for not having a boy when she didn't manage to have one either."

This was why Lissie's roommate was always her first reader. They'd met the first day of class, in Literatures of the Atlantic World, 1680–1860. Mel's laptop froze, and Lissie lent her a piece of paper and a pen, but the pen had no ink, so Lissie took notes for them both. They'd been inseparable English major besties ever since.

"I know Lady Lucas doesn't have a son in the book, but I gave Mrs. Lu one," Lissie explained. "We never see the guy, but they talk about him. He made an app that he sold for a buttload of money, but he still lives at home, and everyone in the family waits on him hand and foot. That's why Charlotte is dying to get out of the house."

"Ha! I like it."

"Good. Because in the real *Pride and Prejudice*, Elizabeth always thinks Charlotte is such a sellout, but I think she actually shows a lot of agency. She *makes* her opportunities, you know? She grabs Mr. Collins because no one else wants him, and by doing so she gets her own establishment and sets it up the way she likes it. She makes lemonade out of lemons. I mean, if Elizabeth hadn't gotten Darcy—and she almost didn't—what would have happened to her? A lifetime of being stuck at home with Mrs. Bennet and Mary probably, because those two sure weren't going anywhere. Charlotte Lucas *chooses* her doom, but Elizabeth just lucks into hers."

"I get it," Mel said, sitting up in excitement and tucking her legs under her. "I like it! In fact, you should cast someone totally hot as Mr. Collins and turn the whole story inside out."

"Yeah, except that completely wouldn't make any sense, Mel, because if Mr. Collins is so hot, then why wouldn't Jane or Elizabeth want him?"

"Oh—right." She shrugged. "Scratch that. Are you still making him a clergyman, though?"

"He's an engineer who volunteers at their Chinese church and is the special pet of the pastor's wife."

"Awesome!" Mel sang. "So what are you making Darcy in contrast? A neurosurgeon?"

Lissie grinned. "He was, in my earlier draft. But now he's meta-morphosed into a Ph.D. scientist type. You know—he could have become a doctor, but he hates people, so he sticks to research."

"I see what you're doing there," Mel nodded, her dark curls bobbing. "Turn your pain into art, girl."

"Except I'm not in pain."

"You're totally in pain. You poison the girlfriend of this bigshot Stanford Ph.D., and he gets you pretend-fired? That's pain."

"No, that's a serendipitous sabbatical," insisted Lissie. "With a few weeks off from the restaurant, I might be able to write another whole act. Besides, I don't think she was his girlfriend. Just a friend who his mom hopes will become his girlfriend."

"If you say so," Mel drawled. "Mrs. Lin sounds like a woman who always gets her way in the end. But seriously, I'm a fan of this, Lis! I wish public speaking didn't paralyze me, or I'd beg you for a part. Especially if you cast a really hot Darcy and there was lots of kiss-ing. But I'll just have to be your ticket-taker and audience plant who laughs at all the right moments."

"You're the best. Do you think you could make me some posters on the cheap, too, at FedEx?"

"For sure. I'll make them when my boss isn't looking. But here's the thing: do you think your title is going to work? *A Doom of One's Own* doesn't sound very Chinese."

"It's Virginia Woolf."

"Duh, but she's not known for writing Asian takes on Jane Austen."

"Maybe I should use that 1950s Chinatown font on the poster so people know what they're getting," Lissie threw her roommate a frown. "I guess I could put some kind of subtitle in small print under the title: 'A Chinese American adaptation of *Pride and Prejudice*' or something."

With a laugh, Mel sprang to her feet, pulling her glasses to the very tip of her nose and clawing some of her hair down to cover her face in imitation of San Jose State's Creative Writing instructor. "Don't edit yourself when you're in creation mode, Cheng," she commanded in a hoarse smoker voice. "Don't revise. Don't censor. Get all the ideas down. Let them flow . . . "

"Okay," Lissie shook out her hands and shut her eyes, playing along. "*A Doom of One's Own*: Jane Austen Meets *Kung Fu Panda*."

"Good! More!"

"*Pride and Prejudice* meets *Crazy Middle-Class Asians*."

"Yes!"

Jenny walked through the door. "Sorry to step in front of the creative firehose, but when you guys get going there's never a good time to interrupt. Lissie, do you have plans tonight?"

"Writing and maybe bingeing *Bachelor in Paradise*. Why?"

Jenny's eyes gleamed. "Because Charles Bing invited me to a barbecue at Stanford. In the grad student housing."

"What? Let me see!" Lissie grabbed her sister's phone and swiped through the brief text thread. "This is amazing. He used three emojis, including a goofy face, and he used it unironically."

"Stop it!" Jenny plucked her phone from Lissie's hand. "He seems like a really nice guy. And he's sorry things went so sideways at the restaurant."

"I thought only Lissie went sideways," put in Mel. "Why would he want her to come with you?"

Jenny and Lissie made the identical face.

"He didn't say so, in so many words," Jenny sighed. "I just asked if I could bring a friend."

"You know the family rule," Lissie confessed. "We promised Auntie we wouldn't go to parties without each other or some other honorary sister. In case one of us is dancing topless on the tables with a lampshade on her head, the other is theoretically only mildly buzzed."

"But what if you're both topless on the table?" asked Mel. "Did your aunt think of that? Maybe I should come along. I can run interference for you, Lissie, in case Mr. Ph.D. and his wannabe girlfriend are there."

"Who says I'm going?" Lissie protested. What if they *are* there?"

"It's not a tea party, Lissie," Jenny said reasonably. "It's a barbecue.

Even if they were, you could avoid them, and they probably wouldn't even recognize you out of context. Who would expect the evil, incompetent waitress to show up on their home turf? Just leave your hair down and don't wear a cheongsam."

"But I never go anywhere without my cheongsam," cracked Lissie, looking down at her ratty T-shirt and yoga pants. "Not that I'm going."

"Please come, Lissie!" Jenny urged. "I really, really would like to see if Charles Bing is as nice as I remember."

"I do, too," Mel said. "So I'm coming, right?"

"Sure, you can come."

Sister and roommate turned on Lissie as one.

"No way," she said. "You don't need me now, with Mel going."

"You know that if the two of us go, you won't get a word written because you'll be dying of FOMO," Mel pointed out.

"Maybe," admitted Lissie. "Or at least of curiosity."

"Well, then?" Jenny made her please-please-please face again.

Lissie groaned. "You guys are the worst. This is so gonna suck."

>—❤—→

Lissie spotted Preston Lin right as her sister pulled into the parking lot in Escondido Village. He wasn't hard to pick out, even across the grassy strip—he was manning the barbecue and seemed to be half a head taller than the other students nearby, among whom, thank God, Lissie did not see Hazel Bing.

"Don't park so close!" she ordered, panicking. "Go down the other way. I knew this was a bad idea! There's that stupid Preston Lin!"

"The archenemy?" Mel swiveled in her seat as Jenny obediently backed and turned. "Where?"

"The tall one by the grill."

"Ooh!" Mel undid her seatbelt and got on her knees for a better look out the hatch window, even as Lissie doubled in half to stay out of sight. "If he wanted to yell at me just once, I might be okay with that. That is one fine young man."

"Whatever. You know what? I've changed my mind. I'm not getting out of the car."

Jenny eased the Civic into an open spot. "Don't be ridiculous. You can't just stay in here, Lissie."

"Watch me," she retorted. "I should have brought a disguise."

"Since when are you such a chicken?" Mel asked.

"Since I almost killed his wannabe girlfriend!" When her roommate cocked her head dubiously, Lissie added, "I'll be fine. Just bring me a plate of food, Mel. And something to drink. And you guys have fun. I'll work on my play. I have it in a Google doc on my phone."

Jenny and Mel shook their heads, but Lissie was already climbing into the back seat where she wouldn't be so obvious.

"I'll crack the windows," her sister sighed. "So you don't fog them up."

"Because that would be even more embarrassing," Mel snorted. "You fogging up the windows of a car. *By yourself.*" She removed her glasses and tossed them on the dash. "If you get brave enough to come out, you can put those on."

It was stupid, Lissie knew. She'd already apologized three hundred times, she'd been "fired," and presumably Hazel Bing had recovered, so if Hazel or Preston Lin were going to have a problem with her, that was on them. Clearly Charles Bing was over it, as all reasonable people would be. But had he told his friends he was inviting Jenny? He must have, right?

Her stomach growled.

"Shut up," Lissie told it. "We're not going anywhere."

Nineties R&B music added to the swell of conversation as more people gathered. They were casually dressed, the women showing less skin than Lissie was used to, and she bet Mel was the only one there with fake eyelashes. With an effort, she bowed her head over her phone, but few words came. She read through what she had so far, deleting and replacing a phrase here and there. As a distraction, she cast the play in her mind, using friends and classmates. Her roommate

Nelson wanted to be the Wickham character, but the poor guy didn't exactly scream sexy, and she was going to have to figure out some way of saying that nicely. Despite herself, her gaze wandered back to the party on the lawn, Preston Lin still highly visible.

A knock on the window made her jump.

"Hey, sorry to startle you. Jenny was going to bring you some food, but I asked if I could do it."

It was Charles Bing, bending down to grin at her.

"Oh, my gosh. Thanks!" Lissie replied, feeling like a dork to be discovered hunkered in the back seat. With the engine off, she couldn't roll down the window, so she opened the door awkwardly.

He handed her a paper plate with a burger and chips as well as a bouquet wrapped in newspaper. "The flowers are for Jenny, but she said you could look after them. And lest I forget," he whipped a beer from the inside of his jacket.

"Tsingtao," said Lissie, raising rueful eyes to his.

His grin widened. "Okay, I saw them in my neighbor's fridge and begged him to let me have a couple. I gave the other one to Preston. You remember Preston."

"Strangely, I do remember. Did he chuck the beer in the trash?"

"Nope. He did make a face, though," answered Charles. "Look, I'm sorry about how things went at the restaurant, and I feel terrible that you lost your job."

His niceness was impossible to resist, and Lissie felt bad for lying about her fake firing.

"But if you won't come join us," he went on, "I'll picture you unemployed and living in this car, and it'll be all our fault. Don't you think you should take pity on me?"

"Seriously—it's fine," Lissie insisted. "I just want to let it all blow over, if you don't mind, but it hasn't yet."

"If it makes you feel any better, my sister, Hazel, isn't here. I told Preston you might come tonight with Jenny and left it kind of vague. He said he probably wouldn't even recognize you out of context unless you got in his face or tried to kill someone else."

When she didn't answer straight away, Charles added, "He was joking about that last bit."

Lissie forced a laugh, but she felt a flicker of annoyance. What Preston Lin said was almost verbatim what Jenny had predicted an hour earlier. But it was one thing for her sister to say he wouldn't recognize her out of context and another altogether from Mister Stuck-Up Ph.D. Was he saying she was nondescript? Indistinguishable from all the other Asian internationals and Asian Americans milling around the Escondido Village lawn? He wouldn't recognize her if she weren't chasing Hazel Bing around with a tube of shrimp paste? The fact that Lissie had picked him out instantly added insult to injury.

"Thanks so much," she said, after a pause. "I'm good for now."

He rapped on the roof of the Civic. "Okay. I tried my best. Jenny said you wouldn't budge. But you can change your mind anytime. Deal?"

"Deal."

Lissie ate her hamburger and chips and drank her beer, her resolve wavering as dusk gathered and Preston Lin finally disappeared. But it was a dribble of cold water leaking from the bouquet onto her sandaled foot that finally propelled her from the car, flowers in hand to shake out the water.

The porch light of the low-rise unit nearest the parking spot flicked on with her movement, and like the fingertip of God, the beam fell across the newspaper-wrapped flowers, spotlighting a byline: *by Preston Lin.*

She froze. Squinted.

Preston Lin? Now the guy was a journalist?

Lissie drew the flowers out and laid them on the hood of the car. Then she gently opened the wet newspaper, oblivious to the rest of the droplets running down. The *Stanford Daily.* Taking a step toward the porch light, she peered at the article.

"When Will Food Allergies Be Taken Seriously?" clamored the headline.

Oh, no. This could not be happening.

She skimmed the article so fast she barely comprehended it. She almost didn't care what Preston Lin had to say about people not taking food allergies seriously. She just wanted to know if . . .

Holy cow. *He went there.*

"Now whether this incident arose through ignorance, negligence, or indifference, it was inexcusable and should never happen again. According to a study published in *JAMA Network Open*, the number of Americans suffering from food allergies continues to rise. Though the factors contributing to this rise remain unclear, over 26 million American adults suffer from food allergies, and of those, almost 3%, or nearly 780,000 people, are allergic to shellfish.

"This being the case, the carelessness of our server must not be allowed to become the norm, and I urge both food providers and allergy sufferers to prepare themselves for this new world order. Food preparers and servers need to be thoroughly familiar with the ingredients in the food they serve and give their full attention to their customers' restrictions. And allergy sufferers, sadly, should 'come prepared in all circumstances,' armed with antihistamines or EpiPens, depending on the severity of their reactions. Sometimes a prawn isn't just a prawn, and a shrimp can have jumbo consequences. Isn't it time we give people who suffer from food allergies the respect and compassion they're due?"

Oh, crap.

"This all hit too close to home a few days ago, when friends and I were dining at the Four Treasures restaurant, in Mountain View. Our server asked, in what turned out to be purely *pro forma* opening chatter, whether anyone at the table had food allergies. She was told that a member of the party was allergic to shellfish. The server then allowed us to order a dish which contained the allergen, and the afflicted party suffered the consequences. Fortunately, the victim's response was not life-threatening, but the server had no way of knowing that."

By the end, Lissie nearly broke out in hives herself. What would Auntie Rhoda and Uncle Mason say? Why hadn't Charles Bing mentioned this? Did he not know about the article or how his stupid friend had yet to dismount from his high horse and was now doing dressage on it? What if every person who read the *Stanford Daily* stopped going to the Four Treasures and told everyone they knew to stop going there? What if the whole thing snowballed from there, and the *San Jose Mercury* and the *San Francisco Chronicle* picked it up? What if every last person in the entire Bay Area got on Yelp or Google to flame Auntie Rhoda and Uncle Mason for something that wasn't even their fault?

Lissie sank back into the front seat of the car, sweating.

Couldn't Preston Lin—*that jerk*—have mentioned that the careless, ignorant, negligent, server had been fired, so no one had to be afraid anymore of dying at her hands? It'd be impossible now for her to go back to the restaurant in a couple weeks! In fact, would there even be a restaurant to return to?

"A boy is something to brag about, but a girl is a blessing," Lissie muttered. Well, Preston Lin was certainly something to brag about, with his looks and his Stanford degree and his holier-and-smarter-than-thou attitude. But what was she, except a disaster—one who might bring her whole family down with her?

CHAPTER 3

Lissie wanted to read the article online, but her phone had little battery left and browsing the Internet would quickly finish it off. She would have to plug in somewhere. This couldn't wait. The paper was several days old. Who knew how many snarky comments and bad reviews had already piled up?

Digging a charger out of the glove compartment, Lissie climbed out of the car and glanced around. It was dark. She reached for Melanie's glasses and smashed them on, almost impaling herself with the little nose pads. At least she was right about the prescription. Almost pointless.

Trash in hand, Lissie cautiously circled the barbecuers, who were now digging into a clamshell of Costco cookies and half-gallons of ice cream. Her brain noted that graduate student barbecues were not the same thing as undergraduate parties. No one looked or sounded drunk. Two people were arguing about Nietzsche. The trash can hadn't been vomited in. Half the nearby doors were open, so she might wander into any one of them in search of a random outlet, but it would be nice to know in which unit Preston Lin lurked.

She would have to take a chance. Keeping her eyes lowered as if making sure her napkin didn't slide off her paper plate, Lissie darted into the nearest open door and almost ran slap into Hazel Bing. At least, she was pretty sure it was Hazel—the lank hair, the bulging eyes. But Charles had said she wasn't here!

"Were you looking for the yard waste bin?"

"Yup, thanks," said Lissie, struggling to keep her expression neutral and speaking in a lower register than normal. She prayed Hazel wasn't one of those people who never forgot a face. Or that the Superman lame-glasses disguise really was a thing. Or that Jenny was right, and Lissie would be anonymous out of context.

Whatever the cause, Hazel, oblivious, led Lissie past the board game going on in the living room, something complicated and Settlers of Catan–like, and past the other couples and groups into the kitchen. Then she flipped open the cabinet under the sink and pointed. "Recycle. Compost. Trash."

"Thanks," said Lissie, sorting her things. "Is there a bathroom I could use?"

Hazel motioned again, this time at a door between two bedrooms, and Lissie zipped away. Locking the door behind her, she hunkered on the floor and let her heart slow. There was an outlet here, but if she plugged in, she was sure to be interrupted. A bedroom would be better.

Lissie waited for a burst of laughter from the board-game players before cracking the door and peering out. No one was looking. She chose the left bedroom, whose door was ajar.

Judging from the pictures on the desk and dresser, this was Charles Bing's room. Lissie gave herself thirty seconds to indulge her curiosity. There was a graduation photo with Hazel and his parents, another of him windsurfing, and then one of a group of guys with their arms around each other, among which Preston Lin figured prominently, though it took Lissie a moment to recognize him because of the wide, un-self-conscious smile on his face.

"So this is what you look like when you're not trying to wreak vengeance," Lissie murmured, picking up the frame to study it. "It must be exhausting to live up to your own standards."

Replacing the picture, she turned in a circle and was delighted to spot cords snaking from an outlet inside the closet. Perfect. She could charge in peace, without worrying that someone would come upon her.

A minute later, she was hooked up and connected to the Stanford visitor network, sitting comfortably on the closet floor, her feet resting on a pair of ski boots, with the door slid mostly shut. But before she could even Google "Stanford Daily," she heard heavy steps and voices. Stifling a gasp, Lissie shrunk down, pressing her phone to her chest to hide the glow.

She peeked out carefully and saw Charles Bing. "But you told me I could invite a friend or two," he said to another guy who had his back to the closet. Judging by his size and shape . . .

"I didn't mean *that friend*," snapped Preston Lin. "You didn't think to ask me before you made everything awkward?"

"How bad could it be? By next weekend it'll all be ancient history. Besides, you've survived her being here at the barbecue."

"Yeah, well, I haven't spoken with her, and it's easy enough to deal with when there are tons of people and we're not all confined to the same house. Look, she seems nice enough, and she's pretty, I'll grant you, but come on! And now you tell me she's that girl's *sister?*"

Lissie held so still she was surprised her heart continued to beat.

"Yes. Jenny is the sister of 'that girl.'" Charles gave a wry chuckle. "I am guilty of inviting the sister of Hazel's would-be killer to hang out next weekend at your advisor's place. But Jenny's the one who helped the situation, remember?"

"Did you tell Hazel you were going to invite her?"

"What for? She lived, didn't she? And I am not going to start running my potential girlfriends past my little sister. What's your problem exactly?"

If Charles Bing had no clue why his friend was so uncomfortable, did that mean he didn't know about the *Daily* article? Lissie's paralysis was loosening. She silenced her phone, lest Mel text her and give her away with the obnoxious honking sound she'd set for herself.

Preston sighed, raising his arms to run his hands through his hair, distracting Lissie despite herself by the play of muscles across his back.

"Call me crazy, but when she broke out in those hives, it was the shrimp crackers all over again."

"Dude. That was, what, second or third grade? She was barely sentient at the time. Let it go."

"I know, I know. Not everyone can blow things off like you, though."

"You mean, not everyone can obsess and overthink like you," Charles retorted.

Preston gave a rueful laugh and held up his hands. "Fine. But there's a lot going on before then. Come next weekend, I'll be dying to get away and relax, and I'm not thrilled at the idea of tiptoeing around someone because of the restaurant incident. But I get it. You can't uninvite her now."

"Attaboy," Charles gave him a playful punch. "Seriously, Jenny's great. Super chill. She's not going to bring it up if you don't. Remind me, Lin, why a guy who grew up in a giant compound in Los Altos Hills with its own lap pool and pool house needs to find another place to relax in?"

"You've met my mom."

"But she falls all over herself to make you happy."

"Maybe it's not relaxing to have someone fall all over herself to make me happy."

Charles shook his head. "I'll take your word for it."

"And now that she's got Hazel working for her, it's gonna get weird," Preston went on.

"How weird can it get?" protested Charles. "You've known each other since preschool."

"My mom wasn't hoping I'd go out with Hazel in preschool."

"Because she and my mom had already arranged your marriage."

"Very funny."

"Oh, come on. Next thing you're going to tell me, you don't want Hazel coming by Bronklin's either." Charles took a few steps toward the closet, causing Lissie's heart to leap into her throat. He stopped, bending to pluck a sweatshirt off the floor. "If you're so worried about your mom playing matchmaker, you could make the whole thing moot by picking someone yourself. Just spitballing here, but Jenny's sister isn't too bad-looking either."

"That's what they said about Amanda Knox."

His friend groaned. "Who's Amanda Knox?"

"Just get off my back." Preston turned to go, but paused in the doorway. "And if you think getting together with a negligent waitress who couldn't keep track of a few simple ingredients or understand basic Chinese would go over well with my mom, you're deluded."

With that, he went. Charles shook his head, chuckling, before grabbing something off his desk and following.

"Wake up, party animal." It was Melanie rapping on the car window. "Unlock the doors."

"What time is it?" Lissie asked, sitting up. She flipped the lock on the passenger door and rubbed her arms.

"It's 11:00, Grandma. Sorry to keep you out so late." Melanie gave a dramatic shiver. "Give me the keys. I'm going to turn on the heat."

"Where's Jenny?"

"Saying goodbye to loverboy. Here she comes."

Jenny climbed in, giving a last wave to Charles Bing. She eyed her sister in the rearview mirror. "Did you honestly sit here all night? And why do my flowers look like you dug them out of a dumpster?"

"First of all, I did not sit here all night. I got out for a little while to charge my phone. Second, you have to see this!" Lissie snatched up the newspaper as Jenny started the engine and backed out. "That stupid Preston Lin, not only did he get me fired—"

"Fake fired," Jenny corrected.

"But now he's trying to finish us off!" Lissie waved the soggy paper until Melanie grabbed it from her. "He wrote an article in the *Stanford Daily* about food allergies, mentioning the Four Treasures *by name*, and now there are already twenty-something comments on the online version and new reviews on Google and Yelp about how 'negligence like this can be fatal,' 'better safe than sorry,' and 'the pepper prawns aren't even that great,' 'that place is overrated,' and more!"

"Easy on the air quotes," warned Mel, clicking on the passenger light. "That's how you get a repetitive stress injury."

"Whoa, whoa, whoa . . . are you serious?" Jenny breathed.

Melanie read the article aloud, powering through Jenny's gasps and Lissie's snipes and giving a low whistle when she finished. "Man. That Preston Lin is so out of pocket."

"Right?" Lissie said, thumping a fist against the back of Mel's seat. "Like he's never made a mistake in his life! And now he's on some personal crusade. Why did he have to name the restaurant? Auntie Rhoda will kill me if business goes down! I've been trying to answer the reviews, saying sorry, sorry, sorry, and the idiot waitress has been fired, and everyone got signed up for remedial food allergy training."

"Oh my gosh," Jenny was still dumbfounded. "I wish he hadn't done that. I know he meant well, but—"

"Did he though?" Lissie sputtered. "Or does he just get off on being so much smarter and more conscientious than the illiterate, negligent waitress?"

"Illiterate?" repeated Mel. "Where did that come from? Negligent, yes."

"Thanks, Mel," Lissie said. Sheepishly, she recounted the conversation she overheard, which took longer than it should have because Jenny kept asking questions and Melanie kept screaming and laughing.

"You stayed in the closet listening to this?" she cackled. "That is gold, you stalker."

"What was I supposed to do, come busting out? Then I would've been the psycho."

"You should have come busting out, yelling something—anything—in Chinese," insisted Mel. "That would've shown him. What do you know how to say in Chinese?"

"Uh . . . 'I love you,' 'Have you eaten?' 'Put socks on.' What else . . . " said Lissie. "Which one would you have gone with?"

"Definitely the socks. It could've been like the Chinese version of 'Put *that* in your pipe and smoke it.' Put socks on, Preston Lin! That would have been epic."

"And what are you invited to, anyhow?" Lissie turned accusingly on her sister. "You need to think twice about consorting with the enemy."

"I'm not doing anything with the enemy. Charles Bing is not the enemy," Jenny replied. "And probably Preston Lin isn't either—he's just zealous . . . about food allergies."

"Or maybe he likes Hyperallergenic Hazel," interjected Mel.

"And he didn't stop to think about the repercussions," Jenny added.

"Or he thought about them, and he didn't care," said Lissie darkly. "But don't dodge the question. Where are you invited to?"

"Apparently Preston Lin is housesitting next weekend for his advisor in Portola Valley. The house is supposed to be amazing, and Charles invited me to go hang out."

Lissie's mouth fell open. "Just you and Charles Bing and Preston Lin? For an entire weekend?"

"No, no. There will be other people. A big potluck or something. I can't stay the whole weekend anyway. I have to study, and I'm working Friday night and Sunday night at the restaurant. I'd just go up after work Friday and probably leave again Sunday."

"That's the whole weekend," Lissie pointed out. "Friday night to Sunday is literally the whole weekend. I can't believe you'd do this."

"It might not be a bad thing," Jenny mused. "It'll give me an opportunity to smooth things over. I could apologize to Hazel again—or to Preston on Hazel's behalf, if she's not there—and tell them again how sorry we are."

"I'm less sorry by the minute," grumbled Lissie.

"We all got off on the wrong foot, Lissie, but this might be just the thing to make it better."

"And Charles Bing is pretty cute," said Mel reasonably.

Lissie frowned at her, but an embarrassed smile lit Jenny's features.

"Yeah," she admitted in a soft voice, "Charles Bing is definitely cute."

CHAPTER 4

Lissie's hope that the *Daily* article would fade away after the initial wave was dashed by Sunday night, when Auntie Rhoda's texts started blowing up her phone. *What is happening? Jenny says you can explain. What is the article? Call me. Come by tomorrow. JoJo has new swim group. Come by. Call me. Are you dead?*

"I told her you'd take JoJo to her swim practices this week," said a tired Jenny when she got home from the Four Treasures. "So you take the car, and I'll take the train and the Marguerite to the hospital."

"How was the restaurant?"

"It was weird. A lot of canceled reservations."

"More than the usual?"

"Way more," Jenny sighed. "And practically everyone who canceled was white. Or had white names, at least. It was still full, but not like a regular weekend night."

Lissie groaned into her hands. "This is all my fault. And stupid Preston Lin's for putting his Eye of Sauron on the Four Treasures. God, I could strangle him with my bare hands!"

"Just help drive JoJo, okay? And talk to Auntie Rhoda."

"Yeah, of course. I'll go over after class tomorrow, I'm out by one. And I'll drive JoJo to her practices. All of them."

"Good. That would really help, I think. Auntie Rhoda seems worried about the swimming for some reason."

The Liangs lived in Milpitas, in the house they'd always lived in, an aging tract home of beige stucco with dark brown wood trim. When Lissie was younger, she always thought of her aunt and uncle as richer than her parents. Their house was five years newer and there were more grass lawns in their cul-de-sac, whereas yards on the Chengs' street had long ago yielded to drought-induced watering restrictions, replacing thirsty turf with pavement, rocks, and succulents. After the girls' parents were gone, the Liangs sold the Cheng home. Lissie, though aggrieved, understood. At least she was a senior, in a town with only one high school, but her little sister had to change elementary schools and start over. In Lissie's file cabinet of worries and regrets was a large folder labeled "JoJo."

Lissie spent the hour between her Comp Lit seminar and her Special Topics in Shakespeare class perched on a metal picnic table outside Sweeney Hall, answering more Google and Yelp reviews. They seemed to be multiplying like bunnies, and the Four Treasures' overall star rating had dipped. "Beshrew me, if I don't start paying someone to write us good reviews," Lissie complained, hitting Send on another groveling response. She stared unseeingly in the direction of MacQuarrie Hall. It wasn't such a bad idea. She could save money by writing them herself, but with her luck, Mr. Perfect would somehow trace all the phony praise back to her IP address and write his next blazing editorial on Internet fakery. Ugh.

At 1:30 she pulled up to the Liangs' in the Civic, hoping to sit a second and gather her nerve, but the front door flew open and Auntie Rhoda marched out. "You coming in?"

"Coming."

Auntie Rhoda poured her a glass of iced tea and shoved a tin of individually wrapped cookies at her. "Okay. You tell me what is going on."

Lissie got through it with a minimum of editing (mainly not mentioning that she and Jenny had gone to the barbecue). The article became something she stumbled across while doing her monthly check on the restaurant's online accounts. Her aunt listened, stone-faced. She asked to see the article and then the reviews. Lissie obliged, pulling the article up on her phone. Auntie Rhoda read silently. Lissie felt smaller and smaller and worse and worse.

"I'm so, so sorry," she said, for what felt like the thousandth time. What more could she do? She'd apologized in person; she'd apologized on the restaurant's behalf; she apologized here again. She was willing to stay away for however long it took.

Lissie finally petered out.

In the silence, the sound of her cousin Jeremy whooping carried to their ears. He must be playing video games.

Auntie Rhoda shut her eyes briefly, and Lissie couldn't help but be glad she wasn't the only disappointment in Rhoda Liang's life. Though even Jeremy's lack of ambition took a backseat to this.

After a glance at the clock, Auntie reached for a knock-off Chinese Pirouline, the tube-shaped cookie Jenny and Lissie used to pretend were cigars when they were kids, the kind which shattered into fragments when you bit into them.

At last, she sighed. "He seemed like a nice young man."

"Who did?"

"The one who wrote the article."

"*Him?*" Lissie boggled. "That's your takeaway? How can you say that? He was yelling at me."

"So smart and handsome."

Lissie rolled her eyes. "Well, if you're hoping he'll marry Jenny, I've got to tell you it's a long shot, Auntie Rhoda."

"I know."

This uncharacteristic admission of defeat made Lissie feel worst of all. She thrust out an impulsive hand. "Tell me what I can do. I mean, besides what I'm doing. I'll keep answering the reviews, and hopefully after a while, all the scared people will come back, especially because it will never happen again. I'll be so, so careful, Auntie Rhoda."

Her aunt shook her head solemnly. "I think you should stay away for at least a few months."

"What? A few *months?* But how will you manage?"

"We will hire another server."

"But . . . but—"

"And you can help us, Lissie."

"How? By robbing a bank?" Lissie suggested glumly.

"You take care of JoJo's swimming."

"Of course," agreed Lissie at once. "I was already planning on it. I'll do all the driving and stuff for you. Jenny said she's in a new swim group."

A faint flash of pride straightened her aunt's spine. "She was moved up to Senior Prep, even though she started the year in the slow middle-school one."

"Was she? That's awesome!"

"Yes. Awesome. You know she wanted it so badly because some of her friends got moved up before her."

Lissie didn't know, but she nodded. "I'm so glad she can be with her friends again."

"But the Senior Prep is much more demanding," said Auntie Rhoda, her shoulders sagging again. "Practice six days a week, and at a later time, when I have to be at the restaurant."

Lissie swallowed. Six days a week? That was a lot of driving and a lot of time. She could bring her books and laptop along, but what would happen if she decided to produce her play? When would rehearsals happen? They just wouldn't. That would have to be her sacrifice, she realized. Rehearsals weren't going to happen because production wasn't going to happen. She kept these thoughts off her face, however, and just smiled. "Don't worry about that, Auntie Rhoda. I'm always out of class by two at the latest. I can get her to the club."

"And then there's two days of 'dry land' workouts."

Lissie swallowed. "But that makes eight days a week," she faltered.

"No, no. Two days she has longer practice because they do both."

"Oh, okay. I hope she can still get her homework done."

Her aunt's brow puckered. "And it's very expensive, Senior Prep.

All that coaching time. But JoJo loves swimming, and she is fast now."

The word "expensive" twisted the knife in Lissie's gut since she was responsible for the business slowdown. She said, with even more fake conviction, "Don't you worry, Auntie Rhoda."

But her aunt was thinking aloud. "More equipment and higher volunteer-hour requirements."

"Volunteer-hour requirements?" echoed Lissie.

"It used to be ten hours a year from a parent or guardian—your uncle would go and help keep time at the meets. But Senior Prep requires twenty-eight hours. And if you don't do them, they charge $50 for each hour you miss."

"Good grief!" Lissie blurted. "What else do they want? Her first-born child? JoJo better make it to the Olympics, at the very least." Seeing the worry on her aunt's face deepen, she slammed the lid down on her indignation. "It's fine, it's fine. This makes up for Jenny and me being total unathletic klutzes. Maybe JoJo will earn a scholarship to college. I'll figure it all out, Auntie Rhoda. It's just a few months. I'll get the lay of the land and schmooze our way into new carpools and stuff."

Her aunt's mouth opened a moment, but then she gathered herself and pushed the cookie tin at her niece again. "Better have some more. You're too skinny. So unhealthy."

Lissie sat cross-legged on the couch, having waded into the misogyny debate surrounding *The Taming of the Shrew* and wondering if she could work a reference to it into *A Doom of One's Own*, when the deadbolt turned and JoJo came in.

At least, Lissie thought it was JoJo.

It had only been, what, five days since she'd seen her? A week, tops. But something had changed in JoJo since school started. Was she taller—or maybe her skirt was shorter, making her coltish legs look like giraffe legs?

"Are you wearing makeup?" Lissie demanded.

Her sister's hand flew to her eyes even as she blurted, "No!"

"You mean you rubbed most of it off already."

JoJo tossed her backpack in the corner. "What's there to eat?"

"Auntie Rhoda made you a plate. She seems to think this new swim group is going to work you to the bone."

JoJo was already halfway to the kitchen, and Lissie had to chase after her to finish her sentence. "Gimme a hug, you little stinker!"

Lissie was right: The little stinker was suddenly not so little. She was now just two inches or so shy of Lissie, who was 5'4", and hugging her felt like embracing a collapsed patio umbrella. And Auntie Rhoda called Lissie too skinny? At least JoJo was doing her best to remedy the matter, practically inhaling the *bao* and sliced oranges she found on the table and then flinging open the fridge to dig out her plate.

"How was school?" Lissie asked, feeling suddenly mournful. She remembered the little girl who used to come running when her sisters came around.

"Fine." JoJo lifted the plastic wrap, gave a sniff, and then loaded the dish in the microwave.

"You like your classes this year?"

JoJo shrugged.

"Did you have any with your friends? With Katie?"

"Casey."

"I meant Casey."

"Social studies and P.E."

"How are the teachers?"

With a roll of her eyes that clearly indicated she thought her sister was being a bore, JoJo offered up a few things about her teachers to make it stop. Then she punched the Cancel button on the microwave and took out her food, making chattering sounds as she almost dropped the hot plate. The ceramic rang on the tile counter, and she whipped off the plastic wrap.

"Are you excited about Senior Prep?" Lissie persisted. "I'm gonna be driving you for a while, which is great because I don't think I've seen you swim since your divisional meet in the spring."

"You haven't," said JoJo flatly, "and I'm way faster now because I grew."

Another wave of bad sister guilt swamped Lissie. And it might have wrecked her had she not already been pinned to the sea floor by the restaurant incident. As it was, she was almost tempted to shrug. Once you sucked, you sucked, and there was really nowhere to go but up.

She pulled her bony sister into another hug, ignoring JoJo's non-participation. "Well, I'm going to see plenty of your swimming now. You'll be wishing I would go away. You'll be begging Auntie Rhoda to let you Uber or hitchhike just to get rid of me. And for starters, let me have a bite of that."

The Mission Valley Manta Rays swam at a community college less than ten miles away, though it took twenty minutes to get there with traffic, JoJo's knee bouncing the entire drive.

"Weren't there any swim teams in Milpitas?" Lissie asked.

"Auntie Rhoda thought a college environment would be more astraditional."

"More what?"

"Like inspirational."

"Oh. Aspirational? Well, if you're swimming faster, it's working. Do you have the same coach in this new group?"

An expression flashed across JoJo's face. Lissie nearly missed it as she slowed for the parking lot speedbump. Uncertainty? Excitement? What was it?

"Coach Wayman is new to the team this year," muttered her little sister. "He came from a club in Southern California." She said no more, grabbing her swim bag and springing from the car the moment Lissie put it in park, leaving her older sister to find her own way into the club.

The desk clerk helped Lissie fill out the form and took her picture for a parent-affiliate card, but when Lissie tried to ask questions about the team and its volunteer requirements, she said, "You'll have to ask the coach." Meanwhile, throngs of kids in sweats with moms in tow pushed past, flashing their cards under the scanner and clamoring to each other. Lissie felt a pang of sympathetic shyness for her sister, but then reminded herself that a few of JoJo's friends had also moved up. It wasn't like she'd be a total stranger.

The total stranger would be me.

Following the moms, who ignored her after a few curious glances and returned to their rapid-fire conversations in Mandarin or mixed Chinese and English, Lissie emerged on the pool deck where the swimmers lined up, stuffing hair under swim caps and adjusting goggles. JoJo looked less gangly when surrounded by kids her age, but she was still one of the skinnier ones, and stripped of her street clothes and her long hair tucked away, she looked strangely vulnerable.

The moms made their way toward the bleachers on the far side of the eight-lane pool, and Lissie noted in dismay that they sat in full sun, which would make it impossible to see her laptop screen. Maybe she could sit in one of the plastic chairs in the shade and pull over a side table?

But no.

"Hey, do you mind sitting with the parents? This is where I set up shop."

Lissie looked up to see someone who must surely be Coach Wayman, and all at once she understood JoJo's weird reaction to naming him in the car.

This can't be a good idea. For one thing, he barely looked older than Lissie herself. For another, he was way too good-looking. Wasian, she guessed, because his eyes and hair were light brown and he had the hint of a five o'clock shadow. He reminded her of Flat Stanley, from the children's book, because he was so lean he was almost two-dimensional, with wide shoulders above a nonexistent waist and hips. The navy team polo shirt with "Coach Wayman" in orange embroidery clung to him for dear life, making it very plain he carried not an ounce of excess body fat. *Who would hire this guy to coach teenagers?*

He grinned at her, even as she hurried to jam her laptop back in her bag.

"I'm not a mom," said Lissie.

"I see that now."

"But I do need to talk to you when you have a second. My sister Joanna Cheng is new to the group."

"Got it. Just let me get them started on their warm-up set, then I'll give you the spiel."

She hurried away toward the bleachers, feeling like the new kid showing up late for class when the moms turned as one to study her.

"*Nǐ shì tā de nǚ péng you, ma?*"

Lissie might not speak much Chinese, but she understood that one. *Are you his girlfriend?* "*Bú shì,*" she answered. "My little sister, Joanna, is starting with the group today."

With that one sentence, two things happened—one which she expected after all her work at the Four Treasures, and the other a surprise. First, her listeners gathered from her barebones reply and her switching into unaccented English that, despite her appearance, she spoke Chinese no better than a year-old donkey. Second, and this was the unexpected part, her announcement that she was not, in fact, Coach Wayman's girlfriend pleased them and made up in some way for her linguistic shortcomings.

"Ah, Joanna. Which one is she?" The question came from one of the bigger moms, Mrs. Pang, her round face stern atop a matronly figure in tunic top and jeans.

Embarrassingly, however, all the kids had jumped in and begun their set, and Lissie hadn't seen which lane JoJo was assigned. In the water, they all looked the same, arms and legs and capped heads and splashes.

"I'm sorry. I can't tell right now."

"Will you be bringing her to practice, or her mom?" Matron Mom asked.

"Mostly me," said Lissie, not wanting to get into JoJo's orphan status.

"Who will be doing the volunteering at the meets?" asked another mom, this one pretty and stylish and wearing makeup.

"Me again, I guess."

"We need help with concessions," said Matron Mom. "I'm Mrs. Pang, by the way."

"Uh—"

"Do anything but concessions," whispered Hot Mom behind her manicured hand. She grinned. "Unless you enjoy working like a dog."

"I don't really know all the volunteer roles yet," said Lissie to Matron Mom. "My uncle used to time at the meets." Then she made a face. So much for not bringing up JoJo's orphan status.

A third mom suddenly sat up very straight. "Who does he want?" All the women looked over as one to see Coach Wayman beckoning.

"Um . . . I think it's me," said Lissie. "Because of JoJo being new. He said he had things to tell me." Self-consciously, she climbed back down the bleacher steps, leaving her bag behind and trying to ignore the feeling everyone at the pool was watching her.

Coach Wayman gave her an easy nod. "So . . . you're Joanna Cheng's sister? Great." He consulted his clipboard. "If you could just give me her mom's email, I can send the usual welcome, with all the team requirements and policies. Or better yet, she can come in and I can give her the speech in person—unless she isn't super comfortable with English?"

"Her English is fine," Lissie waved this off. Poor JoJo! Was it like this all the time? *Where's your mom? Can I speak to your mom?* "But I'm actually going to be Joanna's 'swim mom' for at least a few months, so you can just email me or tell me."

He hesitated, then shrugged. "Fair enough. Let's do it." He stuck out a hand. "I'm the coach, Wayman Wang."

44

"Elisabeth Cheng."

"Great. Okay, Elisabeth. The Senior Prep group of the Mission Valley Manta Rays is pretty serious business. We see potential in your child, er, sister." He looked at his clipboard again. "Joanna's fly times have been dropping like crazy. She has already made regional cuts in butterfly and freestyle for her age group, and her back is on the cusp. Which is pretty amazing since she just aged into the bracket."

"Her back?" Lissie pictured JoJo balanced atop a fulcrum like a teeter-totter.

"Backstroke."

"Oh, right. Backstroke."

"So we demand our Senior Prep swimmers commit to making 90% of practices and missing no more than one meet per year, with all champs meets required. Without that commitment, I can't put Joanna on any relays."

Lissie nodded. "Okay. What can I say? We will."

"Great. We're a tight swim community and hold ourselves to the highest standards. That means all our coaches and parents and other volunteers—anyone around the kids on deck—go through SafeSport training and sign a team covenant of behavioral standards."

"Yeesh," said Lissie.

He softened and grinned at her. "It's not that scary. Just stuff like, all texting and emailing between the kids and me will include a parent—or sister, the guardian person, I mean. No alcohol, smoking, or drugs. That's the kids, not the parental figures. Though, if you're going to do any of that, please don't do it around the swimmers."

"Got it," said Lissie. "Do all my hard drugs at home."

He chuckled and went on, "High level of sportsmanship, abide by USA Swimming rules, clean up after yourself in the locker room, that kind of thing. All the details are in the document."

"Sure. Fine. Where do I sign?"

His grin widened. He had very white teeth. Or it looked that way because he was so tanned. "I'll email it to you." He handed her his clipboard. "If you could just put down your contact info by Joanna's name . . . " When she complied, he glanced at it. "Were you a swimmer, Elisabeth?"

"Not at all. This is totally a JoJo thing. I mean Joanna. You better ask her what she wants you to call her, but I hope you'll call me Lissie. No one calls me Elisabeth except my college advisor."

"You still in school? Ohlone? Foothill?"

"San Jose State."

"A Spartan. Right on. Nice pool. I swam for Chapman."

Lissie had no intelligent reply to this, so she gave him back his favorite word, "Great," before backing away. "Well, I'll let you coach, Coach, unless there's anything else?"

"Just the volunteer hours."

"Yes. The other—the moms—were starting to tell me about that. Timing, working concessions . . . "

"We actually need officials, if you're interested," Coach Wayman suggested.

"Yeah, probably not. Not a swimmer, remember?"

He raised humorous eyebrows. "Just saying, concessions is indentured labor. Being an official gets you free food and a front-row view. And you don't have to be a swimmer. There's a training class, and you take a test. The club pays your fees. Piece of cake."

That made two strikes against concessions. But it wasn't that. She felt herself wavering in the face of the charm offensive. "I don't know. I'll think about it."

"You do that." He turned back to the swimmers, but as she walked away she heard him add, "It'd be great to have you on deck."

CHAPTER 5

After sleeping in almost to noon, Lissie awoke to a note on the fridge: "L— You ate my Greek yogurt. You know I need protein. I hate you. —Nelson."

"Why does he think it was me?" Lissie complained, wadding up the note. "You're the yogurt eater, Mel."

"Because I gave up yogurt and all dairy for the foreseeable future," said Mel, pressing down on her bagel sandwich. "See this? Ham, cuke, mustard. That's it."

Lissie stared. "It's not Lent, is it? I mean, it's October. Is that Lent?"

"You're so ignorant. It's not Lent. Lent is before Easter. But I made a deal with God: I'm going to go to Mass every day and forgo dairy until I get a boyfriend."

"Does it work like that?" Lissie asked.

Melanie shrugged. "I'm Catholic. Bargaining is always the opening gambit."

"But this seems like a goal you could achieve without divine intervention."

"You don't think I've tried? I thought I really hit it off with that guy at the barbecue last week, but it's been crickets. I even texted him to wish him good luck on some project he talked for twenty minutes about, and all I got was the clapping emoji." She huffed out a breath that blew the hair off her forehead. "What does that even mean? That the project went well? That he applauds me for hoping it went well?"

"You got me. But if you didn't eat the yogurt, and I didn't eat the yogurt, then Jenny must have, but Jenny never steals food."

"What would you know about it? I've hardly seen either of you forever. Jenny's been leaving early and getting home late since you have the car every day, and you're always off playing middle-aged swim mom to JoJo. And Nelson . . . he's no fun because he's Nelson. Plus I hate his new boyfriend, who is so condescending to him."

"Well, I'm here right now. JoJo got a ride to Saturday swim because she had a sleepover at somebody's house. I think the daughter of Hot Mom. Too bad they live on the other side of Fremont so it can't happen more often."

"Heck, I'd offer to take JoJo half the time, if I got to see Wonder Wayman."

"That's all you'd get to do. See him. He's pretty serious about his job. It's not like he's said much to me after that first day besides hi and bye."

"I know, I know. You told me. I would just go to window shop anyhow, since it sounds like you and all the moms and all the teenage girls have dibs."

"Don't say that!" protested Lissie. "At least about the teenage girls. Half of them have a crush on him, including JoJo, I'm pretty sure, and if he has creepy tendencies, it's all going to end badly." She considered, smoothing out Nelson's note again and replacing it on the fridge. "All the moms do think he's amazing, though."

"But that's what the pervert training said," Mel observed, waving a tortilla chip in the air. She'd been fascinated by the faces Lissie made and the cries of "ick" that came from her while she watched the SafeSport training and ended in watching the videos with her. "That the pervs also groom the adults so that no one believes it if a kid accuses them."

Lissie threw the sink sponge at her. "I said stop! Besides, he's not going out of his way to win them over. He just stands there and coaches."

"Whatever. Did he or did he not make that half-flirty comment to you about swim official training, and the next thing you know, you went and signed up for the clinic." Mel whistled. "That boy has already got you wrapped around his little finger!"

Before Lissie could retort, her phone chimed. Mel leaped up to look over her shoulder. Just the day before, Lissie had gotten her first coach-swimmer-parent group text, and she'd been kind of fluttery to open the message from Coach Wayman to JoJo: *You forgot your fins. Left them in office.* ("It's code!" screamed Mel. "Code for 'Yo, hot mama, I wanna get it on.'")

"Is it him?" her roommate demanded.

Lissie shook her head. "Jenny."

"Ooh—I bet she tried to apologize to Hive-y Hazel for you and pissed off that Preston Lin all over again, so now he's taking out a billboard along 101." She framed it with her hands. "Four Treasures: License to Kill."

But it wasn't even Jenny.

Hi, Lissie. This is Charles. Jenny has a bad migraine and vertigo. Can you come? Address is 14 Brookhaven, PV.

Lissie and Melanie looked at each other in dismay. "Vertigo? She hasn't had one that bad in years. Poor Jenny! She was so looking forward to the weekend. But when it's like that she just wants to lie in a dark room and tell everyone to shut up and go away."

"Are you going?" Mel asked. "Into the lion's den to rescue your sister?"

Lissie's shoulders hunched. "I don't want to. At all. Ugh!"

"But you can't just leave her there. Unless . . . I guess I could go."

But that wouldn't work. Mel was sweet and well-meaning but also loud and boisterous and exactly what a migraine-sufferer didn't want. *Stop being a chicken, Elisabeth Cheng. Hive-y Hazel and Mr. Perfect probably want to avoid you too and will clear out when they hear you're coming.*

"I'll go," she decided. "I'll get her that green migraine smoothie and try to bring her back if I can."

49

"*Here?*" Mel cried, even as the upstairs neighbors thundered above them like sumo wrestlers and two separate blowers droned outside.

"You're right," agreed Lissie. There was no rest for the wicked at Château Cardboard, their name for the Château Cardoza apartment complex. "Maybe I'll take her to Milpitas so she can sleep in my Uncle Mason's office."

"Yeah, if you wanna be like an Uber driver on New Year's Eve. She has vertigo, Lissie! She'll be barfing all over the Civic the whole way!"

"Then I'll just have to play it by ear."

Throwing clean clothes and sweats for her sister in a duffel bag, Lissie was on the road in fifteen minutes.

She'd never actually been to Portola Valley. The semi-rural air of the town surprised her, next door as it was to the densely populated cities blurring together down the length of the Peninsula. But here were winding roads, horses in pastures, pickup trucks parked beside Teslas, houses tucked so far back they were invisible from the streets. Even the Portola Valley version of a strip mall was wooden and ranchy and charming. Lissie turned onto Brookhaven, waiting at the corner for a pair of people on horseback to cross before creeping along the road so she wouldn't miss the address. Only the ends of the driveways were visible, each marked with either an archway or a pillar made of stacked stones. 14 Brookhaven opted for the pillar, the number painted in blue on a white tile.

There were four cars already parked in front of the long, low house and deer browsing in the drought-resistant, native-planting yard. Not being a wildlife and great-outdoors kind of gal, when she turned off the engine, she hesitated to get out. Should she honk the horn? Yell at them? Didn't deer rear up on their hind legs and kick you in the chest if you annoyed them? Or was that moose? Meese?

Lissie rolled the window down an inch, prepared to give a trial hiss, but it was so silent she didn't dare. Quiet in a weird way—so quiet it was *loud*, with what could only be described as nature sounds: birds, bugs, breeze rustling through grasses.

What is *this place?*

A full minute passed, with the dumb deer generally minding their own business, while Lissie took herself to task. *What's the worst that can happen? At least if a deer kicks you in the chest and you die, you won't have to face Hazel or Mr. Perfect again. And then they'll probably feel guilty and write a nice review of the Four Treasures.*

That convinced her. Taking a deep breath, she grabbed the duffel bag and the smoothie and opened the car door.

And nearly peed her pants.

Because the moment she emerged, Preston Lin popped up from behind one of the cars. She hadn't seen him in two weeks, except from behind, from the floor of the closet, but she remembered that big build and too-handsome face.

Lissie gave an undignified shriek of surprise which did indeed startle the deer and send them bounding off. "What are you doing hiding out here?" she demanded.

He raised one eyebrow like he was Sherlock Holmes and she was Watson asking a particularly stupid question. "Who says I was hiding?"

"I didn't see you!" she accused.

He held up his palms. "A lack of observational skills on your part does not constitute hiding on my part." But when she only frowned at him, he added, "I was cleaning the bottom of my shoes from a hike. In my defense, I was going to let you go in first, but you sat there so long . . . "

"Yes, well." He already thought she was a negligent moron, she didn't need to add that she was afraid of deer. Her chin went up. "Can you blame me? I wasn't exactly eager to see you all again."

He said nothing for a moment, clearly feeling no urge to tell her it was all water under the bridge or they should let bygones be bygones or what didn't kill Hazel made her stronger. Instead, he caught her off guard. "I wasn't sure I'd even recognize you again."

What was she supposed to do with that? "What does that mean?"
He didn't answer her question. "Did you recognize me?"

"Yeah," said Lissie. "Trauma does that to you." Trauma, and the fact
that her world wasn't overpopulated with giant hunky guys.

There was a twitch of his lips that might have been amusement but
might also have been indigestion, and then he gestured toward the
front door. "I think we'd all agree it would be easier if Charles never
asked Jenny out."

"Well, what do you know," said Lissie, marching ahead of him.
"Common ground."

The double doors opened onto an enormous open-plan room, living
and dining and kitchen spaces flowing together and beyond, with a
floor-to-ceiling glass far wall that led to a wraparound deck overlook-
ing the canyon. She had never seen anything like it, and if Preston Lin
had not been on her heels, Lissie would have jumped and clapped her
hands and run everywhere to look at everything and taken a hundred
pictures to text to Mel.

But Preston Lin was behind her, so she had to play it casual, and
lounging on the deck were Charles Bing and his sister, so any incipient
excitement was stifled by dread.

Okay. If she was going to take her medicine, at least she had the
relief of choking it all down at once.

Charles saw her first and came forward quickly to greet her. "Lissie!
Thank God. I know Jenny will be glad you came. She's stashed away
in a downstairs bedroom, the darkest and quietest one in the house,
trying to sleep it off, and she hasn't said hardly anything, but I know
she's miserable. But before you check on her, come out here and say
hi. You remember my sister, Hazel, of course."

Lissie strode forward, determined to get it over with, and she had
to plunge right in because Hazel's surprised, puzzled expression meant
she was realizing Lissie had in fact been at the barbecue.

"Hazel!" Lissie blurted. "Let me apologize again for what happened
at the restaurant a couple weeks ago. I'm so glad you're okay and that

nothing worse happened, and I'm sure Jenny mentioned that steps have been taken, and I promise it will never happen again."

"It'll never happen again because I'll never eat there again," replied Hazel, crossing her arms over her chest.

"Your loss, Hazel," put in Charles, "because I went back for the free meal with some buddies from the biz school and it was awesome."

"You went back for the free meal and to see Jenny," accused his sister.

"That too."

"Well, I hope one day you'll try it again," Lissie said, "because it really is a great place, and I feel bad if I've . . . played a part in damaging its reputation." She had no idea if Jenny had told them the Four Treasures belonged to their aunt and uncle, but she wasn't about to volunteer that information if she didn't have to.

It would have been gracious of Preston Lin to speak up at this point—while he hadn't made a mountain out of a molehill, he had certainly made an Everest out of a standard-size mountain. But he didn't, and his continued silence on the matter ticked Lissie off all over again.

Fine. That was it. She'd apologized again to everyone she needed to, and that was the last time she was going to do it or feel bad about it. He wasn't even the one who'd gotten hives, but he got whatever revenge he deemed appropriate with his name-naming article. They were now even, as far as she was concerned.

She held up the green smoothie. "I'd better get this to Jenny before it's all melted."

"Yes," agreed Charles eagerly. "Come with me."

He really was a good guy, Lissie thought, following as he descended the wooden stairs without a sound and all but tiptoed down the carpeted hall.

"I won't knock," he whispered. "You go on in." And then he crept away again.

The bedroom where Jenny had been tucked away was probably where the family put its least-welcome guests because it was dug into the hillside, with only one small, high window providing a ground-level view of the front yard. But it was ideal if what you sought was quiet and darkness. Jenny lay curled on the bed, a pillow covering her head, but she lifted it when her sister approached.

"Lissie," she croaked.

Silently, Lissie presented her offerings: heavy-duty ibuprofen, Jenny's softest sweatpants and oldest T-shirt, and the green smoothie. Jenny couldn't manage more than a wan smile, and it took the two of them to sit her up and change her clothes.

"You want me to take you to Milpitas?" Lissie murmured.

"No. I never want to move again. I already threw up twice," was Jenny's barely audible answer. "Just leave me here. No one will bother me."

Lissie squeezed her hand and helped her get another sip of the smoothie down. From the taste Lissie had taken, it was a disgusting mix of kale and spinach and celery and other green things, with not nearly enough honey, but the juice-bar lady swore by it for migraines.

"Do you want me to come back tomorrow?" she asked next.

But Jenny's hand tightened on hers. "Please stay." Lissie's eyes bugged, and Jenny clutched her again, weakly. "I won't feel so alone. Please. They won't eat you, Lis. Tell Charles I'm sorry."

Stay? We might have declared a ceasefire, but they don't really want me here, Lissie's inner voice objected, but she tried to keep her face neutral. She managed a valiant nod, and Jenny smiled and shut her eyes.

Argh.

When her sister was asleep a few minutes later, Lissie tiptoed back to the door and snuck out. At least the house was big enough that she could hole up somewhere to stay out of their hair.

But the second her head appeared in the stairwell, there was Charles. "How is she? Was she glad to see you? I feel terrible about this."

"She's not great," admitted Lissie. "In fact, I hope you don't mind, but she asked if I could stick around. Possibly overnight. But I'll sleep in the same room as—"

"Of course! Of course, right, Preston?" Charles wheeled around to consult him. "I mean, what Bronklin doesn't know won't hurt him."

"Who's Bronklin?" asked Lissie innocently.

"My advisor," said Preston.

"Wow," she said, "I should tell my advisor to dump English for . . . microbiology, was it? Because this house is really something. But I'll stay out of your hair, and I promise, no shenanigans."

He didn't really have an option, short of total rudeness, but he gave in with tolerable grace. It was Hazel who shook her head and made a face, which Lissie had to pretend not to see. Charles hurried to smooth everything over. "You don't have to stay out of our hair. The more the merrier. Besides, we're having people from Preston's department for a potluck tonight, so it's no big deal. Did you already have lunch? Want something to drink? There's iced tea."

Glass in hand, Lissie followed them onto the deck. Preston claimed one of the lounge chairs in the shade and opened his laptop. Hazel took the chair nearest him, though she wasn't dressed for lounging around and was actually wearing a skirt and a scarf. This oddity was explained the next moment when Charles asked her, "What time's the open house?"

"From two to five. Not far from here." She glanced at Preston. "I'll go in a little bit and come back after."

"Open house for what?" asked Lissie.

"What else do you have open houses for?" Hazel said, not very nicely. "A listing."

"You have to congratulate my sister, Lissie," Charles declared. "She just got her real-estate license. If you're looking to buy or sell, look no further."

"We rent," said Lissie. "The student life, you know. But when our lease is up at the Château Cardboard—"

"We don't handle rentals," Hazel answered in a cool voice. "Just high-end properties."

"So basically any freestanding house, you mean?" Lissie returned.

"Since even the crappiest shed in the Bay Area starts at a million."

Hazel plucked at her scarf to arrange it. "A little higher than that, I should say. This one today is listed for $7.8."

Round one went to Hazel Bing because Lissie was floored. "You just got your license and you're selling a $7.8 million house?"

"Hazel is working with my mother," spoke up Preston, not even raising his eyes from his laptop screen.

Hazel looked miffed to have her cover blown, but the frown she threw him was wasted. "Yes. I work for the great Penelope Lin."

Lissie shot a quick glance around to see if she was being punked, but Charles was answering a text and Preston was still typing. Apparently Hazel was not being ironic.

"Don't tell me you've never heard of her?" accused Hazel. "She was with us in the restaurant. I bet half the people there recognized her. She's only the biggest name in Peninsula real estate."

"Chill out, Hazel," Preston said mildly, lifting his eyes at last. "Why would she know her? She's still in college and she rents." His gaze shifted to Lissie. "And there was a lot going on that night."

Lissie supposed Hazel didn't enjoy remembering that night any more than she did because she changed the subject. "I thought you wanted to relax this weekend, Pres," she said, "but it looks like you're working as hard as ever."

"I told Bronklin I'd email these results to him by Monday."

Hazel leaned from her chair to his to see his screen. "I don't know how you make sense of all that. Math was fine for me, but chemistry and biology were a slog."

"They wouldn't be much use to you in real estate anyway."

"And working with rats!" she went on with a shudder. "I just couldn't."

"But aren't there plenty of rats in real estate?" he asked. Lissie did a ba-dum-tiss under her breath.

Hazel laughed appreciatively. "Don't let your mother hear you say that!"

He made no response to this, and a little silence fell. Charles had stepped inside and was talking to someone on his phone. Lissie leaned against the deck railing, watching a hawk riding the air currents over the canyon and debating if she, too, could excuse herself.

But before she could decide, Hazel accosted her with, "What were your plans this weekend, Lissie, before Jenny got her migraine?"

Preston looked up.

"Sleep in and then do homework, mostly." Ordinarily she would have worked at the Four Treasures too, except for her ban.

"Jenny says you're studying English at San Jose State."

"Uh-huh."

"Do you want to be a teacher?" Preston asked. Hazel's head whipped around at him.

"Of course she does," Hazel replied. "She wants to shape our country's young minds."

"Actually, I think I'm too lazy and self-centered to be a teacher," Lissie said. "I'd prefer a nine-to-five business job, so after hours I could do my own thing."

Hazel would have let it die there, seeing that Preston was now paying attention, but to her irritation, he asked, "And what thing would that be?"

Lissie had no intention of marching out any hopes or dreams to face the firing squad of their opinions, saying only, "Oh, you know, something business-y."

"Did someone say business?" Charles emerged onto the deck again. "Capitalists of the world, unite!"

"Charles is at Stanford GSB," crowed his sister.

He winked. "Some people want to make the world a better place. Hazel and I just want to make money off it."

"Helping people find houses is important, meaningful work!" she protested.

"That's for sure. And $7.8 million is a whole lot of meaning."

She threw a balled-up napkin that fell short of her brother. "We can't all be Preston Lins."

Thank God, thought Lissie. But then her eyes widened. No way, was Hazel being serious again? "Does that mean he falls in the make-the-world-a-better-place bucket?"

His wry gaze caught hers. "Surprise, surprise."

"Of course he does," declared Hazel. "And I don't mean just his science research—"

"In fact, you especially don't mean that," laughed Charles, "because we don't understand it. He could be building a biochemical weapon, for all we know."

"I mean the volunteer work he does for USA Swimming—"

"Swimming?" interrupted Lissie. "Are you a swimmer?"

"Is he a swimmer," snorted Hazel indignantly.

Preston said, "Yes, I'm a swimmer. Or was. But don't let Hazel give you ideas. I never went to the Olympics."

With great effort Lissie managed not to roll her eyes. Only at Stanford did athletes have to apologize for not making the Olympic team. She supposed she should have recognized the body type: the endless shoulders and slim waist and hips like Coach Wayman. Only Preston Lin was bigger and didn't make her think of Flat Stanley at all.

"He had Trials cuts in multiple events!" declared Hazel, slapping a hand onto the cushion of her lounge chair. She was obviously the self-appointed president of his fan club.

"So did hundreds of people across the country," Preston pointed out with impatience.

"My little sister Joanna swims," Lissie volunteered. "She just turned thirteen and swims for the Mission Valley Manta Rays over in Fremont."

Preston shut his laptop. "What strokes?"

"Oh, here we go," said Charles.

"Well, she just moved up a group, so her new coach wants her to get times in everything over the course of the year. But her favorites are freestyle and butterfly."

"Sprint or distance?"

"I don't know," confessed Lissie. "I actually know hardly anything about swimming, but I'm going to learn more because her club has all these volunteer requirements, and I've said I'll fulfill them and drive her back and forth everywhere since I don't have my job—"

She broke off, remembering too late that: (1) she had vowed never to allude to the incident again if she could help it; and (2) she would rather they didn't know her relation to Uncle Mason and Auntie Rhoda because, well, see reason (1).

The conversation died again, and Charles opened his mouth to say something—anything—but before he could, Lissie charged into the breach again. "Anyhow, what were your favorites, Preston? Strokes, I mean." Saying his name required a Herculean effort, but she managed it.

"100 Fly and 2 IM."

"2 IM?" she repeated uncertainly.

"In-di-vi-du-al med-ley," supplied Hazel, as if Lissie were both hard of hearing and slow of comprehension. "Two hundred yards to-tal—fifty of each stroke."

"Or meters, depending on the season," added Preston solemnly, but there was an unidentifiable gleam in his eye, and Lissie didn't know if he was laughing at Hazel or himself. In any case, Lissie hoped all this would be explained in her training clinic. And that the clinician wouldn't be as patronizing as Hazel Bing.

Preston was still looking at her. "If you're going to be volunteering, I might see you on deck sometime."

"Why is that?" Lissie couldn't hide her attitude. "You don't swim against eighth graders, do you?"

"Only when I need an ego boost," he replied, deadpan.

But Hazel couldn't bear for him to be misunderstood. "Preston is a Youth Ambassador for USA Swimming," she explained.

"How do you even know that?" asked her brother. "Even I didn't know that."

She went a blotchy pink. "I, uh, follow some of the swimming

social media accounts. He's kind of the most famous person I know."
After this confession, which made Lissie cringe for her, she scrambled
up and lunged for Lissie's empty drink glass. "Are you done with this?
I should head for my open house."

Lissie let her take it. "That's a good reminder. I'd better get
some stuff done, too. I'll go check on Jenny and get started on my
homework."

But the first thing she did after retreating to Jenny's darkened
bedroom was look up the Lins. There was plenty to see.

Penelope Lin's website named her as the "number one" this, that,
and the other for anything real estate–related on the Peninsula, and her
glowing testimonies included not just run-of-the-mill, anonymous rich
people who could afford homes in the area, but also tech household
names, a couple of 49ers players, and some influencers who didn't look
old enough to have driver's licenses, much less purchase real estate.

But even Mrs. Lin's online bona fides yielded in length to her son's.
There was his co-authored article in *Cell*. His name on the department roster. His recent article for the *Stanford Daily* (Lissie ground
her teeth), along with older ones, all health-related. (Apparently, he
saw himself as another Atul Gawande.) And endless swim mentions.
Stanford team pages from past years. PAC-12 meet results. NCAA
meet results. *Swimming World* and *Splash* and *SwimSwam* citations.
Preston Lin provided enough Internet fodder to make even a dedi-
cated cyberstalker's eyes glaze over. It no longer seemed lame for Hazel
Bing to call him the most famous person she knew; he now was also
the most famous person Lissie knew.

Not that she would ever tell him so.

CHAPTER 6

Lissie finished reading *Manon Lescaut*, looked over her *Shrew* paper one last time before submitting it, and answered another slew of online complaints, ignoring the rumbles of her stomach. Speaking of stomach problems, one review described a vague digestive issue after a Four Treasures banquet. Exasperated, she took a screenshot and sent it to Mel. Her roommate shot back a GIF of a vomiting cat.

The light from the narrow bedroom window was fading. When Jenny stirred, Lissie tiptoed over. "Are you hungry? Thirsty?"

"Bathroom."

Popping her head out to make sure the coast was clear, Lissie helped her sister up.

Jenny made no sound, but Lissie could tell from her set mouth and colorless cheeks that she still felt terrible.

"Tell me the truth," Lissie commanded, watching Jenny force down more ibuprofen and take a sip from her water bottle. "How are you feeling? Give me a percentage better. Ten? Twenty? Or are you still on the downswing?"

"Fifteen percent better," Jenny answered softly. "The room doesn't spin anymore unless I get up."

"Can you hear anything down here? Because apparently, they're expecting a lot of people. I won't know anyone except Everyone's Favorite Person and the Bings. I wish I could just get a plate of food and hide in here with you. Or that I was invisible."

Jenny made a face. "Please don't bring food in here. I don't think I could deal with the smells."

"Fine, fine," sighed Lissie. "I won't come hide until after I've eaten."

"Are you doing okay, Lissie?"

"Totally fine," she lied.

Jenny lifted a hand and let it drop back to the bed. Then she shut her eyes again. Lissie's stomach gave a louder growl, drawing a faint smile from her sister.

"Go," she murmured. "You'll keep me awake."

Lissie went upstairs. A quick look at her bank balance told her that her best bet for cheap food to contribute to the potluck was going to have to be that little market in the woodsy strip mall she had passed. And she'd better go soon, or people arriving might block her car in.

When Lissie reached the top of the stairs, however, she found Charles and Preston in the enormous kitchen, Charles unloading charcuterie items from Robert's Market bags and setting them on the granite slab countertop next to all the things Preston was pulling from the Sub-Zero fridge. Lissie slid to a stop in her socked feet, prepared to retreat, but Preston spotted her. "Hey!"

"Hey."

"Get a lot of work done?" he asked, at the same time that Charles said, "How's Jenny?"

Considering how Preston's article had contributed measurably to her workload, Lissie ignored him and gave Charles a brief update.

"And I was thinking I would run out and get something for the potluck," she finished.

"Don't bother," said Preston. "It's already too late, and there'll be more than enough."

He was right. There was plenty to eat.

Though there were enough people present and general noise that she might have hidden in plain sight, it turned out Lissie did know someone. Or, rather, someone knew her.

"Elisabeth?"

It was a tall, skinny guy with wire-framed glasses and the posture of a praying mantis.

She looked at him uncertainly, her loaded cracker halfway to her mouth. "Yes?"

"It's me, Darren. Darren Liu. I met you at church a few times. At Christmas. You and your sisters."

"Oh-h-h, right." Uncle Mason's and Auntie Rhoda's Chinese church, where Jenny and Lissie dutifully joined Christmas Eve service every year, despite it being almost completely in Mandarin. JoJo said the middle-school group was in English, which meant, as in so many things, her experience of church was totally different from her sisters'. "Nice to see you again," said Lissie politely. "What are you doing here? And how is your family?"

"My family's fine. And I don't really know what I'm doing here, since the only person I know is my roommate Jay." He pointed to a stocky guy in a baseball cap. "And now you. Jay's in microbiology and he invited me to tag along. Are you at Stanford now?"

Lissie gave a snort. "Nope. My connection to this potluck is even more tenuous. My sister Jenny got invited by Charles Bing," she offered a discreet point of her own. "So I came to keep her company."

Darren perked up visibly, straightening his posture. "Jenny's here?" He followed Lissie's finger to the clutch of people around Charles and proceeded to examine and dismiss each dark-haired woman in turn.

"Don't stare!" hissed Lissie, seeing Preston glance over. Great. With his big, swollen head, he would now think she was talking about him. "Jenny wasn't feeling so good, so she went to lie down."

Darren drooped again. "Oh. Do you think she'll come back out again later?"

"No," said Lissie heartlessly. She was too used to guys yearning after Jenny to be nice to all of them, especially if, like Darren Liu, they didn't stand a chance. "And if she did, that Charles Bing would be glued to her side because he likes her."

She expected her announcement to complete the deflation process, but, to her surprise, he straightened again, throwing another look at Charles. "Yeah? Who's he?"

"A GSB student," answered Lissie. "Friend of the guy whose advisor owns this house." She wanted to put a hand to each side of Darren's head like blinders. Preston was now openly watching them. Argh.

"But he's at Stanford?" persisted Darren. Clearly Lissie had underestimated him in those few meetings at Milpitas Chinese Covenant, writing him off as a shy, awkward nerd.

"Yes. The Graduate School of Business."

"Business," repeated Darren, his narrow chest expanding. "A fuzzy. Probably a schmoozer too."

"Probably. Because he's a nice guy." She tried to get him off the subject. "What are you studying, anyway? Weren't you math at Cal? Or was it CS?"

"It was both. But now I'm here getting a master's in symbolic systems."

Her eyebrows lifted. "You can't mean like hieroglyphics. No, don't tell me. Braille."

"What?" he stared at her. "No, it's interdisciplinary. I'm doing AI."

"That sounds interesting," faked Lissie, but Darren was already back on Charles.

"How did he meet her?" was his next question.

"At the restaurant."

Giving a grunt, Darren shook his narrow head. "The restaurant. Yeah. I heard Four Treasures isn't doing so well lately. My folks told me your aunt and uncle are thinking of hiring a PR firm."

"*What?*" Lissie gaped at him. How could Darren Liu have heard such a thing when she herself hadn't heard any such thing? "What are you talking about?"

He frowned in return. "Didn't you hear what happened? Some person got food poisoning or something—"

"A food allergy," interrupted Lissie. She couldn't help glancing toward Preston again. He was talking to someone, but she had the feeling she had just missed his gaze. "I know about that, but I didn't know about them hiring a PR firm. Where did your parents hear that?"

"They're in a Bible study group together," he shrugged. "They didn't say much more than that to me, but I know my folks have gone to eat there twice in the last two weeks, just to shore things up." An idea struck him. "I should go, too. You and Jenny still work there, right?"

"Shhh!" She lifted two fingers almost to his mouth as she hushed him, suddenly remembering their surroundings. "I don't work there anymore, but Jenny still does. Let's just drop it."

"Why?"

"Because the people who . . . never mind!" Lissie's explanation died on her lips when Preston appeared behind Darren.

"Preston Lin," he said, holding out a hand to the newcomer.

"Darren Liu." To Lissie's bemusement, despite being half Preston's width and devoid of movie-star looks, Darren didn't look daunted by Mr. Larger-than-Life any more than he had by Charles Bing's credentials.

"This is his advisor's house we're in," explained Lissie.

"Thanks for letting me crash the party," said Darren.

"Did Lissie invite you?" asked Preston, giving her a curious look.

She glared right back at him. "No, I didn't. I don't usually invite people to other people's houses, especially when I don't belong here myself."

"But I've known the Cheng girls a long time," Darren explained, his chest swelling a degree. "Their whole family, in fact."

A zing of panic shot through her, and Lissie dumped a dollop of refried beans on Darren's foot. "Oh, crap! Sorry about that, Darren. You'd better go wipe it off."

But he only waved his paper napkin. "No big deal."

"My fault! I'll do it!" she cried, snatching the napkin from him before he could bend down. "Why don't you tell Preston how you came

65

to be here? I mean about your roommate Jay."

"I can clean my own shoe, Lissie," Darren protested, sitting down and doing just that. But he said to Preston, "My roommate is Jay Goldsmith, and he knows somebody here."

"Me," said Preston. "He's in the lab across the hall from Bronklin's. This is Bronklin's house."

Lissie saw a question forming on Preston's lips, and she blurted, "Darren is in symbolic systems. Isn't that awesome? So smart. AI. Tell him about your, uh, project, Darren."

Thank God Darren actually had something he was working on and didn't say anything stupid, like, What project? Though Lissie's insistence made him frown in puzzlement. He obediently launched into the elevator pitch of his proposed thesis. Lissie hardly cared if Preston understood it any better than she did, or if he even listened to it. She just wanted his curiosity about the stranger satisfied so he would go away.

But when Darren stopped talking, Preston asked him an informed-sounding question about large language models, which Darren answered in greater detail. Lissie would normally have been interested, but with Preston looming, she almost danced with impatience. When Darren was done, Preston still stood there like he'd been carved from a tree stump.

"Well, you'd better go mingle with your other guests now," she said pointedly.

"I already have."

"What about you, Preston?" asked Darren. "What are you working on?"

Lissie almost groaned. Did she dare leave them alone? What was the worst that could happen? Surely, if Lissie weren't there, Darren would have no reason to mention her aunt and uncle, for Pete's sake?

"Brain cells," said Preston. "The effect of autoimmune conditions on them."

"Cool," Darren said.

There was a pause. No one showed any sign of going anywhere.

If only the San Andreas fault would choose this moment to strike with an earthquake and swallow them into oblivion, that the half of Bronklin's house holding Preston Lin would tear away with a world-ending, crunching growl and crumble and crash into the canyon below.

No such luck.

Instead, they all stood there like they were in line at the deli counter. Lissie could have bored Preston into moving away by talking to Darren of their mutual acquaintances, but that was far too dangerous a stratagem. So of course, after a minute, Darren began going down that path.

"When is Jenny thinking of taking the MCATs?"

"She's signed up for January," replied Lissie. "That way she can take it again before applying if she needs to."

"How's her studying going?"

"I don't think she's had that much time to study, between working at the hospital and, uh . . . " With a vague wave, Lissie stuffed a bite of chicken biryani in her mouth.

"And working at the restaurant?" prompted Preston.

"Is it so busy there, even with business down?" asked Darren.

Shut up! Shut up shut up shut up, thought Lissie desperately.

Preston frowned. "Is business down?"

"Slow season," said Lissie, scraping her food around on her plate and using the movement to disguise a kick at Darren.

But Mr. Symbolic Systems wasn't so brilliant when it came to social cues. He merely shifted his leg away as if being kicked were a regular consequence of standing beside somebody.

"Since when does the Four Treasures have a slow season?" he asked. But before he could say more, Lissie tossed her half-finished plate aside and seized his hand.

"Come out on the deck with me, Darren. I want to show you something."

"What?"

"Just come!"

Shrugging, he nodded at Preston Lin and let Lissie drag him away.

CHAPTER 7

"Did you just say you kissed Darren Liu?"

"I said I pretended to kiss him."

Jenny rolled onto her side to scrutinize her sister in the dim morning light that filtered through the closed curtains. When no dizziness followed, she tentatively sat up. "Explain."

"I will. But first, how are you feeling?"

Jenny thought about this, making a slow survey of the little bedroom, looking up to the little window and back to where her sister lay on an inflatable mattress on the floor. "I feel much, much better."

"Oh, thank God. Then we can get out of here. Or at least I can if you can't bear to leave without seeing Charles Bing."

"No, I'd better go with you. I haven't done any studying this weekend and I'm supposed to work tonight." She pulled on a pair of socks. "I'll leave Charles a note. Let me pee and brush my hair, and then you have to get back to what happened with Darren Liu."

When she returned, Lissie described Darren's unexpected appearance the evening before. "And he kept hovering around the topic of the restaurant and our family, and I was freaking out because I didn't want Preston Lin to know we're related to Uncle Mason and Auntie Rhoda! He doesn't know, does he? You didn't tell Charles?"

"I didn't. Believe me, other than apologizing when I got here, I didn't want to bring any of it up either."

"That's what I figured. But stupid Preston kept hanging around for some reason, like he wanted to make me uncomfortable, and stupid Darren kept talking too close for comfort, so I dragged him out on the deck to show him the view. Not that you could see anything then because it was dark." Lissie giggled. "And there were a few other couples out there, so it was awkward because then it looked like we were a couple, and I kept pointing into the darkness and saying dumb things like, 'There's a nice view of the canyon when the sun is up'—"

"Get to the kissing!" ordered Jenny.

"I am, I am! But Darren acted like he wanted to go back in, so I grabbed his arm and told him to please, please, please shut up about the restaurant and our aunt and uncle because the less said about the whole thing, the better, given the publicity. And he said, 'No, we should put the word out that it's a great place, to counteract the bad publicity,' and I said, 'No, just listen to me,' and he said, 'No, I'm right about this,' and I said, 'No, trust me,' and then I see fricking Preston and some other people coming out on the deck! I knew they could see us in the light coming from the house, Darren and me, close together and clearly having some intense *thing*, so I panicked. I threw myself at him and spun him so his back was to the light, but the idiot started to ask me what the heck I was doing, so I had to slap a hand over his mouth and get really close and hiss at him, 'Just stand here like this for one second.'"

Jenny had covered her face with her hands and doubled over with muffled laughter. "Get. Out. No! You didn't! Darren Liu?"

Lissie covered her face, shoulders shaking. "Shhh! It gets worse! I mean, better and worse. Better because, when I peeked again, Preston was gone. So it worked. But worse because, when I finally let go of Darren, he said, 'Lissie, we've known each other a long time, and you're great, but I need to tell you I don't feel that way about you.'"

A tiny scream escaped Jenny, and Lissie hit her with the pillow. "Be quiet! You'll wake somebody up, and I want to get out of here."

"Tell me more!" cackled her sister. "What did you say back?"

"No way. I'm not telling you another thing till we're safely in the car."

The two sisters snuck up the stairs a few minutes later, Jenny wincing when she saw the mess left over from the potluck. Someone—probably Hazel Bing—had rinsed out the banquet-size plastic containers and stacked them, but there were still Solo cups everywhere, open bags of chips, stray paper plates, indoor chairs out on the deck, dish towels draped over a statue.

"Who cares?" said Lissie. "Just shut your eyes."

"I can't stand it. You know my eccentricities. Just give me five minutes," pleaded Jenny.

"You didn't make any of this mess! Why would you clean it up?"

But her sister was already whisking here and there, stacking, wiping, arranging. With a sigh, Lissie joined her. "Then I'm at least eating something out of the fridge."

"Go for it."

Therefore, five minutes turned into twenty, but finally they were out the front door. With a quick check for lurking deer, Lissie dashed down the walk and around the corner of the house, where she promptly collided with Preston Lin. Bouncing off him for the second time in their brief acquaintance, Lissie thought at this rate she could probably blindfold herself and pick his chest out of a lineup. At least she caught herself this time and could avoid the hand he stuck out.

"Don't tell me," said Lissie. "Another hike?"

"Swim, actually," he said, tapping the shoulder straps of his swim bag. He looked at her a few ticks longer than she thought necessary before turning to her sister. "How are you feeling, Jenny?"

"Much better, thank you. We don't mean to be sneaking out, but I thought Lissie and I should make an early start because I really need to hit the books today. I left a note for Charles, and thank you, too, for letting me—us—come."

He grinned at her that engaging grin which Lissie remembered from the picture in Charles's room, the smile that transformed his entire appearance. "You were no trouble at all," he told Jenny. "In fact, if not for your sister coming, I would have hardly known you were there."

"I hope Lissie wasn't any trouble either," Jenny replied.

"She had her moments."

Lissie shot him a dirty look and grabbed her sister's elbow. "Thanks, anyway. Gotta go." Honestly, just for variety, couldn't he say the nice, well-mannered thing?

Instead of going inside, he lingered while they threw their things in the Civic. He wasn't watching them, exactly—he took a drink from the hose, picked up some detritus from the party—but he wasn't *not* watching them.

"Does he think we're going to steal one of the potted cacti on our way out?" Lissie snorted.

"You're just paranoid about him now," answered Jenny. "He seems nice!"

"Would you do me a favor and not talk about things you know nothing about? 'Nice?'"

Jenny chuckled. "Maybe you're being a little hard on him. He may be a little socially awkward, but I can't imagine someone as nice as Charles Bing being friends with a jerk."

Lissie could, but there was no point in arguing the matter. Jenny would just have to see for herself when she was around Mr. Big Man more.

"Speaking of awkward," Jenny resumed, looking both ways before turning onto the main road, "go on with your story. What happened after Darren Liu let you down easy?"

Lissie gave a bark of laughter. "Shut up! It was the worst. Because I told him that actually I didn't think of him that way either, but I could tell from the look he gave me that he thought I was just trying to save face."

"Ah, Darren Liu," marveled Jenny. "I didn't know he had it in him."

"Seriously, Jen. I think getting into his program at Stanford has totally changed how he thinks about himself. He didn't even seem insecure around Charles Bing or Preston Lin!"

"That is pretty impressive," Jenny mused. "Symbolic systems. I'm kind of amazed Auntie Rhoda hasn't tried to push him on me again."

"Maybe because she already made that suggestion three times and you were pretty emphatically 'No, thanks' each time."

"Probably."

"But Jenny, I've decided he could actually be an okay guy."

Her sister regarded her skeptically. "Are you saying *you* might like him? I know he turned you down, but who knows, maybe he could be persuaded."

"No, no. I'm good. It's just that he said he wanted to bring some friends to the restaurant to help boost business again, and I thought that was sweet of him to suggest. He may only be doing it to catch a glimpse of you, but whatever it takes. I really don't want Uncle Mason and Auntie Rhoda to have to pay thousands of dollars to some PR firm. They don't have thousands to spare!"

"I know."

"So when he told me he and I would never be a thing," Lissie went on, "I was worried he wouldn't want to go to the restaurant after all."

Jenny gave her a wary glance. "So then what did you do?"

"I invited him to Château Cardboard for dinner tonight," Lissie answered in a rush.

"No-o-o-o-o," breathed Jenny. "Are you *trying* to mislead him? Thank God I won't be there."

"I need to explain everything to him so he doesn't go around shooting his mouth off. Plus, I want him to tell me when he's going to go to the restaurant. I honestly didn't remember you wouldn't be home when I invited him, so at least I didn't lie to him. But if you're not there, Mel and Nelson better be, or this will be totally awkward."

"That's for sure."

"Is it okay if I tell him the days you'll be at the restaurant, though?" Lissie pressed.

"No! Don't tell him. Auntie Rhoda will put him in my section and give him all sorts of free food. It'll be so embarrassing."

"But the poor guy has to have some reward for his good deed," wheedled Lissie. "You'll just have to give him the same speech he gave me. Please, please, please? Take one for the team?"

Jenny groaned, beating on the steering wheel with her palms.

"You kinda owe me," Lissie was not above saying. "I spent my whole Saturday, day and night, where I didn't want to spend it, just to be there for you."

Her sister's mouth pressed into a line, and she didn't speak until they were on the freeway. "You are the embodiment of evil."

Lissie leaned over and kissed her cheek. "Thank you, Jenny, you're the best!"

"Is he cute?" was the first thing Nelson wanted to know. Jenny had already grabbed her backpack and headed for the library, leaving Lissie to deal with it.

Nelson Nguyen was wispy but good-looking, with fine bones and soulful eyes. "If you hooked him to a bike pump and put about fifty more pounds in him, he'd be hot," was how Melanie put it. Nor was Nelson oblivious to this shortcoming, which was why he ate almost nothing but protein.

"Darren . . . shows promise," Lissie said. "But he likes girls."

Nelson stirred his protein shake, making a face at the new, flavorless brand of powder he was trying. "I figured, Lissie. I didn't think you'd be kind and thoughtful enough to invite someone for dinner for *my* sake."

"He's honestly not super cute, so there's no need to be bitter and guilt trip me. Besides, he's a nice guy, and you don't like nice guys, even if he were gay. I'm just asking you to be around for dinner to dilute the situation. You'll get free food out of it."

"Can I invite a friend?"

"One of your mean boyfriends? No way."

He pouted a moment. "What are you going to make?"

"I don't know. But there will be at least one protein-heavy dish, okay?"

"Fine."

"I've got your back, girl," drawled Mel from the couch. Her glasses were on her forehead and a copy of *America Is Not the Heart* open across her chest.

"How's the book?" asked Lissie.

"I can safely say it's the best Filipino American novel I've ever read, since it's the only Filipino American novel I've ever read. It makes me feel guilty for being middle-class. On the other hand, Milpitas is in it. Kind of."

Lissie cheered. "Woop woop! Milpitas! I was so jealous when Fremont and the Berryessa Flea Market got to be in *The Kite Runner*. Skipping over the city in between was like a deliberate snub. But if you spent yesterday where I did, you would not feel guilty for being middle-class."

"Yeah, no. Don't try to make me pity you."

What the Château Cardoza Apartments lacked in beauty, newness, construction quality, ambience, amenities, off-street parking, and manager responsiveness, they made up for in convenience, being walking distance to both the San Jose State campus and the Diridon Caltrain station. Though Lissie had advised Darren Liu to take the train, rather than drive, he ignored her advice, arriving fifteen minutes late.

"I think I parked in Gilroy," he groused when Lissie opened the door. He thrust a bottle of wine at her while surveying his surroundings with a critical eye. "Is this place safe?"

"You hear sirens, of course, from time to time, but not gunfire," she replied, backing up to admit him.

"No, I meant is it up to code. It looks like it's about to collapse."

She sighed. "Yeah, well, we joke about that. It's basically made of cardboard, so the good news is, if it does collapse, it shouldn't hurt too badly. Darren, these are my roommates, Nelson and Melanie."

"Where's, uh, Jenny?" he asked, after nodding to the others.

Lissie gave a placating smile. "To be honest, when I invited you, I'd forgotten that Jenny was working tonight. So it's just the four of us." Seeing his disappointment, she hastened to add, "But she's hoping she'll see you when you eat at the Four Treasures. You look great, by the way." He looked surprisingly passable without his glasses, and he'd gotten a trim or down permed his side hair or something. As soon as she said it she could have kicked herself, however, because now he would really think she was after him.

Sure enough, he looked uncomfortable. "Thanks."

Mel had to clear her throat to cover her laugh, but then she charged in to help, inviting Darren to have a seat. "Take the armchair, though, if you don't want to get an unexpected spring in your butt."

"Only the pros know how to sit on that couch," agreed Nelson.

"Did you want to open the wine?" asked Lissie. "Or we have beer or water or iced tea or some LaCroix." Nelson's head shot up and he threw her a scowl. They all knew the LaCroix was his.

"Just water," said Darren.

Mel pushed the chips and salsa toward him. "So," she said, "long-time friend of the family, huh?"

"It's more like my parents are friends with Jenny's and Lissie's aunt and uncle. They go to the same church."

"But Darren didn't grow up in Milpitas," Lissie put in, handing him his glass. "He went to Independence High School."

"Oak Grove," Mel raised her hand.

"Overfelt," said Nelson.

"Nelson and I are natural rivals," explained Mel.

For a minute they all occupied themselves with the chips and salsa, mood music provided by the thumping bass from the apartment overhead. Darren looked up dubiously at the popcorn ceiling. "Do you ever worry about asbestos dust?"

"Never," Lissie answered.

"Too much else to worry about," added Mel. "Like the Four Treasures. Lissie says you want to help counter the bad PR."

He blinked. "Uh, that's right."

"I think that's pretty awesome of you." She blinked right back at him, but with her fake eyelashes, it produced quite a different effect.

"Darren," Lissie began, "when you suggested it yesterday—eating there, I mean—and mentioned that my aunt was thinking of hiring a PR firm, I got an idea. I've had to spend lots of time lately answering bad Yelp and Google reviews. What we really need are some new ones to bring the rating back up and bury the bad ones."

"You want me to eat there and write a review?" he asked.

"Yes, exactly! And one with pictures, because those get better placement by the algorithm. I can tell you which dishes are the most photogenic—"

"I don't take good pictures," interrupted Darren.

"Maybe you could invite someone who's good at social media to go with you?" suggested Lissie. "And who might also be willing to write a good review with different pictures?"

"Lissie, everyone I know stays up all night coding and eating Domino's and Hot Pockets. They like Chinese food and they're not picky, but they're also not super eloquent, and I'm not sure they post reviews on Yelp and Google."

"Nelson and I could go with you," Mel blurted. "We take awesome pictures. And I could help people write their reviews."

"It's not the usual sort of thing I post about," spoke up Nelson.

"Not even for a dozen Greek yogurts?" Lissie cajoled.

He sighed. "I'm such a cheap date."

"But will *you* do it, Darren?" begged Lissie. "Go with Nelson and Melanie and whoever else you can round up?"

"Sure, fine," he agreed, smiling when she screamed with joy. "What nights will Jenny be working?"

Whipping her phone out, Lissie consulted the text Jenny had sent her. "Looks like Thursday, Friday, and Saturday this week and Friday and Saturday next week."

Once they settled on a date, Lissie rose to get the enchiladas out of the oven, and she waited until Darren was on seconds before hitting him with the parameters. "Listen, Darren, just a few more things about Saturday night . . . "

"Let me guess. You want me to wear a wire." There was a little silence, and then he smirked. "It was a joke."

Lissie's mouth popped open. Darren Liu told jokes? Who knew? "No, no wire. But there is kind of a secretive element to it."

"You mean besides trying to game the review algorithms with biased reviews by friends of the family?"

"Yes. Besides that one."

He sighed. "Let's hear it."

"You need to pretend not to know my aunt and uncle when you're there."

"What? Why? You think someone will comment on the review, 'This guy knows the owners so he clearly can't be trusted'? I don't think anyone would tie the two things together."

She gave an uncomfortable smile. "No—it's because you know people at Stanford. And . . . people know people."

Darren frowned at her, pushing his chair back from the table. "Okay, Lissie. Cut the BS. What else is going on here?"

There was no alternative. She had to tell him about the restaurant incident. Darren Liu wouldn't rat her out, would he?

"So you get it?" she asked when she had finished her story. "Your roommate knows Preston Lin, and I don't want it getting back to him that Jenny and I are related to Uncle Mason and Auntie Rhoda. He already made such a big stink over my mistake. If he heard that the Four Treasures firing me was a total scam because we're all related to each other, he is going to lose his mind. I'm talking more articles, more bad press, more bad reviews—"

"Think Super Bowl ad," said Mel solemnly.

"I don't know if I want to get involved," Darren said after a minute.

"Darren, *please!*"

"Even if I pretended not to know the Liangs—I don't mean to sound cocky, but they kind of like me, Lissie."

"We all do," she assured him. "I'll tell my family to play it cool. Come on, Darren." Lissie could see him softening and pushed further.

"And when you go with Nelson and Mel and anyone else you can get, it'd be great if someone could pretend to be allergic to something. Anything. It doesn't have to be shellfish. It could be nuts, gluten . . . "

"There's a woman in my program with celiac disease," he suggested. "I don't want to give her the wrong impression, though."

"Just say you're inviting a whole group of friends." Lissie was beginning to wonder if this version of Darren Liu actually did have to fend women off right and left.

"You can say your girlfriend will be there," Mel proposed. When Darren looked confused, she pointed at herself. "That can be me. Just for the dinner, I mean. Unless you'd rather be gay and claim Nelson."

"Uh-uh," said Nelson, "I don't do arranged marriages."

"It's not a marriage, you dork. It's a romance trope, a super popular one: the fake relationship."

"You know what you should really do," said Darren, "is go on that *Check, Please!* show." He took in their blank faces. "It's on public television. My folks watch it. You know, someone sends in a restaurant recommendation, and they send people, not professional reviewers, just normal people, to review it in secret. And then they sit around a table and talk about what they liked."

"Great idea!" Lissie responded, thinking this a time-insensitive longshot. "I haven't seen the show, but that's really helpful."

"I doubt you could nominate your own restaurant," he continued, frowning, "but I'll take a look at the application. Maybe I could do it."

"That would be so awesome of you," she praised. "We would be thrilled. But in the meantime, could you please do this other thing?"

"Okay, okay," he agreed. His face relaxed into a becoming grin. "I just have to not know who I actually know, invite someone I hardly know, and pretend to be dating someone I don't know at all."

Lissie couldn't help herself. Never mind the mixed messages. She leaped up from her chair to hug him around the shoulders, while Mel banged on the table and set the silverware rattling. "Let's hear it for Darren! Man of the hour!"

CHAPTER 8

Apart from the swimmers, Lissie was by far the youngest person on the pool deck at the Mission Valley October Challenge. She had done her training clinic; bought herself a white polo shirt, navy shorts, and white tennis shoes (Mel: "Did you get a job at the post office?"); and now stood paired with someone who looked twice her age, Ed Simmons, watching eight-year-olds flop across the pool in attempted butterfly strokes.

"What do you think of lane two?" asked Ed, a burly, teddy-bear-shaped man and hairy everywhere but the top of his head.

Was there anyone in lane two? Lissie saw only ripples and the occasional bump of a swim cap breaking the surface. "Uh . . . " She consulted the damp and wrinkled disqualification slip in her hand. Ed's slips stayed pristine on his clear acrylic clipboard. "Something wrong with the arms?"

"Swimmers' arms can go wrong two different ways during the swim," Ed informed her. "What are the two ways?"

Dutifully she read back to him, "Non-simultaneous or underwater recovery."

"And?" he prompted.

Lissie blew out a breath. "Well, if I hadn't seen that the kid had two arms when he was on the starting block, I'd have a hard time believing he had any arms at all. I haven't seen them since he dove in, so does

79

that make it underwater recovery?"

"Ah," said Ed, raising pedantic eyebrows, "but 'arm' is defined as any-thing from shoulder to wrist, and something is making those ripples. Which means that if even two millimeters of some part of the arm break the surface, it's legal. It isn't pretty, but it's legal. It's hard for the little kids to get their entire arms out of the water. It takes a lot of core strength."

"So . . . lane two is fine?"

"Lane two is fine."

To become an official "official," Lissie had to complete a certain number of sessions under various watchdogs—mostly other swim par-ents or people like Ed, who did it for a hobby, his own swim children long grown and gone. Not being a swimmer herself, Lissie could tell she was going to take the maximum number of observed sessions to feel confident, but Coach Wayman was right about the job giving her the best view of the pool. Too bad JoJo wasn't in the darned thing except for a couple minutes at a time, widely spaced apart.

Lissie glanced up in the stands to where her little sister clustered with her friends, snacking and playing on their phones. JoJo and Emma Yeh, the daughter of Hot Mom, were thick as thieves by this point, but the whole clutch of thirteen-year-old girls got along decent-ly well, apart from JoJo having displaced one of them from the fastest relay. Unfortunately, the displaced girl also hailed from Milpitas, and Lissie had so far refrained from trying to worm JoJo into their carpool.

She was relieved, moreover, to see them all acting like kids. The girls had taken to showing up to practice with curled hair and traces of makeup, despite the efforts going totally to waste the second they put their caps and goggles on. Much as Lissie wanted to chalk it up to ado-lescence, she was afraid it had equally to do with their handsome coach.

"What is your sister swimming next?" asked Ed.

Lissie looked at her heat sheet, where she had carefully highlighted JoJo's events. "100 backstroke."

"Good. Observing flip turns is one of the trickiest things you'll learn."

"It all seems tricky," answered Lissie. Her phone vibrated in her pocket. She was dying to check Darren's updates on who would go with him to the Four Treasures but wasn't allowed to take out her phone on deck.

The meet was one of the earliest of the season, and the disqualifications among the youngest kids kept Lissie busy filling out slips and running them to the deck referee, Matron Mom's husband. "Give these to Coach Penny," Mr. Pang commanded, signing them and noting the infractions on his heat sheet.

Coaches Penny and Wayman sat together at the Mission Valley Manta Rays table, she conferring with her little swimmers and he looking at his phone. Club tea had it that Penny had a crush on Wayman, but since everyone was accused sooner or later of liking Wayman Wang, Lissie hadn't paid much attention.

He glanced up when she drew near, his mouth curling into a smile. "Hey there, Lissie. How are you liking your first meet so far?"

"It's fun. I don't know what I'm doing yet, but it's fun."

He took the slips she extended to Coach Penny. "Let's have a look at these."

"They're Ed Simmons's calls, so don't blame me."

"Don't you know officials are supposed to present a united front against the coaches?" he chided.

"They are? Oh. Then I totally stand by those."

He tossed them to Penny's end of the table and tilted back in his chair. "How's JoJo liking Senior Prep?"

"She loves it," said Lissie. "I thought she'd be tired or try to beg off practice once in a while, but it's like she can't get enough."

"Great. That's what I like to hear."

Lissie imagined everyone told Coach Wayman what he liked to hear. Certainly every bit of his coaching advice was repeated by kids and moms alike, and there was plenty of "Well, Coach Wayman said . . . "

Coach Penny had the loud, singsong voice of a preschool teacher, but even her troop of younger swimmers divided their attention between her and Wayman, giving him shy glances when they came to the table to check in before and after their races. The navy-and-orange team colors, which drained Penny of all color, only flattered him, and Lissie thought it must be hard to play second fiddle to him in every possible way.

For her own part, Lissie did her best to avoid looking at him too much so everyone wouldn't start accusing her of liking him too. Not that a pairing between them would be as shocking as other possibilities—at least she was over eighteen and unmarried—but neither Lissie nor JoJo needed the drama.

Giving a nod, she scooted back to her position beside Ed and was relieved when the event switched to freestyle so she could let her mind wander.

By the time her break came, JoJo was in the warmup pool. Making herself a lunch plate and grabbing a drink, she sat on the end of the bleachers and scrolled through her messages, tapping back appropriate replies.

Mel: *Cute guy was looking at me at Mass today.*
Lissie: *Are you sure he wasn't thinking, Didn't I see her here yesterday and the day before and the day before and the day before?*

Darren: *Three from dept plus Melanie and Nelson make six.*
Lissie: *That's great! Thank uuuuuuu.*

JoJo: *Can I have $ for Cup Noodles?*
Lissie: *Sorry. Didn't see this. Hope you borrowed $.*

Wayman + JoJo + Lissie: *Dryland warmup and 400 drill before each race.*

Jenny: *Charles came by hospital again.*
Lissie: *Don't they ever go to class in grad school?*

Jenny must have been on break because her answer was immediate: *Says we should all go to Fall Ball.*

Making a face, Lissie typed: *What the heck is Fall Ball? And what do you mean ALL?*

"Something funny?"

She looked up to see Coach Wayman again, holding a plate of veggies and hummus.

"Just texting my sister."

"Isn't JoJo warming up by now?"

"Oh, she is. I meant my older sister, Jenny."

He whistled. "No way. Three Chengs?"

"You can never have too much of a good thing."

"I believe it. How's the Spartan life, by the way?"

She was surprised and, yes, flattered, that he remembered. "It's good. Busy. Especially with JoJo's swimming."

"You commute to school from Milpitas?"

"Nope. JoJo lives there with our aunt and uncle, but Jenny and I live with friends in San Jose, near the campus."

"I can't tell you how awesome that sounds. I've moved back in with Mom and Dad to save money. I'm hoping it's a six-month thing to scrape together first, last, and security deposit."

"Smart," said Lissie. "We have four of us in a two-bedroom to keep costs down."

"Yeah. Hey, if you're near the campus, there's a really good boba and noodle place with a Star Wars-y kind of name—"

"Boba Fête!" she exclaimed. "I keep waiting for George Lucas to sue them over the name, but I guess he has bigger fish to fry. It's walking distance from our place."

"Wow, now I'm even more envious! If JoJo gets any personal bests today, we should take her there to celebrate." His watch vibrated, and he glanced at it. "Gotta go. Emma is in the next event."

Lissie fumbled out a parting word, but in truth, she was too stunned to make much sense. Had he just asked her out? Or was

83

that some weird extension of the coach-swimmer-parent-equivalent group texting?

Her own phone vibrated, and she looked down, dazed. Jenny again. *Fall Ball is some kind of themed dance on Stanford campus. Real dancing. Swing, ballroom etc. Nov. ALL means crew from PV weekend I think.*

Lissie shuddered, spared having to respond right away by her break ending. She loved dancing. When Jenny and she were in elementary school, their grandmother used to take them to her dance classes at the Milpitas Senior Center. Line dancing, Chinese folk dancing, swing, ballroom. Never mind that the girls were decades younger than the other participants. When their *năinai* died a few years later, it was one of the things they missed most about her.

But going to a dance with the Bings and Preston Lin? Not on your life.

"Did you see that?" JoJo asked Lissie breathlessly, pointing to the scoreboard when she climbed out after the backstroke. "I took two seconds off my best time! Coach Wayman said he would get boba with us if I got a PB, and I did!"

"Wow," said Lissie, aware of Ed over her shoulder. Call it too many SafeSport videos, but Lissie felt as if she were participating in something inappropriate.

But Ed merely smiled and told JoJo, "Good job. Nice clean turns, too."

An hour later, JoJo blasted through her 100 fly PB again, then positively danced with excitement to the coaches' table for feedback. Coach Wayman gave her a high five and replayed her race on his tablet, pointing out various things while she nodded and grinned hugely. Before she went back up to the bleachers, JoJo darted back to her sister.

"I told him we really have to go to boba now, and he said just tell him when!"

Lissie peeked over, and there was Coach Wayman watching. He

gave a thumbs-up, which she dorkily returned. Okay, so apparently this was happening, for better or worse.

By the end of the meet, Lissie was spent. Although it took some time for the referee to finish wrapping things up so he could write in her training log, JoJo still wasn't out of the locker room. Wandering out to the parking lot, she decided to take a lap around the outside of the building to stretch her legs, making it as far as the first corner before a raised voice stopped her.

"I don't know what to do about this! It's making me crazy. *You're* making me crazy!"

Figuring she had stumbled upon a mom berating a child, Lissie turned casually around the corner. But it was not a parent and child. It was Hot Mom, Mrs. Yeh, giving Coach Wayman the business. She stood facing him, stylish as ever in a flowing maxi-dress, pointing a finger in his face, her dark eyes flashing fire. How he was receiving this tirade Lissie couldn't tell, as his back was to her. The instant Mrs. Yeh realized she had a witness, she dropped her hand and retreated a step, trying to regain control of her expression.

Coach Wayman whirled around to see who had come up behind him, his face impassive.

It was Lissie who was most embarrassed—for all of them. For catching Mrs. Yeh behaving like a Tiger Mom on steroids, for Coach Wayman having a witness to his telling-off, and for herself getting caught in the middle.

"Sorry! Excuse me," she said inadequately, backing up.

"Never mind, Lissie," declared Mrs. Yeh with a toss of her head. "I was just mad about the relay." And with that she swept off, the skirt of her dress billowing behind her.

"I am so sorry I interrupted," murmured Lissie.

He gave a mirthless laugh. "I'm not sorry. That was going to be a doozy."

"It must be hard coaching a bunch of kids from Silicon Valley. Every parent is trying to get their kid into Stanford."

A slow nod. "That they are." But then he gave himself a shake to clear his head. "That's why it is so refreshing that, not only is JoJo fast, but the sister in charge of her Olympic dreams is pretty low-key."

Lissie returned his rueful grin. "I hope it wasn't JoJo who messed up the relay, in Mrs. Yeh's opinion. I mean, it wasn't Emma who JoJo knocked off—"

"No, no. Don't worry about it." He waved a negligent hand in Mrs. Yeh's direction. "She'll calm down. Swimming is pretty cut-and-dried. It's all about the times. All there in black and white."

"Okay," agreed Lissie, still worrying over the hit to his approval rating.

"Really," he insisted. "Forget about it. And tell me, did you and JoJo decide when the victory boba is happening?"

"We didn't. But you pretty much know our schedule. If she's not in school, she's swimming, and if I'm not in school, I'm taking her to swimming."

"How about next Saturday afternoon, then?" he suggested. "Unless you have something else going on?"

"Okay," said Lissie again, feeling a prickle that was half-anxiety, half-anticipation. "Let's do it."

"Great. I'll text you guys later to hammer out the details."

She nodded, turning to go and still totally unclear on what she was getting herself into.

CHAPTER 9

The new reviews for the Four Treasures were showing up by Sunday afternoon as Lissie sat at the student information desk on the fourth floor of the King Library. Six of them, thank God, each with different pictures, of different length and emphasis, and a four- or five-star rating. With a huge smile on her face, she responded to each with a version of "We are delighted you enjoyed your meal at our restaurant." Blessed Darren thought the Sichuan prawns had "exactly the right amount of heat to enhance the flavor." His colleague "Celia" praised the number of gluten-free options. Mel called the sesame noodles "to die for" and the service (a.k.a. Jenny) prompt and "just the right amount of attentive." Nelson mentioned the "very clean bathrooms." The two other people from Darren's department only left a line apiece saying, "tasty if u like Chinese" and "I would go here again," but at least they gave it four stars.

Logging back in as herself, she marked each review as helpful and shot texts to Darren, Mel, Nelson, and Jenny to remind them to do the same. Would it be enough? There were a lot of negative comments to bury, but hopefully these six would be like clods of dirt thrown on the coffin at graveside. Up until stupid Preston and the Bings' fateful visit, the Four Treasures had always averaged over four stars. Jenny said reservations were still only 50% of normal and walk-ins at 75%, but maybe, just maybe, they could turn the corner.

"What are you so happy about?" asked Silas Alarcon, the head librarian for the university floors of the library. The students' nickname for him was "Collapso-Man" because of his lanky, bony build, and Lissie had written him into *A Doom of One's Own* as Mr. Bian. Silas wasn't Chinese, but he was fittingly myopic, detached, and happier to be with books and information than people.

"The satisfaction of a job well done," Lissie replied, tucking her phone away and randomly straightening items on the desk.

"Oh, don't pretend like you're working. You think I can't tell the difference?" He slapped a mailing tube down on the work surface. "Here. Go swap out all the posters for past events on the information board with these new ones, okay?"

"Yeah, sure. And Silas, if I ever finish my play, and if I ever find money to put it on, and if I ever make a poster for it—"

"Yes, yes," he interrupted, making the sign of the cross over her and moving on, "then you can hang your poster front and center, over the top of whatever's going on at the Center for the Performing Arts."

The announcement wall was a colorful holdover from when people actually got their information from bulletin boards. Lissie had suggested several times that they put a coffee kiosk in front of it to encourage people to linger and look at what was on offer. Silas nixed this as too messy, adding, "First comes coffee and then you'll want tchotchkes. This isn't Barnes and Noble."

Armed with a step stool and staple remover, Lissie made quick work of the outdated posters, admiring a few of them one last time before they went in the recycle bin. But opening the mailing tube always felt like unwrapping new toys on Christmas morning.

Fifteen minutes later, Silas caught her doing nothing again, sitting on the stool texting away, with only three new posters hung.

"What is happening now? Or, I should say, *not* happening?" he demanded over the stack of books he held. "We have budget cuts, you know. Are you trying to make me fire you?"

Lissie leaped up. "Silas, you will totally understand that I had to stop because—look!" She held up a poster with silhouetted dancers in silver foil against a black background. The elegant script read, "Fall Ball: Silver Screen."

He set his books down on the stool and took it from her. "What's this?"

"And look, they're going to have lessons for newbies: the dance Elizabeth and Darcy do in *Pride & Prejudice* and the Hand Jive from *Grease*! And a special performance of a Fred-and-Ginger dance from *The Gay Divorcée*. I think I've seen clips of that, but I'll watch the whole thing now."

"Get out," said Silas. "Is this ball open to the public or just Stanford students?"

"It'd be pretty rude to send posters all over if it was just for Stanford students," Lissie laughed. "No, it's for everyone, as long as tickets last. That's why I was texting. My sister Jenny mentioned going yesterday, and I shot her down, but I didn't know it was going to be movie-themed! I want to dance like Keira Knightley and like Sandy from *Grease!*"

"I'm going as Fred Astaire," Nelson said, the moment she came in the door. "Or Ginger. I can't decide."

"I thought about going as Frenchie with the yellow hair and dress, like at the dance-off," Mel announced from her usual place on the couch. "But with my luck, my wig will fly off at a pivotal moment, like when Nelson dips me. Or Darren."

"Darren!" yelped Lissie. "Is Darren coming too?"

"Maybe," Mel said evasively. Then, "Okay, so I texted him to ask him if he liked dancing."

"You mean you asked him out?"

"I was giving him the opportunity to ask *me* out," she clarified, "but it backfired. Because I think he wants to ask *you* out."

"What are you talking about? I told you Darren already warned me at the potluck not to get my hopes up about him."

"Well, it was clearly an effective reverse-psychology ploy he used on himself because it got him thinking," she sighed. "I admit I was working on him, going to the Four Treasures and everything, but between him pretending not to know Jenny and him thinking you like him, there wasn't much room left for me. And it's too bad because he's kind of a cool guy. And super smart."

"Did I say he was dumb?" Lissie countered. "But if he reverse-psychologized himself into considering me, he did not reverse-psychologize me into considering him. If he mentions it, I'll just say he can join our group. Because we have to have our own group, so we don't have to join the Bings and Jenny and Preston Lin."

On cue, the door opened and her sister appeared, holding a full laundry basket. She smiled at Lissie. "Judging by your excitement, I clearly should have led with the theme of the event and the costume aspect instead of the company."

Lissie took the basket from her, pushing Mel's legs aside so she could pour the laundry out on the sofa.

"Do *not* fold underwear in front of me," complained Nelson.

"If you're considering dressing up as Ginger Rogers, you should be able to handle seeing women's underwear," Mel retorted.

"How big is this thing, anyway?" Lissie asked Jenny. "Is it possible for you to go with Charles and Company and for the rest of us to go separately, so we don't have to deal with each other?"

"You act like I've been to one of these before," Jenny said dryly. "And that's not really a question I can ask, since it was Charles who suggested we go in the first place. But since it's held in a studio gym space, I think you should prepare yourself for dealing with people."

Lissie began matching her sister's socks. "There are two things I cannot get my mind around. First, why would Preston let Charles invite me along? Was Weekend at Bronklin's so awesome? And second, why would he even go in the first place? Can you picture him hand jiving?" The second she said it, however, Lissie had a fleeting vision of a happy, grinning Preston Lin doing just that.

"Hand jiving might be a stretch for him," Jenny admitted, "but Charles told me it was Preston who first got him to go to one of these things. Apparently Preston had a girlfriend a couple years ago who came back from a semester in Austria and made him go to the Viennese Ball, and he thought it was fun."

"If you say so," Lissie said doubtfully.

"Charles says the Fall Ball is always a different theme, but the Viennese one is formal—you know, women in gowns and men in tails."

Preston Lin must have looked marvelous in tails, waltzing with some model-tall girl, Lissie thought, before she could catch herself. "Somehow it's easier to picture someone like him dressed formally than in costume. Did Charles say if he and Preston were going to grease their hair and go as T-Birds?"

"Be still, my heart," said Nelson. "Maybe I'll switch to *Grease* too, then."

"He didn't say," Jenny replied, folding a T-shirt precisely in KonMari style. "But I told him I didn't have the time or money to do a costume, so I would just wear a nice dress, and he said that was fine."

"But Jenny, I thought Mel and we could go as the Bennet sisters," Lissie said eagerly. "There are five of them in the book, but we could each just pick one, and you should be Jane Bennet. If I find something for you to wear when I go thrifting, will you be Jane?"

"What about me being Frenchie?" protested Mel. "No way am I giving that up to be Mary Bennet."

"If you were a Bennet, you wouldn't have a wig that fell off," Lissie pointed out. "And you could be whichever Bennet you want. I thought I'd do the Jena Malone Lydia Bennet—you know how she wore her hair in those long pigtail ringlets? And I have a greenish dress like she wore if I don't find a better one."

"If you're all going to be Bennets, then I should match you," complained Nelson. "Do they have a brother?"

"They don't, but you don't have to match us, Nelson, because if Darren comes, I'm betting he's not coming in a costume."

"I dunno," said Mel. "Now that we know how effective reverse psychology is on him, you would probably just have to tell him absolutely not to wear a costume, and next thing you know he'd show up as Napoleon or something."

As predicted, later that night, Darren sent Lissie a text asking how the restaurant reviews were paying off and casually mentioning the Fall Ball. She replied with fervent gratitude for the former and a friendly group invitation to the latter.

The talk continued off and on all week, whenever any of the roommates were home to share costume or hair ideas. Relevant TikToks and YouTube videos shot back and forth among them. One night, they made as much noise as their upstairs neighbors, pushing the furniture aside and imitating some of the moves and steps from the film clips.

The passing of the days brought the trip to Boba Fête ever nearer. But Coach Wayman made no reference to it at Monday practice, to JoJo's disappointment, and when Tuesday passed, she was beside herself.

"Do you think we're still going?" she demanded of Lissie as they drove away. "Or do you think he's forgotten?"

"I don't know. I don't think you should ask him about it, though."

"Yeah, yeah," said JoJo impatiently, ripping open the wrapper on her granola bar. "Because you think it might create jealousy. You already told me."

"Well, have you heard of him celebrating other people's personal bests this way? Did Emma get any at the meet?"

"Emma added time," JoJo said, her mouth full of crunchy oats.

"Another one of your friends, then."

"Melissa dropped in breaststroke, but she didn't say anything." Melissa Pang was the daughter of Matron Mom and the meet referee. "And Olivia isn't talking to me because I bumped her off the A relay."

Lissie sighed. Olivia Wei was from the Milpitas family who would have made convenient carpool buddies. "I wish you'd bumped off someone from Newark, instead of the girl who lives a five-minute walk away from you. Look, JoJo, the problem is, we're so new to this group, we have no idea if Coach Wayman always does this kind of thing, and everyone keeps quiet so it doesn't sound like bragging, or if he never does this kind of thing, which means it's weird, and maybe we shouldn't do it either."

"What's wrong with it?" protested JoJo. "It's just boba! It's motivational! And it's not like I'm going with him by myself. You'll be there, and you're an old and responsible adult. Can't you ask in the group text, Lissie? You could say you're trying to set your schedule, and is it still on?"

"We'll give him a little more time. If he hasn't said anything by Thursday after practice, I'll ask."

On Wednesday, when the kids were climbing out of the pool and heading for the locker room, and Lissie was typing away and hadn't yet gathered her things, she looked up to find Coach Wayman.

"Oh, hey. Do I need to clear out of here?"

"No, no hurry. I was just checking if you and JoJo were still on for Boba Fête this Saturday."

"Sure!" Lissie said, torn between relief and discomfiture. "We're still available. My aunt will bring her to morning practice, but then anytime afterward should work."

"How about three, then?"

"Perfect. Three at Boba Fête." She hesitated. "Did . . . will anyone else be coming?"

"Anyone like who?"

"Well, like, I don't know, Emma Yeh or anyone?"

A shadow crossed his face, and Lissie belatedly remembered Mrs. Yeh chewing him out after the meet. But he only said, as JoJo had, "Emma added time."

"Right," said Lissie, grasping at this straw. "And this was for JoJo's two personal bests. It's great. She's excited."

"Awesome." He gave one nod. "Here comes my next group. We'll talk to you later, Lissie."

She wondered if, by "we," he meant the group text, or if swim coaches had some equivalent to the royal we. Anyhow, weird or not weird, JoJo would be ecstatic. And Lissie herself had a funny flutter in her stomach to think of the impending . . . celebration? Recognition? Get-together? Not-date?

It was not a date. He was probably too old for her. One afternoon, the swim moms had cyberstalked him, trying to figure out how old he was based on when he swam for Chapman and how long he had been coaching for various clubs. They settled on late twenties. Not old, per se, but older than anyone Lissie had ever gone on a date with.

Mel was convinced it was a date. "He can't just ask you out, of course," she reasoned. "SafeSport doesn't cover this. I mean, you're supposed to be on the text chain to protect JoJo, but actually JoJo is the one chaperoning you two. Crazy!"

"It's not a date," insisted Lissie.

"Whatever. I might just happen to get boba at the exact same time," Melanie said. "Total fly on the wall. I just want to see the guy. You and I can act like we don't know each other."

"I can't control you, but I wish you wouldn't. It's getting confusing for me to remember who I'm supposed to know and not know, and where. First the Four Treasures, and now Boba Fête."

Fortunately for Lissie, a giant project came in at the FedEx Office where Mel worked, and she got called in to help. Which meant that Lissie and JoJo could encounter Coach Wayman without an audience.

"Do you think he's paying?" JoJo asked. She was particularly dolled up that afternoon, her hair curled and lips glossy and eyes outlined. Lissie regretted that there would be no swim gear to hide it all or chlorine to wash it away.

"I don't think swim coaches get paid a lot," answered Lissie. "We'll split it."

"Hey, there are the Chengs," called Coach Wayman. The line was out the door, and he was at the end of it. Lissie had never seen him out of Mission Valley Manta Ray attire, and she wasn't surprised to see that he looked equally appealing in a brick-red pullover and jeans. Several people in line who had already been eyeing him checked Lissie out to see how she measured up.

Having no idea how to greet the off-duty swim coach of one's little sister, she hung back and let JoJo go ahead of her. Coach Wayman solved the problem with a fist bump for JoJo, fist bump for Lissie.

"How has your Saturday been?"

"Pretty quiet so far," said Lissie.

"You worked us hard for a Saturday practice," accused JoJo.

"I have to! Only two more chances to make champs cuts, and not everyone is as lucky as you are to already have six of them."

JoJo preened. "Does that mean I can have the crème brûlée tea with 100% sugar? Or, no, wait, the strawberry with lychee jelly?"

"Gross," he said. "You know both of those are just dessert disguised as tea, right? I'd say if you absolutely have to have one, do 30% sugar." He laughed at the face JoJo made. "Besides, you picked drinks that are almost $7. You got personal bests, not Olympic Trials cuts!"

"Coach Wayman always drags us about eating junk," JoJo sighed to her sister.

"Don't worry about treating her," Lissie spoke up. "I can cover hers."

He lifted a hand. "Nah. This was my idea. I got this."

The day was cool and overcast, the kind of weather where a jacket was too warm and a long-sleeved shirt too cold. Lissie wore an oversized SJSU sweatshirt which she thought about leaving in the car when she saw how JoJo had taken pains to look cute. On the other hand, it would not do to show up looking like she had expectations of this being some kind of date. Lissie had worn the sweatshirt several times while sitting out on the bleachers during JoJo's practice; if she wore it today, it meant, *I am not reading anything into this.*

But it was impossible not to analyze what was going on. They spent the time in line talking about JoJo's swimming: how she was liking Senior Prep; what her goals were at the next meet; whether it made more sense in the relay for Emma to swim the backstroke and JoJo the fly, or would more time be saved by putting JoJo on back, where her split was nearly two seconds faster than Emma's, and putting Melissa on fly, etc.

So Mel was wrong, and this really was just a celebration of JoJo's swim achievements.

Once they got their drinks, however, and squished into a corner table, Wayman Wang turned his attention to Lissie.

"How's it going for you, diving headfirst into the swim world?"

She sat up straighter, feeling like she was at a job interview. "I like it. It's really time-consuming, but I'm enjoying it more than I thought I would. I love watching JoJo swim, and the meet was just plain fun." Lissie stirred her milk tea. "I was even thinking I might try out the pool at our rec center sometime."

"Great idea! We'll turn your sister into a swimmer yet, won't we, JoJo?" he asked. But the girl shrugged her skinny shoulders, and Lissie could see she was annoyed to share her handsome coach. Her own brow knit as alarm bells rang in her head. If she could see that her sister had a thing for Coach Wayman, was it equally obvious to him? She almost wished Mel had come after all, to provide an objective-ish opinion on whether Coach Wayman was a SafeSport bomb waiting to blow or the innocent victim of a paranoid world.

Not that Lissie wouldn't have enjoyed a little flirtation with a hot guy if her younger sister hadn't been present, but there had been enough trouble in her life lately without starting some with JoJo. Therefore, all such thoughts must be suppressed.

"How long have you been swimming, Coach Wayman?" Lissie prompted. "I don't know your story."

"Since he was eight," JoJo supplied, before shrinking back in embarrassment. "I mean, it's in his bio on the team website."

Her coach gave the rickety table a pleased smack. "Swimmers

reading the team website! That's what I like to hear. JoJo's right, I've been swimming since I was eight. Grew up in Sunnyvale but eventually swam for clubs in Mountain View and Palo Alto. Distance freestyle, 4 IM, 2 Fly. Basically, the longer the better, because if you're 5'11" like me, you need to make up in endurance what you lose in height and wingspan."

"That makes sense," said Lissie. "Do you come from a swimming family, or are you the lone ranger, like JoJo?"

He shifted in his seat. "More of a loner. Swimming becomes its own community, doesn't it, JoJo?"

"Yeah," she agreed, smiling again to be addressed. "I text my swim friends more than my school friends."

"Did you tell them about getting boba today?"

"Um, no . . . I didn't know if I should."

"Tell them," he declared. "I want word to get around that working hard and getting your head in the game and swimming the best you possibly can at the right time get you rewarded. I probably should have announced it to the whole team, but I couldn't decide if it was weird or not."

Lissie was unutterably relieved to hear him say exactly what she had been thinking. Then this was not a secret, and he was not "grooming" JoJo! Thank God. It was all Preston Lin's fault, making her think everyone was sinister and out to get her. Her smile was as big as JoJo's.

"Okay, I will," said JoJo, not altogether pleased. "I'll tell them." Lissie guessed that part of her was sorry not to be special, singled out. Hoping Coach Wayman wouldn't notice her sister's reaction, she jumped in again.

"You better watch out, or the team might bankrupt you," she joked. "At least, the girls will try their hardest to."

"Never underestimate the power of boba," he answered, matching her tone. He glanced at his watch. "So what else is on the agenda for the Cheng girls today?"

"We're going thrifting for costumes!" announced JoJo.

"Halloween costumes?" he guessed. He raised an eyebrow at Lissie.

"Aren't you two a little old for trick-or-treating?"

"I'm not trick-or-treating," said JoJo indignantly. "Emma and Melissa and Olivia and Ava and I are gonna bake pumpkin muffins and answer the door and give out candy."

"To old folks like your sister?"

"I'm not trick-or-treating either," laughed Lissie. "I'm going to a costume ball the Saturday after the Age Group Invitational, and I have to find a dress for my older sister."

"Costume ball?" He looked amazed. "Is that even a thing?"

"It's the Fall Ball at Stanford," she explained, "but it's open to the public. It's 'costumes admired, but not required.' It's not usually my thing either, but this year the theme is the movies—'Silver Screen'—so it might be dorky, but a group of us are going together."

"The theme is movies in general? *All* movies? So somebody comes as Godzilla and dances with the Godfather?"

JoJo crossed her arms over her chest and looked annoyed again, so Lissie tried to keep it brief, but it was hard to hide her enthusiasm on the subject. "They did narrow the focus a little to this schizophrenic mix of *Grease* and *Pride & Prejudice*, with a little Fred Astaire thrown in. So there'll be some Danny Zukos doing English country dance and some Mr. Darcys hand jiving. They're even going to have lessons! So nerdy and fun, if you like that kind of thing. And my roommates and I like that kind of thing."

"I like that kind of thing too!"

"You're kidding."

"I'm not! You might not guess it to look at me, but I was a champion square dancer in middle school." He grinned at JoJo. "When I was your age, I owned that P.E. unit. All of us in the gym, with our glasses and braces, rocking the do-si-dos."

Her scowl deepened, but he didn't seem to notice. "Ah, good times. I still never miss a chance to line dance at weddings. How big is this group of yours that's going, Lissie?"

She swallowed. Was he doing what she thought he was doing?

Was Wayman Wang asking to tag along to the Fall Ball with them? "Uh, well, we're kind of in two groups, but my group is four people so far."

"I guess I'd be a fifth wheel, then?"

He *did* want to come! Lissie glanced at her surly sister, but what did JoJo expect her to do? She couldn't tell him he couldn't come to a public ball when she'd already said she and her friends were going as a group.

"We're not couples," she answered at last. "We already bought tickets, but they're general admission, so it would just be a matter of if there were any still available."

"Cool," he said. "Would it be a problem if I invited myself to join your group?"

"No." She managed a smile. The thought streaked through Lissie's brain that she wouldn't mind Preston Lin seeing her show up with a handsome partner. Wayman Wang might never have made Olympic Trials cuts like the mighty Preston Lin, but he could certainly compete in the charm department.

"No," Lissie said again, the smile reaching her eyes now. "It'd be no problem at all."

CHAPTER 10

"Lissie, since you're not yet officially signed off as an official," Fred Pang said, "I thought I might put some of your other skills to work at this meet."

Dismayed, Lissie glanced around at the room of "official" officials. It was the November Age Group Invitational, and they had just gone over the stroke briefing and were being given their deck assignments. "You're gonna make me work concessions? How will I ever get signed off, then?"

"No, no, not concessions," Fred assured her, "But from now until the session break, I figured you could play handler."

She tried to hide her reluctance. "Is there . . . a special-needs swimmer today?"

The meet referee waved away her fears. "Nothing like that. The USA Swimming Youth Ambassador is at today's meet. We just thought it would be more fun for this guy to have someone younger look after him. You just make sure he gets something to eat and tell him where the bathrooms are and help him hand out the ribbons and awards to the little kids. Okay? Piece of cake. Didn't you say you used to work in a restaurant? You know how to be friendly and welcoming."

It wasn't like she had any choice. In this setting she was lowest on the totem pole, both in qualifications and in age, so there was no use crying about it. It wasn't until she was sitting at the entrance desk to the pool and her special charge strode in that she connected the dots.

She had already met this USA Swimming Youth Ambassador.

"What are you doing here?" demanded Preston Lin, looking down at her. He was in full Stanford swim team regalia: warmup jacket with its giant "S" and matching track pants.

"I happen to work here," she said, scrambling to her feet. "Kind of. I mean, I'm working this meet. Because my sister JoJo is swimming. And I'm your handler today."

His eyebrows lifted. "You volunteered for that?"

"No, I didn't volunteer for it. The powers that be made me do it. I didn't remember it was you or that there even was such a thing as a 'youth ambassador.'" She threw a pair of air quotes.

"There you go, bursting my bubble." There was the barest flash of a grin, but it was enough. Lissie backed down.

"Well, anyway," she resumed, beckoning him to follow her. "I'm supposed to show you where you can put your things and find something to eat or drink. After the anthem and before the first event, I introduce you and you say a little something. Here's the breakroom."

"How have you been, Lissie?" The polite question that seemed to come out of nowhere made her hackles rise in suspicion.

"Fine. You?"

"Fine."

She pointed to a place where he could stow his bag. Several officials were milling around, grabbing coffee or breakfast, but none were from Mission Valley. They gave Preston curious looks but didn't try to address him. He tucked his bag obligingly where she'd indicated, and she pointed wordlessly at the food table.

"You're good at this handling business," he said dryly, "though I seem to remember you having more to say at the restaurant."

"That was work me. This is volunteer me. But if it's details you want, there's breakfast sandwiches and fruit and yogurt. Coffee. Tea."

"I see that." Taking a plate, he loaded it up while she stood stiffly to the side. "You don't want any, Lissie? I remember you having a healthy appetite at the potluck."

"I already ate this morning, thanks."

When he took a seat at one of the tables, she had no choice but to join him. He unwrapped his first bacon-and-egg sandwich, and Lissie's nose twitched. Yes, she had already eaten, but just a boiled egg and fruit and yogurt. The sandwich was next-level. As if she had spoken aloud, he raised his gaze to her as he chewed. "Man, this is good."

"Okay," she gave in, and he grinned. "Maybe I'll have one."

It is hard to maintain a shell of cool reserve while eating a sloppy breakfast sandwich. Her first bite pulled one of the bacon slices clear out of its English muffin and onto her chin. "Ugh," said Lissie, dabbing at her face with a napkin.

"I'm glad it happened to you first," Preston chuckled.

"Me too," returned Lissie. "Bacon sloppiness would be most unbecoming for a youth ambassador."

"You're not going to leave that alone, are you?"

"Leave what alone? I'll be the first to applaud if you bring about the long-awaited détente between swimming and the youth of today."

At that he actually laughed, and Lissie felt pleased with herself.

"I'll do my best," he said. "But since you're not a swimmer, you might not believe me when I tell you it can be a love-hate relationship."

"Really? What does Preston Lin, Stanford star and USA Swimming Youth Ambassador, hate about swimming?"

Having finished his first sandwich, he started to unwrap the second. "Sometimes you work so hard—every day, you work *so hard*, and you get nothing for it. Nothing to show for it in your times. And sometimes you're even slower than before you busted your butt trying. So you wonder why you bothered in the first place. It's not like science either. In science, you can put in a lot of work and not get the result you want, but the failure is at least directional. You learn something. You refine your hypothesis. In swimming, you just want to quit."

"Oh." His admission surprised her. It was so . . . vulnerable. Candid. She herself had never tried anything so hard she felt like she was failing. Lissie saved all her failing for things she didn't care about. "Why didn't you quit, then?"

He shrugged. "I needed a sport, and I wasn't good at anything else."

She looked at him. He didn't look like he was joking. Who was this guy? Was he admitting to actual cracks in his armor?

"What?" he asked, noticing her regard.

"It's just . . . I didn't think you thought you were bad at anything."

"Nobody thinks they're good at everything." He crumpled up his empty sandwich wrappers and then fixed her with his unsettling gaze. "Unless you do."

"Of course I don't think that," retorted Lissie. "Even if I did, you took pains to show me I suck at waitressing, for starters."

Up went the eyebrows. "For the record, I would like to point out that you brought it up this time."

"Granted," she conceded. "But it's always the elephant in the room."

His eyes dropped to the surface of the table where the concessions minions had scattered Hershey's kisses. "I don't think you suck at waitressing. But you did have a significant lapse in focus."

"Yes. For which I apologized that night, didn't I? Multiple times."

"You did, and I don't doubt your sincerity, but I think it's also fair to say you thought I was overreacting."

She chewed her lip a moment, wondering whether to deny it. "Okay, fine. I did think that." It was on the tip of her tongue to mention the *Daily* article, which was what had tipped his overreaction into irrational vengeance in her book, but this was not the place to get into it. "But that didn't mean I wasn't sorry."

"I've made you angry again."

"Just . . . can we take a time-out from this?" She made the sign with her hands. "Change the subject?"

"Sure. I'm . . . sorry."

They watched one of the concessions people wheel in a cart full of water bottles to unload in the cooler. Lissie wondered if handlers were allowed to excuse themselves and kill time in the bathroom when conversation got burdensome, or if she was supposed to wait and synchronize her bladder with the VIP's.

She tried again. "So why did you need a sport?"

Preston gave her a look. "So I would be 'well-rounded.' So I would get into a good school. Did your parents honestly never give you that speech?"

She avoided the question. "I did drama myself. But then, I suck at sports. And I think I didn't end up quite as round as you."

"You mean you didn't have violin lessons?"

"No."

"Piano?"

"I didn't make it past the books where you could sing along as you played," Lissie admitted.

"I'm guessing no Chinese school on Saturday mornings, then."

"Nope. My parents didn't even speak Mandarin to each other," she said carefully.

"Why not?"

She shouldn't have gotten into this. This was quicksand territory. "Oh, you know. They were both second-generation, and their parents came when they were teenagers, so Chinese was mostly something their grandparents spoke to them. I mean, my dad and his sister grew up speaking Chinese at home, but not my mom." *Don't talk about families!*

Before he could ask another question, Lissie rushed them in another direction, saying, "But back to your well-roundedness—"

He laughed. "I said my folks wanted me to be well-rounded. I didn't say I actually was."

"Oh, come on. You're nearly a perfect sphere. But you didn't mention your dancing skills."

"I didn't know I had any."

"Jenny said you're the one who first got Charles to go to a Viennese Ball."

"Yeah, but you don't have to be an amazing dancer to go. They give lessons, like at the Fall Ball." He hesitated. "I think you'll have a good time. It's fun."

She thought for a second he was going to say more. His lips parted and then shut. Once more, she had a brief vision of him in tails and wondered if he was bringing a date. Or if his ex-girlfriend would be there. An ex-girlfriend Lissie pictured looking like Gemma Chan in *Crazy Rich Asians*.

He didn't say anything.

She said nothing right back.

The concessions mom dropped a water bottle that bounced and rolled to Lissie's feet. Bending to retrieve it, she got up to give it back and said over her shoulder, "You better get some coffee if you want any. It's almost time."

"I'm good."

Lissie didn't really drink coffee, but she took her time at the table, dumping in sugar and creamer and going back and forth between the caffeinated Starbucks box and the decaf.

"Whoa! What's going on there, Boba Fête? You pretended to be so low-maintenance when you ordered your milk tea."

Lissie smiled at Coach Wayman who appeared beside her, giving his own coffee a topping-up. "Coffee needs more work than tea to make it palatable."

He elbowed her playfully. "Lucky for you, I see more tea in your future. Word has gotten out, Lissie Cheng! I think we'll need to rent a bus for the next boba run because the kids are all talking big today, including JoJo." He fitted a plastic lid on his cup. "And I wanted to tell you, about the ball, I got a ticket so count me in. Just text me where to meet you guys and when."

"Great," she said. She wished he would lower his voice so they wouldn't become grist for the Mission Valley gossip mill. JoJo had been monosyllabic and pouty all week, and despite finding some goodies, thrifting together hadn't been the fun outing Lissie had hoped.

"What do they have you doing today?" was his next question. "Did they finally cut you loose to watch over your very own lanes?"

She shook her head ruefully. "Still not qualified. In fact, they demoted me. Today, I'm a 'handler' for the USA Swimming Youth Ambassador," she said, pointing with her chin over Wayman's shoulder. She'd expected to find Preston Lin watching, but she was surprised by the narrowness of his gaze and the tension in his frame.

Wayman glanced back.

Then he did a double take.

Preston's mouth tightened.

"Do you two know each other?" asked Lissie.

"The, uh, it's . . . " fumbled the coach. He gave Preston a sharp nod, which was not returned. The youth ambassador rose to his feet. "It's a small swim world," said Wayman. "Um, catch you later, Lissie." And then, without a word to Preston, and without even taking the coffee he had just filled, he slipped from the room.

"That was weird," offered Lissie.

She had a feeling Preston didn't even hear her. His face was dark, and she could see he was breathing quickly. But there was no time to ask anything because Fred Pang popped his head in.

"Are you two coming? They're about to play the anthem."

Streamline Aquatic Club had a beautiful facility with a ten-lane, fifty-meter pool and a sound system that didn't reduce everything to a fuzzy mumble, but Lissie hardly appreciated any of this in her distraction. The anthem played. Preston handed her a card with his bio. Someone handed her a mic. She read the card. She handed the mic back. The mic was handed to Preston. Preston said something. The crowd applauded. He handed the mic back. Then he turned and disappeared into the men's locker room.

What was the youth ambassador's handler supposed to do when the youth ambassador went places the handler couldn't follow? After a minute, Lissie sat down on the bleachers by the starter box. Maybe Preston had to pee. A little declaration of intent would have been helpful, but when had he ever been helpful?

He stayed in the locker room so long that, after watching JoJo's first race, Lissie considered sending in a boy from the team to check on him. Supposing he had gone straight through and out the other door? Was it the handler's fault if the handlee bolted?

Just in case, Lissie went back and peeked in the break room. No youth ambassador. She sheepishly asked the ladies sorting ribbons if they had seen him. One handed her a paper bag and replied, "How did you manage to lose that nice-looking young man? He's not here, but here are the ribbons for him to give to the eight-and-under winners."

"Do you know where he goes to give them out?" Lissie asked.

"The room behind the diving platform. The coaches will start sending the kids over around 10:30."

"Okay. Thanks. And, if you see him before I do, will you tell him that too?"

Taking the bag, she returned poolside, trying not to look around too obviously for her lost charge.

It was Coach Wayman who found her first, catching her elbow as she passed the lower diving boards. "Hey, Lissie, can I have a word?"

He cast glances fore and aft, an uncomfortable half-grin coming and going. Even though Lissie was dying to have her curiosity satisfied, she was sorry he pulled her aside in plain view of everyone in the stands, if not the entire deck. This would do it now—every mom and girl on the team would want to know later what he had to say to her.

"You probably, uh, noticed that Preston Lin, the youth ambassador guy—we recognized each other."

"I did notice that."

"Do you know him yourself, or did you just meet him today?"

"I've met him before," she answered, uncertain how to put it. "He's a friend of a friend of my older sister. But he and I are not friends."

Wayman nodded, absorbing this. "Me, I met him probably seven years ago now."

"Seven years?"

"Yeah, I was a new assistant swim coach, just out of college, thrilled to be hired by a great club and a great head coach I'd admired for a long time."

"And he was on the team?" Lissie guessed.

"Yeah, he'd been on it since his freshman or sophomore year in high school. He'd grown a lot that past summer, apparently, and his times just took off. So much so that he started thinking our club was too small for him. That if he was going to get a big college scholarship, he needed a flashier team."

"So he left the club?"

Wayman shrugged. "That wouldn't have been such a big deal. I mean, there's always a certain amount of club-hopping that goes on. It would have hurt to lose him, of course, but every club can survive losing one swimmer, even if it's the star swimmer." He paused, and Lissie waited, resisting the urge to prod him and tell him just to get it all out already.

"But the way he left . . . it was like, not only did he want to feel like he'd made the right choice, but he wanted everyone else to feel like they'd made the wrong one by staying."

She could believe that. Par for the Preston-Lin course. "He bad-mouthed your club?"

"For starters. I tried to tell him to be cool about it, but it got worse from there. He poached a few of his friends—the other guys on the A relays, basically—and then convinced the head coach to jump ship too. At Lin's new club, when the head coach's contract was up, they didn't renew him. Instead, they hired *our* head coach. Well, our little club couldn't survive that. Not so many blows in succession. Other swimmers and coaches started leaving. Pretty soon, it was clear there wouldn't be enough income to secure the pool rental space we needed."

"That's terrible!"

"I could see the writing on the wall. I was looking for a new job and finally found something in Nevada. The cost of living was cheaper there, at least, but it's taken me all this time to work my way back to California. I still wonder about some of the poor swimmers who got lost along the way while Lin was making his big push to get into Stanford.'"

And here she had been, beginning to think he wasn't the irredeemable oversized jerk she had imagined!

"That's terrible," said Lissie again. "I'm sorry you all had to go through that. No wonder you were so shocked to see him! I can't imagine how USA Swimming could pick someone like that to be their youth ambassador."

"I can," Wayman replied. "You've got to admit, on the surface he's everything they want as a role model. Let's just hope that none of the kids follow closely in his footsteps."

"Maybe USA Swimming doesn't know. How could they, unless someone told them?"

He waved this away. "Nah. It's not going to be me. It's all water under the bridge now. He's done swimming, and I'm still coaching. I've moved on, but I thought you should know, Lissie, so you aren't taken in."

When Wayman was gone, Lissie, her heart burning with indignation, went into the award room and laid out the ribbons by event. By the time Preston Lin deigned to reappear (with no explanation whatsoever for his long absence), the squirrely eight-and-unders were already congregating, chattering and laughing and slapping each other with the empty sleeves of their swim parkas, while their parents crowded in behind, phones at the ready.

Coach Wayman was right. On the surface, Preston Lin was the perfect role model. He made a big fuss over presenting the ribbons to the wide-eyed and admiring winners. He teased and joked and made little encouraging speeches. He patiently took picture after picture with them, and the engaging grin put in several appearances. If Lissie had not encountered him before or known anything about him, she probably would have left the meet halfway in love.

It's a good thing Wayman warned me, Lissie told herself. Because she had the funny feeling that if he had not, she would have been all too willing to be charmed.

CHAPTER 11

L issie had originally wanted the three "Bennet sisters" to arrive at the Fall Ball together, but when she heard Charles and Hazel Bing intended on picking Jenny up and joining Preston, she abandoned the idea.

"Mel and Nelson and I are not going to caravan behind you," she told her sister. "We'll just meet you there."

"But if Wayman Wang goes with you guys, it'll be a tight fit in Darren's car."

"Wayman's a Flat Stanley, remember?"

Better a tight fit in Darren's car than being stuck with Preston Lin all evening, was Lissie's opinion. Lissie had told Jenny about Wayman's history with Preston, and Jenny had reminded her there were two sides to every story. To which Lissie replied, only half in jest, "That's what Stalin said."

Lissie wasn't telling the entire truth. If she didn't want to join a party which included the likes of Preston Lin, neither was she eager to be squished up against Wayman. Could going to the Fall Ball in a group be looked at as "getting involved" with JoJo's coach? Her little sister clearly thought it could, given her recent coldness to Lissie. But the man himself was hard to read. Was Wayman Wang interested in her or not?

If he was, she decided she should not encourage that interest in any way, for a hundred reasons. It'd be too messy, for starters. There'd be messiness with Auntie Rhoda, who had given her a penitential assign-ment, not a new dating avenue. Messiness with the Mission Valley Manta Rays—the coach dating the sister of a swimmer fell in a gray area, but in that tight-knit group, the area was so dark gray as to be charcoal. And above all, messiness with JoJo. If Lissie and Wayman became a thing, it'd be bad enough; it would be exponentially worse if they then broke up. Things might get so awkward that JoJo would have to find a new club.

To make up for the limbo she found herself in, Lissie was all busi-ness at JoJo's practices during the week, not saying a thing to Wayman beyond basic greetings nor seeking him out in any way, even though they really needed to nail down the logistics for the Fall Ball. Nor did he seek her out or make mention of the thing. It was the boba all over again. Had he forgotten, or was this just how he rolled? He couldn't have forgotten! He'd bought a ticket, after all. But the days passed and . . . nothing.

On Friday, Uncle Mason agreed to take JoJo to practice so Lissie could put the finishing touches on her costume. Melanie, a sewing whiz, had made subtle refinements to Lissie's green dress, adding a lace "tucker" and tiny pleats to the bodice. Lissie had cut her bangs and experimented with putting her hair into loose pigtails at her chin, and then curling three separate ringlets in each tail. She set the curling iron down and spun around. "Blammo. Jena Malone as Lydia Bennet."

"If Jena Malone were Chinese," said Mel, looking up from the stitching she was doing to her own dress.

"Exactly." Satisfied with her dress rehearsal, Lissie went to bed, checking her phone one last time before she slept, again when she got up to go to the bathroom in the middle of the night, and once more after waking up.

Nothing.

By eleven on Saturday, she broke down. She sent Wayman her first-ever text that did not include JoJo: *Did you want to ride with us tonight?*

She knew he ran practices for Senior Prep and the Seniors all morning, but it was nearly two before he responded. *Stomach issues. Not going to make it. So sorry.*

"Stomach issues!" Lissie stomped into the living room to show Mel and Nelson. "He couldn't find one second earlier this morning to say something?"

"Maybe the heaves came on last minute," said Mel. She was taking in Nelson's vest in return for a 12-pack of LaCroix. "But that sucks. I really wanted to see this guy for myself."

"Not me," Nelson said with a shudder. "Not if he has the runs. I'll just have to feast my eyes on Jenny's boyfriend and Preston Lin."

"Well don't forget in all your drooling that you have to partner Mel and me," Lissie reminded him. "It's probably better that he can't come. At least we'll now be an even foursome."

"Is Darren my date or yours?" he asked Mel.

"Ha-ha, I would have said he was mine, except he's been effectively AWOL since the Four Treasures. I swear I'm giving up on boys completely," Mel said. "But not until I've gone to this dumb ball. What if God has something dramatic planned for me?"

At six-thirty, Darren Liu knocked at the door of Unit 114. Lissie threw it open and was about to drop an elaborate curtsy when his appearance froze her mid-knee bend. "Wow. You . . . went all out."

He struck a pose. "You like it?"

Then Nelson and Melanie were beside her, oohing and aahing, with Lissie very careful not to make eye contact with Mel.

Darren Liu was a T-Bird. Not that Lissie thought he would look better as Mr. Darcy, but as a T-Bird he was . . . she didn't know whether to laugh or cry. It wasn't the black leather jacket, which hung on his angular frame like a coat on a hanger, or the wife-beater or the shiny pompadour—it was the whole ensemble. She was going to have to make sure her bladder was reliably empty all night.

"Are you *Pride & Prejudice?*" he asked, looking her up and down.

"I'm one of the characters from the movie, and so is Mel. And Nelson is Fred Astaire." Lissie stepped aside so Darren could admire her roommates, but he only tossed them a cursory glance.

"Your hair looks very nice," he said, his gaze returning to Lissie.

"Thanks. I think it took as much product as yours." She had a moment's unease that had nothing to do with showing up at the Fall Ball with this T-Bird rather than the handsome partner she had imagined. No, it had more to do with Darren's lingering look. He had said he wasn't interested, but what if he had forgotten? Was Mel right, and Darren had reverse-psychologized himself?

They headed out almost immediately, climbing into Darren's Camry after Mel did the requisite bit from "Greased Lightning."

"You know how weird that looks in your Bennet girl dress, right?" asked Nelson.

"Not any weirder than everyone else is going to look tonight, at one point or another."

When they entered Roble Gym after their supper in Japantown, Lissie's and Mel's first reaction was disappointment. Lissie had pictured a silver-screen wonderland: silver streamers, gray and white balloons, white flowers in silver vases, iridescent sequins scattered across white tablecloths, giant black-and-white posters of Hollywood stars from all eras. But apart from a few garlands, it basically looked like a gym. A nice one, but still a gym.

"Could they not decide between Netherfield Hall or Rydell High, so they went with nothing?" Lissie hissed.

"Maybe they wanted all the Dannys and Sandys and Darcys and Elizabeths to look equally out of place," Mel hissed back. "Or they blew all the money on the deejay and the poster."

A couple was working on a dance routine in the center of the floor as Cole Porter's "Night and Day" floated over the loudspeakers, and there were several photo booths and refreshment tables by the entrance, but that was it. At least the lion's share of people were in some sort of costume, or Lissie might have turned right around and gone home.

"We might as well take pictures," Nelson suggested, "because we, at least, look amazing."

"Good idea," agreed Lissie. "Before the dancing starts and my ring-lets unwind."

"But we can't take a Bennet Sisters picture without Jenny," said Mel, craning her neck and looking around. "Is she here?"

"We'll get one with Jenny later. If we meet up with her now, we'll have to deal with the Bings and Preston Lin. Come on."

It was when they had finished clowning around in the booth and were bent over the pictures critiquing them that Lissie heard a familiar voice.

"Hi there. Darren, wasn't it? And Melanie? Hi, Lissie." Preston nodded and met her startled eyes, then turned toward Nelson and introduced himself.

True to form, Nelson stared, and Lissie couldn't blame him.

Preston Lin wasn't just dressed as Darcy. He *was* Darcy. It was all there: the swoony navy-blue tailcoat fitted to his broad shoulders, the white shirt and cravat, the knee breeches. Behind him, Charles was dressed similarly, but Lissie could hardly tear her gaze from Preston to give Charles his due. But would he want to talk to her, given the stiff near-silence in which they had ended his time at the Age Group Invitational?

Yes, as it turned out.

"Lissie, if no one has asked," he said, "I wondered if you'd be my partner when they teach us the English country dance."

"What? Oh, okay," she croaked.

"Great. Oh, and I like the pigtails." He added, before accompanying the Bings and Jenny into one of the photo booths.

"I thought the four of us were dancing together," Darren said.

"I didn't mean for this to happen," Lissie replied faintly. "I'm just as surprised as you are."

"Well, you're dancing with Darcy Lin now," said Mel. "And not only that, but you have to learn some dance you don't even know but Mr.

Marvelous has probably had private lessons in."

Lissie groaned. "How do I get myself into these situations? Everything I know about that guy, I don't like." Even as she said it, she realized it wasn't true. She liked how cute—how *adorable*, frankly— he'd been as he handed out awards to the eight-and-unders at the meet, for instance. But did that count? That was his obligation as a youth ambassador, and clearly he played a role, every bit as much as a role in a play.

Everything else she knew about Preston Lin was no bueno.

"Then dance with me now," declared Darren Liu, sweeping a positively dorky bow in his T-Bird outfit and adding cringily, "milady."

So things could get worse, apparently.

Without even looking, Lissie could sense Mel deflating beside her, and Nelson must have too because he grabbed Mel's hand and said, "Yeah! Let's get out there and dance, milady."

The deejay put on "Blue Moon" from *Grease*, which meant Lissie couldn't even get away with just shuffling her feet and bending her elbows as she faced Darren. No, he had to take her hand and put an arm around her waist, and start rotating her clockwise, like leftovers in a microwave.

Kill me now, she mouthed to Mel, but Mel and Nelson were hamming it up and not looking.

"Lissie," said Darren, "I know I told you I wasn't interested—"

"You totally did, and it's fine, Darren," she cut him off, "because I love things to be crystal clear."

"You probably didn't know, but I always kind of had a thing for Jenny—"

"I actually did know," Lissie said. *Everyone did.* "I mean, I guessed."

"You must have been watching me pretty closely, then." His arm around her tightened a fraction, and Lissie went stiff as a two-by-four.

"Watching you? I wasn't!"

He gave her a little pat. "Hey, loosen up. It's okay. Because what I wanted to say was that you got me thinking. You know, talking to me at that potluck, inviting me to dinner, and then the whole thing about the reviews."

"Yeah. Thank you again for that." She looked around, hoping something might happen to rescue her from what was coming.

"I read your reply to it online," Darren continued. "How you said you so appreciated me coming by and taking the time to write such a thoughtful review, and how you hoped I'd come again soon. I read some of your other replies to see if it was just a template, but it wasn't."

"I tried to mix it up a little," said Lissie. Weren't songs on average only three minutes long? This one was lasting an hour.

"What I'm trying to say, I guess, is that I'd like to edit my original response."

"To the Four Treasures?" she asked, feeling sweat break out in her armpits.

"No, Lissie—to the question of going out with you."

"Darren—"

"I think we should give it a try. Because you're not seeing anyone, are you?"

"I don't really have a lot of time for that kind of thing right now, between school and the job I still have and being JoJo's 'swim mom.'"

"What about your cousin Jeremy? My mom says he still lives with your aunt and uncle and plays video games all night. Why can't he drive JoJo half the time?"

"He works at the restaurant too."

"I still don't see why he couldn't on his day off."

"Anyhow," struck in Lissie again—she had enough on her hands without trying to defend her cousin from charges of not carrying his weight—"Thank you, Darren, but no thanks."

"I know I probably hurt your feelings at the potluck—"

"No, no. It was totally fine."

"But you caught me by surprise—"

"Darren!" she raised her voice, losing patience. "Look. I was not coming on to you at the potluck. And I was completely, totally fine with you not wanting to go out with me. I appreciate your friendship and your being such a good sport about the Four Treasures and everything. You're a great guy, but I'm not interested in going out with you."

The song wound down at last and the deejay started talking. Darren raised his own voice in turn. "I don't get it, Lissie. You gave me mixed messages—"

"What? My messages weren't mixed, it's your head that's doing the mixing! I like you, and our families are friends, but I don't like you that way." The music started up again, and it was a fast song, but the two of them kept circling, still gripping each other.

"I have a lot to offer."

"I know you do."

"I'm at Stanford, and my advisor is already trying to get me to join his company, and—"

"I know all these things. I don't care."

"And—no offense, because you're pretty and everything—but you are an English major at San Jose State."

Lissie stopped moving and Darren stepped on her foot. Her right hand dropped from his shoulder and the other pulled away from his grasp. "I think, for the sake of our relatives' friendship, I'm going to stop you right there. I'm sorry there was a misunderstanding, but there's no need to be an obnoxious jerk."

Darren's narrow face went Christmas-stocking red. Lissie was pretty sure hers wasn't a normal shade either. They looked like a couple breaking up, she was certain, right there in the middle of the dance floor, with other couples jumpin' and jivin' around them. This would certainly lead to awkwardness in their relatives' Bible study. Darren would tell his parents, and they would take his side (he couldn't have come by his assessment of her all on his own). And poor Auntie Rhoda and Uncle Mason would be forced to defend their niece again. Lissie could already hear her aunt's deprecating "Aiya, young people. You can't make them like what's best for them."

"Should we leave?" she asked. "Or just me?"

He shook his head and walked away, a dejected T-Bird, leaving her on the dance floor.

Mel found Lissie in one of a row of folding chairs along the wall, under a sagging garland.

"What are you doing, Lis? You're literally being a wallflower right now."

"I'm recovering."

"From what, 'Blue Moon?' I don't get it."

"From Darren asking me to go out with him."

Mel sagged into the chair beside her. "What's the big deal? I gave you a warning. I told you he was interested so you should have been prepared. Or are you regretting saying no?"

Lissie put her face in her hands. "No, I'm just feeling beat down. I was so looking forward to this evening, and then Wayman bags on us and Darren has to make things uncomfortable."

"And don't forget you still have to dance with Mr. Darcy."

"No, I didn't forget. Maybe I should claim stomach issues too. I bet he doesn't want to dance with someone with the runs any more than Nelson does."

"I dare you," Mel taunted. "I'll give you five bucks to tell Preston you have diarrhea."

"And have him write another *Stanford Daily* article about how Elisabeth Cheng, former employee of the Four Treasures Restaurant of Death, was Patient Zero at a deadly Fall Ball norovirus outbreak?"

"Well, you better think of something, because he's headed this way."

"Kill me now," said Lissie.

"And you probably don't want to hear it, but he looks hella fine."

"You're right, I don't want to hear it."

"Mm-hm, that's what I'm talking about! Just watch those heads turn."

"Stop staring at him!"

"It's either stare at him and listen the whole time he talks to you, or go try to comfort Darren Liu."

Lissie shook her head. "Go comfort Darren Liu."

CHAPTER 12

"A re you feeling all right?" Preston Lin asked, looming over her. "Of course," said Lissie. "Just gathering my strength for the country dancing. It isn't time yet, is it?"

"In a few minutes. There's a swing-dance performance first."

She thought he would go away—if it wasn't time, what was he even doing there in the first place?—but instead, after a hesitation, he sat in the chair Mel had occupied. They stared straight ahead, watching the performers go through their routine.

"You say you've been to a few of these?" she asked when she could stand the silence no longer.

"Yeah, as an undergraduate, and I still know some of the organizers."

"Oh? Why did you start coming in the first place? Did you have dance lessons as a kid?"

He gave her a measuring look, as if surprised by her nosiness. "No lessons, unless you count elementary-school and junior-high P.E. But I thought back then it was kind of fun."

Who knew school dance lessons were so effective? Wayman Wang had said the same thing, not that she was about to bring him up. Preston's eyes were still friendly. It was apparently going to be the affable version of him tonight.

"How about you?" he asked. "Did you have lessons as a kid?"

"No, but I used to dance with my grandparents and other old folks at the Milpitas Senior Center when I was younger, many years ago. Where did you get the costume?"

"Rented it. Bing and I got the same one. It's the 'Mr. Darcy.' I didn't know if I could pull off the *Grease* look like your friend Darren."

Lissie gave him a sharp glance in case he was making fun of Darren, but nothing in her companion's face gave anything away. "I think we girls had it easier. *Pride & Prejudice* and *Grease* are both pretty bold looks for guys."

"This is the first time I've ever come in a costume, actually," he admitted. "I'm surprised you and Liu didn't coordinate. Isn't he your date?"

"We're a group," said Lissie quickly. "It only looks like a date be- · cause Waym—because one of our group couldn't come. Oh, look. Is it time?"

It was indeed time. The swing group made its bows and yielded the floor again to the evening's emcees, the "Night and Day" couple who had been practicing earlier. Everyone at Château Cardboard Unit 114 had watched *The Gay Divorcée* YouTube clips ad nauseam to advise Nelson on his costume, and Lissie was pleased to see Nelson's was just as good as the male emcee's.

Fred gave Ginger a fancy twirl before she announced, "And now, the moment I know I've been waiting for, Mr. Beveridge's Maggot, a.k.a. the dance we've seen so many times in Jane Austen movies! We're going to learn it tonight!" When the applause died away, Fred gave a brief background on English country dance, then encouraged everyone to find a partner and line up on the floor.

Preston stood up and extended a hand to her, and Lissie found her heart suddenly racing. She was glad she had put her long gloves back on because her palms were instantly sweaty. Nor did the gloves insulate her from the shot of warmth that zinged up her arm when his fingers closed lightly on hers. She had a terrible feeling her face was going as red as Darren's had, so she avoided meeting his eyes as he led her out. But looking elsewhere meant noticing what Mel had noticed. Heads were turning to watch them.

I am going to have stomach issues, thought Lissie. *I feel like I swallowed a bag of butterflies.* What on Earth was her problem? Bad pork katsu? Or the fact that, in spite of everything that had happened with this guy, some unruly part of her still thought he was attractive?

Pathetic. *Come on, Cheng. Control your hormones*, she admonished herself. Thank heavens it was a dance lesson. It would give her something to concentrate on besides him.

"The key to English country dance," Ginger said, "what makes it so tense and expressive in the Austen movies is eye contact. Am I right? If we can't have much physical contact, it's all about the eyes. Not making eye contact with your partner in English country dance is disrespectful. Ill-mannered. So I don't want anyone looking at their feet! The steps aren't complicated. It's more about patterns, so staring at your shoes won't help. So let me see those eyes up!"

Crap. Lissie looked warily at Preston and found his expression frustratingly calm. Ginger walked them through the steps, and she had told the truth—they weren't complicated. "Honoring" your partner was merely bowing or curtsying. Right-hand turns and left-hand turns were similarly straightforward. When Lissie had to take his hand for them, she pretended they were polite business handshakes and ignored the internal fireworks that accompanied them.

The difficulties were the patterns: figure eights and skirting around the other couples and trying to keep track of whether you were a first or second couple moving up or down the room. This precipitated a fair amount of crashing into others and laughter and sheepish apologies. Lissie supposed it was part of Preston Lin's tiresome brainpower that he grasped patterns so quickly, or maybe it was just that he was taller and could see over people's heads for the bigger picture. In any case, he didn't crash into anyone, and though she stepped on his feet twice when she wasn't where she was supposed to be, he never came near stepping on hers.

"Don't worry," he interrupted her apology, when Lissie veered left instead of right for the back-to-back and collided for the third time in her life with his chest. "I kind of like it." Which only made her more confused. He liked her klutzing into him? Did he like seeing her off-balance, or English country dancing mishaps in general?

When she made the requisite, good-mannered eye contact, she found a gleam of amusement and even encouragement there, and she felt herself relax. Okay, fine. If his good mood was going to last the duration of the dance lesson, she had no complaints.

Even more surprising, Lissie started having fun. After a dozen repetitions of the pattern, she began to get the hang of it, enough so that she could look around some as she traveled. She saw Jenny and Charles farther down the line and Mel and Darren on their other side. And either Nelson had asked Hazel to dance, or vice versa, because there they were at the very end.

Fred signaled for the music to stop again, and Ginger clapped her hands. "Beautiful! This is really coming together. Which means we're ready to try it for real, as they would have experienced it in the ballroom, as opposed to lessons with a dancing master. So we're not going to start and stop, start and stop this time. When we get to the end of the full pattern, we just repeat. Which means, first couples, you will gradually, with each repetition, be working your way farther down the room, while second couples, with each repetition, will be working their way up the room. When first couples reach the bottom of the room, they become second couples, meaning you will then work your way back up the room, but you will switch to the steps and positions of second couples. Likewise, second couples, when you reach the top of the room, you become first couples and head back down in the first couple pattern. Got it?" This news was met with groans of dismay, but Ginger clapped her hands again. "It's not so bad! Really. I'll be at the bottom of the room helping, and Arvin will take the top of the room. This is going to work if we have to keep at it all night!"

"We just might have to," said Lissie.

"One can only hope," said Preston.

The deejay started the music once more. Preston bowed to her;

Lissie curtseyed to him. And they were off. But without Ginger shouting out the steps, there was only the music and the obligatory eye contact and a rising tension in Lissie's midsection. *Keep it together*, she told herself.

Lissie couldn't understand how Austen heroines carried on conversations on the dance floor. As Preston and she executed the right- and left-hand and took hands with the second couple to step forward and back, the silence grew in size and heaviness, with each pattern they traced as they went down the room. But if he didn't care, if he wasn't uncomfortable, why should she? He was the one who asked her to dance, after all.

They reached the bottom of the room, where Ginger held them out for one repetition. "Remember," she said, "when you go back in on the next repetition, you'll be a second couple."

And being a second couple meant they had that period in every pattern where they just stood there with nothing to do but look at each other, while the first couple figure-eighted around them and crossed in front. Still Lissie said nothing.

Finally her stubbornness was rewarded. "So," Preston said at last, "was Wayman Wang going to be part of your group tonight?"

"He was. He got sick."

They turned in place and were parted by the first couple. When he took her hand again, he continued, "Have you known him long?"

"I think he began coaching at the club in September, and JoJo didn't get put in one of his groups until October. So a month, maybe. You've known him a lot longer than that, yes?"

Dutifully making eye contact, Lissie saw the tightening of his jaw and flare of his nostrils; he did not respond right away. She began to think he would not respond at all, but when they had completed the pattern and moved farther up the room, he said, "I have."

"He seems like a good coach. The kids and the parents love him."

"I'm sure they do."

"You say that like it's a bad thing."

"Let's just say Wayman Wang has never had a problem getting people to like him."

Lissie's eyebrows rose. "Well, a little charm never hurt anybody."

To this he said nothing for another pattern. Lissie was about to relent and begin a new subject when he asked, "So he admitted to knowing me?"

"He could hardly deny it, you two were so weird in the break room." The first couple intervened again, and they took hands and marched forward a step, back a step.

"But he hasn't been as fortunate as you in his swim career," Lissie ventured as they faced each other again. "Owing to circumstances beyond his control."

She drew back the next instant at the angry glitter in his eyes. "I wouldn't believe absolutely everything I heard, if I were you," he replied in a hard voice. "There are two sides to every story. What happened to him was very much under his control."

"Stalin," murmured Lissie to herself.

"What?"

"Nothing. What's your side of the story, then?"

If he wasn't careful, he would grind his teeth into oblivion. "It doesn't matter. What's past is past. Just—"

"Just what?"

"Nothing," he bit off. "It was all a long time ago." In a galaxy far, far away, apparently.

He relapsed into silence, a surly one this time, and Lissie was sorry the specter of Wayman Wang had driven away the affable version of Preston Lin. Or maybe it only removed the veneer of affability, leaving behind the authentic person, one who yelled at waitresses and wrote vindictive articles and stole coaches and cared about no one but himself.

After what felt like an eternity, the dance finally wound to a close, and Lissie joined politely in the applause. Two partners alienated in two dances, which had to be some kind of record. Preston nodded at

PRIDE AND PRESTON LIN

her, and she returned his nod, darting away before he would have to think what to do with her. She couldn't catch Mel because Darren, too, must be avoided, so that left Jenny.

"Come get some air with me," she urged her sister, throwing Charles a smile. Lissie's clutch on her arm left Jenny little choice, but Charles helpfully said, "I'll get us some punch."

"Aren't you having fun?" Jenny asked when they went through one set of the double doors into the courtyard. It was chilly out, but working on Mr. Beveridge's Maggot for a steady hour made the change in temperature pleasant.

"You saw me dancing with Darren Liu and Preston Lin, and you ask me if I'm having fun?"

"Come on. I know you don't like Preston, but what's so bad about Darren?"

"He decided if he can't have you, I would do."

Jenny gasped. "What? He didn't!"

"He did. So I had to tell him no, thanks. So awkward."

Laughing, her sister patted her shoulder. "I'm sorry. And then what did Preston do? Threaten you with a lawsuit?"

"No, but he brought up Wayman Wang and then got all huffy about him and said I shouldn't believe everything I hear and that there's two sides to every story."

"Exactly," said Jenny. "I asked Charles about him since you wanted me to, and Charles said, Yes, Preston changed swim clubs in high school, but it was to be closer to home so his mom wouldn't have to drive him so far six days a week. After he switched, he carpooled with friends until he could drive himself."

Lissie frowned. Given how much time she spent driving JoJo, this explanation made sense, even if it did sound more thoughtful than a teenage Preston Lin would likely have been. "Okay, I mean, that sounds plausible, but what about the head coach and all the best swimmers following him and the old club going under?"

Jenny shook her head. "Lissie, you can't blame a fifteen-year-old for what an adult does after that. Charles said there's always lots of churn with coaches and swimmers at any club, anywhere. That's why there's some rule in place about not being able to earn points for your new team for a certain period after you change."

"But Wayman said the old club collapsed because Preston left," Lissie insisted. "Coaches like him lost their jobs, and other swimmers had to find new places to go. Not everyone is a star, welcomed with open arms like he was!"

"If a club couldn't survive losing one good swimmer and the head coach, it was probably on pretty shaky ground to begin with," her sister reasoned.

"There you guys are!" It was Nelson, sweeping through the same set of double doors they had used. "I couldn't see you through the reflection of the glass. Ladies, I'm afraid we have a capital-S Situation on our hands, and I take full ownership."

Accustomed to Nelson's drama, Lissie said, "Let me guess. You asked Fred to dance and Ginger got mad?"

"No, I'm serious. You're gonna kill me."

"Let's hear it then, so we can bury the body and get back to dancing."

He covered his face with his bony hands. "I let out your secret."

"What secret?"

"The secret that the Four Treasures is owned by your aunt and uncle," he blurted, still not looking.

Lissie and Jenny froze.

"I know," wailed Nelson. "I suck. I know!"

"Who did you tell?" breathed Jenny.

Lissie had to give her chest a thump with her fist to get her voice working again. "It was Hazel Bing, wasn't it? I saw you dancing with her."

His hands dropped, revealing his guilt-ridden expression. "Yes. Hazel. It just came out! She asked how I knew you guys, so I was talking about Château Cardboard, and then she wanted to know if Darren was dating one of you ladies, and I said, no, he was a friend of your family. Then she asked if your parents all knew each other, and I said, no, his parents knew your guys' aunt and uncle, and I added like a moron, you know, the ones who own the restaurant. Oh my God, if you could have seen my face! And her face! I am *so* sorry. I am *such* an idiot. And then I should have played it off better. I should have said they owned an In 'n' Out or something, but it was too late! She would have known anyway by how I stopped talking and stopped dancing and stopped *everything*!"

"Nelson." Jenny took him by the shoulders. "Nelson, it's okay. It's not your fault. It couldn't have stayed a secret forever. I was already thinking I would have to tell Charles soon if I kept seeing him."

"No, it's not okay!" shrieked Lissie. "What is wrong with you? Do you know what that freaking Preston Lin is going to do now? How could you do something so stupid?"

"Lissie!" Jenny chided. "It was our lie to worry about, not Nelson's."

"I don't care! Nelson, I've never blown any of your secrets! Like the time I pretended to be your girlfriend at your cousin's wedding because you said your parents weren't ready to hear you were gay. Everyone gave me the third degree, but I managed to keep my mouth shut for an entire three-hour reception!"

"I know, I know," he groaned. "How many times can I say I'm sorry?"

Hearing that particular phrase, one Lissie had been forced to say so many times since the restaurant incident, took the wind out of her. She shut up. Looking through the row of French doors behind Nelson, in all the light streaming out, she picked Preston out easily—somehow, it was always easy to pick him out. And there were the Bings next to him. Even at this distance, Lissie could feel Hazel had told them about Auntie Rhoda and Uncle Mason. She had no reason not to.

"Maybe we could text Mel and Darren to meet us out here and just go," suggested Lissie. "It would give everyone time to calm down."

"But we'd miss the Hand Jive!" protested Nelson, his anxiety fading now that Lissie wasn't laying into him.

"And I didn't come with you guys," said Jenny. "If Charles doesn't want to take me home after this, he doesn't have to, but I'd rather talk about it now."

Lissie sighed. "I figured you would. I was just fantasizing. Can we at least get our story straight before we go back in?"

Jenny regarded her sternly. "Wouldn't we just say, yes, we're related, but things were so contentious we hated to mention it, and we're sorry?"

Lissie could picture Charles graciously understanding, but Preston was another matter. If Jenny spoke to them right now, would he still think it necessary to bring it up with Lissie later? Of course he would. He was the sort of person who liked to put people in their place. How vindicated he must feel to learn that, on top of everything else, the Cheng girls were liars.

But the more she thought about it, the less guilt she felt. Let him pound his chest and look down on her one last time. Because Preston might have the upper hand again, but what a relief it would be, at long last, to tell him exactly what she thought of him!

CHAPTER 13

"There are some inconsistencies of tone," Professor Bach-Peralta told Lissie, pushing Acts I–III of *A Doom of One's Own* across her desk to her. "It started as a rom-com, but by Act III, I began to think it was going to turn into a slasher."

"Is that bad?" asked Lissie. She was glad to see a minimum of red ink on the front page. "*Into the Woods* was like that—all sunshine in the first half, and then the dark underbelly."

"Mm-hm." Her advisor removed her readers. "But why do I feel like that wasn't your original direction? Is this going to end in the dark place, or will you pull it back to the happy-ending side?"

"Probably the dark place."

"Are we talking *Hamlet* dark? *Jude the Obscure* dark? Because if it is, it turns the title from wink-wink, tongue-in-cheek to painfully earnest."

"You think I should retitle it?"

"I think you should finish it and then decide. As long as it's wrapped up by, say, the first month of spring semester. You have time—which is a good thing, since I'm not positive you know where you're going with this yet. Remember, we agreed that this project wasn't just a play for a play's sake. If you want senior thesis credit for it, you need to be able to tell me why you make the choices you make and what that says about the literature and writers you adapt and/or respond to. Yes?"

"Got it."

Emerging from the Faculty Offices building to a gray and overcast sky, Lissie wandered across the lawn absently, riffling the pages of her incomplete play. What she had not told her advisor was that *A Doom of One's Own* had been a far more consistent, uniform creation a couple weeks earlier. Before the Fall Ball, when things went south.

>—❤—→

Not that things went immediately south that night. Nelson and the Cheng girls returned inside, Lissie braced for impact. And then . . . Nothing.

With her blood up, Lissie made a beeline for Preston Lin. *Look at me!* she commanded telepathically. *You want to call me a liar? Then look at me!*

Her laser-beam glare worked. As if he felt it boring holes in his back, he turned slowly.

His eyes met hers.

Held.

And then, without the slightest change of expression, he turned away. He bent and said something to Hazel, to which she responded with a sudden, eager brightening, and he led her to the dance floor.

"What the heck?" Lissie glanced over at her sister. Charles was leaning toward Jenny to make himself heard over the music. Calmly, Jenny nodded, and the two of them walked through the French doors to the courtyard. He, at least, was going to talk to her about it like a mature adult. But what about Preston? Didn't he want to come point a righteous finger in her face and deliver his lecture?

There was still Nelson. Whipping around, she seized his hand. "Dance with me."

"Ow! Stop crushing my phalanges, or I won't be able to hand jive!"

He let her drag him to the floor, where the deejay was playing some twenties number. Swing had been a favorite of hers at the Senior Center, but she was too tense to enjoy it, and she kept fighting with Nelson over who was leading.

"What is your problem?" he complained.

"Can we dance closer to Preston and Hazel?"

"You should be thrilled he doesn't want to talk to you. I wouldn't want to be on his bad side."

"Well, I've never been on any other side," she retorted.

But before they could get much closer, the song ended, and Fred and Ginger leaped to the mic to announce the long-awaited Hand Jive. A scream went up as seemingly every person in the entire gym charged the dance floor. Not only did Lissie lose the ground she had gained, but a horde of people walled her and Nelson in. Hopping up and down, Lissie glimpsed Preston leaving the floor, trailed by a dejected Hazel. *Where is he going? Doesn't he want to confront me?*

Now that Preston did not appear inclined to have it out with her, Lissie wanted all the more to have it out with him. But she could hardly abandon Nelson, who was in hand-jiving heaven. The second the music ended, while everyone was still whooping and clapping, she poked her dance partner in his Fred Astaire lapels. "I'm gonna try to catch him," she yelled in his ear.

"It's your funeral!" he yelled back, shrugging. But Lissie was long gone, threading her way off the floor. When she reached the edge, she spotted him near the photo booths at the entrance, texting. Hazel was claiming her coat.

Hiking up her dress, Lissie almost ran across the gym.

He saw her, of course. Watched her with that same expressionless expression, eyes impassive and cool.

She slid to a halt in front of him, all too aware of her undignified scramble and of Hazel now looking over.

"Are you leaving?"

"We are."

"Don't you want to talk to me before you go?"

His brow furrowed, and he looked toward the ceiling, as if considering. Then his mouth twisted and he gave a shrug. "It turns out . . . no."

Lissie stared. "You don't? Why not? Nelson told us that he told Hazel . . . and she told you, didn't she?"

"Told me what?"

"That Jenny and I are related to the owners of the Four Treasures! That the Liangs who own it—they're our aunt and uncle!"

"Oh. That."

"Yes, that. And you're clearly pissed about it, or why are you acting like you don't know me, or something?"

"Because clearly I don't."

"So now what? You're just gonna do this passive-aggressive thing now? I thought your style was more aggressive-aggressive."

He slid his phone into an inner chest pocket of his frock coat or whatever it was called. "I'd better explain because I don't want to be thought of as passive-aggressive. But I wouldn't characterize this as aggressive-aggressive either. I'm just . . . we're done here. I don't know you, as it turns out, and now let's keep it that way. We don't know each other. We *won't* know each other."

Lissie thought she would explode with . . . rage? confusion? hate? hurt? a mixture of all of the above? She was angry, certainly, but some immeasurable portion of her anger was directed at herself. But why did she also feel hurt? How had she given this impossible, insufferable person the power to hurt her again?

"You want to be strangers from now on?" she spat. "Good. We'll be strangers. But did it ever occur to you, you giant smug jerk, that the reason Jenny and I didn't bring up our relationship to the restaurant was that we were trying to contain the poison? That we wanted to protect the only family we have from your self-righteous vindictiveness?"

He said nothing, of course, since he didn't know her anymore. Maybe his brain had already reclassified her voice as a vague insect-like buzzing, ignorable and not worth the trouble of swatting at.

With one final growl, Lissie spun on her heel and stalked off, no clearer destination in mind than away from him. She was nearly to the chairs lining the wall when she heard footsteps and turned to find

Hazel scurrying after her. What could she possibly want? Preston was all hers now, as far as she was concerned. They deserved each other, the way Hazel had gone straight from Nelson to broadcast his indiscretion.

"What?!" snapped Lissie rudely.

But Hazel didn't look triumphant. She looked almost apologetic, and she bit her full lips. "He can't stand being lied to," she said, as if that explained everything.

Lissie made an impatient face. "Neither can most people. Which is why, for what it was worth, I planned on apologizing. Or at least explaining."

Hazel nodded. "Yeah. It's just . . . that's his trigger. He can stand most things, but not dishonesty."

"This would be really helpful information," Lissie replied dryly, "if it mattered. But since he and I no longer know each other, it doesn't. Thanks, Hazel."

Dismissed, Hazel walked away. Lissie dropped into the closest folding chair to wait for the night to be over.

Darren dropped the group back at Château Cardboard at one in the morning. The sisters had been quiet in the Camry, leaving the chattering to Mel and Nelson, with occasional interjections from the T-Bird. But after the latter was thanked and had driven away, the foursome dashed into sweatpants, heated up hot water for cocoa, and gathered in the living room for a debrief.

"What did Charles say when you went outside?" pressed Lissie. "Was he angry?"

"A little," Jenny answered. "For him, I mean, which isn't much at all. He said I should have trusted him, that he wouldn't have told anyone else if I'd asked him not to."

"Not like his sister," Lissie said grimly.

"Or our roommate," Mel added, kicking Nelson with her slippered foot.

He groaned. "Lissie already punished me by crushing my hand and abandoning me on the dance floor, so you can shut it, Espinosa."

"So then what happened, Jenny?"

She heaved a slow sigh. "We broke up."

"*What?*" chorused her roommates.

"Why?" demanded Lissie. "You said he wasn't that mad!"

"He wasn't." Jenny's eyes filled, and she dabbed them with the cuff of her sweatshirt. Melanie and Nelson fussed over her, refilling her mug and passing her a blanket to wrap around herself.

Lissie was preoccupied with a new idea. "Did he break up with you because Preston Lin told him to?"

"What? No, Lissie."

"How do you know? Did you ask him?"

"Why would I ask him?" Jenny answered, an uncharacteristically waspish note in her voice. "The Preston paranoia is your issue, not mine, remember?"

Mel bugged her eyes at Lissie in a what-is-your-problem way, and Lissie pressed her lips shut.

"He said the usual," her sister went on. "'That maybe we should take some time to think about things and what we both were looking for in a relationship." She shifted on the couch, grimacing as one of the springs jabbed her. "And I said that made sense, and I apologized again for everything. I told him things had gotten off to such a shaky start that it didn't take much to bring the whole thing tumbling down."

Lissie covered her face with a cushion and screamed into it, but Jenny ignored her, taking a deep breath. "I was thinking of breaking up with him anyway." Seeing their incredulity, she frowned. "It's November. I take the MCATs in January. Between working two jobs and hanging out with him, I've hardly done any studying. I'm so behind. If I don't get serious about it, I'll get a terrible score, and there won't be enough time to improve it before the first applications are due. So tonight was the last hurrah. If anyone wants me from now until January 15, I'll be cramming."

With that pronouncement, she heaved herself off the couch. "I'm going to bed."

The others soon followed, but as Lissie lay in her top bunk, wide awake, she couldn't help but reflect that, with Charles and Jenny broken up, she might never see Preston Lin again. Which was great, right?

Just before she finally dozed off, a last thought streaked through her dimming consciousness: *at least Wayman Wang will have no reason to avoid me now.*

It only took a few more days for that nascent romantic flicker to be extinguished. On Monday, JoJo greeted her coldly when she came home from school. Lissie grabbed her nonetheless and spun her around. "The ball would have been more fun with you there, you little brat. You need to have a sleepover at our place to watch the movies they did dances from."

"I don't want to have a sleepover at your place," JoJo said with a scowl. Lissie could see traces of the blue sparkly eyeliner her little sister had missed wiping off. "You guys are old and boring."

"You're not the only one who thinks so, apparently," Lissie returned, "because your dumb Coach Wayman said he was sick and bailed on us."

At once JoJo's face brightened. "He did?"

"Yup."

"But he seemed fine Saturday morning."

"Well, he was not fine by midday."

JoJo was too young to dissimulate successfully, or even to make much of an attempt. She grinned and galloped into the kitchen for her usual pre-swim meal.

At practice, Wayman caught Lissie before she reached the bleachers. "Hey there, how was the dance?"

There were three possible replies: the truth ("a day that will live in infamy"), a partial lie ("pretty fun"), and a total lie ("so much fun!"). Naturally, Lissie went with the partial lie. "I had a decent time. There were lots of great costumes, and the dance lessons were my favorite part."

He nodded. With a glance at the bleachers where all the moms were taking their seats, he added in a low voice, "I know I told you it was stomach issues, but I decided, on second thought, that spending a whole evening in the same room with Preston Lin would be more unpleasant than pleasant. Not only for me, but possibly for everyone in the group, if the weirdness between us spilled over."

"I get it," said Lissie. And she did. Who could know better than she?

"He has a way of making you feel at fault, even if you're not," Wayman went on.

"Yup," agreed Lissie. She felt the coach studying her response, and it brought the heat of awareness to her face.

"Maybe I'm too hard on him, though. I mean I know I made it sound like his leaving made that old swim club collapse—"

"You mean his leaving and poaching the head coach and the best swimmers."

"But maybe a stronger swim club would have survived, and it's wrong to pin everything on him."

It was what Jenny had said, but on the contrary, it made Lissie even more certain it had been Preston Lin's fault. "Don't make excuses for him," she frowned. "He clearly doesn't seem to feel bad about it, so why should you? You already suffered the consequences. Don't take on the blame as well."

Wayman relaxed into a smile. "Well, I didn't want to make things awkward with you, if you're going to be friends with him. I didn't want you to feel like I was asking you to choose or anything."

"Have no fear," Lissie laughed humorlessly. "I may never see the guy again. My sister and his friend broke up, and it's not like I'm ever on the Stanford campus in the normal course of my existence. So even if I were inclined to take his side—which I'm not—it's all moot. I can be totally, wholeheartedly Team Collapsed Club."

His smile widened, and Lissie could feel his charm begin to operate on her. Did he like her? Would it be inappropriate to like him back?

When she made her way into the bleachers, the moms converged.

"You're very chatty with Coach Wayman, Lissie. Are you dating him?" Matron Mom teased.

"No, no."

"You can tell us! We see everything."

"Including what isn't there," she said archly.

Now that Lissie officiated with her husband, Fred, Mrs. Pang was friendlier than she used to be. On the other hand, Mrs. Yeh had been chilly ever since Lissie caught her chewing out the coach. Mrs. Yeh turned narrowed eyes on her. "Has he asked you out?"

"No." Lissie assumed her best poker face. "We were just talking about someone we know in common."

She pulled out her laptop to work, and Mrs. Wei leaned past Mrs. Yeh to click her tongue. "Now she's going to write him love letters."

"Just homework, Mrs. Wei." Lissie could handle not being Hot Mom's favorite person in the world, but she hadn't abandoned hopes of JoJo catching rides with Olivia Wei. If only Lissie's attempts to get on her mom's good side weren't undermined every time JoJo beat Olivia in a race!

"Another paper to write?" asked Mrs. Pang.

"I'm an English major, so it's safe to say I always have a paper to write."

Mrs. Pang sighed. "My Melissa . . . I want her to read more. I tell her there is more to life than getting perfect scores on her math tests." A ripple of pursed lips and averted eye rolls greeted this humblebrag.

"All the kids need to read more," said Mrs. Yeh. "It's all phones, phones, phones."

"I like the phone for one thing: knowing where my kids are," Mrs. Wei declared, but Mrs. Yeh dismissed this. "I don't turn those things on, or my husband will be checking on me all the time. 'Why did you go to Valley Fair?' 'You said you were home all day, so why was your phone in Palo Alto?'"

The other moms laughed. Mr. Yeh was an outsize legend at Mission Valley, yet no one had ever seen him in the flesh. He commuted between Taiwan and Fremont and apparently made gobs of money—JoJo said the Yeh house was palatial—and both his wife and daughter seemed to prefer his absence. "He's a little Chinese Napoleon," Mrs. Yeh had once complained. "He wants to rule the world." Emma only said, "He doesn't talk much, but my Westie hides under the coffee table when he's home."

Conversation ebbed and flowed the rest of the practice, with Lissie left to whip up her two-page response to George Sand's *Indiana*, and it was only as everyone gathered their things at the end of practice that Mrs. Yeh stalked over to her, pausing to adjust the strap of her boot.

"He likes you, I think," she muttered.

Lissie glanced up, surprised, her lips beginning to form the question.

But Mrs. Yeh gave an impatient shrug. "Who else? Don't let the teasing stop you if you're interested. Just know that it could be . . . messy." Well, yeah, Lissie knew that already. Even if the whole swim club weren't there to witness everything and pass judgment, there would be JoJo's fury.

But it all turned out to be moot: the moms' curiosity, Lissie's uncertainty, Mrs. Yeh's "permission." That Friday, Coach Penny stopped by the pool to go over something with Coach Wayman on the clipboard she held, and when that was done and she turned to go, he reached out to tug her back. The kids were in the middle of a set and saw nothing, apart from Adam Patel, who was sitting on the wall adjusting his goggles; but every mom present saw Coach Wayman lean in and say something in Coach Penny's ear. She blushed, looked around her, and then hurried away. Wayman glanced toward the bleachers, but every pair of eyes had instantly found another object. Lissie thought she need not worry any longer whether Wayman Wang was interested in her. Yet instead of feeling 100% relieved, she discovered she was only 40% relieved and 60% disappointed.

Hence the dark turn her play had taken had many root causes, none of which could be explained to her thesis advisor. How could they when Lissie could hardly account for them herself? *A Doom of One's Own* turned gloomy and pessimistic for every reason and for none at all.

T hat fall and early winter, once JoJo thought Lissie and she had a common enemy in Coach Penny, she warmed to her older sister.

"We don't know what he likes about her," JoJo confided, folding over the green-onion pancake Lissie had warmed for her and dragging it through the soy sauce. "She's kind of shy, except with the little kids."

"Maybe that's what he likes," replied Lissie, dabbing the tip of her own triangle of pancake in JoJo's sauce puddle. "Someone not as clamorous and demanding and opinionated as all you guys and all the moms."

The door from the converted garage opened, and there stood their cousin Jeremy, tousle-headed and sleepy-eyed, wearing a wrinkled T-shirt and baggy sweatpants.

"Good morning, Sunshine," said Lissie. "Hope we didn't wake you. I didn't even know you were here," Lissie added, unable to help glancing at the clock on the microwave. "Aren't you usually at the restaurant by now?"

"It's Wednesday," he grunted. "I don't work Tuesdays and Wednesdays."

"How did I not know that?" she marveled.

"Because you don't work Tuesday or Wednesday either."

"I mean, I've been driving JoJo to practice for a couple months now, and I've never even known you were home." She pushed the near-decimated plate of scallion pancake toward him over JoJo's protests, and he helped himself. In age, Jeremy fell between Jenny and Lissie, and he had always been the family's golden boy, earning a coveted spot in Cal's Electrical Engineering & Computer Science program, though he hated the engineering part and soon dumped EECS for the straight CS degree from the Letters & Science college. After graduation, however, his luster began to fade. He put off getting a tech job by claiming he was going to go to graduate school, but then he put off grad school applications with a gap year, supposedly to recover from four years of all-nighters. Never mind that a gap year from applications would result in a gap of *two* years from starting a program. And now all Jeremy did, according to Auntie Rhoda, was work at the restaurant, play games online, and sleep. And Lissie believed her because his color was nonexistent and he had big dark circles under his eyes.

"If it was Tuesday or Wednesday, I was home." He paused, chewing, seeming to consider something. Then he poked JoJo. "Tell her why."

JoJo gaped. "Really? I can tell her?"

"Tell me what?"

"Yeah. But it goes no further than this room." Jeremy pointed to the four corners of the kitchen.

"He streams Wednesdays on new patches," said JoJo triumphantly. "Jeremy's niche is DPS and arena." Her cousin shoved another piece of scallion pancake into his mouth.

Lissie had no idea what she was talking about but gathered it was gaming-related. She frowned at her sister. "How come you never mentioned Jeremy was home on Tuesdays and Wednesdays?"

"Why would I?" JoJo asked reasonably.

"I just thought—" Lissie studied her hollow-eyed cousin, who had polished off the food and was getting a glass pitcher of coffee out of the fridge. "I just thought maybe we could have been splitting chauffeuring duties."

"But Jeremy is *working* on Tuesdays and Wednesdays," insisted JoJo.

"Is that what Auntie Rhoda would call it?" Lissie asked, before she could help herself.

"Nope," said Jeremy. "Which is why she doesn't know about it."

"How many viewers today?" JoJo asked, leaning her elbows on the counter and bouncing on her toes.

"Almost 3,000. About a hundred more than last week and 155 new subs."

JoJo drew numbers on the counter with her finger. "So, 155 plus 5,042 equals 5,197. Not bad! Remember how happy you used to be if you got twenty in a day? Which pair of glasses did you wear?" Turning to Lissie, she added, "I got him red glasses and purple glasses, so we could test over two weeks and see which ones get him more subs."

"Purple." He twisted off the lid and drank straight from the pitcher. "Two weeks isn't enough time because there are too many variables. Like how significant the patch is."

Peering more closely at her cousin, Lissie realized Jeremy didn't have bedhead. His hair was gelled into position. "Hang on," she said, awareness dawning. "You have almost 3,000 people watching you?"

"Yup. Live. And then more later when I put it on YouTube."

JoJo jumped in again. "Patches are updates to the game. Fixes and tweaks and changes and stuff. People freak out over them. Jeremy figures out what happened each week and explains it all to his viewers. Walks them through it."

"So . . . you're not working on grad school applications?"

"Nope."

"He's building a brand, Lissie," insisted JoJo. "This is his job. He makes money."

For the first time that afternoon, Jeremy's face cracked in a grin. "At least now it does. Took long enough."

"Then it's working, whatever you're doing?" Lissie asked.

He shrugged. "Oh, there's money out there, but how to make it is always changing. I'm only recently making more than I did in high school."

"You made money in high school?"

He held a finger to his lips. "Now you *really* can't talk about that. My mom would flip."

"But . . . how?"

"Gold farming. JoJo can explain. But remember, you can't even tell Jenny."

There was no time to dig more deeply if JoJo was going to make practice, though Lissie tried on the drive. "How long have you known about this? I thought Jeremy was just sitting in his room playing games!"

"Well, he does a lot of that too, but it's work-related." JoJo answered, focused on rethreading the straps on her goggles, like this was all no big deal. "I don't know, since he graduated and moved back home? I was being nosy and so I bugged him a lot and watched him play sometimes and asked lots of questions. I think he let me because he felt sorry for me. You know, Mom and Dad. But he swore me to secrecy because Auntie Rhoda wants him to get a job or go to grad school, and he doesn't think he can convince her that he can do this instead until he shows her the money, you know?" All at once her eyes widened, and she shook her head slowly at Lissie. "You know what this means, don't you?"

"I have no idea what any of this means."

"If Jeremy was willing to let you in on the secret, he must be feeling really confident! He didn't know if it would work at first—most people with big followings on Twitch and YouTube have big personalities or they're funny or they're dramatic. But you know Jeremy, he's not the world's biggest talker and he can be kind of quiet and intense. That's why he had to pick a niche that played to his strengths. Where he could just be quiet and Methodist and teach people."

"Methodist? We're not Methodists, and what does that have to do with gaming?"

"You know what I mean! Like, careful."

Lissie snorted and slapped the steering wheel. "You mean 'methodical?'"

143

"Whatever!" groused JoJo, but she smiled after another moment. "Anyway, that's what he is. So explaining these patches was a good fit. You don't have to be loud or funny or handsome or crazy to do it, just a good explainer."

"Why the purple and red glasses, then?"

"Because it doesn't hurt to make yourself recognizable."

"So how much money do you think he's making?"

"Beats me."

"And what was the 'gold farming' he did in high school, that was an even bigger secret than this?"

"*World of Warcraft.* People paid him to mine gold for them, and he ran a whole team of people in China. Big money and totally under the table."

Lissie looked at her sister with new eyes. As JoJo warmed to her again, Lissie was becoming the recipient of confidences she didn't always know what to do with. Some were typical adolescent things: whether her best friend at school was still her bestie; wondering if a boy bothering her constantly meant he liked her; complaints that she still had to do P.E. at school when she swam a zillion miles per week. Others were harder to hear: Auntie Rhoda and Uncle Mason were arguing about money and the restaurant; Jeremy was refusing to go to church with the family; and Uncle Mason wanted to charge Jeremy rent, but Auntie Rhoda wasn't there yet. But Lissie felt closer to JoJo than she had in a long while, and she knew her sister felt it too.

JoJo performed respectably at Short Course Champs that December, by which point Lissie had been made an official official and completed most of the required volunteer hours. Nor was she troubled by any appearances from the USA Swimming Youth Ambassador. Best of all, when the champs meet ended, Olivia Wei's mom caught up with her in the parking lot with an unexpected request.

"Lissie, congratulations on JoJo making the 100 fly final!"

"Thanks, Mrs. Wei. Olivia had a good meet too. And how nice for them to have a few weeks off from practice, and us from driving them!"

"That's what I wanted to talk to you about—you know we live only five minutes from the Liangs."

"Yes," said Lissie, her heart beating a little faster.

"Well, I thought maybe we could do a little trade." Mrs. Wei and her daughter had the same round face and plump lower lip, which Mrs. Wei bit now. "I mean, you are an English major, and Olivia could use some help with her writing. I don't mean I want you to write for her, but maybe you could look at her assignments and make some suggestions before she hands them in? And in return, JoJo could ride with us to practice a few days a week? Three days, maybe?"

Entire vistas of free time opened in Lissie's mind. It was too good to be true. However long it might take to read Olivia Wei's eighth-grade assignments, getting back three solid afternoons a week was a heavenly prospect.

"Or, if you would rather be paid—" Mrs. Wei began again at Lissie's silence.

"Oh, no, Mrs. Wei! Carpooling three days a week would be wonderful. I was just thinking of my schedule next semester. In fact, it'd be perfect because on Tuesdays I have a class that doesn't get out until three o'clock, and I was worrying about cutting it so close. Would Tuesdays, Thursdays, and Fridays work for you?"

"Yes. Perfect. We will start in January." Mrs. Wei and Lissie smiled at each other.

Surprisingly, it was JoJo who protested. "Three days a week! Don't you like driving me? I'll never see you again, just like before."

"You'll see me Mondays and Wednesdays, dopey, and I'll be at all your meets. That's not never seeing me."

"It'll be just like before," said JoJo darkly, glaring out the passenger-side window. "It'll be like it is with Jenny." Lissie felt a dagger of that familiar guilt. JoJo would understand when she was older, when she herself was pulled in a dozen directions by work and studies and obligations and deadlines. But by then, would she still care about seeing her sisters? Would she have given up on being close to them? Lissie would have been glad to share her guilt with Jenny, but her older sister was bleary-eyed from studying, studying, and more studying. Even Auntie Rhoda had cut back her hours at the Four Treasures, and there was talk of sneaking Lissie back in one weekday night per week.

—❤—

Jenny and Lissie joined the Liangs at Milpitas Chinese Covenant for the Christmas candlelight service. Darren Liu was there with his parents and younger sisters. Lissie didn't think she imagined Mrs. Liu's coolness toward them for turning down her prize of a son, but Darren was warm enough. He had been an absolute trooper, eating at the Four Treasures several more times with anyone he could coax to join him, including Melanie and Nelson. Those three had become partners in crime, creating dummy accounts so they could leave additional good reviews and shoring up the credibility of those accounts with group visits to a few boba places and the Ginger Market on campus.

"Has he reverse-psychologized himself into falling for you yet?" Lissie asked Mel after her roommate returned from an outing with Darren.

Mel crossed her fingers on both hands. "Don't jinx it. He's close, he just doesn't know it yet."

On Christmas Eve, after "Silent Night" had been sung in a cacophony of English and Chinese and the snuffed candles returned to the plastic bucket, Darren took Lissie aside in the lobby.

"Lissie, I wanted you to hear it from me first, but I'm going to ask your friend Melanie out." He rubbed his hands together nervously, but Lissie hardly ever thought of him as a praying mantis now.

"I'm really happy for you two, Darren," she assured him. "You know I think both of you are the best. In fact, I was surprised it took you so long."

"Well, you know how conservative my folks can be. They needed some time to get used to the idea of me dating someone who is not Chinese. I had to invite them to one of the Four Treasures dinners when she was there, so they could just get to know her as a person first."

"Everyone loves Mel," said Lissie stoutly. "Have you already talked it out with her? Because then I'll be mad at her for not telling me."

"No, I didn't say anything yet, just in case it was going to take more time to get my parents used to the idea. My mom is disappointed but says it's okay."

"She will love Mel," Lissie insisted. "Though if you guys do go out and it all ends in a blazing dumpster fire, promise me you won't make things totally awkward."

"How could I?" he demanded. "If I didn't go down to your place, and she didn't come up, we'd never see each other again. Ask Jenny how many times she's run into Charles Bing since they broke up—and she's on the Stanford campus all the time! If Mel rejects me now or dumps me later, I'll just vanish into the millions of people living in the greater Bay Area. Promise."

CHAPTER 15

There might be millions of people living in the greater Bay Area, but in the New Year, Preston Lin popped up in her life again. It was her own fault, Lissie supposed, for going anywhere near Stanford, but Mel had begged.

"Darren and Jay are having this open-house-slash-dinner thing at their place, and I hate being the only non-Stanford person there," she complained. "I end up either hovering around him or being pity-talked to by the spouses. It sucks. If you come, Lissie, I get points for being there without having to work so hard."

"That sounds horrible. Can't Nelson go?"

"Come on! You owe me for all my Four Treasures reviews. And besides, Nelson can't, I already asked him."

Which was how Lissie ended up sitting beside Mel on the circular sectional in the Lyman Graduate Residences common area, holding a plate of Korean barbecue, when Preston Lin walked in. It had been over two months since the Fall Ball. Thank God there were enough people present that they could choose to ignore each other. While he greeted his department colleague Jay, Lissie angled herself toward Mel. "Oh crap, it's Preston Lin. Talk to me. No—don't look around! Just be really, really absorbed in conversation. He won't come over, but I'd rather not deal with him at all."

Mel leaned in obediently. "Have I ever told you that bibimbap is the only time I ever like my egg yolk not cooked all the way through? Because the runny yolk gives the grains of rice that nice sheen. Some people like to mix all the bibimbap ingredients together before they eat, so they get some of everything in every bite, which is totally fine, but—"

"Hi."

You have got to be kidding me. They looked up to find Preston Lin doing his usual looming above them, and since they were seated, it was like running their eyes up a giant sequoia. A giant, unreasonably masculine sequoia.

"What are you two doing here?" he asked, when they said nothing. "You mind if I . . . " Without waiting for an answer, he pulled over a chair. Lissie berated herself for sitting where she could be got at, but how was she to know Mr. I-hate-being-lied-to would seek her out and risk being the victim of more of her evil machinations? Hadn't he told her that he didn't know her and didn't want to?

"Does this mean you're talking to us?" she said at last, since Mel had slid her foot against Lissie's and pressed it.

He swallowed, and Lissie knew he was regretting his last words to her.

"Darren invited us," chirped Mel. "Lissie's my plus-one."

He nodded.

The three of them sat there a minute, Mel resuming her bibimbap consumption, Lissie paralyzed, a bulgogi skewer in her hand. She was not going to drag the meat off with her teeth with him watching. Preston had no plate at all. He merely sat, elbows on knees, tapping the fingertips of his big hands together.

"How are . . . how have you guys been?" he ventured.

"Great," said Mel, munching away. "Darren and I are a thing now, did you know?"

He glanced at Lissie, as if she had anything to do with anything. "I didn't. That's great. And you, Lissie? How are you?"

"Fine, thanks." Silence. Mel nudged her foot again, and Lissie blurted, "What's new with you?"

"Same old, same old. Research, classes . . . " An inspiration struck him because he sat up a little straighter. "How did your little sister do at Champs?"

She was surprised he remembered. "All right, though she didn't get any personal bests. But her 400 medley relay got a Regional cut, and Coach Wayman thinks she's close on three individual events." Lissie's voice faltered over these last words, remembering the bad blood between the two men. She saw his brow knit. She half expected him to go away, but he didn't. He kept on sitting there, and she kept on holding the dumb beef skewer, and Mel kept on eating.

"Did Jenny take her MCATs yet?" He tried again.

"Next Saturday."

Another wordless abyss yawned. Finally, to Lissie's relief, Darren and his roommate Jay joined them.

"So you're the famous Lissie," Jay addressed her, after general greetings passed. He was redheaded and milk-pale, a cross between Ed Sheeran and that actor who played Ron Weasley.

"Am I famous?" she asked warily. It was hard to imagine Darren talking about her, but maybe Mel had?

"I heard you're a stone-cold killer," he grinned, tipping back on his chair. "The shellfish slayer. The Hunan hitwoman. Didn't Darren tell you? I got lunch at the Four Treasures with him last week and left that review from 'M. Beijerinck.' You wrote me a nice response."

She perked up. "That was you? Is Jay your middle name, then?"

"Nope, it's Paul."

"Martinus Beijerinck was a pioneer Dutch microbiologist," muttered Preston. Another glance at Lissie. "You're the one who responds to reviews?"

"You should have come with us, Lin," Jay urged before she could answer. "Good stuff. And I'm not just saying that because Darren said I couldn't say anything else. Apparently Lissie here nearly finished off some poor allergic customer a few months ago, leading to a wave of bad PR that Darren is trying to stem." At the suddenly alarmed expressions facing him, Jay broke off. "What?"

"Awwwk-ward," sang Mel.

Preston's face was darker than ever. "I was there that night, Goldsmith. It was actually someone in our party with the shellfish allergy."

Darren and Mel made half-smiling, half-pained grimaces at each other. Lissie jumped in. "It's true. If you've met Preston's friend Charles Bing, it was his sister with the allergy. It's really sad that there aren't many places I can go without my disgraceful reputation preceding me."

"Sorry," said Darren, but Preston said abruptly, "Hazel was okay. And, uh, these things happen." Lissie stared at him, but he was inspecting the seam of his jeans like he was a quality-control supervisor.

"That's news to me," she said under her breath. She set her skewer down, still untasted. "What's worse," she went on to Jay, "it's my aunt and uncle's restaurant. Nothing like that has happened before or since at the Four Treasures, so it's caused them a lot of stress."

"Has business picked up any?" Preston darted her a glance and then returned to picking at his seam.

It was on the tip of her tongue to retort, *What do you care? Worried we'll get back on our feet?* But trying to follow the twists and turns of his mind wasn't worth the trouble. Apparently he was willing to "know" her today, his cutting words at the Fall Ball notwithstanding, but Lissie would be a fool to bare her throat to his knife again. Bad enough that he now knew she handled the Four Treasures' online presence! Would that be his next target?

"It's a little better," she answered. "Not pre-shrimp-paste-debacle better, but better than it had been."

He nodded again, and then Mel skillfully introduced a new subject, the latest Marvel blockbuster. Lissie hadn't seen the movie, and judging from his silence, neither had Preston. But Darren and Jay and Mel started chattering obsessively about it, Lissie silently blessing her tact.

After a few minutes of this, Lissie said to no one in particular, "I'm going to get more food," and squeezed her way out. If the mountain wouldn't get away from Mohammed, Mohammed would have to get away from the mountain. She took her time reloading her plate, peeking sidewise to see if Preston had left, but nope, there he sat, and she had the prickly awareness that he was only staying because of her. Argh.

It being January, the garage-style doors that opened onto the patio were closed, and she had no clue if it was raining or hailing or clear, but Preston-free was good enough for her at this point. At least outside, she could eat her bulgogi in peace.

It was freezing in the open atrium. Lissie dashed to the circular bench in the center, crossing her legs and hunching over for warmth. She took her phone out while she inhaled her food, so that the people passing would think she was absorbed in something. From time to time, the door to the lounge opened and voices and laughter floated out. She rose to dump her plate and debated going back in when the door closest to her opened. A girl emerged, her pink fleece contrasting with the shining black lacquer of a grand piano behind her. "Did you want to practice?" she asked. "I'm done."

Lissie almost laughed at the thought of playing "Twinkle, Twinkle, Little Star" on a grand piano, but she caught the door before it closed. The practice space was warm and bright, and while she was no pianist and her fingers were a little greasy, the Yamaha was so beautiful she was tempted to trill the upper keys.

Instead, she nestled in one of the two oversized beanbags anchoring the far corner of the room and texted Mel: *Gone yet? Hiding out till coast is clear.*

Mel's answer was immediate: *Just left. You can come back* (three chicken emojis followed).

Grinning, Lissie started to tap her reply when the atrium door opened. She glanced up, figuring it was another earnest grad student clutching an iPad of sheet music, but she was wrong. It was Preston.

This is inexcusable, she thought. Her first instinct was to scramble up, but she squelched it. She could sit there. It wasn't against the law.

It wasn't his beanbag. If he wanted to play, fine, whatever, she would go. But otherwise, he was the intruder.

She stared at him.

He stared back at her.

I am not going to speak first, Lissie vowed. *Not even to tell him to shut the door because he's letting all the cold air in.*

Lissie saw Preston swallow hard. Then he finally moved into the room, letting the door swing shut behind him. He went, as Lissie had, to the gleaming black piano and let his fingers fall on the keys, playing just the trill she had imagined.

She nearly asked, *Do you play?* but she stuffed it back down, giving herself a mental high five for the achievement.

What on Earth did he want? Did he really come into the music room just to plink on the keys? And even if he did, shouldn't he at least say something?

I don't care, she thought. *I don't care about his motivations. I refuse to care. I refuse to be curious. I refuse to ask. I. Will. Not. Speak.*

He lowered the cover on the piano keys and took a seat on the bench, in the posture he had assumed in the lounge: elbows on knees, fingertips tented. But that only lasted until he glanced at her again. Then he sprang back to his feet and wandered to the nearby music stand and inspected the sheet someone had left there.

Lissie found she was clutching handfuls of the beanbag, and she pictured the little Styrofoam pellets deforming in her grasp. She was going to give in. She felt it. She couldn't outlast him. He was unnatural.

"I thought you didn't play," he blurted at last, face flushed. Lissie wanted to pump her fist in triumph. That only lasted an instant, however, before she was fighting the urge to apologize. *You did lie to him,* said the devil's-advocate side of her brain. *By omission.* Lissie gave that side of her brain a firm shake. *Yes, but I wouldn't have needed to, if he hadn't been such a first-class jerk in the restaurant, yelling and accusing. I was trying to defuse the situation.*

Helpfully, Preston Lin shored up her resolve by saying, "I was upset at the Fall Ball. And you *did* lie. I mean, I understand why you did it, but a lie is a lie."

There. That was better. He was pissing her off again.

She shut her eyes briefly, but they flew open when she heard the woosh of a chair being pulled across the carpet.

"Lissie."

All the guy did was loom. And now he was going to lecture her again from the superior height of a chair.

"Yes?" she asked, heaving herself ever so slightly up. It was graceless, but she felt less like a turtle on its back.

"I . . . wondered if you wanted to grab dinner sometime."

Her lips parted in surprise, and she sunk back into the beanbag.

"I've been thinking for a while—after the ball, and before the ball— that I wanted to ask you out." He gave a mirthless chuckle. "I mean, I wanted to, but didn't want to. I've been fighting the idea for a few months now, but it hasn't gone away. You were so pretty and funny at the restaurant—before everything happened, I mean. And every time I see you, I like you more. Tonight . . . " He shook his head slowly. "After two months, it's still not out of my system, despite everything that's happened. Not to mention, my mom harbors dreams of me marrying Hazel, so imagine what she'll think when I say to her, Hey, Mom, remember that waitress who couldn't speak any Chinese and almost killed your favorite person? Here she is! And even better, she's an English major at San Jose State who lives in a crappy apartment with three other people. Which is fine, of course, just that my mom's kind of hung up on prestige and appearances. I don't think she ever goes south of Mountain View or north of Menlo Park, if she can help it."

He was grinning at her like he thought this was all very funny, but for once, she didn't find the look engaging. In fact, as she listened and felt her blood pressure rise, she wanted to slap that grin right off his face.

This was how he felt about her? This was what had been going on behind that unreadable face? Before she could even decide what she thought of the revelation, it was smashed to atoms beneath the boot of his arrogance, a superiority all the more maddening because it was so casual. Her astonishment at his confession had robbed her of words at first, but by the end of his speech, they'd come flooding back—and then some. She blinked at him with glittering eyes.

"Was that my cue to crawl out of the beanbag and fall at your feet in gratitude?"

"What?"

"Let me save you some worry. You won't have to deal with your mom's reaction," she ground out through her clenched jaw as she scrambled up, "because you'll never have to drop that bombshell on her. Because there'll never be anything to tell. Because you and I are not going to go out. And your dear mom will never need to learn how you went slumming for dates."

"Who said anything about slumming?" He got to his feet.

"You did! You just did, when you talked down about me going to San Jose State and living in a crappy apartment."

He threw up his hands, his face reddened. "What is your problem? You're the one who called your place 'Château Cardboard!' I was half kidding."

"And half not kidding. And what do you mean, 'What is my problem?' If someone says no to you, they've got a problem?"

"Are you this rude to everyone who asks you out?"

"Are *you* this rude to everyone *you* ask out?"

The color drained from his face, replaced by stony anger. "I'm sorry. I forgot that you prefer things to be smooth, whether you have to bend the truth or not. So I should have just told you I liked you, and stuffed all the rest down? If I pretended like I never had any qualms, you would have found that plausible?"

She could hardly see him, her own anger blinding her. "You can tell yourself that if you want, but I promise you, there was no universe in which you were going to ask me out and I was going to say yes."

"Because I told you the truth, and you couldn't take it."

"Oh, I knew before then. Way before then. I knew within half an hour of meeting you that you, Preston Lin, were a smug, self-righteous, everything-handed-to-you-on-a-silver-platter, superior, bullying asshole that I would be grateful never to meet again in the whole course of my existence!"

For a second, she thought he might throw her back onto the beanbag, and if he weren't so much bigger than she was, she would have dared him. But he held completely still—stiller than she was, because she could feel herself trembling with adrenaline. When he spoke again, his voice was very low and quiet. "Wow. That was heartfelt. If your dislike of me began so soon after we met, I can only assume you were offended by how I reacted when Hazel broke out in hives. I was upset, yes. I made a big deal of it. I'm sorry. I was harsh. I admit it. So how is it that, for all the times you've apologized for that night, somehow I still feel like you believe I'm more to blame?"

"If only you had yelled at me," Lissie answered, "and gone away, I think I would have been remorseful. I *was* sorry. And I was determined it would never happen again. But that wasn't all you did."

He looked at her sharply.

"I saw the article you wrote for the *Stanford Daily*. You have no idea what that did. You have no idea the hit the Four Treasures took after that article came out. The drop in traffic, the nasty and undeserved online reviews and comments. My aunt and uncle don't pay any attention to the Internet! They had no clue what was happening. You have no idea how hard I've had to work to try to fix things. I answered every stupid fear and complaint. I begged every person I knew to eat there and leave positive reviews. I gave up my server job and income so they wouldn't have to deal with my embarrassing presence, so instead, they've had to deal with some new person who's incompetent and unreliable in totally different ways. Why do you think I've been acting as my little sister's 'swim mom?' It was to help my aunt and uncle because it was my fault they were stressed for money. I'm sure you know—I'm sure Charles told you—that Jenny and JoJo and I have been their responsibility since our parents died. As if taking JoJo in and paying for our college and everything weren't enough—I almost sank their life's work, not to mention their only source of income! Yes, it was my fault, but can you blame me for thinking I had the worst luck ever? That out of all the people on the entire planet, I happened to screw up in front of *you*?"

He said nothing to this. She shrugged. "I pressed one of your buttons. And it was a real button. I get it. So you went DEFCON 1 on us. Whatever. The restaurant is getting better. Slowly. And it's a good thing, because I'm going back soon to take Jenny's shifts until the MCAT is over. Just do us a favor and stay away. From me and from all of us."

She thought he might step back then and leave her a clear path to the door, but he stood there in his characteristic Rock of Gibraltar fashion. "So if I hadn't written that article, maybe this might have gone differently?"

"I don't think so. If anything, it just showed me your true colors sooner than I might have discovered otherwise. When I heard other things about you, they only confirmed what I already knew."

"What 'other things?'" His voice was even quieter, but it was the quiet of menace.

She glared at him, resenting what she saw as an attempt to intimidate her. "Wayman Wang told me about how he came to your swim club as a new assistant coach, only to have you jump ship to someplace sexier and then proceed to poach the head coach and the top swimmers. You got your Stanford scholarship, but that old club collapsed, and Wayman had to move to another state to find another job. Striking a match to things and watching them burn seems to be your MO."

His mouth twisted. "Wayman Wang has always managed to land on his feet. He's popular wherever he goes."

"And why shouldn't he be?" she countered. "He's friendly and personable. Optimistic, even though he's had some tough things to overcome."

"Tough things," he sneered. "Of his own making."

"You always manage to put the blame on someone else, don't you?" accused Lissie. "When bad things happen to other people, it's always one hundred percent their fault and never the slightest bit yours!"

"The parts that are their fault are always their fault, no matter the percentage." He waved this away like a buzzing fly. "If this is what you think of me, this was an exercise in futility."

"Like I said." But her voice shook the tiniest bit.

"Forget it. You may have withheld the entire truth about other things, but you've sure let it rip now." His face was shuttered, closed off, and he shoved his hands in his pockets. "Have a good weekend."

Without waiting for a reply, he stalked away, ramming the door with his shoulder on his way out.

Lissie wilted into the chair he had pulled over. She wished she could lock herself in some quiet closet and have a good cry.

Preston Lin *liked* her? Had liked her all this time? The big, arrogant, brilliant swim star, with his accolades and his pool records and his Ph.D. program?

"He sure hid it well," she told the empty room. She couldn't help but feel flattered, even though he was such an unlikeable person. She had to remind herself that he'd barely apologized for jeopardizing the restaurant. And toward Wayman Wang's hardships, he'd been downright contemptuous.

"He's a jerk," Lissie announced to her invisible auditors. She stood up and brushed herself off. "Imagine dating a guy who never thought he was wrong. Who would never admit when he was wrong. It would be impossible."

Sheet music fluttered from the stand to the floor as she passed.

She was right to have turned him down. There was no question. But she still wanted a good cry.

Of course, she had to tell her roommates about it.

Nelson clicked his tongue and shook his head like Lissie had been diagnosed with a terminal illness. "Ooh, too bad. He's so hot. And not many boys like smart, mean girls like you. He was probably the best fish you'll ever catch, and you tossed him back, girl."

"What if the fish was shiny on the outside and rotten on the inside?" she demanded.

"Everyone's rotten in their own way," he said with a shrug. "At least you knew what his was. And it was all wrapped up in that nice, pretty package."

"Poor Preston," was Jenny's opinion. She was lying on the sofa with a cold compress across her forehead, staving off a migraine and stressing that the MCAT was only days away.

"I don't know what's so poor about him," Lissie turned on her next. "Are you all forgetting how he yelled at me and then dissed me at the Fall Ball? Not to mention how he made Coach Wayman suffer a serious life setback. And somehow it's 'poor Preston?'"

"But he liked you. And he did put himself out there. No one likes to be rejected. That's all I mean."

Lissie rolled her eyes, but even Mel wasn't fully on her side. "You could've at least kissed him before you rejected him."

"Kissed him? Why would I have done that?" sputtered Lissie,

throwing a cushion at her.

"Me, I would have kissed him. Just saying."

Nelson raised his hand. "I would've kissed him too." He reached for Jenny's limp arm and held it up. "So would Jenny. That makes it unanimous. Why don't you call him and say it's still no way, but if he wanted, you know, to make out a little, you would be willing to kiss him?"

"With friends like these, I'd rather have enemies," she muttered. "Thank you all for sharing your opinions, but it's not going to happen. I'll do whatever I have to do to make sure of it. Because if I can help it, I'm never going to see or talk to the guy ever again."

Lissie managed to keep her vow for all of a week, and when she did break it, it wasn't her fault.

It was Saturday afternoon, and she was back at the Four Treasures, rolling silverware and taking bites of the beef with broccoli Carlos had whipped up for her.

"It's the customer killer!" he had shouted in greeting, not even pausing as he whacked at a whole chicken with a cleaver. "Ray, look who got paroled."

"Here comes trouble," Ray crowed, whipping a pan off the flames and setting on a new one. "Your aunt had to print up all new menus with the ingredients listed."

"Haha," said Lissie. "Nice to see you too. And I'm the one who suggested the menus."

"Sure, sure, killer."

David the waiter told her, "Thank God. I thought you were a moron, but Stacey who replaced you not only couldn't speak Chinese, she was late so often I decided she couldn't tell time either."

Auntie Rhoda patted Lissie on the shoulder every time she passed, and Uncle Mason emerged from his office in the back to offer the special Chinese New Year menu for her perusal. Ten minutes before the doors opened, Lissie was tucked in the rejects' booth, going over Olivia Wei's latest writing assignment in Google Docs—a book report on *The Giver*, which Lissie had never read and which had clearly bored the pants off Olivia. She didn't even notice anyone entering the restaurant until she heard Auntie Rhoda say, "We're not open yet, sir! Give us a few more minutes."

"I'm sorry—I wasn't going to eat. I was seeing if Lissie was working today."

At the sound of Preston Lin's voice, Lissie's head jerked up. Her heart began to pound, and something seemed to be lodged in her throat.

"Oh, yes. Lissie!" Auntie Rhoda called. And then, turning back to him: "I remember you. You ate here before with the poor girl with the shellfish allergy."

"Yes."

"How is she? Is she okay? We were so sorry for—"

"She's fine. Completely fine. Thank you. Oh, hey there."

"Hey," said Lissie around her throat obstruction.

"I didn't know how else to get this to you." He held out an envelope, and she took it. Then, before she could even glance back up at him, he turned on his heel and left.

It was the longest night ever. Not the busiest night ever, but traffic was steady. Lissie had one break around eight o'clock, and she stole to the back room to satisfy her consuming curiosity. But before she could do more than finger the envelope in her pocket, Jeremy popped his head in.

"Lissie, got a second?"

"What?" she asked impatiently.

"Check this out." He showed her his phone screen. She expected to see some gaming meme or joke picture JoJo had taken, but instead, bizarrely, it was Zillow.

"You're showing me a house?"

"It's a townhouse. What do you think?"

"What do I think? I think it's a townhouse."

"But it looks good, right?"

She grabbed his phone and looked again. "Sure, it looks nice. Why?"

"I was thinking I would go to the open house tomorrow."

"What? What for?"

"Because I'm thinking of getting my own place."

Lissie's jaw would have hit the floor had it not been attached to the rest of her head. "What are you talking about? You and who? Some friends?"

He didn't answer her. "I thought about surprising the folks. But if I move them, then what about JoJo and her swimming?"

"Jeremy, you're not making any sense. Are you telling me you're thinking about buying real estate?"

He grinned. "Shhh, keep it down. And don't sound so surprised."

"How am I supposed to sound? I know you've been doing the streaming thing and saving up, but you're telling me you saved that much?"

"Yup. Hey, it's not like it happened overnight. It's been eight years, ever since high school."

Lissie thought of the $437.29 in her own checking account, which might just buy her a tent at REI. She had dozens of questions, but Auntie Rhoda appeared over her son's shoulder. "Come on, you two, break's over. There's a large party for you, Jeremy, and Lissie, tell the man at table six that he can't order any more drinks."

When she was finally done at the Four Treasures, she could only drive as far as the Whole Foods down the street before pulling into the well-lit parking lot to open the envelope. The outside was blank. She slid a finger under the flap and found a handwritten letter. Spiky, dense handwriting covered both the front and back of two sheets of paper.

Lissie,

I hope you'll read this because I didn't have my thoughts together enough to respond properly to the things you said when we spoke. I'm not writing to ask you out again. You made yourself clear there, believe me, and the sooner it's all forgotten, the better. I'm writing to address your two accusations.

You claim I vindictively tried to destroy your aunt and uncle's business. That was not my intention. You read the article I wrote for the Daily, so you know how strongly I feel about the dangers of food allergies, and not merely because of Hazel Bing. While you apologized for your carelessness on that occasion, there continues to be a defensiveness and even dismissiveness in your response. But I do appreciate the changes the Four Treasures has made as real and undertaken in good faith. Exactly the sort of thing my article was working toward, not only at the Four Treasures, but at all places where food is handled and served.

Lissie paused here to release a groan. Could the guy sound any more pompous if he tried?

But there was more going on that night which might help you appreciate my response. Two things. The first is, when we were kids in school, Hazel had a bad reaction to something I'd brought in my lunch, so it's made me jumpy where her allergies are concerned. And the second is, if you recall, the party included my mother. You weren't formally introduced, of course, and I don't expect you to know anything about her, but she's a successful businesswoman with a reputation as a tough negotiator. She has also gone to court more than once to make her point. I am not saying she would have sued the Four Treasures for what happened to Hazel that night, but I also couldn't promise you that she would not have. Hazel is, as I said, one of my mother's favorite people as well as her employee. My father and I have learned that my mother can be deflected or redirected if she feels like a situation is already being handled to her satisfaction. If my dad had been at the dinner, you might have seen the strong response come from him. He and I have become adept at these efforts. All of which is to say, as I was dealing with it appropriately, she didn't feel the need to do it herself.

"Oh, I get it," Lissie muttered. "Here I thought you were being a self-satisfied jerk, but you were actually throwing yourself on a grenade for me?" The bit about Hazel's childhood incident was harder to dismiss, but she shook her head and resumed reading.

Which leads me to your second accusation, that I single-handedly took down the Los Altos Flyers Swim Club. I have never talked about this with anyone outside my immediate family, and to tell the truth, we haven't talked about it more than once since it all happened eight or nine years ago. I have no alternative but to share what I know and to ask for your discretion. When I was a freshman in high school, I got moved into the senior group of the club. I had had a growth spurt and was suddenly showing lots of improvement. That was also the year Wayman Wang came to LAFSC as our new assistant coach. He was a couple years out of college, I think, and was immediately popular with both swimmers and parents. I admired him because I dreamed of being a college swimmer as he had been. I remember my mother saying to my father that she worried about the club hiring someone so young and handsome because all the girls were in love with him.

Lissie smashed the letter to her chest, a wave of dread swamping her. "Please don't let him say what I think he's going to say," she prayed aloud. "Please don't let him say that Wayman Wang was a pervert who molested all the girls on the team. Please, please, please." Her heart was hammering. She had the wicked hope that Wayman wouldn't pick JoJo as his victim, which she immediately revised to include all the other Mission Valley Manta Rays, lest her selfishness be punished.

It wasn't like people had never heard of coaches or adult leaders abusing their position, and my mother was probably not the only one to worry, but in light of what happened afterward, I guess she was hiding concern of a different kind.

This is really hard to write. I had to take a break for a while and come back. But here goes. Sometime after the December champs meet that year, my mother disappeared for 72 hours. No one knew where she was, and nothing like that had ever happened before. My dad's casual calls to family members and to her coworkers the first night turned into anxiety and then panic. He is a very private person, and it was mortifying for him to admit that he didn't know where she was and to have to cast a wider net. But he had no choice because he thought something terrible must have happened to her.

It was the police who found her by tracking her cell phone. My dad told me where she was when he first found out. She had run off with Wayman Wang, and he had to get on a plane to go get her. She had had a midlife fling of some sort. When my dad returned with her, my mother kissed me and made some joke about taking a secret vacation, and how she wouldn't have gone if she had known everyone was going to get so excited about it. That was it. No other explanation. And if I hadn't seen my dad's face—he had aged ten years in a week—and if he hadn't told me where she'd gone in that one unguarded moment, I might have believed her.

I decided I would never swim again. It wasn't only to punish her. I couldn't bear the thought of showing up at the club with Wayman on deck and no one the wiser. I knew my family was not going to bring this shameful incident to light. My dad, even though he had always loved to watch me swim, understood. He had no more desire for me to go back to LAFSC than I did, though he didn't press me one way or the other. He was probably too busy trying to save his marriage, in any case.

What Wayman did was not something he could have been fired for, even if it had become known. However inappropriate, it was

*between consenting adults and thus not illegal, though I'm sure
most clubs nowadays would strongly encourage him to move on.
My mother protested my decision to quit. She tried everything from
lectures to guilt trips to bribes to get me to go back, but I refused.*

*As time went on, however, I found that I missed swimming
horribly. There is something therapeutic about following a line at the
bottom of the pool back and forth, back and forth, with all the world
shut out and the pain of your own body driving out every other kind
of hurt. I asked my dad if I could join a different swim club, and
he agreed at once. I was so glad to be back in the pool with a place
to channel my anger and hurt. And when my old head coach and
some of my old friends joined my new club, that was just a bonus.
I never knew what happened to LAFSC or heard the details of its
collapse. I only know I was grateful not to run into Wayman again.
I never forgot him or the destructive impact he had on my family,
but I tried to put it all behind me. To pretend it never happened,
as my mother does.*

*It was a shock, obviously, to see him at that meet. It's been years,
and people can change, but since he coaches your younger sister, it can't
hurt to make you aware. Again, what I have shared is known only to
my parents, Wayman, and myself, and I ask you to keep it that way,
unless someone might be endangered by your not speaking up.*

*I'm sorry again for how everything went and wish we could at
least be friends.*

Preston

The Whole Foods parking lot had emptied out by the time Lissie
finished reading and re-reading the letter. Finally, she inserted the
sheets in the envelope and started homeward. Could it possibly be
true? There was no one she could ask about it except the very people
he had mentioned. How could it not be true? Why on Earth would
he fabricate such a mortifying story?

It accorded at several points with what Wayman had said: the timing of it, who left the club, Wayman leaving the state entirely for years. And why didn't Wayman just get another job nearby? He was talented, attractive, popular. He might even have applied for a position at the club Preston Lin transferred to, as his boss had. But instead, he went all the way to Nevada. And why had Wayman bailed on the Fall Ball, when he had expressed interest before he knew Preston would be there and that Lissie knew him?

Preston's story accounted for more than the demise of the Los Altos Flyers Swim Club. It also explained the odd comments she had overheard while hiding in Charles Bing's closet. Preston had said to Charles that it wasn't relaxing to be around his mother—whom he always referred to as "mother," Lissie had noticed, though he called his father "dad." More memories followed: he had stiffened when Mrs. Lin touched his shoulder in the restaurant. Lissie had chalked it up to his general standoffishness, but now it took on deeper undertones.

And then there was the Fall Ball. "He can't stand being lied to," Hazel Bing had said, as if that were something unique. But Preston's extreme reaction made more sense in light of what had happened to him. Could a lie in his family's past have scarred him enough to leave him hypersensitive even to comparatively harmless or understandable fibs and omissions, as hers had been?

Unit 114 at Château Cardboard came with one narrow parking spot between a post and a dumpster, requiring up to a seventeen-point turn to squeeze into, but when it was accomplished, Lissie made no move to go inside. It occurred to her that if the latter part of Preston Lin's letter were true—and she admitted to herself that she did in fact believe him—what did that mean about the first part? She had thought him arrogant and overzealous. Which he was. But now she understood what else had driven him. His past experience with Hazel, yes, but more than that. Now that she knew the complexity of his relationship with his mother, she felt more inclined to believe that his overreaction had been a protective move. Would Penelope Lin have sued her aunt and uncle? She would never know.

And what about Preston Lin himself? Did his intensity predate his mother's betrayal, or was it another consequence? He wasn't always awful, she conceded. Before the shellfish disaster, she had thought him uptight, yes, snobby about the beer, yes, but also kind of fun to tease. He couldn't have been at his most comfortable that evening, considering it was a dinner with his mother and the girl his mother wanted him to marry. Probably the whole thing had been her idea. And at his advisor's house, he had been cool and polite with her, even though she knew he didn't want her there. He said he'd liked her since the restaurant. Lissie had been too on edge to think about whether or not she enjoyed his company—how could she, when she didn't even want to be *in* his company?

Lissie was honest enough with herself to recognize she would probably have fallen for him under different circumstances. At the November meet, he had been at his most winning, joking with her, showing some vulnerability, making a big deal over the little kids getting their ribbons. If the shellfish disaster had never happened, she likely would have nursed a full-blown crush. But there it had always been, like a curtain wall between them: her carelessness and the aftermath. And thus her heart was spared.

Lissie felt for the first time that she understood Preston. She recognized for the first time how her own assumptions and embarrassment and personal snobberies had prevented her from seeing him clearly. From giving him what she gave to most people: the benefit of the doubt. At every swim officials' meeting, they hammered home the point that "the benefit of the doubt goes to the swimmer." That is, if you didn't actually witness the infraction, you could not disqualify them. But she had done precisely that with Preston Lin. He had yelled at her and written a damning article, and that was all she needed to know. She hadn't asked herself—nor had she cared—what might be going on in his life to make him the jerk he was. And yet not a jerk, it turned out. Or less of a jerk. Less and less and less. *Oh, dear.*

CHAPTER 17

Although Lissie may have blown her chance with him, Preston at least trusted her discretion, and she intended to live up to that trust. Therefore, she told Jenny and Mel about his letter but only revealed parts of it.

"Let me get this straight," said Mel. "He faked being angrier than he actually was because he was trying to prevent his mom from going off on you?"

"Pretty much."

Her roommate sighed and fluttered her fake lashes. "That is so hot. I wish Darren had a reason to defend me from his mom, but she only ever threatens to overfeed me."

"You think it's plausible, then?"

"I don't know. I didn't see the woman. I'm just saying it's hot. Jenny, what do you think?"

Jenny looked up from her MCAT prep book. The test was over, but she was deep in the post-test beating-herself-up phase. She jabbed the page before her with a disgusted finger. "I *knew* that. I can't believe I forgot it when I knew it! I should have cut my hours back sooner. I never should have gone out with Charles Bing. I am not making those mistakes again. I've got one more chance in March, and I am going to crack down and be serious this time."

"You always do this, Jen," Lissie pointed out. "Maybe wait and see your scores before you make all these vows?"

"But I won't get my scores for a month! If I find out then that I did badly, that won't be enough time to get serious. I have to buckle down now, and then I can let up later if I do better than I thought. Which I didn't."

"Just take a half hour off, then," Mel urged her, "so we can have this critical conversation, and then you can go back to flogging yourself."

Jenny gave a deep sigh and pushed the book away. "What was the question?"

"Did Preston Lin's mom look like the type who would sue the Four Treasures for giving Hazel Bing hives?" Mel repeated.

Jenny considered. "I don't know about that, but Charles did say she's pretty intense and that Hazel feels a lot of pressure trying to live up to her expectations. So, yeah. I could be persuaded of that. Do you not think so, Lissie?"

"No, I could believe it," Lissie said in a small voice.

"So if he wasn't trying to blow up the Four Treasures after all, did he say anything about his other purported victim?" Mel pursued. "Did he mention his ex-swim club?"

Lissie had thought about how to phrase this. "He did. He said he left the club because he quit swimming altogether. But after a while he missed swimming, so he made a fresh start somewhere new. And he had no idea the head coach from the old place was going to come over, much less any former teammates."

"Correlation is not causation," said Jenny. "If p, then q. Q, therefore p. That's a fallacy."

"What?" Mel rolled her eyes. "Never mind. You're agreeing, I think, that it wasn't his fault? Maybe you really should go back to studying."

"I'm agreeing that with the little we know, we can't be sure what went on," Jenny laughed.

Though Lissie was dying to tell them the more she did know, she held it in. But if only she could ask them if she ought to worry about JoJo having Wayman for a coach! She wanted to think there was no danger. He had gone after an older woman eight years ago, for Pete's sake, not any of the kids. And he was with Coach Penny now. And he had flirted (hadn't he?) with Lissie. Maybe it wasn't that he liked women of any particular age, but that he had liked that particular woman, Mrs. Lin. What could she say, in any case, without revealing what Preston had not given her permission to reveal? And if there was no danger to the kids, and Lissie revealed the secret, wouldn't she then be trying to destroy Coach Wayman's career—exactly what she had thought Preston guilty of?

Lissie decided she would keep an eagle eye on the coach on the days she took JoJo to practice. In the meantime, she wished she could respond to the letter. It would be easy enough to send an email to the address listed in Stanford Profiles. But what would she say? "Hey, thanks for your letter. It helped me understand your side of the story. I wish you would rethink going out with me because I think I maybe possibly would give you a different answer now." Ugh. No way. If it were even wise. Just because he had his reasons for being overbearing did not change the fact that he had been overbearing.

Not that she didn't own her percentage of the blame. Preston might have liked her, but he was no more blind to her flaws than she to his. He had called her defensive and dismissive. Persistently so. Worse, Lissie had to acknowledge there was truth in his words. She had said she was sorry over and over, but apparently he had seen through her apologies to her underlying glibness.

So it never would have worked between them, right? *Right?*
Still.

She continued to think of him. She read his letter until she could have recited it. At the Four Treasures, her heart gave a little flip if anyone his size came in, which admittedly was rarely. Auntie Rhoda asked about the letter the next time Lissie worked since she had not volunteered any information, but she only straightened the menu stack, making sure they were all facing the same way, and mumbled, "He said he was pleased with the restaurant's response to the shellfish incident."

"That's it?"

"Pretty much."

Auntie sighed in disappointment. "If that's all, he didn't need to write that. He could have told me face to face. Such an impressive young man. I thought maybe he wanted to ask you out." She scrubbed at the fish-tank glass with extra vigor when her niece made no reply. "So sad. Jenny and that nice Charles Bing broke up. And then this handsome friend, no interest."

Knowing better than to get into it, Lissie moved on to setting the tables. But her aunt had one last innocent remark before the Fongs arrived. "It is good to have you back, Lissie," she said, "but I know JoJo misses seeing you almost every day. I wish she was better friends with Carpool Olivia but she is always texting that Emma Yeh. Always doing things with Emma Yeh. I ask her what was there to be texting about all the time and make her put her phone away, but she is se-cretive like you. I hope it isn't boys. She is too young for boys, right?"

Lissie too hoped it wasn't boys, and out of all boys JoJo and Emma might be discussing, she especially hoped it wasn't Coach Wayman. She could now only take her to practice on Mondays and Wednesdays, and that left a lot of unsupervised time in which anything might happen.

"Are Coach Wayman and Coach Penny still a thing?" she asked her little sister the next week when they drove to practice. "What do you and your friends think?"

JoJo made a face. "She hasn't come by the pool again, but every-one thinks probably. Emma asked her mom if Coach Wayman ever showed up during her little brother Henry's practice, and Mrs. Yeh said he had, once or twice, but it wasn't like Emma could say, 'Well, did they make out on deck?' So we're waiting to decide at the January Challenge because the afternoon session is the eight-and-unders and the thirteen-and-overs. You'll be there, won't you? Or are you trying to quit my swim stuff altogether?"

"I'll be there, you little brat. Now that Jenny's done with her big test, I've convinced her to do Saturday night shifts at the restaurant specifically so I can work your upcoming meets." *And keep an eye on Wayman Wang,* Lissie added to herself.

"Lightning Swim Club supposedly has a really fast pool," JoJo volunteered, something almost defiant in her tone. "Emma and Princeton already qualified for the All-Stars Meet, and they're going. I think I can qualify this weekend because Coach Wayman finally put me in the 100 fly again. I'm only three-tenths off."

"That's great! I bet you will. I know he wanted you to get times in all the other things, but that's still your favorite race."

JoJo picked at the vinyl armrest. "If I don't make it at this meet, I'll have to at the next. All-Stars is Presidents Day weekend."

"You'll for sure get it," Lissie encouraged her. "I'll have to write that one down to make sure I sign up to work it."

"You can't work it," JoJo said flatly, "because it's in Seattle, not here. But even if I make the cut, I can't go. I don't think Auntie Rhoda and Uncle Mason can afford to send me. I'm not even going to ask them."

"In Seattle? How much could it possibly be?" floundered Lissie. "You'd share a hotel room, right, and only swim the event you qualified for—"

"You get two bonus events."

"Okay, so three events total," Lissie calculated, "plus airfare and meals. Since it's a holiday, airfare might be a little more, but that'd be maybe $500 total?" It was one thing for Jenny and Lissie to deny themselves things like fun little trips, but another altogether to think of JoJo missing out. Jenny and Lissie could find the money, somehow, some way.

"Really? JoJo perked up at once, her face glowing with excitement. "Because Mrs. Yeh already said if I make it, she could chaperone me, and I really, really want to go!"

"Wait, what?" Now that her brain was catching up with her mouth, Lissie wished she had thought this through before she got JoJo's hopes up. Because clearly she would have to go along, or some family member would have to, because the Liangs would never send JoJo alone, even if Lissie thought it was a good idea, which she didn't. And how could Auntie Rhoda or Uncle Mason ever get away on a weekend? But for anyone to go along meant coming up with about $800—a steep sum on relatively short notice.

"I mean, that's really generous of Mrs. Yeh to offer, but if you go, I need to go too—"

"I don't think they'd pay for you to come along, Lissie."

"I don't want to bum off the Yehs! I'm talking about the meet itself. You wouldn't want to have nobody there to cheer for you, would you?"

JoJo's lower lip began to protrude. "But we can't afford two people. Which means neither one of us will get to go. Why don't you just say so?"

"Because I don't know so, not yet," Lissie insisted. "Why don't you worry about your times and let me think about the money? This will all be moot if you can't find three-tenths of a second."

To her surprise, JoJo lunged at her and hugged her, almost causing Lissie to veer into the next lane. "You promise? Promise you'll find a way?"

"I promise," said Lissie, grinning in spite of herself.

Of course, Jenny had no moneymaking ideas besides contributing $100 of her own meager bank balance, but an idea struck Lissie in the middle of the night. On Wednesday, she wasted no time hurrying from campus and banging on the door to the garage the second she got to the Liangs.

"Don't ever do that," groused her cousin Jeremy, emerging scowling and tousle-headed. He was wearing the purple glasses. "I just finished streaming, and that would have been so embarrassing to have someone knocking in the background."

"Sorry, sorry," said Lissie, thinking Preston Lin would have accused her of dismissiveness had he been there. "You should hang a sign on your door when you don't want to be interrupted."

"No one ever interrupts me."

"Okay, fine. I'll text you next time. But I had to talk to you before JoJo gets home."

"Why?"

"Because I need $600, and you're the only person with any money I can ask. I don't want to ask your parents."

"Why would I give you $600, and why do you want it?" he demanded.

"One, because you're the closest thing JoJo and I have to a brother; and two, she has her heart set on going to an away meet in Seattle, but it'll cost $800 to get her and me as a chaperone there. Jenny and I can manage $200, but not the whole $800, and that's where you come in. We hope."

He groaned and shuffled past her to the kitchen.

"I know you have the money, Jeremy. You wouldn't be talking about buying a place if you didn't have the money."

"I wouldn't have the money to talk about buying a place if I spent it on unnecessary things."

"She's just a kid, Jeremy. She never asks for much."

"Because her swimming already costs a mint."

"I know. It's true. But I'll pay you back. You can garnish my wages over the next six months."

This made him roll his eyes, but he didn't object right away, and Lissie pressed ahead. "I was just about to warm up some food," she coaxed. "Come join me in the kitchen. You can make a better decision on a full stomach."

Jeremy chewed silently, rather enjoying Lissie's fidgety impatience. He finally put down his fork and said, "Okay. I'll give you the money. And instead of you scraping together $100 a month to pay me back, you can pay me back in labor."

"What kind of labor?" Lissie asked warily, picturing herself having to play some first-person shooter game for which she had neither the skill nor the temperament.

He laughed. "Don't look so worried. I meant real estate. Go to a few showings for me and make walk-through videos. No big deal."

"What's the point? You'd still have to go look eventually."

"But you can rule some out for me. I'm looking on the Peninsula, and you know what a pain it is to get out of Milpitas. You're already halfway there, you can just jump on 280. I'll just send you some listings, and you schedule them at your convenience."

"How many are you talking about?"

"How would I know? It depends on what comes on, and when. I might love the first place and you get off totally easy, or it might take a while. Either way, you're done after I get a place or after, say, twelve showings. That means you're getting paid anywhere from $600 per showing down to $50 per. What do you say?"

"I say yes!" Lissie responded, clapping her hands. Even if she had to drive all the way up to San Mateo, if she could stack several showings on a Saturday, how long could it take to go from one to the next? Her brow furrowed. "How do I see a house, though? Doesn't an agent have to let me in?"

Jeremy grinned. "Yep. Unless it's an open house. Another reason I don't want to do it myself. Once you show any interest in a place, the agents come out of the woodwork and start trying to call and email and be your best friend. I've had to pretend I don't speak English a few times, but that only works if the agent isn't Asian."

"Okay. Some time and some hassle, you're saying. I'm still in. Can I tell JoJo?"

"Yep. But you're going to have to think of some explanation for how you got the money. My house-hunting is a secret, remember?"

Lissie sighed. "No worries. I'm good at that."

JoJo greeted the news with a scream, spinning in a circle and throwing her arms around Jeremy and Lissie in turn. "Thank you! Thank you, thank you, thank you! You won't believe how fast I'll go this weekend!"

She was as good as her word, taking a full half-second off her best time. Lissie was working the turn end of lanes five and six, but she could see her sister hopping up and down at the coaches' table, Coach Wayman fist-bumping her, and Emma Yeh flapping her swim parka sleeves in excitement.

After the meet, Mrs. Yeh sashayed up in a slinky knit wrap dress. "She did it, Lissie! I'm so glad. Emma will have much more fun in Seattle with a friend along."

"Yes. And how would you feel about the four of us sharing a hotel room—unless you and Emma wanted your own room . . . ?"

Mrs. Yeh shrugged. "I've already told Emma I want my own room. But if you and JoJo wanted to split hers, that'd be fine with me. It would mean I could be on the top floor, and she wouldn't have to be adjoining. I'll send you our flight and hotel information."

"Oh, thanks. Or I could get it from Coach Wayman."

"Coach Wayman?" Hot Mom frowned. "No—he won't be there."

Lissie's mouth popped open. "He won't? Then who will coach the girls and Princeton?" *And what am I doing, going on this trip, if I don't need to make sure there's no funny business?*

"He assigned them to Coach Paul from Streamline. They have seven swimmers going. And Mission Valley has the Fremont Invitational that weekend."

For a second, Lissie thought of sending JoJo with the Yehs after all. It would save $400. But who would scream for JoJo at her races if she didn't go? Besides, without Coach Wayman there, Lissie could relax and enjoy her first-ever trip to Seattle. Not to mention canceling now would require renegotiating her deal with Jeremy.

Nah. I'll go.

Lissie would think back to that decision with relief later, but in the moment, her gratitude was all for JoJo getting her heart's desire.

CHAPTER 18

Lissie failed Jeremy right off the bat. When he sent her some listings on Thursday, she pleaded a paper and a midterm and promised fervently she would go the following Saturday. The semester promised to be dreadful because, as a fifth-year senior, she actually got all the classes she registered for and all her remaining graduation requirements had to be stuffed in, lest she become the unthinkable: a sixth-year senior. She had her thesis project; British Drama before 1800; The Victorian Age; and the only Physical Science G.E. which fit her schedule, Geology 9: Earth Disasters. It totaled fifteen units, but the Victorian class covered one thick novel per week (along with a chunk of *Bleak House*, which they were reading in serial installments, as Dickens's original audience would have), and creative writing had become like pulling teeth.

"Are you sure you don't want to switch to writing a standard senior thesis?" Bach-Peralta asked over the top of her reading glasses. "When you proposed this, you had grand ambitions of staging the thing, and now I'm worried you won't even finish."

"What if I did a hybrid?" Lissie suggested. "Like, turned in the three acts I have, revised, of course, along with a shorter paper explaining why I made the choices I did, and then I performed part of it?"

"Are we talking a monologue?"

"Probably, unless I can recruit another person. But I don't want to overpromise."

Her advisor shook her head and expelled a slow breath. "Okay. Fine. I'll accept a hybrid. I'm trying to pass you, Lissie. I don't remember you being this scattered in my Ethnicity in American Lit class."

That was because Lissie had only been juggling school and two jobs at that point, as opposed to juggling school, two jobs, JoJo's swimming, Olivia's tutoring, and now Jeremy's house-hunting. But she spared the professor her excuses, thanked her once more, and escaped to the library for her shift, praying Silas would have nothing for her to do so she could get through *Wuthering Heights*.

Things weren't much easier the next weekend because she had another paper due ("compare and contrast Shakespeare's *The Tempest* to Davenant and Dryden's Restoration reboot *The Tempest, or the Enchanted Island*"), and she was now two chunks behind in *Bleak House*, but Jeremy sent her three listings and the message, "All open houses! No need to talk to anyone." Lissie glanced at Zillow to note the times and plan her route: start in Redwood City, then hit Menlo Park, and end in Mountain View. *Honestly, no wonder he wanted it hush-hush. He must have robbed a bank if he thought he could swing any of these*, she thought.

The Redwood City listing was part of a tired and old string of beige-brown townhouses two blocks off El Camino, but the sight of it unexpectedly filled Lissie with optimism. It might not be pretty, but it sure was convenient, and this part of town gave off a comfortable, humble vibe like the Liangs' Milpitas neighborhood. But there was competition—the door stood open, and two couples were going in as one family emerged.

An agent stood by a table in the living room, a middle-aged woman with brassy blonde hair and sensible shoes covered in blue booties, which the visitors all donned while balancing or leaning against the walls in the cramped entry. But none of these things made Lissie almost turn and run. No, it was that on the agent's table beside a fan of flyers stood a sign reading, "Another property brought to you by the Penelope Lin Team," above a big picture of the woman herself.

"Is she here?" Lissie croaked, pointing at the sign.

"Who? Penelope? No, but I'm Jillian, and I'm happy to answer any questions for you," replied the blonde. "Is this the first house you're looking at today?"

Lissie's heart resumed its normal position in her chest. "Um, yes."

"Great! Are you meeting your agent here?"

"No, not at this one," said Lissie vaguely. "And it's not for me. I'm looking for a friend. He couldn't make it, so he asked if I could do a video walk-through."

The woman's lips tightened, but when one of the other couples approached with a question about the water heater, Lissie seized her chance to get away, hitting record on her phone camera and setting off on a high-speed tour. It was exactly what she had imagined from the outside, its tired interior matching its tired exterior, the modest staging making it look nicer than it ever would if Jeremy occupied it. The only drawback Lissie noted was the scarcity of outlets, a possible dealbreaker given Jeremy's livelihood. He was more likely to care about the number of outlets and the Internet speed than the cramped galley kitchen or the burn ring on the countertop.

"What do you think?" The agent caught up with Lissie in the second bedroom as she was thinking about where a Wi-Fi router might go.

"It's nice. I think it would work for him."

"Wonderful. Can I answer any questions for you?"

"It looks like there's been a lot of interest."

"There has. A couple people already said they'd like to put in an offer, so I'm going to talk to the sellers about a review date of Tuesday at noon. Which means your friend will probably want to set up a showing ASAP if he's serious."

"Thanks, I'll tell him," Lissie replied breezily, sweeping past her as briskly as the ridiculous blue booties allowed.

Back in her car, she sent Jeremy the video. *Redwood City a thumbs-up. But agent says at least two offers coming in.*

His response came as she got out of the car in Menlo Park. *Meh. Kinda dumpy. Where are the outlets???*

Lissie shook her head. It might have been a little dumpy, but it was listed for $80,000 less than this significantly smaller place. Not that Jeremy took up a lot of room. The agent, who was on the phone, held up a finger and smiled at Lissie to indicate she would be right with her. But Lissie, blessing her luck, slipped on the booties and whisked after a middle-aged Asian couple and their agent into the kitchen. This place was newer, and Lissie grinned as she hit record, being sure to pan over every electrical outlet in slo-mo. Her luck held and she escaped back outside before having to answer any questions.

Small. Nicer. Expensiver. More outlets.

This time he answered almost immediately. *Any offers on it?*

At a stoplight she typed back: *Didn't ask but less crowded.*

Lissie's last stop was a beige-with-brown-trim 1980s development in Mountain View, equidistant from El Camino and Castro Street. This unit was bigger than the Menlo Park dollhouse but older and between the two other properties in price. Before she even got out of the car, she texted her cousin: *Mt View. This is the one! I've got a feeling. Did you get preapproved? Heard agent at RC place asking someone else.*

Jeremy didn't reply, and Lissie pictured him rummaging through the fridge for lunch. Her own stomach growled, and she thought longingly of the restaurants nearby. She could grab something at the Four Treasures, of course, before she went home, but that would mean detouring north again, and sometimes you just wanted to try something new. Maybe a black sugar Assam boba tea from Teaspoon? The splurge could be balanced with a grilled cheese at Château Cardboard, but if she showed up at the apartment with no drinks for her roommates, she'd have to divvy hers into pitiful servings the size of shot glasses.

To Assam or not to Assam, that was the question. But when she walked up to the unit, all thoughts of expensive drinks fled, for by the open door was a sandwich-board sign: "Another property brought to you by the Penelope Lin Team." *You've got to be kidding me.* And there again was the picture of the queen of Peninsula real estate, arms crossed and smile fixed.

Whom would Lissie find inside this time? Another Jillian? Because surely Mrs. Lin didn't bother holding open houses at piddly million-dollar properties. But what if it was Hazel Bing?

"Excuse me."

Automatically, Lissie stepped aside to let the person pass, but then, as if she had conjured everything by the force of her fears, Hazel appeared in the doorway and the person beside her halted, the boba drinks in his hands dropping a full six inches.

"Lissie?" in stereo.

Oh, dear Lord.

What happened next was a full out-of-body experience. Lissie watched the scene unfold as if she were seated in the mezzanine. She saw herself turn and greet Hazel Bing and Preston Lin in slo-mo, her attitude casual, like they ran into each other weekly and this was no big deal. She saw her mouth comment admiringly on the bobas in Preston's hands and ask which flavors they were. Just a normal Saturday afternoon, out living her best life.

And then everything snapped back to normal speed and normal volume, or maybe it sped up, because Lissie was suddenly aware Hazel had said something to her she didn't catch, and she was sweating despite it being only 55° out. She wished she were wearing a cuter outfit.

"Wh-what?" Lissie managed.

"I said, what are you doing here?" Hazel repeated. She strode forward, heels clicking on the pavement, to take the green-and-white beverage from Preston's unresisting hand. He seemed as paralyzed as Lissie was. More, even, because he had said nothing since he blurted her name.

"I'm, uh, here to see the property," answered Lissie lamely.

"You're here to see *Preston's* property?" A skeptical frown.

Preston Lin owned property? Or had he dropped out of Stanford to become an agent? "This is your house?" Lissie gulped, raising sheepish, please-believe-me-I-am-not-stalking-you eyes to his.

"A graduation gift," he muttered.

"And now you're regifting it?"

"Flipping it, actually."

"Oh." This was all Greek to Lissie. It made her head spin. She had hesitated over a $7 boba drink, and he was flipping real estate?

"Are you in the market for a place?" was Hazel's insistent question. "Or did you just happen to be walking down this street?" Hazel Bing had never been friendly to her, but now she was being borderline hostile. Lissie rallied. Or she intended to. But just as she opened her mouth, she shut it again, running over the circumstances in her head and trying to sort out what, if anything, could be shared.

"Uh, no. I came here on purpose. But I didn't know this home was . . . " She waved a vague finger around, encompassing Hazel, the Penelope Lin sandwich board, Preston. "Anyhow, I was looking at this place for a friend who couldn't be here. But this is probably not what my friend is looking for." Never mind what she just texted Jeremy, she could lie and say it was a pit inside.

"You mean this is not the exterior your friend is looking for?" murmured Preston.

"What?"

"Because you haven't gone inside yet, have you?"

"Well, no," she admitted. "But I mean, you know, the location—"

"Is too convenient?"

A jittery laugh escaped her. "Okay, the location is wonderful, but he—" she broke off instantly, having meant to leave any identifiers out of it, but her hesitation only drew more attention to the masculine pronoun, freighting it with unintended significance.

"He . . . ?" prompted Preston.

If she didn't say something, her suspicious behavior would leave them thinking she was moving in with some boyfriend. "'He' is my cousin. I was looking on his behalf. But please don't tell anyone."

That questioning eyebrow she well remembered rose at this. "Don't tell anyone?"

"Yes, please. Don't tell anyone that he's looking. Or that I'm looking for him. Because it's a secret."

Lissie didn't have to read minds to know he was thinking, *Another one?*

"I assume 'he' knows about it, at least?"

"Yes," conceded Lissie. "Duh. Surprising someone with a house would be worse than surprising them with a puppy."

At this Hazel gave a little gasp and glanced at Preston, and his lips quirked in response. All of which communicated to Lissie that, unbelievably enough, the graduation gift of a townhouse must have been a surprise! A million-dollar surprise! Who did that? The Lin family, apparently.

"Cousin?" said Hazel, stirring her matcha drink. "I thought you said you were looking for your friend?" Lissie wished she could take her oversized straw and use it as a pea shooter. Ping! A boba right to the forehead.

"Yes, my cousin," Lissie said, beginning to back away. "In any case, not important. It was nice to see you both again."

"Wait." Preston held up his empty hand. "Seriously, you don't want to look at it? For your cousin?" He was half-smiling now, and it was doing disturbing things to Lissie's insides.

"There's no point, even if 'he' made an offer," Hazel said. "How could we negotiate effectively? There's a conflict of interest."

"What have I got against Lissie's cousin?" He sounded teasing, but Hazel was not amused. She rolled her eyes and marched back inside, clearly having no intention of working the sale.

"How are you, Lissie?" Preston asked, when Hazel was out of sight. He didn't seem in any rush to go inside now.

"Good. Busy. You?"

"Same."

She thought about mentioning his letter. But where to begin? She expected him to fall into cool silence as he so often had in the past, but he surprised her by beginning again.

"How's school?"

"All right. I mean, I'm keeping my head above water."

"I bet you're doing more than that." This chatty, interested version of Preston Lin unnerved Lissie. He swirled his boba thoughtfully. "And how about Jenny? How did her MCAT go?"

"She should find out soon, but she's already planning to take it again, just in case." She glanced toward the open townhouse door, half expecting a grouchy Hazel to reappear and demand if she was coming in or not.

"That makes sense. It's a bear." Another swirl of the boba. He lifted it toward his mouth but then thought better of it. "How's your little sister's swimming going?"

Lissie bit her lip. She had been dreading the question without realizing it. JoJo was still swimming with Coach Wayman. Would he think Lissie didn't believe what he had said in the letter?

"She's doing amazing. She even qualified for an All-Stars meet in Seattle in February, and I'm going with her. We've never been there before." Lissie delivered this news to the coiled-up garden hose behind him, so she missed the sharp look Preston gave her. She wondered whether she should add that Wayman Wang wouldn't be at the travel meet but decided that would sound defensive. And wasn't that Preston's criticism of her, that she was defensive and dismissive?

"That's awesome," he said absently.

She gave herself a shake. "What about you? How's your research going? Had any directional failures lately?"

This made him grin. "You make those sound like a good thing."

"*You* made them sound like a good thing when we talked about them at that meet."

"I only meant that scientific failures weren't as utterly demotivating as swimming failures. But, no, my project is the one thing going well right now." Even as he said it, he colored, and she felt her own face warm in sympathy. Not that it took much. Lissie had already been castigating herself for bringing up the meet. Preston might think it was an attempt at flirtation, considering how they had had a few minutes of fun together before stupid Wayman entered the break room.

But what made him flush? "I appreciated your letter," she ventured. It was vague enough. It could mean anything. He could make of it whatever he wanted.

"Thank you." Right back at her. A tennis match. While Lissie considered her next move, Preston straightened and spoke again in a louder voice. "Anyway, I'm hoping to unload this place, and Hazel is helping me out."

"Are you sure you don't want to live in it? It's no Bronklin's, but it looks nicer than Escondido Village." Then she turned redder still, remembering he didn't know she'd hidden in the closet of Charles Bing's room months ago.

"EV works for now. And I'd rather convert this to a future down payment on wherever I do end up living." He took a sip of his drink then, and Lissie tried to tear her gaze from the muscles of his throat working. He had a nice neck. But Preston Lin's mind was focused elsewhere because he lowered the cup again, frowning. "So . . . this cousin of yours, he's saved up quite a down payment."

Lissie swallowed, alarmed to find Jeremy's secrets hovering into sight again. If Preston Lin hated deceit and lies and flipped out over things like Hazel Bing getting hives, he certainly wouldn't take well to hearing how Jeremy earned the high-school portion of his nest egg. Which she wasn't supposed to talk about anyway. But she hated to be evasive when they might finally have a chance to overcome their bad beginning. How unfair everything was!

She shifted away a step. "Yeah, I guess so."

"Is this a cousin on the restaurant side?"

"Uh-huh." Another step.

"Lissie, I hope you won't take this the wrong way, but—"

"No good sentence ever begins with those words," Lissie cut him off with another jittery laugh. "So I'll just stop you right there. If you don't mind, I'd rather not talk about my cousin. Like I said, he wants to keep his house-hunting quiet for the time being."

"Is that why he's having you do it?"

"One of the reasons." Her voice sounded higher than normal, and she backed away one more step. His eyes narrowed, making him look again like the Preston Lin she was too familiar with. What was it about him? Lissie could feel a confession rising to her lips, and it wasn't even her confession to make!

"I'm just trying to get an idea of your cousin as a potential buyer."

"Just . . . Not necessary. Because I think this place is not going to be a fit for him."

"Meaning you don't like me asking questions."

"Not around this, no. Let's just drop it."

There was a pause. His mouth disappeared in a thin line. Then, with an effort, he said, "Lissie, I know you haven't wanted to come clean with me in the past, but you can tell me—"

"Some things aren't mine to tell!" she protested, goaded. "I would think you of all people would understand that."

His head jerked back as if she had thrown his mother's past in his face, which she had.

"You're still here?" demanded Hazel, reappearing in the doorway. "Two people just scheduled showings, so if you want to see it by yourself, you'd better come in now."

Lissie held up her hands, relieved to get away before she added more fuel to the present fire. "I'm good," she called. "Thanks, Hazel. Good luck selling the place."

With a vague nod in Preston's general direction, she turned away, forcing herself to walk in the most carefree manner she could muster. And if half of her wished irrationally that he would follow her—well, that half was disappointed.

CHAPTER 19

"I don't see why you didn't even go in," Jeremy complained on
Monday afternoon. "I looked at the virtual tour and that place
was perfect."

"It was owned by Jenny's ex's friend, you dope. The guy who yelled
at me about the shellfish allergy and who singlehandedly dealt a body
blow to Four Treasures' business the past few months. What part
don't you understand? If you're still dying to make an offer, nothing's
stopping you."

He blew out a defeated breath, pushing up his glasses and rubbing
his fingers along each side of his nose. "Actually, after you asked if I
was preapproved, I looked into it because I wasn't. And it turns out
they want two years of verified income if you're self-employed. Two
years! My lame Four Treasures income is not going to qualify me."

"Oh, that sucks," said Lissie. "Does that mean you can't buy a place
for at least another year?"

"That, or someone with a steady income has to cosign with me. Or
I have to pay cash."

Lissie thought of the Lins, dropping nearly a million dollars as a
graduation gift to their son.

"Do you want the money back from JoJo's swimming?" she asked,
bracing herself.

To her relief, he snorted. "Forget it. Like that would make a difference at this point. This just means you don't have to look at any more houses for now."

"Well, if it'll take you another year before you can get a loan, I bet Jenny and I could pay you back the money before then. That's just $50 each a month from us."

"Whatever. I'm not thinking about the stupid $600. All I know is I'm not waiting another year to get my own place." Lissie supposed spending his life in the Liangs' converted garage had bothered Jeremy more than she thought.

"Are you going to tell your mom and dad, then, so they can cosign with you?"

"No, I'm not telling them! It's a surprise, remember? You haven't said anything to anyone, have you?"

"Of course I haven't. Though I don't see why I couldn't tell Jenny."

"It's not that I don't trust her. It's just that one person tells just one person, who tells just one person, and the next thing you know, everyone knows."

"Fine," Lissie huffed. "Though Jenny is studying so hard she'd have no one to tell besides her books and our roommates, and they don't care that you want to buy a house."

"See? This is what I mean," Jeremy insisted. "One person leads to another."

"I didn't tell anyone else! Relax, I was giving you a hypothetical."

"Then just keep it hypothetical, okay?"

"Okay, okay. The lip is zipped. So if you don't want your folks to cosign, what's your plan?"

"My plan is that I'll just have to put more money down. The lenders aren't going to be so picky if I'm just asking for a couple hundred thousand."

Lissie stared. "You think you could come up with that kind of money in less than a year?"

His chin with its uneven stubble lifted. "Yeah, I think so."

"Wow. Just . . . wow. But in totally aboveboard, legal ways, right?"

Jeremy groaned. "I should never have told you about the gold farming. That was a few years ago now, Lis." *As if shady activities were only shady if they took place recently*, she answered silently. "Yes, everything I'm doing now is totally legit. And you haven't told anyone about that business, have you?"

"Even if I totally understood how it worked," she retorted, "I can keep a secret, as we just discussed."

She had been unable to stop thinking about her encounter with Preston Lin. What went through his mind on Saturday when she popped up at his place? That she had read his letter and changed her mind about him and decided to stalk him, only to have her plans thwarted by her incorrigible tendency to lie and hide things? It was so frustrating! Because she hadn't changed her mind, but she hadn't 100% *not* changed it either. Did he still like her, and did he think she liked him back? How else could he have interpreted her sudden reappearance?

Wherever he was today, he was surely thinking, *She wants me*. But if that was the case, why didn't he follow her to her car? Was it because of her tendency to lie, or because he was over her, or because he was too embarrassed to do it in front of Hazel? What was it?

Too, too frustrating.

With Jeremy tying her hands, Lissie had been unable to analyze the matter with Jenny and Mel. Not that they had been lounging around Château Cardboard much lately. Jenny had redoubled her study efforts, and Mel and Darren were spending more and more time together. To Lissie's surprise, it was Nelson she saw the most at home lately. Nelson, who had been dumped by his latest bad boyfriend, Kev.

"Kev made you feel bad about yourself anyhow," she tried to comfort him. "Didn't you say he was always criticizing you?"

"Yes," sighed Nelson, retrieving another Greek yogurt from the fridge. "But he was better than nobody. I'm not like you, Lissie. I'm not happy with no one."

"Who said I'm happy alone?"

He ripped the foil lid off as if it were the scales from her eyes. "You have no one, right? And you're happy, right?"

"Okay, yeah, but that doesn't mean I would never want to have someone," she argued. Opening the fridge, she grabbed one of his cans of LaCroix, and such was his moroseness that he didn't notice.

"Oh, 'never,'" Nelson waved this away. "That's what I mean. I want to have someone special *now*, all the time. Not that you girls aren't amazing, but it's not the same. Not to mention, how much longer will I even have you? We're almost at the end of our road."

"Don't say that." Now that they were, fingers crossed, officially into the final semester of her college career, Lissie was doing her best to ignore the fact. Because what on Earth happened after graduation? What would she do to earn enough money that she wouldn't have to join Jeremy and JoJo under her aunt and uncle's roof? Jenny would be around another year at least, since the med school application process was so long, but if Lissie wasn't employed and able to pull her own rent weight, Jenny would likely find new roommates and move closer to her Stanford and Four Treasures jobs.

She hadn't expected Nelson, of all people, to stress her out about the future. Nelson was studying finance like his parents wanted and actually liked it, so he rarely brought up any sort of agonizing over his career with others. But now, in one conversation, he touched on both her singleness and careerlessness?

"If I get a job, you could still live with Jenny and me next year," Lissie said.

"Girlfriend, my job will be in the city, and I am not going to commute from down here. Plus, I am not letting my life ride on you getting a job."

"What's that supposed to mean?"

"Did you even go to that career fair I told you about in the Student Union?"

"Did you tell me about a career fair?"

He sighed. "What are they teaching you English majors in Dudley Moorhead Hall? Nothing practical, I see."

"Whoa, whoa. No need to knock DMH. Just pass along your advice and hold the judgment."

"Well, I saw something there your lame ass might be good at." He grinned to himself, scraping the sides of the yogurt container as he let her impatience build.

Sure enough, she broke first. "What?"

"The City of San José is looking for a PR-intern-slash-gopher." Nelson always said the "José" part as Spanish-sounding as possible because he loved any and all accent marks.

"You think I could do public relations?" she marveled. "I haven't got any experience."

"What are you talking about? You mean you haven't got any 'official' experience. What did you do for your aunt and uncle's restaurant, except an unofficial PR campaign? You brought their rating back up, didn't you?"

"Not in a way I could brag about on a resume."

"Whatever. You think people aren't doing that whenever and wherever possible and asking their friends and family to help them out? And you know how to write and how to talk in front of people because of drama. Which is not to say you'd have a realistic chance if you were just competing on the PR. I'm just telling you how to spin that part. You'd have to play up your strength as a gopher—fetching, carrying, running errands, taking crap from everyone. You've done plenty of that. Plus, the position barely pays over minimum wage. But it's government! Benefits! Job security, if you made it out of intern status. Sane hours, leaving you plenty of free time to work on your own stuff. You should fix up your resume and apply."

"Wow." Lissie eyed him with newfound respect. "You may not pick great boyfriends, but you're really great at this career stuff!"

He licked his spoon. "Boccardo Business Complex, baby. BBC all the way."

Lissie took Nelson's advice. Putting aside her halfway-revamped senior project, she visited the ballroom on the top floor of the student union for a copy of the job listing. She asked for references from Silas at the library and Mrs. Fong from the restaurant and even Ed Simmons from the Mission Valley Manta Rays. It was Ed who said, "Public relations? You want to do public relations? I'm adding you to the club website as our public-relations intern, okay? I doubt we can find you more than a couple hundred bucks for it, but it'll look good on your resume. The booster club was just talking about publicizing how we achieved Level 2 Club recognition from USA Swimming. Why don't you write us a press release to put on the website and send it to the *Mercury* and the *Milpitas Post* and the *Argus*? And while you're at it, you could pick up our new banner at the Zone office and ask Laurie there if she wants publicity for anything."

When Lissie reported her progress to her roommate, Nelson reached out a hand to shake. "Congratulations. You're now a nepo PR consultant and honorary BBC padawan. I'd tell you to change your major to Business if it wouldn't delay your graduation for another two years."

The Western Zone office was a tollbooth of a space in a strip mall between a nail place and a UPS Store, and it was only staffed a couple days per week. It had taken days for anyone to respond to Lissie's email, but at last a time was agreed upon, and she entered to find one middle-aged woman with fluffy gray-brown hair at a desk surrounded by cardboard boxes on the floor and along the walls, some opened and others taped shut. Every inch of visible wall space above desk height was covered in framed pictures: swimmers of all ages on podiums; groups of officials; several shots of Michael Phelps with various individuals; and several more of Katie Ledecky with still other individuals. But it wasn't the clutter which made Lissie halt in her tracks. It was the life-size cardboard cutout of Preston Lin, shirtless and clad only in a swim jammer, medals around his neck.

"Isn't he dreamy?" asked the woman with a wink, seeing Lissie's stunned face. "I like to keep him by me while I work."

"Yeah, he's, uh, dreamy," gulped Lissie, when she could breathe again. She had seen him with his shirt off in pictures online, of course, but life-size was another matter altogether. Even 2-D. Because somehow his chest and shoulders seemed sculpted like bas-relief, tempting her to run a hand along the surface.

"Plus he's an absolute angel," the woman continued.

"Angel?" Not the first word Lissie would have applied to him.

"Like a cherub," said the woman with a smile. "He's our youth ambassador for the Zone this year. Preston Lin. He swam for Stanford, but he's a local boy from Los Altos who grew up in Pacific Swimming. The nicest, most polite boy. A good role model for the little kids. I was not the least bit surprised when he got chosen."

"Why, um, do you have a life-size cardboard cutout of him?"

She laughed. "They made it for the ceremony where his appointment was announced because he was at NCAAs and couldn't be there. And then we couldn't bear to get rid of it because"—gesturing at her surroundings—"we never get rid of anything. You're from the Manta Rays, right? If you play your cards right and get a little lucky, you can schedule him to visit your next meet. He tries to do at least one thing a month, which is super generous because now he's a Ph.D. student in microbiology at Stanford. So busy saving the world!"

The woman was already digging out a plastic bag containing the club's new recognition banner and pushing it across the desk to her, and it would have been easy enough to thank her and leave, but Lissie heard herself say, "Is he really that nice? I thought I heard someone mention they thought he was a little arrogant."

At once the woman dropped her friendly manner. "Well," she drew herself up coolly. "If you haven't met him personally, I would wait to make such pronouncements if I were you."

"Sure," said Lissie. "Of course. Maybe I heard it wrong."

"Last month," the woman continued through lips which had narrowed to a slot, "at Christmastime, he visited Lucile Packard Children's Hospital and gave out teddy bears we had from the last PanPacs."

"So nice of him!" The snarky side of Lissie noted that the children's hospital was in Preston Lin's backyard and the teddy bears left over, so he wasn't exactly curing cancer, but there was no denying it was more than she herself had done at Christmas. With this realization, she added with more sincerity, "Really sweet. I bet the kids loved it."

"They did. And no one but me and the kids, and now you, even knows he did it because it wasn't on the calendar. He just came and got the teddy bears from me." With a shrug, she glanced at the club recognition banner Lissie now clutched. "Not everyone does things for recognition banners."

Zing! Lissie did grin now, finding contrarily that she liked the woman more for sticking up for Preston.

The feeling was clearly not returned. "Is there anything else you need today?"

"I'm good, thank you. And . . . I'm sorry I said that about him. I hope I do get to know him myself."

Without waiting for an answer, Lissie backed out and hurried to the car.

It was true. More and more, she wished she could know him better. The *real* Preston. Would she have rejected him if she'd seen these other sides to him? If she'd even known they existed? If only in his letter he had put one little line, one little hint, that if his letter succeeded in changing how she felt, he wanted to know.

CHAPTER 20

The Rising Stars Meet wasn't exactly in Seattle, but rather a sub-urb south of it. In fact, once Mrs. Yeh got them their rental car from the airport, they didn't even see the city, instead heading south down the interstate toward Federal Way.

"At least it's not raining!" JoJo crowed from the backseat of the Nissan Sentra-or-equivalent. Emma seemed rather blasé about new places, but Lissie and JoJo had never before been this far north of San Francisco, and they were hard put to contain their excitement. "I wish it were lighter so we could see what we were passing. And too bad Princeton's grandma got sick and he couldn't come."

"Are we at that crummy hotel again, like last year?" demanded Emma of her mother. Lissie suppressed a smirk at this clear effort to highlight her previous experience with both the place and the meet.

"I guess Streamline didn't like that place either," replied Mrs. Yeh, "because this year we're at the Hampton Inn. A little farther away from the pool, and three people per room." That last bit was for Lissie and JoJo's information because Mrs. Yeh had persisted in booking her own hotel room. At least JoJo and Emma and Lissie made three (if Emma didn't bail and escape to her mom's), so they wouldn't have to share with strangers from Streamline.

Lissie's chaperone duties began the second they were checked in when Mrs. Yeh said, "You've got this, right, Lissie? Girls, don't stay up late, if you want to swim fast tomorrow. Warmups are at eight, so breakfast no later than seven-thirty, okay?"

"Where are you going?" asked Emma.

"To the aquatic center to check in with Coach Paul," her mom answered. With a languorous wave from her manicured hand, she turned right around and left.

JoJo and Emma clamored to check out the pool and the fitness room and the snacks. In the room, they flipped through all the channels and begged to rent a movie. Only by dint of threats and bribes did Lissie get them in their beds at ten o'clock, and at eleven, she ruthlessly confiscated their phones. "You can't swim like slugs tomorrow. Emma, your mom will blame me if you add time. I don't care if you can't fall asleep. Just shut up, shut your eyes, and count to a thousand."

The King County Aquatic Center was a long, low-slung, rectangular building of gray blocks topped by a pointed roof. "It smells way strong of chlorine inside and the water is freezing," JoJo informed her. Both girls were subdued that morning, but they were positively sprightly compared to Mrs. Yeh. She wore her sunglasses even in the breakfast room and nodded curtly to them, urging her daughter to keep her voice down. Lissie was glad she wouldn't have to sit by the woman in the stands all weekend. Much better to work on deck.

Stuffing some cash in JoJo's hand and reminding her to text if she needed anything, Lissie took the stairs down while the rest of them headed up to stake out a spot in the bleachers. Seeing someone else in a uniform like hers, she scurried after him down a long concrete, windowless corridor, following him through a set of doors which led to the pool deck. He almost eluded her then, turning into a room to the left, but she was determined not to lose her way and put on a burst of speed. She slipped through before the door shut and ran full tilt, for the fourth time in her life, into the solid and unforgettable chest of Preston Lin.

"Sorry about that," he said automatically. Then, "Lissie?"

"That thing is a deadly weapon," she muttered, feeling her face heat. "What are you doing here? I mean, I can guess what you're doing, but why didn't you mention you would be? Here, I mean." She was babbling.

"I didn't know at the time, when I saw you, that I would be," he answered, hardly more coherent. "But now I am."

"I see that."

"So . . . have you had breakfast yet?"

"I could have more," she said, more eagerly than she would have liked. Embarrassed, she went to sign in and pick up the bag tag with the events listed on it. When she turned back, he was still standing there, waiting for her, and her pulse did a funny little skip.

The break room was on the other side of the building. They walked between the Olympic-sized pool on one side, divided by a bulkhead into two shorter pools, and the deep blue dive tank with its platforms on the other, dodging noisy kids in a rainbow of team swim caps. A Taylor Swift song blared over the PA system while coaches directed warm-up traffic. Thankful that Wayman Wang's absence meant Preston and she would be spared a repeat of November's awkward scene, Lissie glanced around trying to remember what Coach Paul of Streamline looked like. But it was JoJo who appeared out of nowhere.

"Lissie, my goggle strap snapped!" she wailed, thrusting the pair at her, its bungee ties dangling. "And I left my other ones at the hotel. *And* my phone *and* my shampoo!"

"Where was your head this morning? Well, the phone and shampoo don't matter, but can you borrow someone else's goggles?"

Preston took them from her hand. "I can fix them."

JoJo's mouth dropped open, and she stared at him, her eyes taking in his height and model looks and navy polo shirt with "USA Swimming Youth Ambassador" embroidered on it.

"You were at my other meet," she said.

"I was." He was feeding the end of the bungee strap carefully back through the slot by the eyepiece.

"Lissie introduced you before the national anthem."

"That's right."

JoJo made googly eyes at her sister, who gave her a comic warning glare and said, "This is Preston Lin, here in his capacity as USA Swimming Youth Ambassador."

"I can read," JoJo said, pointing at the embroidery on his pectoral. "Hi, I'm JoJo."

"I can read, too," he answered, pointing at her swim cap. Instead of her last name, JoJo always insisted on having her first name printed on it, likely to forestall questions on why her last name didn't match the Liangs.

Nimbly, he tightened the tiny double knot he'd tied in the strap and tugged on it before handing them back to her. "You're Jenny and Lissie's younger sister."

"You know Jenny, too?"

"Yup."

"How?" JoJo accused, as if her sisters were secrets she hid under a rock.

Preston's glance slid to Lissie. "I met them at the Four Treasures last October. Your sisters make an impression."

"Like a bad case of food poisoning," put in Lissie, in spite of herself.

"Wait," said JoJo, looking from one to the other. "Were you there when Lissie fed that girl shellfish and almost killed her?"

"What?" yelled Lissie. "How do you know about that? I didn't feed her shellfish and I certainly didn't almost kill her!"

"I've got ears," said JoJo calmly. "I heard Auntie Rhoda and Uncle Mason talking about it."

"You *did* feed her shellfish," Preston pointed out, equally calm. "Shellfish paste is shellfish ground into a paste."

"Oh, is that how it works?" Lissie snapped.

"Just a wild guess."

She took a deep breath. She could swear she saw the corner of his mouth twitch, but then remembered she wanted to show him she was no longer defensive and dismissive. Which meant no more sarcastic cracks or denials. It probably would have helped if she hadn't just done both again. Defended and denied.

"Yes," she told her little sister. "Preston was one of the party that night. They ordered a dish that had shellfish paste in it, and his friend Hazel ate some. She was allergic. It was my fault it happened. I should have remembered the ingredients. And it's fortunate her allergy was milder. Some people are so allergic they might die because their throat swells up so much they can't breathe."

JoJo nodded. "My friend Dylan has that from peanuts. Anna relaxes."

"What?" said Lissie.

"Anaphylaxis," supplied Preston. He clapped his hands together. "But this story had a happy ending. Hazel recovered, with Jenny's quick help, and the restaurant learned from your sister's oversight. Better try the goggles on so you can warm up. What are you swimming this weekend?"

"The 50 free, 100 fly, and 100 free."

"Awesome. I'm not supposed to cheer openly for any one person, but I'll cheer for you inwardly."

JoJo pulled on the repaired goggles and gave him a toothy grin. "Thanks, Preston!"

When her sister was gone, the two of them continued toward the break room, Lissie feeling warm and shy. Could it be any cuter how good he was with kids?

"Thank you for that," she said. Meaning the goggles, the shellfish. Everything.

"Yeah," he said, equally vaguely.

"So . . . how's your townhouse? Did it sell?"

"It's under contract. And your cousin, did you find him something?"

"He's decided not to buy right now. Preston, look," she halted by the heat sheet posted on the wall. "I did want to apologize for being evasive the last time we spoke—"

"No," he rejoined quickly, "It's your cousin's business. I thought about it afterward. What you said about some secrets not being yours to tell."

Her eyes widened at this. His unexpected flexibility made it easier for her to say, "And that's the other thing. I didn't mean to throw that remark in your face like that. And I want you to know I've never said anything to anyone about . . . what you wrote in your letter. Not any of it."

"Okay. Thanks." He gave her a slow smile, and Lissie might have swayed and smiled back at him like a fool if a clutch of little boys didn't choose that moment to crowd up to the heat sheet and force them to move on. In the break room, they loaded up plates and drifted to the picnic table farthest from everyone else.

"I've only got fifteen minutes until the officials' meeting," Lissie announced. "Will you be here all day? Did they give you a handler?"

"Mww," he said, pointing to his mouth full of breakfast strata.

"Just tell me with your mouth full."

But he held up a finger and chewed and swallowed. "I'll be here all weekend. And I have a handler, though I told them, 'Anyone but Lissie Cheng.'"

She laughed, despite an irrational pang of jealousy for whoever got to babysit him. "You should pick someone with experience. Not everyone can read through your list of accomplishments before the meet's over."

"Very funny," he grinned wryly.

She took a huge bite of her own breakfast, covering her mouth with a hand while she spoke, to show him how it was done. "I met a lady at the Zone office. I forget her name—"

"Probably Laurie Stafford? Fluffy gray-brown hair?"

"Yes. Laurie Stafford. She said you generally do one thing a month."

"Generally. Why were you hanging out with Laurie Stafford?"

Lissie preened a little. "I was picking something up for JoJo's club.

I'm their new public-relations intern."

"No way! Congrats."

He seemed sincere, though Lissie figured it was pretty small potatoes in his universe. What made up the meat of her resume wouldn't warrant a footnote on his. Cautiously, she added, "And I've made it to the second round of interviews for an entry-level PR position with the City of San Jose. But that might be because no one else applied. It pays like a penny over minimum wage."

"Nope. I bet you made it to the second round because you knocked the first interview out of the park."

Who was this guy? Lissie had a sinking awareness that she was going to forgive him for everything and, worse, fall for him if he didn't blast her with a good dose of repellent arrogance soon.

But he chilled her warming thoughts another way. "I'm guessing JoJo's not changing clubs, after what I told you."

"No. She's still at Mission Valley," Lissie admitted in a small voice. "You know, that was all a long time ago . . . what you wrote about."

He skewered a cube of pineapple on his fork but didn't lift it to his mouth. "Did you not believe me?"

"I did. I do. I'm so sorry that happened to you. It was not good. Inappropriate. Awful." *Stop with the lame synonyms, dummy!*

"But you think people can change."

Did she? Of course people could change. But could people who lacked a sense of right and wrong grow that sense later? Could Wayman?

Because she had no answer, she turned the question back on him. "I guess you don't think so, then."

He chewed the pineapple thoughtfully.

"You form your opinion of someone, and nothing will budge it," she blurted.

"Is that what you think? I can change my mind. I have changed my mind about some people."

"I'm not saying you're wrong, in this case," she hurried on, "but how could I ask JoJo to change clubs without giving a reason? And how would I explain it to my aunt and uncle? They pay for her swimming, you know. They pay for nearly everything. And if JoJo changed clubs, it would mean she'd be unattached for Regionals and couldn't be on any relays, and she loves relays! And all her friends are at Mission Valley—" Lissie heard herself being defensive. Again.

She shut up.

They finished their meal in silence.

Before Lissie could excuse herself to go to the officials' meeting, a positively adorable young woman with a long brown ponytail and big brown eyes wearing a skort and a teal South Sound Aquatics polo approached the table. "Excuse me. Are you Preston Lin? I'm Maddy James, your handler for this weekend."

"Oh, hi. Great. Nice to meet you." He rose and held out a hand to shake, and Lissie thought the girl might faint. When he turned to dump his paper plate, Maddy fanned herself and threw Lissie a droll look. "Oh, my God. Best volunteer assignment *ever*," she whispered to her before skipping off with him.

Lissie knew exactly one other official at the meeting, a bald guy from Streamline whom she'd never actually spoken to before and who only gave her a brief nod. But everyone else seemed nice enough, and another woman who was assigned to the two lanes next to Lissie's came and sat beside her. "The bulkhead is the best if you don't fall off the back," she said with a smile, "because you can see the races in both pools."

"USA Swimming sent us a special guest for this meet," the meet referee announced from the head of the room after the deck assignments had been given. "A former NCAA Division One Finalist in 100 Fly and the 2IM for Stanford University and a gold and silver medalist in those events at Junior PanPacs, now in his first year as a USA Swimming Youth Ambassador, please give a warm welcome to Preston Lin! He'll be handing out the medals at finals, giving a talk on college swimming between sessions, and signing for the kids at other times in the room behind the stage."

Applause and craned necks greeted this speech as Preston waved from the back of the room, Maddy holding her hands in a ta-da pose beside him.

"Oh, my, isn't he a nice young man," said the woman beside her. "And Stanford, too! I'm going to go to that talk, for my son. All he does when he's not in the pool is play on his phone."

"That's not entirely a waste of time," murmured Lissie, thinking of her cousin. But Jeremy was forgotten the second she locked eyes with Preston, who picked her out in the seats. He gave her the merest flicker of one eyelid. A wink? A facial tic?

At the beginning of the meet, Maddy James announced him flawlessly over the PA system, robbing Lissie of the chance to feel superior. But she had to put on her big-girl pants and do her job and try not to care that Miss Ponytail was free to trail after him all day long, undoubtedly making a better first impression than Lissie had.

Both JoJo and Emma had two events apiece during the Saturday prelim session, and such was the level of talent at the All-Stars Meet that while Emma was a shoo-in for the 200 Back A Final, Lissie was praying JoJo could scrape into the B Final for the 100 Fly. Officials weren't supposed to cheer openly any more than the USA Swimming Youth Ambassador, but Lissie couldn't help clenching her fists and urging her sister under her breath. It didn't help that JoJo was swimming in the pool at the scoreboard end while Lissie was assigned the turn end of the other pool, which meant she had to rotate all the way around on the bulkhead to see how her sister was doing.

Fearless JoJo swam her heart out in the outside lane, shaving off a full half-second off her PB! Lissie bounced when she saw the time flash up on the scoreboard, unable to contain her thrill to save her life. And when JoJo climbed out, there, wonder of wonders, was Preston Lin to give her a high five. Admittedly, he gave the entire heat a high five as they passed, but he hadn't done that for the other heats, and Lissie just knew it was for JoJo.

Her time held up through the remaining heats, and one of the girls who were expected to be fast added time. All of which meant Joanna Cheng made the A Final that evening! Lane 8, yes, but the A Final! When Lissie's break came, her sister was waiting for her, and they screamed and hugged each other.

"Did you text Jenny and Auntie Rhoda?"

"Yes! And Jeremy," Lissie assured her. "I only wish I could have taken a picture of the scoreboard."

"I think Mrs. Yeh did. I'll tell her to send it to us. I added a tenth on my 50 free, but that was my bonus event. This was the final I cared about."

"You did great!" Lissie gave her another hug. Then she added in her most casual tone, "And when you have your phone again, we should send the scoreboard pic to Coach Wayman in case he's not following the results."

JoJo got a funny look on her face, and Lissie drew back. "What?"

"Oh, nothing."

"What? He's your coach. He'll want to see how you did."

"If he wanted to see how I did, he should have come," retorted JoJo.

Lissie laughed. "You and Emma aren't the only kids on the team, you know, even if you're the fastest. He had to stay back with the rest of the Manta Rays at the Fremont Invitational."

JoJo's lower lip began to protrude. "I thought he was going to surprise us up here."

"What are you talking about? Why would he do that?"

"Because he's not at the Fremont Invitational," she blurted. "Olivia texted Emma and said Coach Penny said he was sick with a stomach bug."

Another one? Or was this another excuse, as it had been at the Fall Ball? "Ew. Too bad," said Lissie. "But if he's barfing, he isn't exactly going to jump on a plane and come up here."

"But that's just it!" JoJo protested. "He isn't barfing. Because Ishaan said his mom saw him at the airport on Friday morning!"

She stared. "At the airport? Well, maybe he was picking someone up."

"No, he was past security, at one of the gates," argued JoJo. "And Mrs. Karwhal said the board read Seattle. He was on his phone so she didn't bother him, but she was thinking it'd have to be a pretty short trip if he was going to make it back in time for the meet. That's why Emma and I thought he was going to surprise us. But he didn't."

"Just because he got on a flight to Seattle doesn't necessarily have anything to do with anything," said Lissie, though it came out sounding doubtful. Was it just a weird coincidence? Why would Wayman Wang come to Seattle this weekend if not to watch his star swimmers? And if it was, why wouldn't he make himself known? No need to saddle Coach Paul of Streamline with Mission Valley swimmers if their own coach were there.

Seeing her little sister shiver, she put the mystery out of her mind for the moment. "We'll ask him about it later. I'm sure there's a good reason. But if you and Emma are both done, after you warm down, Mrs. Yeh can take you for an early lunch and then back to the hotel to rest."

"But what about you? You're stuck here till the session ends, aren't you?"

"Yes, but I really want you to go now so you can get a nap in. You know you and Emma were up half the night! I'll be fine. I'll finish the session and work time trials, and they'll feed me here. Then I'll just find a place to sit and do homework. I'll see you for finals, okay?"

"Okay. Emma's mom said we could get Panera!" JoJo said excitedly. "Auntie Rhoda and Uncle Mason never let us eat out."

"You wouldn't either if you spent your whole life in a restaurant. So enjoy Panera, but promise me you'll nap afterward," ordered Lissie. "Or pretend to nap. And do exactly what Mrs. Yeh tells you, okay? Don't run around and get too tired."

"Yeah, yeah, yeah. Did you see Preston Lin gave me a high five?"

"I saw."

"Emma and I are going to have him sign our T-shirts on the shoulder. Emma says he's even better looking than Coach Wayman. And younger."

"Whatever. Both of them are too old for you."

"I knew you'd say that. See you later."

Retreating again to the break room, where she was allowed to pull out her phone, Lissie sent her own message to Jenny and Jeremy: *If you could see her face! Best $800 we ever spent.*

CHAPTER 21

"Hey there."

Lissie looked up from her ratty copy of *Barchester Towers* to see Preston Lin doing his usual looming. Before she could think of getting up, he hunkered down, resting on his heels and nodding at the thick volume in her hands. "A little light reading?"

"Homework for my Victorian Novel class. We read one of these puppies each week."

He whistled. "Better you than me."

"Actually, I love it," said Lissie. "My roommate Mel was saying I should have taken Renaissance Lyric Poetry with her because the assignments were only eight short poems a night, but I'd rather read a novel than a poem any day, and this one is super funny." She might have added that Mr. Arabin in *Barchester* reminded her the teeniest, tiniest bit of him: overeducated, and socially a little awkward. And so quick to believe the worst of Eleanor Bold! Instead, she carefully inserted one of JoJo's million swim ribbons as a bookmark and laid Trollope aside. "What happened to your handler?"

He grinned. "She's a better handler than you ever were. Tenacious. I thought she might excuse herself after the talk I gave the parents about swimming in college, but no such luck."

It made Lissie grin back to hear that he wasn't interested in Maddy James. "Well, where is she then?"

"You know what they say, 'Desperate times' and so on. I tried everything I could think of to get rid of her, but finally had no choice. I asked her if she knew Jesus Christ as her Lord and Savior."

Lissie clapped a hand over her mouth to stifle her laugh. "Unbelievable! It would have served you right if she'd said yes."

"No, because then I would have said, 'Then you'll understand why I need to spend part of every day alone in prayer.'"

"That's brilliant. Weaponized evangelism."

"She couldn't get away fast enough." He hesitated and then said, "It looks like you already had lunch."

Lissie would have lied, but the detritus from her box lunch lay between them, and not wanting to repeat the morning's eagerness by offering to eat more, no ready response came.

He stood up, shaking out his legs. "So have I. Do you want to go for a walk, get some fresh air?"

So much for hiding her enthusiasm. She sprang up so quickly her chair skidded away. "But what if Maddy sees us?"

"I'll say later that I couldn't shake you, no matter how hard I tried."

"Nice."

"You know your way around here," she said as he led her across the busy street outside the aquatic center and they began climbing the hill into the neighborhood. It was chilly, but the sky wasn't entirely overcast and there was no rain.

"I've been coming here since I was JoJo's age for travel meets and Winter Juniors, and then for the Pac-12 Championships and Nationals."

"Wow." But she couldn't help but think what they would do if JoJo turned out to be as good a swimmer as Preston Lin. How would they ever afford it? Lissie had had to swing a deal just to get JoJo to this one piddly travel meet! And if—when—Jenny went to med school, she would be so burdened by loans, Lissie wouldn't be able to ask her to contribute anything at all.

I've got to get that job, Lissie fretted. *I've got to get two jobs.*

"Hey, Lissie, I hope I didn't offend you with the evangelism joke."

"What? No, it was fine."

"I grew up going to church when it didn't conflict with swimming or some other extracurricular, which was half the time," he explained. "I think for my mom, church was more of a networking opportunity."

"I get that." She pictured Penelope Lin working the room in a country club sort of place in Los Altos Hills.

"What about you?" he asked. "Did you go to church growing up?"

"Some," she said evasively. It wasn't the truth. In fact, the Chengs had gone fairly regularly. "The church we went to before my parents died doesn't exist anymore. It merged with my aunt and uncle's."

"I didn't say so before, but I'm very sorry about your parents."

She threw him a look, but he kept his eyes on their route. He hadn't had a chance to say anything previously, because the first time she had told him about her parents, it was in the middle of their shouting match at Darren and Jay's party. Maybe there were never non-horrible circumstances in which to talk about dead family members. Heaven knew Lissie avoided doing so whenever possible.

"It's been six years," she answered, muted. "But thank you."

They turned down a side street of big homes with big yards, all nicely landscaped. Bright green grass and shaped shrubs and purply-gray plants that looked like cabbages. Coming from the perennially drought-stricken Bay Area, she wasn't used to seeing so many lush lawns.

"Now I go occasionally with my aunt and uncle and cousin, and Jenny and JoJo too. But the sermons are mostly in Mandarin and my Chinese sucks, as you know."

"I know," he said, and Lissie didn't know whether to laugh at his baldness or hit him for it. "You're complicated," he added. Then she was indignant, and it was on the tip of her tongue to argue, but he drove any retort straight out of her head by asking, "Were you close to your folks?"

"Is anyone *not* close to their folks?" she sputtered, before halting on the sidewalk. "I'm sorry." She reached a hand toward him. "I forgot about you and your mom. That is, if you're not close. Actually, it was a stupid thing to say. Lots of people aren't that close to their parents. It's just that I was. It wasn't perfect, of course. Jenny and I were already teenage girls when my mom got sick, with all that being teenage girls entails. Though my mom's cancer was so unexpected and fast that it shut down all that rebellion and snark." She pressed her fingers to her eyes. "I'm babbling again."

"It's all right. I want to hear it."

"And my dad—well, we didn't even get to say goodbye. I don't want to talk about it. Can we not talk about it?"

"Of course. Sorry."

But then she went on talking about it. "It's why we want JoJo to have everything, Jenny and I. Because she got less of them than we did. A lot less. And Jenny and I still have each other because we're so close in age. Not that she doesn't have us, but we don't live in the same house, you know? I mean, she has my aunt and uncle, and they're wonderful people, but it's not the same, you know? It's like the extra years we got, we feel like have to make them up to her." For a dreadful moment, Lissie thought she was going to burst into tears. "But that's another reason I didn't ask her to change clubs after reading your letter. I couldn't. I can't bear to take anything else away from her."

Suddenly, she really did start to cry, standing in the middle of a strange suburban neighborhood far from home, with the almighty Preston Lin looking on. And the second she registered the sobs as coming from her own person, she tried to choke them down, hiding her face in mortification and wishing a giant meteorite would conveniently hurtle through the atmosphere and take her out before she had to look at him again.

But then his arms were around her, and she found herself gathered to his chest while he murmured sounds with no words in them. Or maybe Lissie couldn't make out the words with one ear crushed against his body and the roar and thump of her own heart working overtime.

It worked.

His comforting, that is. If only because the sheer astonishment of it distracted her from her grief and guilt. And no sooner did the astonishment astonish her than it threatened to be eclipsed entirely in the physical awareness which overtook her. Because Lissie suddenly felt like butter melting on toast.

Kiss me, she urged him silently. *I know I made myself clear in January about not liking you, but I've changed my mind, in case you haven't.*

He didn't kiss her.

And even she, ex-wannabe actress that she was, couldn't prolong the moment with fake sobs after the real ones dwindled. She straightened a fraction of an inch at the precise moment that he dropped his arms and released her.

"Sorry about that," she croaked.

He might have apologized as well. They weren't looking at each other. Wordlessly they started walking again, Lissie wondering if there was a non-squirm-inducing way to tell him she thought differently about him and hoped he had changed his mind about her too.

But she didn't dare make a move. Because how awkward would that be if he had, in fact, gotten over her? He would have to let her down easy, and then they'd have no other option but to walk together back down this enormous hill. No, it was better not to throw herself at him, not to force things. Because assuming he had gotten over her, wouldn't her chances of resurrecting his affections increase if she could first lure him into an uncomplicated friendship? Or would friendship with her always be complicated because he already thought of her as "complicated?"

Be uncomplicated, she told herself. Friendly and uncomplicated. But she must, in fact, be complicated, because it was impossible for her to come up with anything harmless to talk about. The longer the silence stretched, the more fraught it became.

"You haven't asked me yet if Jenny got her MCAT scores," Lissie blurted. Total non sequitur from everything that came before, but it would have to do.

"I meant to," he took this up willingly, his voice tinged with a note of relief. "They were good, I hope?"

"They were good," agreed Lissie. "They fell in the middle of the range for all the schools she's looking at."

"Will she skip taking it again?"

"She hasn't decided. She's been studying like a crazy person, so she's thinking she might as well."

"Plus she broke up with Charles expressly so that she could study more."

So much for uncomplicated.

"Yes, kind of," conceded Lissie, "but it was more mutual than that. He suggested taking some time off to think about what they each wanted after he found out we were related to the restaurant owners."

"Yeah. Well."

The road bent into a cul-de-sac, and they had to retrace their steps.

"Is Charles . . . seeing somebody else now?"

"Nope."

Did Charles Bing still like Jenny? Lissie wanted to ask, but that seemed too indiscreet. Besides, if Preston said yes, what difference would it make? This wasn't junior high. Preston wouldn't tell Charles to try with Jenny again. Or would he? And even if Charles did try, there was no guarantee Jenny wanted to get back together with him. Lissie knew her sister had liked Charles. A lot. But she was also determined to become a doctor and might think ambition and Charles Bing were mutually exclusive at this stage.

Lissie and Preston reached the road that had led up the hill and asked at the same time, "Do you need to get back?"

Lissie smiled. "The officials' meeting isn't until four o'clock."

"You don't need to check on JoJo?"

"Her friend Emma's mom was taking them to lunch and then the hotel. So right about now, they better be napping if they know what's good for them. They were up till all hours last night. I'm pretty sure I fell asleep before they did. Mrs. Yeh is in charge of bringing them back for finals. What about you? When do you need to be back?"

He checked his gleaming silver wristwatch. "Not till the medals for the first final get handed out. Though I should check in with Maddy before then so she doesn't stress out. It's only three now. Wanna keep going? There's a little lake trail at the bottom of the hill."

Time for another attempt at being friendly and uncomplicated. She nodded and gestured for him to lead the way.

"I see why the neighborhood was so quiet and empty," said Lissie, stepping aside to allow a family with three little kids and two dogs to get around her. "Everyone in town was on the Panther Lake Trail."

"Saturday and not raining," was his laconic reply.

The lake was modest in size, outlined in trees and reflecting the gray-streaked sky, the encircling path sometimes graveled, sometimes paved, sometimes dirt, always level.

"How's the Four Treasures doing?"

Another subject they would have to tiptoe through. Lissie turned to watch a muddy dog pass so she could gather her thoughts. "It's better than it was a few months ago. Business is nearly back to P.P.L. level. Pre-Preston-Lin," she added when he raised a questioning eyebrow.

"When I wrote that article, I really didn't think through the impact it might—"

"Didn't you?" she interrupted, but there was barely a flicker of fire in her tone. Mostly there was teasing and a teeny bit of provocation that his mother might have condemned as flirtatious. "You named names, after all. I think every bad reviewer gets a little satisfaction, a little power trip, from being able to tear something down. It's easier to tear something down than to build it up. Easier and faster. Because a million things go into running a successful restaurant, half of which are outside your control. Case in point: having a waitress niece who gets distracted for a minute by who-knows-what, and suddenly, the whole thing is in jeopardy."

"Lissie—"

"No, wait." They had reached a wooden bridge, empty for the moment, and built over no water that Lissie could discern. She held up a hand to silence him, mock stern. "I'm going to stop you right there. Because if you're thinking you'd like to be defensive or dismissive, that's my territory, you know."

"*Lissie*—"

But she held up both hands now. "Uh-uh-uh! I *forbid* you."

He expelled an exasperated breath and reached for her hands to push them down. But Lissie jerked them away, only to shove them in his face again when he swiped at empty air. "You brat," he laughed, grabbing for her again. Again she whipped her hands away, but this time he seized her around the waist with one arm and tried to wrangle her flailing and slapping hands with his own free one.

"You stop that!" shrieked Lissie, gasping and giggling. "I forbid you to manhandle me!"

"You call this manhandling?" Pinning her against his chest, he thrust his other arm under her knees and picked her up, lifting her off the ground while she screamed and kicked. "You don't weigh a thing," he said, panting nonetheless as he wrestled with her. "Let me say what I want to say, or I'll drop you off the bridge."

"Put me down!"

"If you say so." He pretended to let her fall, only to catch her again, mid-screech, a few inches lower.

"If you drop me in poison ivy, I will rub my rashy self over every inch of your exposed skin!" threatened Lissie.

The next second, they were both tumbling off-balance, Lissie banging her elbow on the bridge railing, because two men had yanked Preston backward.

"Miss, are you all right?" Her surprise liberators were a pair of pale and lanky runners in short shorts and singlets.

She gripped the railing to steady herself and managed to say,

"I—yes. I'm sorry. We were just messing around!"

With Lissie off his chest, Preston's embroidered monogram became visible again, and the two rescuers now scrutinized him from head to toe while he stared bemusedly back. Lissie stifled an urge to snicker. It was obvious to her he had never in his life been mistaken for the bad guy. He stood there now, palms raised in innocence as if he were about to be arrested, the muscles in his jaw clenched.

"Really," she spoke up again. "Thank you. But we're friends. Working the meet at KCAC. Sorry if we worried you. But if he *had* been assaulting me, that would have been amazing that you intervened. Most people wouldn't have."

Probably the quaver of amusement in her voice didn't help Preston's cause because the men still hesitated. "You sure you're all right?" Asked the paler and lankier of the two. He had a man bun.

"All good," repeated Lissie. "Put your hands down, Preston, and stop looking so guilty!"

When he obeyed, a snort of laughter escaped her. She grabbed his hand nearer to her, winding her fingers through his, to give his arm a swing.

"Friends," she insisted to her champions. "See? Just goofing off." Lissie even went so far as to pat Preston on the chest to indicate said friendliness and because she had wanted to do that since the first time she saw him.

The men nodded, persuaded by this unasked-for show of solidarity. With a glance at each other, they bobbed once or twice on the balls of their feet and continued over the bridge on their run.

Lissie gave her amusement full rein then, releasing his hand to grip her own sides as she howled. "Oh my gosh, I just totally saved your behind! Let's get out of here before someone tries to save me from you again. That'll teach you not to mess with Lissie Cheng, Mr. Youth Ambassador! I have friends in high places. Or low, leafy places, as the case might be."

"If you hadn't been screaming so loudly—"

216

"If *you* hadn't been dangling me over the side of a bridge," she jeered back, delighted to see the beginnings of his cute grin.

"I wasn't 'dangling' you! I had you in a firm grip."

"Yeah, yeah. Just imagine if I hadn't stuck up for you against those guys. They were so earnest! Imagine the USA Swimming Youth Ambassador being thrown in jail! Not to mention the black eye that would have given Stanford once anyone learned you were part of that hallowed institution. And with no money for your legal defense, we would have had to set up a GoFundMe. I want you to know the Chengs would have given at least five dollars. Maybe even ten."

Preston's smile was in full evidence now. "I could have paid my own bail."

"That's even sadder. In Victorian novels, the accused always has at least a couple friends who believe in him and put their money where their mouth is. Paying your own bail would be like admitting that not only did you commit the crime, but everyone knows you did, and you have no friends."

He rolled his eyes heavenward. "Where did you get this mouth?"

"From the Lord, of course," she replied promptly. "Speaking of which, do you know Jesus Christ as your Lord and Savior?"

For the second time in their entire acquaintance, Lissie had the satisfaction of making him laugh openly, and she was tempted to skip as they made their way back to the aquatic center. Their leisurely way back. Because now that they were at last, Lissie hoped, uncomplicated friends, there was so much to chat and laugh and tease about.

Which was why she was almost five minutes late for the officials' meeting. And why she didn't notice, until finals were starting and she took her place by the starting blocks, squinting and scanning the stands in vain, that her sister wasn't there.

JoJo was nowhere to be seen.

CHAPTER 22

W here was she?

As the lowest person on the totem pole, Lissie was assigned the inside position on relay takeoffs, meaning she would be
showered with water whenever the kids dove in from the blocks. It
also meant she had little time to scrutinize the stands for her sister.
But at the first break, during which Preston Lin emerged on deck to
hand out medals after being introduced again over the PA system by a
noticeably less enthusiastic Maddy James, Lissie dashed to the officials'
room to dig out her phone.

She called JoJo.

No answer.

She texted her: *Where are you? Your event is coming up! Are you here?*
Nothing.

Then she tried Emma. Mrs. Yeh. Nothing. Nada.

The next block of events were announced, and Lissie stuffed her
phone back in her bag before dashing back out to her post observing
lanes seven and eight, start end. The swimmers in her lanes might have
been playing Marco Polo and she wouldn't have noticed. When the
heats for the 200 Backstroke C Final began, she was too busy worrying about Emma missing her event to notice the official on the turn
end of her lanes raise a hand. The chief judge rushed over to stand by
Lissie, prepared to deliver the bad news when the swimmer got out.

"Did you see anything on your end?" he asked her. He was a giraffe of a man from Sierra Nevada Swimming.

"No, nothing," admitted Lissie. "Am I in trouble?"

"Nope. I'm just here to tell the swimmer she was disqualified."

Emma was a no-show for the A Final.

As soon as the last swimmers touched the wall, Lissie grabbed Giraffe Man's sleeve. "Can I go now for the break? I'm worried my little sister will miss her event."

"Go ahead. They've got to hand out this batch of awards, so you have at least ten minutes."

Here came Preston again, Maddy trotting after him with the tray of medals. He caught Lissie's eye, and she must have looked freaked out because he frowned and came to a dead stop. But duty called, and he couldn't turn and follow her.

She thrust her arm in her bag for her phone, expecting and hoping to find apologetic texts and voicemails, to which she would reply with scorching anger, followed in due time by grudging grace. But the only messages were from Mel of a GIF of a camel chewing (she thought her boss at FedEx Kinko's chewed like a camel); and from Nelson, a pic of his latest crush to the apartment thread: *Celebrity sighting! Hassan M aka Hot Man at 7th St Plaza handing out frisbees for BofA. Took 4 one for each of us <3 <3<3.*

What was going on??

After trying JoJo, Emma, and Mrs. Yeh again, she called the hotel and asked them to ring both rooms. No answer.

"Have you seen them today?" Lissie asked. "Attractive Chinese lady and two thirteen-year-old girls?"

"Uh . . . " said the desk person. That is, she had likely seen dozens of that combination.

"Can you please, please go knock on their doors and just make sure they aren't in or passed out or something?"

Lissie finally convinced the woman to check with the manager and call back. What else could she do?

What else? There was Coach Wayman, of course. Lissie tapped her phone screen with her nails restlessly. Who cares why the guy was secretly possibly in Seattle? She could pretend ignorance of all that, and just maybe he knew something about the girls' whereabouts.

Taking a deep breath, she opened the group thread with JoJo, frowning when she realized her sister hadn't sent the scoreboard picture. Resentment? Forgetfulness?

Hey, Wayman. Good news and bad news. Emma and JoJo had great prelims, but now I don't know where they are. Mrs. Y took them between sessions but none of them are back yet for finals. Emma missed event. If you've been in contact, can you pls tell them to get their butts back here or at least message me???

She waited, staring at the phone as if she could will him to reply to her. Then she pushed it away from her because a watched phone never rings. But that didn't last long, and soon enough she was holding it in her palms again, praying for something, anything.

"You're Elisabeth Cheng with Mission Valley, right?"

She snapped her head up to find Coach Paul of Streamline standing in front of her, and she must have looked a sight because his bushy eyebrows rose. "Are you okay?"

"I'm okay. And yes, I'm Elisabeth. Coach Paul—"

"Where are your swimmers? They didn't show up for warmups, and Emma Yeh just missed her event!"

"I don't know where they are!" Lissie said, deflating. "I was hoping you did. When I last saw them, they were headed to Panera and then back to the Hampton Inn at about eleven, and that's all I know. No one is answering my calls and texts."

He threw up his hands. "They should have declared their intention to scratch if they didn't want to come back tonight."

"But they did want to come back tonight," Lissie insisted. "That's what's so strange. I don't know what could have happened to prevent them from coming back."

He gave a grim shake of his head. "Since she was a no-show, I'm afraid Emma is going to be penalized on her next swim tomorrow."

"Oh, no," breathed Lissie, not really caring about Emma's next swim and worrying instead about JoJo. If she missed her race, she would be disqualified from the next day's 100 Free.

"This is not my fault," muttered Coach Paul. "Wayman Wang told me those two girls would have family members as chaperones—"

"They do! Mrs. Yeh and me."

"He said they just needed a club to warm up and down with and someone to answer questions for them."

"No one is saying this is your fault," said Lissie, her eyes narrowing. Really? At a moment like this, he was more concerned with avoiding blame than with helping to find two AWOL young swimmers? Anger felt better than fear, and she nursed it. "I'll find them so you don't get blamed for anything, Coach," she snapped. "I'll make them come and apologize to you, and I'll explain to my club that it was Mrs. Yeh and I who lost them. You're off the hook. They're kids. They've just lost track of time or something." Never mind that Mrs. Yeh was the one responsible—and why wasn't the stupid woman answering her phone? Stuffing her own phone back in her backpack and zipping it closed, Lissie rose to march past him. "I'd better get back on deck."

But her resentment lasted only until the next event. With each passing minute, her anxiety reached new levels. Where were they? Should she call Jenny? Auntie Rhoda? No, no, that would do nothing except freak them out. Maybe Wayman had answered by now. Even if he knew nothing, maybe he could at least pass on Omar Yeh's phone number, and Mr. Yeh could use Find My iPhone to locate his stupid wife. And that woman had better have the girls with her if she knew what was good for her.

The 200 Breaststroke took a mini-eternity. With each gender and age group having three heats apiece, and even the fastest swimmers requiring several minutes to finish, an hour crawled by. Lissie scanned the stands when she could, alternately shivering in the aquatic center's air conditioning and sweating from stress.

A hand tapped her arm.

"No, thank you," she said automatically, thinking it was the volunteers who came by from time to time with water bottles and snacks. But it was Preston.

"Are you all right? That last kid took two giant dolphin kicks at the start."

"What? Did he? I . . . must have missed that."

"Maybe it was because you were staring up at the bleachers."

She threw him an anguished glance before returning her gaze to the water. "It's JoJo!" she hissed from the side of her mouth. "Her friend Emma missed her event, I don't see JoJo anywhere, and no one is answering my calls!"

Lane eight must have taken two dolphin kicks off the first turn as well, because Lissie's counterpart's hand went up. Which meant the chief judge came scurrying over again, and Preston had to back away. When the heat ended and Lissie returned behind the blocks, he was beside her again, asking questions: What had she tried? Where did she think they were? Had JoJo ever done this before?

The referee whistled the next heat up, and Preston retreated again, waiting for Lissie's swimmers to leave her jurisdiction.

"I'm going to get in trouble for chitchatting," Lissie worried.

"This isn't chatting," he answered. "Who knows the girls are unaccounted for besides the Streamline coach?"

"No one. I mean, I did message Coach Wayman." A shadow fell over his features, but he was the only one present she didn't have to explain things to, and she couldn't help what came spilling out. "I messaged him on my last break, but he didn't answer. Maybe he has now. I hope he has. But he might not because there's something weird going on with him too."

"What do you mean 'something weird?'" Preston's voice was tight.

Lissie explained briefly how Wayman had called in sick the day after being seen at the airport. "And this is all third- or fourth-hand info, but Mrs. Karwhal supposedly saw Wayman at the gate for a flight to Seattle. Which makes no sense at all! JoJo and Emma thought he might be coming to surprise them at the meet, but obviously he didn't. But why would he come up here secretly at the last minute if he wasn't coming to the meet? Maybe he didn't want Coach Paul to know he was here since he'd already asked him to keep an eye on the girls? But that doesn't make sense either—"

She broke off, belatedly noticing he had gone white. "I'm sorry. I know you don't like to hear about him. It's just—"

"Go on," he said, still sounding unlike himself. "It's just what?"

"It's just, I mean, even if Wayman is up here, I don't care at all about that. I just want to know if he's heard from them or knows anything. At the very least, he could give me Emma's dad's number, who might be able to tell me where they are."

The heat ended, and Lissie scooted back to the chairs behind the starting blocks, followed slowly by Preston. There was only one more heat of breaststroke, and then she would have another ten or fifteen minutes to hunker over her phone. The ponytailed Maddy James emerged from a side door to glance around for her charge.

"You'd better go," said Lissie. "You're almost up again."

"In a minute."

"Thank you for listening to me," she added quietly, though no one was likely to hear her over the announcer calling out the swimmer's name and club in each lane to cheers from the stand. "I know this isn't your problem."

"It's okay, Lissie." He straightened and ran a hand through his hair.

"If JoJo doesn't show up in the next half hour, she's going to miss her event, and then she won't be allowed to swim tomorrow. If she's not dead in a ditch," Lissie fretted. "You don't think she's dead in a ditch, do you?"

"She's not dead in a ditch," Preston declared, so firmly that Lissie took irrational comfort from it. "If she doesn't turn up, we'll find her."

Lissie's throat tightened, and she could only manage a nod.

It would be okay. It had to be. Preston said JoJo wasn't dead in a ditch, and however little the universe cared for the Cheng girls, it treasured Preston Lin. His word counted for something.

The heat ended, and Lissie dashed for the break room. At the next medal break, Lissie retrieved a voicemail from the hotel saying that there was no answer at the room doors and no replies to calls. The manager said she'd call again if they learned anything new, and if the party showed up they would certainly let them know she was trying to reach them, etc., etc. Lissie thought she was braced for no news about JoJo, but it still hit her like a gut punch.

JoJo missed her event.

Lissie continued to stand over her lanes, but she saw nothing, heard nothing. She was going to have to tell Auntie Rhoda and Jenny she'd lost her baby sister. "Where will you be when I'm done here?" Preston asked before his final handout of medals.

Lissie held out her arms. She was wet again from working medley relay takeoffs. "I'm going to change and wait for you out front." *Trying not to bawl my eyes out*, she added inwardly.

"We'll find them," he told her again. "Together."

Even her excitement at their new friendship was forgotten in the terrible turn the day had taken. Thrilled as she was to spend more time with him, she was stupefied to realize she had lost her sister. She sank down on the curb, pressing her face to her knees. Should she call the police or wait until Preston came out?

She should call the police. If the girls were really missing, every minute counted. And that meant she had to tell Auntie Rhoda and Jenny what was going on.

Swimmers and parents pushed through the sets of doors and strode by, but no one stopped to talk to her, thank God. If they noticed her at all, they probably figured she was a swimmer disappointed with her times, in which case they all knew to leave her alone.

The phone in her back pocket began to vibrate. Lissie's head shot up so fast the tears running down her face flew off. The hotel!

"Hello?"

"Hello, Ms. Cheng? This is Casey from the front desk again." The woman sounded like she was in a closet and trying to keep her voice down. "Did you hear from the girls you were looking for?"

"No. Have you?"

"Not exactly, but we know where they were as of about 5:15 p.m."

"What? Where? But I called you after then!"

"I do apologize for not letting you know about the message sooner. We had a shift change, and the new person didn't realize a message had been left earlier for the other guest until she came back a few minutes ago and asked."

"She's back? Mrs. Yeh?" Lissie leaped up, brushing herself off. "Can you please put her on?"

"Sorry, but she's gone again. She was very upset, wanting to know where the girls were too."

"Why didn't she call me?" Lissie shouted. Heads turned, and she stalked farther away.

"Of course we suggested that to her, Ms. Cheng," said Casey, barely above a whisper, "and offered to give her your number if she didn't have it, but she got very upset and said if she wanted to call you, she would call you. But then Bernard told her there were messages for her. I tried to hush him because I thought it was just the message you had left and I was afraid she would get even more upset, but Bernard said, No, it looked like one of the messages was from earlier. So of course Ms. Yeh wanted to hear that one, and the second she did, she started saying things in Chinese, and the next thing we knew, she was gone."

"Never mind that," said Lissie, waving it away. Waving Gloria Yeh away. Mrs. Yeh knew Lissie was panicking and didn't even bother to call her? Screw her! "Please keep going. Where are the girls? Did she say? Was she going to get them?"

"We don't know, Ms. Cheng," Casey replied apologetically, "because none of us speak Chinese, but we did, uh, decide to listen to the earlier message, which of course we don't ever do, but this time we were justified in doing so because—"

"I don't care if you listened to it," Lissie screeched. "What did it say?"

A hand touched her shoulder, and she jumped and whipped around. It was Preston. Lissie pointed at her phone and mouthed the word "hotel."

"What did the message say?" she repeated.

"It said, 'Mom and Lissie, if you get this, we are at Ivar's Acres of Clams in Seattle—'"

"*Seattle?*" Lissie hollered, as if Emma had announced they were on Mars.

"Yes, Seattle," repeated Casey. "That's what she said." She continued reading: "'Ivar's Acres of Clams in Seattle. We had to borrow this phone to call because JoJo doesn't have hers and mine got taken—'"

"Taken?" If Lissie's voice got any shriller she would leave the audible spectrum.

"Excuse me, Ms. Cheng, if you would just let me finish," said the long-suffering Casey. "There isn't much more."

"Of course, of course. I'm sorry. Please go on."

"'Mine got taken, and we borrowed this one from a lady who works at the restaurant. Can somebody come get us?' That was the end of the message, and it was left at 5:15 p.m."

"Okay. So they're at a restaurant in Seattle and need a ride," said Lissie. "What was the name of the place again?"

"Ivar's Acres of Clams," Casey said again, more slowly. "I-v-a-r, Ivar's. It's a restaurant right on the waterfront, kinda touristy—"

"Got it. Ivar's. Thank you," Lissie interrupted. "If you hear from them again—any of them—please tell them I'm headed there. If Mrs. Yeh shows back up with them before I do, tell them to call me immediately. Thank you, Casey, so much. Thank you."

Hanging up, she looked at Preston, her eyes filling. "That was the

226

hotel. The girls left a message for Emma's mom earlier—"

He was already digging the car keys from his pocket. "Ivar's?"

"On the waterfront in Seattle."

"Let's go."

"But Preston," she hurried after him, trotting to keep up with his long strides, "I should tell you it might be a wild goose chase. I think Mrs. Yeh is already on her way there."

Lissie was prepared for a long hike to the upper lot, where Mrs. Yeh had been forced to park that morning, but apparently the USA Swimming Youth Ambassador got his own parking space right to the side of the entrance, reserved by an orange cone. *To him who has, more will be given*, she thought wryly.

"Mrs. Yeh hasn't seemed too interested in keeping you in the loop," he pointed out, clicking the key fob. The headlights blinked.

"You're right, she hasn't," Lissie admitted, climbing in on the passenger side. She waited until he folded himself like origami into the compact rental car's driver seat. "Which is why I want to go there too, in case she doesn't bother to now. I couldn't bear to go back to the hotel and just sit there waiting and hoping they'll come directly back."

"Makes sense." When he had backed out and they were waiting to turn onto Campus Drive, he spoke again. "Did the hotel say anything about . . . about Wayman Wang?"

Her breath caught, her eyes on his profile. "No. Nothing. Why would they?"

He didn't answer, hands clenching the steering wheel. His face had a greenish cast, which might have been from the traffic lights.

"Tell me," she whispered. A guess stirred in her gut, but she didn't dare put it in words.

There was a silence which felt endless to Lissie, and it lasted until they were getting on the freeway. She saw him swallow hard, but at last he said, "He's up here, and she doesn't want to talk to you. Those are the two things we know."

"I understand," she blurted. "You don't need to come with me,

Preston. I totally wouldn't blame you for not wanting to. Only, if you don't come, may I please, please, please borrow your car? I'll drop you off first. Please." Even as she spoke she prayed he wouldn't take her up on it. She had no idea where she was. Where anything was. And there was something so reassuring about his presence next to her.

"I'm coming." His voice was heavy. "I don't think you should go down there alone."

He sounded so unhappy that she should have argued with him, told him it was fine, she would be fine. But she couldn't bring herself to. She compromised. "Are you sure? I know this is probably a situation— if it is what you think it is—that you never thought you'd never have to deal with again. I mean, you wouldn't be involved, that is, except for me, helping me. And I wouldn't ask you, except—"

"I'm coming."

She sagged back in her seat, renewed tears of relief and gratitude threatening. Because JoJo was alive and okay, and they were going to get her. And Preston was coming with her because he was amazing.

CHAPTER 23

H e might be amazing, but he was done talking. Other than asking her to punch the name of the restaurant into his phone and turn up the volume, he said nothing more. He just drove. Brow knit and jaw locked, he drove.

If he had his own demons to wrestle, there was nothing Lissie could do about it at the moment, knowing as little as she did about what was going on. She wasn't a nail biter, but she did pick uneasily at the nubs of the vinyl armrest cover as she watched the strip malls and streetlights and then freeway taillights go by. As the skyline of Seattle blossomed amid the surrounding darkness, the Google Maps lady broke the silence with another instruction.

"Maybe I'll try texting Mrs. Yeh again," spoke up Lissie in the darkened car. "To say we're getting close."

"She doesn't want to talk to you."

They were passing the stadiums now, and Lissie knew the dark patch beyond was the water.

"Still, I'll try again."

"Suit yourself."

As he predicted, the text went into the same void which swallowed her earlier ones.

Silence fell in the car again, apart from the navigation commands, more frequent now. When they took the downtown exit from the freeway, Lissie twisted her neck to peer up at the high-rises.

"I didn't know Seattle had hills," she said. "Like San Francisco."

He didn't answer.

It did look a lot like San Francisco. Not just the hills and the setting by the water, but also the abundance of unhoused people and the mix of urban luxury and urban seediness. The irony didn't escape her that she was getting to see Seattle after all, just not in the way she had expected.

At the bottom of the hill, they turned on Alaskan Way, which ran along the waterfront, Lissie stifling an exclamation when she saw the giant lighted Ferris wheel ahead.

"We'd better park," said Preston. "The restaurant's just over there."

He turned into the next lot with what Lissie thought was unwarranted optimism. A space here, in the heart of things, on a Saturday night? But she'd forgotten how the universe smiled upon Preston Lin because, sure enough, there was one narrow spot for him right in the second row. If they ever got together, would some of that gold dust rub off on her?

Ivar's Acres of Clams overlooked the Puget Sound at Pier 54. In another world, one without little sisters MIA and unwanted blasts from his past, she and Preston might have lingered beside the railing to gaze out on the water and the wheel and the passing ferry boats before ducking into the restaurant for dinner with a view. In this one, however, they crossed the street and headed directly inside. The spacious entry, featuring exposed fir beams and historic pictures lining the walls, buzzed with people waiting to be seated, but Lissie noticed none of this in her rapid circuit through the groupings of padded benches.

"I don't see them," she said to Preston, trying to keep calm. "Mrs. Yeh must have beaten us here and picked them up already."

"Check the bathroom before we go," he advised. "I'll talk to the hostess."

JoJo and Emma were not in the restroom. Lissie even called their names to be sure. When she emerged again, Preston was speaking with the hostess, who was clutching a set of menus to her chest but seemed to have forgotten all about seating the next group as she eyed him with the wonder Lissie was starting to recognize.

"Yes, and one of them asked if she could call her sister first, just so she wouldn't worry, but the woman said they'd see her soon enough and just hurry up because she was so mad at them, and then she busted into Chinese and the girls didn't say anything after that. Then they left."

"Did they look okay? Did they sound okay?" Lissie demanded.

The hostess looked affronted at this interruption, but, with a glance at Preston, she grudgingly replied, "They looked fine. Maybe a little nervous. I didn't even notice them until they came up to the stand and asked if they could borrow my phone for a minute to call their hotel."

"Did they say what happened to their phones?"

"The one girl just said she had lost hers."

"And did they tell you anything else?" Lissie pressed. "Like why they were here?"

"They said they got separated from one of their moms and asked if could they wait here till they were picked up." The hostess frowned, clearly enjoying the interview less when Lissie was the interrogator. "It's Saturday. We've been really busy."

Preston touched the back of Lissie's arm, and she relented. "Thank you," she muttered. "For helping them."

"Uh-huh. Have a good night."

When they were outside again, crossing the street to return to the car, Lissie said, "I understand Mrs. Yeh doesn't want me in her business, but I could still wring her neck. She could at least have let JoJo take two seconds to call me and say she was okay."

"It wouldn't have taken two seconds," said Preston.

She groaned. "Yeah, okay, probably not. But still! Well, I told you it might be a wild goose chase. Thank you for driving me here anyhow.

It was a relief to hear the girls were alive and well fifteen minutes ago."

They reached the teeny car again, and this time Lissie laughed when she saw him fold up to get inside. "Did they not have any bigger models at the rental place?"

"I didn't ask."

His sober tone surprised her. Was he annoyed that she had wasted his time? Or resentful because Lissie was now cracking jokes after dredging up the Wayman Wang memories he'd spent years burying?

"Preston—"

"Lissie, would you mind if we made one quick stop before I dropped you off?"

She blinked at him. "A quick stop? You mean like at the grocery store?"

"I mean like at a hotel. The Edgewater. It's just down the waterfront a ways." A glance took in her mystified expression, and then he stared straight ahead out the windshield. "It—I just want to check something."

"What kind of something? I mean, of course, we can stop there if you want."

He was already starting the car. Lissie sat on her hands and pressed her lips together. Had the Ivar's hostess said something about the Edgewater when Lissie was still investigating the bathroom? Was there more going on? Was JoJo not, after all, okay?

She couldn't hold the last question in. "Do you think JoJo isn't okay?"

"I'm sure she is," he answered, with another swift glance at her.

She couldn't think of anything else to say then besides *What is going on in that head of yours?*, so she said nothing at all. If he was sure JoJo was okay, Lissie didn't care if he made one quick stop or a hundred. Besides, now she got this bonus drive along the waterfront and more time in his company.

To one side of the street lay the dark Sound and lights of the piers, and to the other a serrated wall of hills and high-rises. Colored lights outlined the Great Wheel. In the gap between buildings Lissie saw a ferry boat headed to points unknown. They passed the Seattle Aquarium and glittering condominium buildings offering glimpses of other lives through their windows. She wondered if they would see the Space Needle. But no, at the next light, he turned into the Edgewater Hotel, the road into the parking lot flanked by a lodge-like building on one side and a row of evergreens on the other.

Circling a tall stone fireplace, they pulled up at the hotel entrance, where a couple was loading their luggage onto a trolley before a set of multiple wood-latticed doors. A tall, well-built man on his phone paced nearby.

Lissie gasped before she could help it. She recognized the movement even before her brain identified the person. How could she not? She had seen that pacing, back and forth, back and forth, day after day beside the Mission Valley Manta Rays' practice pool.

"Preston, look! There's . . . that's . . . isn't that—"

Preston put the car in park even though he wasn't yet at the curb and yanked on the door latch. Wayman Wang glanced over, taking a few steps toward them before he froze as if turned to stone.

"You!" growled Preston, springing out.

Wayman blanched, stumbling back. "What the hell are *you* doing here?"

"I'm not the one who has to explain myself," Preston snarled, advancing. "Where is she?"

"Oh my God," Lissie breathed. She fumbled at her own door latch, but it was locked.

"How did you know where to find me?" Wayman countered, drawing himself up.

"Must have been a lucky guess, asshole," Preston flung at him. "Looks like when you blow up people's lives, you stick with the same sleazy game plan. You think I don't remember? What you did to my mom and my family? You think I don't know you brought my mother here?"

"'Brought her here?'" Wayman's lip curled. "If that's what you want to call it. She came here herself, dude. Because your mom wanted it!"

Preston roared out a curse, and before Lissie could even scream, he hurled himself at Wayman. Unprepared for the impact, Wayman staggered back, the two of them crashing into one of the rock-lined posts.

Everyone was screaming and shouting at the same time: Preston and Wayman, the people with the luggage, Lissie. Her fumbling fingers finally managed to unlock the car door as the two twisted and grappled, and she sprang out, tripping over her own feet. "Oh my God! Stop! Preston! Wayman! *Stop!*"

At her scream, Preston glanced toward her for a split second, and Wayman seized on his distraction to rear back and throw a punch. With a sharp huff, Preston threw his left forearm up to block it and then landed a clean right squarely against Wayman's jaw. His head snapped to the right and his body followed, sprawling to the ground. Wild-eyed, Wayman looked up at Preston, who loomed over him as he had done with Lissie so many times before. Then he stumbled backward, trying to escape the scene. He'd caught a whiff of Preston's fury, and he wanted no more of it.

"Somebody call the police!" screeched the luggage-trolley lady, her head volleying back and forth between the two men as if they would turn on her next.

"Where are the girls?" shrieked Lissie as Wayman began to flee. "Oh, God," she gasped, her every muscle tensing though there was no way she could catch him. "Stop him! Kidnapper!"

Lissie wondered if she'd sustained a blow to the head herself because the universe slowed. A bellhop swung open one of the double doors and Wayman leaped toward it. Preston, a blur, flew past her with arms outstretched to tackle him. He crashed into Wayman's back, knocking him into the couple's overburdened luggage trolley. Wayman's mouth twisted in a "Oh, fuuu—," the final consonant drowned by the woman's shriek as he tumbled headlong into the tower of matching Tumi aluminum cases.

"Lissie!"

At the sound of her name, Lissie's perceptions of space and time caught up with reality, and she saw her little sister dashing toward her through the open door of the Edgewater. The next instant, JoJo's skinny arms strangled her, and both of them burst into tears.

"How did you know I was here?" sobbed JoJo. "Coach Wayman was calling me an Uber. They were going to send me back to the hotel by myself."

Wayman was straggling up, muttering to the couple whose luggage he had used to break his fall while the woman tried to put distance between them. Preston looked on, his expression like someone who'd received his own blow to the head and couldn't remember precisely how it happened.

The desk manager joined the group outside, and the clamor and confusion increased before it could be determined that, no, the female hotel guest had not been assaulted; and, no, the crying girl was not being held against her will, she was in fact now with her sister.

"Why were you running away?" Ms. Luggage accused Wayman. "It makes you look guilty." And then, whipping to confront Preston: "And why did you chase him and hit him?"

"It's a long story," said Preston wearily.

"Shut up, man," said Wayman. "Let it go."

"If you hadn't involved friends of mine—"

"I didn't involve friends of yours," retorted Wayman. He jerked his chin toward JoJo, who was still clinging to Lissie, watching him quietly, her little features crumpled in a scowl. "Can I help it if they chose to involve themselves?"

Lissie gave her sister a gentle shake. "He didn't pick you and Emma up or ask you to come to Seattle?"

"N-no."

"Where is Emma?"

"With her mom," whispered JoJo. "Upstairs. In the hotel."

"She's a guest here?" asked the desk manager.

"Yes, I'm a guest here," came a new voice. "Gloria Yeh."

Lissie's head whipped up, and she locked eyes with the woman she'd been trying to get a hold of for hours and hours. Mrs. Yeh's lips were tight and her eyes hard, but she was otherwise her usual self, from her expensive haircut to her body-hugging knit dress. And somehow the sight of her—so put-together, when she had been out of her mind with worry and probably looked like she'd been through a hurricane—pushed Lissie over the edge.

Putting JoJo firmly away from her, she marched over to the woman, her heart hammering like mad. "What is the matter with you?" she asked hoarsely. "How could you not call or text me back all this time? I frankly don't care about whatever it is you're doing, Mrs. Yeh. That's your own private business. But how could you possibly not respond to me when you knew I was going crazy, not knowing where the girls were or if they were okay?"

"I didn't know where they were either, for the longest time," retorted Mrs. Yeh, crossing her arms over her chest.

"But you *should* have known! They were in your charge!" Lissie railed, her finger coming up accusingly. "And if you weren't going to be with them the whole time, you should at least have told me! Or told me you lost track of them, so we could put our heads together!"

"They weren't supposed to follow me," hissed Mrs. Yeh, "and of course, I didn't want to advertise my personal life—"

"I get it," interrupted Lissie, "but if that's the case, maybe don't schedule your getaways when you're supposed to be chaperoning young girls in a strange city! Especially when other people are trusting you to do what you say you're going to do and be where you say you're going to be!"

Gloria Yeh gave a sharp shrug. "You think you know everything, don't you? You think you always do the right thing, so you can judge me? Right. Call me again in twenty years." With that, she spun on her heel and went back inside, and if Lissie had had anything in her hands, anything at all, it would have sailed after the woman and hit her smack in the back of the head.

There was a heavy pause, as if they were all onstage, waiting for the curtain to drop. The desk manager was the first to recover. He turned to Mr. and Ms. Luggage. "Wow. How about that. I do apologize for the ruckus. Why don't you let Oscar take your things now, and they'll get you all checked in inside."

Reluctantly, the couple obeyed, but not without Ms. Luggage glancing back several times lest she miss something. When the doors shut behind them, the manager folded his arms over his chest. "Now, then. If this is a matter for the police, I'd be happy to call them, but I cannot have these scenes disturbing our guests."

"It's not a matter for the police," said Wayman, his eyes locked with Preston's.

Preston took a deep breath. "It's not," he conceded.

"Let's go, JoJo," urged Lissie. "Get in the car."

"Come with us, Preston," her little sister pleaded.

"We're all going, don't worry," said Preston, backing away slowly.

The three of them retreated to the rental car, leaving Wayman Wang standing alone in the lot, running a rueful hand along his jaw.

"Okay," Lissie said, when they were getting on the freeway again and JoJo was tucking into the fish and chips they'd gotten her. "Let's hear it. The whole story from the time I last saw you."

"We went to Panera, like I said we were going to," JoJo began, folding one leg under the other so she could sit higher. With the food and the company, she was rallying. "But then, instead of going back to the hotel, Mrs. Yeh said she was going to drop us at the mall so we could watch a movie while she ran errands. I knew you wanted me to nap, Lissie, but I figured there would still be time for a quick one after the movie, and if the movie was boring, I could even nap during."

"Keep going," said Lissie. "You went to the movies."

"We went to the movies," repeated JoJo. "The new Marvel one. And it was pretty good, so I didn't fall asleep, but you know how long those things go, with all the previews, and then you have to watch all the credits so you don't miss the secret scene. We finally got out of there, but Emma's mom wasn't outside waiting for us. She didn't even text to say where she was."

"Wait," Lissie interrupted. "That reminds me, what happened to Emma's phone?"

"It got taken later. By this weird guy. I'll get to that part."

Lissie moaned and covered her eyes. "I'm not sure I want to hear this after all."

"You don't?"

"No. I do. It might kill me, but I do. Go on."

"Okay, so like I was saying, She didn't text Emma, but there was a message on Emma's group thread—"

"What group thread?"

"Like we have," said JoJo. "With me, you, and Coach Wayman. They have one with him too. Coach Wayman texted their group."

"Okay." Lissie was careful not to look at Preston. "What did he say?"

"He didn't mean to text them, I think," JoJo went on, "because it said, *Babe BRB.*"

Lissie frowned. "Be right back?"

"Uh-huh. *Babe* be right back," JoJo nodded. "And so I grabbed her phone and answered, *Wrong thread, dummy, this isn't Coach Penny.*"

"And what did he say?"

"Nothing," said JoJo. "He didn't answer. So we thought, whatever, and Emma texted her mom to come pick us up, but Mrs. Yeh texted back that she was still running errands, and we should get a ride to finals with someone else!"

Lissie couldn't believe what was being said. "Wasn't Mrs. Yeh even going to watch Emma swim in finals?"

JoJo shrugged. "She said Emma didn't swim till six, so that gave her plenty of time to get there. But Emma was upset, so she tried calling her mom, but she didn't pick up. She just texted back and said she couldn't talk because she was 'in a quiet place' and was even going to have to turn her phone off. So Emma got suspicious and looked on Find My iPhone and saw that her mom was at the Seattle waterfront!"

"So, not running errands," said Lissie.

Swirling her fish chunk in the tartar sauce and taking a big bite, JoJo shook her head. "Emma was like, 'What is she doing there? She said there was no time to sightsee on this trip! No fair, she gets to go do fun things without us!' Emma thought we should go meet her there, but I was like, 'No, there isn't time, and Lissie told me to take a nap, so we should just go back.' The Hampton Inn wasn't far from the theater. We could even walk."

"All totally true," rejoined Lissie. "So how the heck did you end up in Seattle?"

JoJo blew out a long breath. "I knew her idea was stupid, Lissie, but then she said we had to go to Seattle because she had her performance suit in the car, the one everyone wears at the big meets, it looks like a jumpsuit and goes down to your knees," she explained. "Emma said if she didn't have hers for finals, she'd have to wear just a regular swimsuit and that would make her slow, so we had to go get it." JoJo jammed a few French fries in her mouth while Lissie absorbed this.

Lissie looked over at Preston, but he didn't react. In fact, he seemed to have withdrawn completely into himself. "Okay." Her shoulders slumped. "So you two had the brilliant idea to go find Emma's mom in Seattle and make it back in time for warmups."

JoJo squirmed. "Uh-huh. So we called an Uber."

"You Ubered to Seattle," Lissie repeated. "Two thirteen-year-old girls. Alone. What could go wrong?"

"It was a woman driver," said JoJo.

"That was luck. You didn't know it was going to be a woman driver." Were all thirteen-year-olds this dumb? "Go on," she sighed.

Relieved that Lissie didn't explode, JoJo complied. "So we went to Seattle and got out at the big Ferris wheel, but we didn't see Mrs. Yeh there even though we were standing right where Find My iPhone had said she was supposed to be. We kept trying to text and call, but then realized her phone must be off, that's why the dot didn't move."

"And then?"

JoJo's swallow was audible. "And then we looked all over the waterfront in case she was still around. We even went up to the Pike Place Market. But we didn't find her, obviously, and it was getting late. So then we thought we'd better Uber straight back to the pool, and Emma could just buy a new performance suit at the stand in the lobby."

"So why didn't you?"

JoJo's voice rose in indignation. "Because the driver wouldn't take us! After we waited over fifteen minutes for him to get there! He said it was against Uber rules because we didn't have an adult with us, and then he left, even though we begged!"

"If it was against the rules, why did the first lady take you?"

"I guess because she didn't care about the rule, but he did. Totally our bad luck, getting him. So after he took off, it was starting to get dark, and I said we had no choice but to call Olivia to get your phone number and you would find a way to come get us."

"You don't know my phone number?"

"It's in my phone, and my phone is still in the hotel!" JoJo jammed her paper fish-and-chips basket into the paper bag and crumpled the whole thing up. "Emma was afraid you'd be mad when you heard where we were, but I said too bad. Not that it mattered. Olivia didn't answer. Then we tried every other kid from the team in Emma's phone: Melissa, Ava, Ishaan, Ji-Hwan. Nobody had your number. So Emma said she'd just call another Uber because it wasn't like you had a car anyhow, and maybe the next driver would be nicer. We were standing at the railing and arguing and so we didn't see this weird man come up behind us. All of a sudden, we turned around and he was muttering something we couldn't understand and gestating—"

"Gestating?" said Preston. It was the first word he'd spoken in fifteen minutes.

JoJo nodded and waved her hands and arms. "Like this—"

"Gesturing," said Lissie. "Or gesticulating."

"Yeah, gesticulating like this, and we tried to pretend he wasn't there, but he got right in our face, and he smelled bad, and then he yelled at Emma and out of nowhere he grabbed her phone and threw it over the railing! We saw it fall down and down, like in slow motion, and we saw it splash into the water!"

"Oh my God! Then what happened?" Lissie asked, smacking her forehead.

"Then we screamed and ran away," said JoJo sensibly. "But we couldn't see if he was following us. We just ran into the restaurant because it was the closest building."

"You mean Ivar's?"

JoJo nodded. She flipped her door lock back and forth a couple times. "We just wanted to get away from the weirdo, but you saw how they have those benches at the entrance where the host can't even see you, so we stayed. It was crowded, so that made us feel safe. We sat there trying to think of what to do . . . " She leaned her head against the car window. "By then we knew we were going to miss finals and get DQed. Because we did, right?"

"I'm afraid so. And they penalized you from swimming tomorrow."

JoJo sighed, her eyes moist. "After a while, the restaurant people finally noticed us, and when we explained everything, the hostess lady said we could use her phone to call the hotel."

"Why didn't you leave a message at the pool, too? Maybe they could have paged me or something."

"Oh, yeah. We didn't think of that."

Lissie rolled her eyes, but there was no point in pursuing it. Water under the bridge. She wanted to ask what happened when Mrs. Yeh showed up, but that would mean bringing up Wayman Wang again, and heaven knew she'd already put Preston through enough in the past couple hours. He was probably dying to be rid of them.

But it was Preston himself who asked. "Did you and Emma know Mrs. Yeh was with . . . your coach this weekend?"

JoJo didn't answer right away, and when Lissie peeked back at her, she saw her sister staring down at her hands. "I didn't, for sure. I mean, I knew he might be in Seattle, but I didn't know what he was doing if he wasn't coming to watch us swim. I thought his text was meant for Coach Penny. But after we looked for her mom and couldn't find her, Emma said he'd done it before."

"Done what before?" Lissie tensed.

"Texted their group by accident. One time he sent heart emojis, but her mom laughed it off and said he must have meant to send it to someone else. And Emma said her mom's been acting weird for a while now. Always saying she needed to ask him about Emma's times or events or what suit to buy. It was like she just wanted excuses to go meet him."

Lissie remembered stumbling upon Mrs. Yeh and Coach Wayman at that first meet. Had that been one of those occasions?

JoJo's voice dropped lower. "Emma said her dad and mom were fighting a lot. She was worried they might get a divorce."

Lissie squirmed. It was childish, but she didn't want to know. She didn't want to know about the Yehs' private business. And she didn't want Preston to have to hear it and think whatever he might think.

But he was inexorable. "So Mrs. Yeh came to get you at the restaurant?"

"Yes," whispered JoJo. "She was really mad and went off on us about why were we in Seattle and why didn't we do what we were told, and how she'd gone all the way to KCAC only to find out we weren't there, and then she had to go to the hotel and look like a fool who couldn't even find her own children. By the time we got to the car, Emma was crying and saying, no, it was her mom's fault for turning off her phone and what was she even doing in Seattle anyway, and they were both yelling at each other nonstop." JoJo choked to a halt and covered her mouth with a hand.

Neither Preston nor Lissie spoke. After a few gulps and hiccups, JoJo went on. "So Mrs. Yeh said, 'You want to know what I was doing?

I'll tell you what I was doing! I was leaving your worthless father.' And then Emma started crying even worse, and I was crying too because I felt so bad for her. Then, instead of going back to the Hampton Inn, Mrs. Yeh took us to the Edgewater."

"Oh, Jo," said Lissie, reaching back to squeeze her knee, which was all she could reach. "I'm sorry you had to hear that. And poor Emma."

It was like a poison JoJo had to get out of her system. "Emma said, if they got a divorce, her dad would go back to Taiwan because he goes there a lot for business anyhow, and she and her little brother, Henry, didn't want to live in Taiwan. But Mrs. Yeh didn't answer her. We got to the hotel, so we had to try to stop crying and be quiet, and Mrs. Yeh took us up to the room. It was a really nice room—you could see the water and the lights—but *he* was there."

Lissie didn't ask who. Neither did Preston.

"Did . . . he seem to be expecting you?" Lissie ventured.

"No! He looked totally shocked. And Emma and I didn't know what to do, we were so freaked out. But Mrs. Yeh told him, 'This is the point of no return, Wayman.' And he just stood there until she said, 'Well, aren't you going to say anything?' and he finally looked at us and said, 'How did prelims go?' Like nothing was happening! Like we were at a regular meet and not in some sketchy situation in a hotel room!"

Lissie again felt that strange stir of pity. What a mess! Was this what the guy pictured when he first started messing around with Gloria Yeh? Or Penelope Lin?

"And then Emma yelled, 'Don't talk to me! Don't anybody talk to me! I hate you!' and ran in the bathroom and shut the door," JoJo resumed, her eyes misty again. "And I didn't want to be there either, so I said I wanted to go back to the Hampton Inn. Mrs. Yeh started banging on the bathroom door. Coach Wayman he said he'd call me an Uber. He followed me down to the lobby and went outside. And that's when you guys came."

They were back in Federal Way, and the Google Maps lady roused herself to issue instructions again. A knot formed in Lissie's stomach.

In a minute, they would pull up to the Hampton Inn, and who knew what would happen afterward? Preston was back to staring straight ahead, mouth tight. Their afternoon walk felt like a lifetime ago.

JoJo leaned forward, her face appearing between the bucket seats. "Did you beat him up because you're the youth ambassador?" she asked Preston.

In spite of herself, Lissie gave a bark of a laugh. "I don't think 'physical assault of creepy coaches' was in the job description, JoJo."

But Preston didn't crack a smile. "I . . . I didn't know what I was supposed to do," he said.

"Yeah," JoJo agreed. "It was weird. That's okay. I'm just glad you came."

When Preston dropped them at the hotel, Lissie leaned back in to say, "I can't thank you enough for helping me tonight. With everything. If you hadn't suggested the Edgewater, and we had gotten back here and JoJo still hadn't turned up, I would have lost my mind! I'm really grateful. I know that must have been . . . hellish."

He nodded, his gaze fixed somewhere past her right ear.

And then he drove away.

CHAPTER 24

A hundred times in the days that followed, Lissie brought up Preston's number and stared at it. Should she call? Text? Curiosity burned. How had he found Wayman Wang? And, even more pressing, did he hate her for forcing him yet again into the presence of the person he despised? But it was impossible to ask him these questions without seeming to pry, without picking at the wound she had forced him to reopen.

Therefore, she pried secondhand. *Did you hear from Emma?* she texted JoJo on Tuesday. There had been no practice Monday because of the holiday.

Not at practice. Neither was Coach W. They said he's still sick.

But did you text Emma?

I did to her old number in case she got a new phone, but no answer so maybe no new phone yet?

When Lissie wasn't pondering the mystery of Preston Lin, she was recalling wistfully their walk together before everything went down the toilet. And when she wasn't thinking of those things, she was worrying about JoJo's swimming. Her sister would have to change clubs, Regional relays or no relays. Because how could Lissie let her continue to be coached by such a person?

What was worse, Wayman and Emma's mom were two consenting adults, but would any Manta Rays parent want their child to continue swimming on the team in such a situation? Was Lissie obligated to expose him, or should she simply remove her sister, as Preston had removed himself years earlier? Preston had been hardly older than JoJo's age himself, and it was his family's shame that would have been exposed, so of course he did what he did. He left—and left Wayman Wang to fate. But Lissie had neither excuse. She had to act.

On Wednesday, she drove JoJo to practice, determined to corner Emma's mom there. She had rehearsed different scenarios when she was supposed to be writing her *Barchester Towers* paper, but concentrating on schoolwork was impossible until this was dealt with. They arrived at the pool to find the swimmers and parents gathered on the deck. And in place of Coach Wayman, there stood Head Coach Flight, a grizzled veteran who had never before been seen at a weekday Senior Prep practice.

"Is Coach Wayman still sick?" asked Mrs. Pang as the swimmers went through their usual ritual of donning caps and stuffing hair in and tightening goggles.

"He is not. If you all would gather 'round, I have an announcement. I'm sorry to say Coach Wayman has decided to take some personal time and won't be finishing out the year."

Uproar met this, a babel of Chinese, Hindi, Vietnamese, Spanish, and English. Coach Flight held up his hands and clipboard against the barrage. "Now, now. Let's be calm. I know it's a surprise and that it's upsetting. I hardly know more than you do at this point. I don't know if or when he will return, and in the meantime, we will find a replacement for him, of course. The rest of the coaching team will be filling in through the end of the year or until we hire someone, and you can be assured the Senior Prep group will be taken care of."

Some of the girls began to cry and the moms were hardly better, but there were a few with dry eyes. JoJo, for one. And Mrs. Yeh and Emma, who weren't there. And Lissie, who was more in danger of crying for joy than sadness. Coach Flight bore with them another minute before blowing his whistle. "All right, all right. I'll let you know more when I know more. In the meantime, let's get started. We're here to work. 200 swim, 200 drill, 200 kick. Go, go, go."

It was enough of an excuse to reach out, Lissie told herself. It was almost a duty. She sent Preston a text: *Head coach told team that WW quit.* But she didn't have an iPhone, so she had neither the joy nor the torture of seeing the three little dots appear, indicating a response. She had only silence.

>———♥——→

Lissie was unloading the industrial dishwasher in the kitchen of the Four Treasures when her cousin tapped her on the shoulder. "Some lady is asking for you, Lis."

She straightened, flushed and damp with dishwasher steam. "Who?"

"Beats me. But Mom brought her tea, so she must think she's important."

"We're not even open yet," Lissie complained, but Jeremy was already tearing open the plastic holding the linens.

Dumping forks, knives, and a thousand plastic chopsticks into a clean towel and folding the corners to carry the unwieldy load, she emerged from the back of the house. Auntie Rhoda was seated at the two-top nearest the entrance, pouring jasmine tea for a woman in a knit suit and silk scarf whose back was to Lissie. As she approached the pair, her armload slipped from her grasp and dropped with a crash on the nearest table, sending her scrambling for the pieces skidding off the surface. "Excuse me."

Mrs. Lin turned while Auntie Rhoda clucked disapprovingly at her agitated niece. "Lissie, this is Penelope Lin," she said. "She ate here months ago. On that . . . unfortunate evening. Mrs. Lin is the mother of—"

"Yes, I know," said Lissie. "Hello, Mrs. Lin."

Why? Why did it have to be like this? In the restaurant? And if only Mrs. Lin had come an hour later, she would have seen Lissie clean and neat in her cheongsam. Despite everything she knew about the woman, she still wanted to put her best foot forward, she realized unhappily. She still wanted Preston's mother to forget their first meeting. And to like her.

Mrs. Lin's gaze took her in, from her damp hair in its messy bun and her overheated face and neck to her ratty T-shirt and jeans. "Won't you join us for tea?" she asked. Auntie Rhoda fetched another chair, and, like a robot in need of oiling, Lissie marched stiffly over.

There was an awkward pause. They could hear Carlos in the kitchen, singing as he always did when he prepped. "I don't know if she told you," Lissie began suddenly, "or if anyone told you, but this is my aunt Rhoda Liang." Gesturing. "She and my uncle Mason own the Four Treasures."

Auntie Rhoda cleared her throat, startled by this burst of honesty, and took another sip of tea, but Mrs. Lin's face gave nothing away. She was an imposing woman, not lovely, exactly, but handsome. She might be pretty if she smiled. Her eyebrows were artfully drawn into skeptical arches.

"Ah," Mrs. Lin said.

Giving herself a thump to the sternum, Auntie Rhoda managed, "We have made some changes since that night you were last here."

"You hired your niece back, I see."

"Yes. After she had time to think about her actions. We also worked on training—"

Mrs. Lin cut her off with an abrupt address in Chinese, of which Lissie only caught *if it's not too much trouble*. What she had said became plain, however, when her aunt rose, replying, "*Méi guān xi*": It's fine. She laid a brief hand on Lissie's shoulder and vanished into the back.

Great! Now what? She had no idea what Mrs. Lin could have to discuss privately with her but prayed it wasn't Wayman Wang. What had Preston told her about the weekend? What could Mrs. Lin have to ask her that she couldn't ask her son? One thing was clear: Lissie could not begin the conversation. She would have to wait her out, as she had become used to doing with Preston. She pulled a pile of clean napkins sitting on the far end of the table toward herself and began to roll them up.

When she was on her third fold, Mrs. Lin said, "You've probably been expecting me."

Lissie didn't have to pretend her surprise. "Expecting you? No, not at all, actually."

"Don't give me that."

Swallowing a flare of indignation, Lissie returned, "I'm sorry. I don't mean to 'give' you anything, Mrs. Lin. We've never spoken, so how could I be expecting you? But I'll be happy to hear what you have to say."

"I'm not sure you will be. Tell me: were you in Seattle this past weekend?"

Oh, boy. Here it came.

Wayman Wang.

She would tell Mrs. Lin she knew nothing—because she didn't! She hadn't seen or spoken to him; all she knew was that he had quit the club. Why on Earth would Mrs. Lin want to ask her, a perfect stranger, about him? It could only be because she did not know her son had revealed her secret, and she was too ashamed, even after all these years, to talk to him about it.

With an effort, she continued her work. "Yes, I was. I took my little sister to a swim meet."

If Lissie guessed Mrs. Lin might blush or falter at this point, she was wrong. Instead, the woman's eyes narrowed, and her nostrils flared.

"I see," Mrs. Lin said in clipped tones. "That's what I thought. Convenient, wasn't it?"

"What? What was convenient?"

"Elisabeth, I'll cut to the chase. I should tell you straight off that there is no point in you pursuing my son. Even if he had the time for a girlfriend now—which he doesn't, between his Ph.D. program at Stanford and his volunteer obligations—you are not the sort of girl who would succeed with him."

The gap between what Lissie thought she was going to hear and what she actually heard was so vast that for a second, she could hardly make sense of the words, except to realize they were insulting.

Mrs. Lin's lips thinned further, and she raised an imperious hand. "That's right. No matter what you do, it won't work. There is no point in you pursuing my son."

Still confused by the attack, Lissie's retort was instinctive. "Then if I have no chance of succeeding, I'm surprised you wasted your time to come tell me."

"Because I know you'll try! I know you *have been* trying! Your sister failed to catch my son's good friend Charles, but you still hope to catch Preston!"

"What on Earth are you talking about?" cried Lissie, her anger catching up to her now that Jenny, too, had been slighted. "When have I tried? What have I tried?"

"Going to the dance to see him! Hanging around Stanford to see him! Coming to his listing to see him! Getting involved in swimming to see him!" Mrs. Lin counted off each accusation on her fingers and ended by thumping her fist on the table, causing her tea to slosh.

With each groundless charge, Lissie's temperature shot higher. "Is this what he's told you?" she demanded, ready to toss Preston Lin onto the bonfire of her outrage. "That I'm chasing him?"

Mrs. Lin tossed her chin. "What does it matter who told me?"

"Well, all those things you mentioned, all my so-called 'attempts,' it was only him or one of the Bings who knew about them."

"And why shouldn't the Bings tell me?" countered Mrs. Lin. "The Bings are very old family friends. Preston and Charles and Hazel have known each other all their lives."

Then it was Hazel, Lissie decided.

The pounding in her ears began to subside, as quickly as it had come. It must have been Hazel. Because Lissie doubted Charles Bing would have any objection to Preston and Lissie dating. And of course, it wasn't in Preston's nature to make such accusations, and even if he were, his mother and he weren't exactly bosom buddies swapping secrets about their love lives.

Taking a slow breath, Lissie resumed folding the napkins. "How did you know I was in Seattle this past weekend?" she asked quietly. "Did Hazel tell you?"

Mrs. Lin considered, then after a beat, nodded. "They were going to have a birthday dinner for him. It was planned for a month. But then he told Hazel he decided to work a meet in Seattle." Lissie didn't look up, but her hand hesitated an instant before she reached for another napkin. So the Rising Stars Meet hadn't originally been on his calendar? She remembered the look he'd given her when she told him JoJo had qualified. And that weekend had been his birthday? Some present she had given him! Here, come rescue my little sister and confront the nemesis of your teenage years.

But Mrs. Lin wasn't through with Lissie.

"I know he was with you this weekend," the older woman pursued, cool and hard. She pulled her phone from her quilted Chanel handbag and waggled it at Lissie. "Oh, don't pretend you don't know what I'm talking about! On Saturday night. Who else would he go to dinner with?"

Lissie stared.

A scoff. "Don't bother with the innocent act."

"You track your son's location on your phone?" Lissie marveled. "What did he turn this weekend, eight?"

"It's none of your business," said Mrs. Lin. "You listen to me. I know about the dinner, and I know about the hotel. But though he might have slept with you this weekend, Elisabeth Cheng, you will never be his girlfriend."

If Lissie's jaw had fallen any farther open, it would have hit the table. She couldn't even shake her head, much less speak. Astonishment had knocked the words right out of her. Mrs. Lin nodded again, taking Lissie's silence for confession. "My son is meant for better things. Who are you? An orphan nobody, with no parents, no money! At San Jose State! What were your SATs?" With a pang, Lissie remembered the grief-stricken haze in which she had taken her tests in the immediate aftermath of losing her parents. Not to mention the hit her grades took or her college applications . . .

"You're not studying computer science or even marketing," continued Preston's mother. "But English! Of course, you have to study English because *you can't even speak Chinese*. How can your family be here this long and you still haven't managed to do better than this?" She waved a hand around, encompassing Lissie's dishevelment and the Four Treasures altogether. "No. He might use you for fun, but he'll never marry you."

Marry me? What the actual what? This must be a nightmare, Lissie mused, dazed and having a slight out-of-body experience. *Or else, when I was emptying the dishwasher, the biggest stockpot fell off the shelf and concussed me. This cannot be happening.*

"I think you'd better go, Mrs. Lin," she heard herself say. She was pleased her voice sounded so steady, and it occurred to her that she should switch back to drama again. "You've said what you came here for."

"No. Tell me, did you sleep with my son?"

"I am not going to answer that question. You already think I did, it seems. But if you want confirmation, why don't you ask him, or better yet, Hazel?" Getting to her feet, Lissie gathered up the folded napkins. Mrs. Lin rose as well, and it gave Lissie a stab of satisfaction to note that, while they were eye to eye, she was wearing tennis shoes but Mrs. Lin needed two-inch heels to get there.

"Did Preston tell you that you were his girlfriend?" Mrs. Lin demanded.

Lissie looked up at the ceiling, as if she were trying to remember the detail, in all the hours of pillow talk she and Preston had supposedly shared. "Hmm . . . no, I don't think he did. But we were otherwise occupied."

Mrs. Lin gritted her teeth. If she had been a cartoon, steam would have erupted from her nostrils. "Shameless girl! Selfish! No values, no . . . no . . . no respect! All right, then. But you remember what I said. It will never work. He may sleep with you for a while, but you will never get more from him!"

"I'll just have to enjoy sleeping with him then," said Lissie, incorrigible.

She thought Mrs. Lin might explode into a million expensive, well-groomed pieces, but the woman had steel in her. She smoothed her skirt and tucked her purse under her arm.

"He will never marry someone like you, Elisabeth Cheng."

A mock sigh. "That's too bad. Luckily, people our age don't care much about marriage anymore."

"Girls from good Chinese families do care!" shrilled Mrs. Lin. "But you are obviously not a good girl."

Lissie turned and walked away, but Mrs. Lin followed her like a pecking bird. "I will tell my son you are just a girl to sleep with, then. Not to marry."

"Mrs. Lin, you are free to say whatever you want to your son, but I need to set the tables now because it's almost time to open. I know the Four Treasures doesn't look like much to you, but we're proud of it."

"I will go," declared Mrs. Lin, as if she were a queen granting a boon. "After you promise me you will never marry Preston."

Lissie counted out four napkin rolls and centered them on a lazy Susan. "I thought you said he would never ask me."

"He won't! He wouldn't! But if you kept at him, you might wear him down. So promise me."

Lissie stopped in her table setting and met the older woman's gaze squarely. "I'm afraid I can't help you there, Mrs. Lin. It's ridiculous to talk about marriage, but when I reach that point—if I reach that point—who I marry is completely my own business. And I wouldn't promise you, or anyone else, a thing about it."

Then Preston Lin's mother went red as a Tien Tsin pepper. With magnificent scorn, she rapped her knuckles on the nearest table (presumably because she couldn't rap them on Lissie's head) and whirled away, stomping like she wanted to punch holes in the carpet with each step. At the door, she turned again, her dark eyes glittering and her mouth a thin line.

"I will never set foot in this restaurant again. I will never recommend it. I will refuse to come if anyone invites me. And I will never sell a house to you or anyone in your family. Ever."

"I thought we weren't making promises to each other," was Lissie's muted reply.

But Mrs. Lin was already halfway out the door, and as it swung shut, Lissie turned back to her work with a sigh that was all too genuine.

"And that's the last I'll see of the Lins," she told the empty room. "Any of them."

CHAPTER 25

"And . . . action." Mel hit the record button on her phone, and Lissie descended the steps from the porch to the brick walkway, launching into Mrs. Lu's opening monologue from *A Doom of One's Own*. She was costumed in a knit suit, two-inch heels, and silk scarf, all scored at the Thrift Box, her long hair hidden under a short black wig, and her eyebrows penciled in skeptical arches. She had staked out the perfect McMansion for the shoot during one of JoJo's practices, circling Fremont neighborhoods in the Civic until she found one on a deserted street with no front-door camera.

A few takes later, it still wasn't perfect, but Lissie called it good. "I just need to turn it in," she said as she watched the replay. "I have to hand in something, *anything*, and Bach-Peralta is as sick of this project as I am. I think she's already entered the B+ in her gradebook, sight unseen."

"Better than a C+," said Mel. "Let's get out of here before someone complains about us on Nextdoor."

Lissie had an email to her advisor already queued up and ready to go, but before she could attach the video, her phone began to ring. Auntie Rhoda. Lissie groaned. "This better not be Jeremy flaking on his shift for some esports tournament."

"Lissie!" cried her aunt, her shriek so loud that Lissie pulled the phone away from her ear and stared at it a second. "*Xīngānbǎo*, what did you do?"

255

"What do you mean? I didn't do anything. Why, what happened?" She was as startled by the endearment—"heart's treasure," one Lissie hadn't heard since her grandmother died years and years earlier—as by her aunt's unusual excitement.

"Your uncle Mason and I, we got this email! Was this your idea?"

"Was *what* my idea? Auntie Rhoda, is everyone okay?"

"Yes. Fine. But here is this email to say, 'It is with great pleasure we invite the Four Treasures to be featured on *Check, Please! Bay Area*—"

"*Check, Please! Bay Area*," Lissie repeated, frowning in thought. Then her eyes flew wide. "Wait, the TV show? They want to come to the Four Treasures?" Then she was shrieking as well, jumping up and down in the middle of the quiet Fremont street, Mel joining in once she understood what was going on. Much was said or shouted, but not much absorbed, for a full minute, until Auntie Rhoda promised to forward the email. Mel brought up episodes on YouTube while Lissie tried to explain that she wasn't the person to be thanked for this stroke of good fortune. "It's because of Darren, Auntie! Darren Liu. He first mentioned this months ago, way back in October. He said his parents watch the show. Yes, it's on public television. He said he would apply for it, but I forgot all about it."

"Your uncle says if you and Jenny won't marry him, we will have to give his family complimentary meals for life," laughed Rhoda.

"It'll have to be the free meals, then, because he's going out with Mel. Maybe she should get them too." At this Mel clapped a hand over her mouth and shook her head, but Lissie waved her off, listening to her family's continued rejoicing. It required multiple promises that she would thank Darren profusely and more promises to invite him to the restaurant ASAP before Lissie could end the call.

When they were back in the car, Lissie read the email Aunt Rhoda had forwarded. "The producers want to come shoot 'B-roll' footage next month—you know, all the background shots, people ordering and eating and having a good old time—and we can all be in it! I mean, I'll be a server, but Nelson and you can sit at a table and be customers!"

she exulted. "Darren can't because he's the one who nominated us, and he gets interviewed on the show itself, but everyone else can. I can't believe he kept this secret! Did you know? Did he tell you? Where is he? Why isn't he answering my messages?"

"Because you left them like thirty seconds ago, and he's hiking in Big Sur this weekend."

"Darren Liu? Hiking? In Big Sur?" repeated Lissie incredulously. "Why didn't you go with him? Was it because you had to help me?"

"No . . . not that. I broke up with him."

"You did what?" Lissie's eyes bulged. When Mel just looked at her hands, she breathed, "Was it a good breakup or a bad breakup?" And she couldn't help it—her brain went there. Darren wouldn't bad-mouth the Four Treasures because he was upset about Mel, would he? Because Mel and the Four Treasures were two entirely separate things, right?

"I suck as a friend," mumbled Lissie after a minute. "I was worrying about the restaurant just now. I'm sorry. Are you okay?"

"Yeah. But I'm worried about the restaurant too," Mel admitted. "It has to be a good thing that he never mentioned *Check, Please!* to me, right? Because it means it was totally separate in his mind, even though it was how we met in the first place. He totally does not associate it with me, right?" When Lissie only bit her lip, Mel began to insist. "If he was mad at me and planned to take it out on the Four Treasures, he would have said, 'Oh, yeah? Well, now I'm going to say mean things on TV about your best friend's restaurant!'"

"But you didn't even know about the TV thing," Lissie pointed out, "so that would have been a super random thing to say."

"Good point." Mel blew out a disgusted breath. "I can't believe he kept it a secret! I mean, he totally should have told me—when we were still together, of course. Who knew he could be so shady?"

"Not me," said Lissie. "Mel, what if he's dumpy from the breakup when they go to film him, and they decide he'll kill ratings, and they cancel his segment?"

"TBH, he's not the most telegenic guy in the first place," Mel said. "I wonder if he submitted a picture as part of the application."

Lissie took her hand off the wheel to grip her stomach. Maybe this was how ulcers began: you get a tiny pinprick in your gut, which gets larger with each successive crisis and worry, until fear eats you from the inside out. If that was the case, between driving Preston away, getting chewed out by his mom, and now possibly having to tell her aunt and uncle that *Check, Please!* might not happen after all, Lissie thought the ulcer must be approaching the size of a black hole.

But, no. Auntie Rhoda said the other show guests had already secretly visited the restaurant to do their reviews. That meant it was too late to cancel, didn't it? It had to. It was out of her hands in any case. Short of convincing Mel to get back together with Darren until the episode was safely in the can, which was ridiculous.

"I don't get it, Espinosa," Lissie said. "You've been MIA for weeks because you spend all your free time with him! I thought you liked having a boyfriend. Don't tell me you're going to start going to Mass every day again."

"Nope. Darren's a good guy, but this makes me more certain that I've made the right decision. Who knows what's really going on with him? Because he asked me to get fake-engaged, and I decided I'd rather for-real break up."

"Who, what? What are you even saying?" Lissie scolded. "Darren doesn't know a romance trope from a rocking chair. What do you mean fake-engaged?"

"He asked if I wanted to move in together when the lease at Château Cardboard is up," explained Mel. "But I told him, no way in a million years would my Catholic parents go for that unless we were engaged, so he said why didn't we get fake-engaged, then? It's my fault. I told him about fake relationships in books, remember? Anyhow, I considered his suggestion for about five minutes, but then I decided I would just end it."

"Because you want to be real-engaged?"

"Not even. But I definitely don't want to lie to both our parents. His mom loves me, Lis! Not to mention, my mom would start reserving the church and planning the wedding, and I do not need to build a giant pyramid of deception. If he'd said, 'Why don't we just say we're engaged now because chances are we will be in a year,' that would've been a totally different thing."

"Yeah. I get it." She did. "So what's the sitch now, Mel? Are you friends? Friends later? Deadly enemies? When he gets back to me, should I mention it? 'Hey, too bad about Mel dumping you, but thanks for getting us on *Check, Please! Bay Area!*'"

"Mm. I'd better butter him up a little," said Mel, pulling out her phone. "Let's hope he hasn't blocked me and that he reads my message first." She read as she typed. '*D, so amazing about 4 Treasures and TV show. L told me!*'"

"That'll fix it," Lissie snorted.

"It will!" vowed Mel. "I refuse to be the restaurant's downfall! If I have to fake-fake-engage myself to him until they're done filming, I will do it. You hear me, Elisabeth Cheng?" She raised a dramatic fist in the air, throwing her head back. "As God is my witness, I will come through for you and for Jenny and for the Four Treasures!"

"All right, already," Lissie laughed, slapping her fist down. "You lunatic."

"Seriously. Let me know if he's weird about it, and I will make it happen. Be happy, Lissie! The Four Treasures is about to have its game elevated. When this show airs, Hazel Bing is gonna brag that she got poisoned there."

Though Darren still had not responded by the afternoon, Jenny wasn't concerned. "He's a fair person," she told Lissie while the sisters refilled the condiment bottles and jars with soy sauce and rice vinegar and chili garlic sauce. "Not childish or vindictive. And we'll just have to check on him before he's due to film to make sure he looks his best."

"If you say so. Clearly there are layers to old Darren, though. Auntie Rhoda said his folks claim he didn't tell them either. If he went all CIA operative on this, how well do we really know him?"

Jenny laughed. "Okay, true. I should just say the Darren we thought we knew doesn't seem childish and vindictive. But I can't help feeling optimistic about everything now that I've decided not to retake the MCAT. It's such a burden lifted. All this next year, I can just work on my applications and save money for med school. Simple. And I'm glad Mel wants to live with us again. I've been feeling sentimental about Château Cardboard."

"You sure you don't want to be closer to work?"

"Closer equals more expensive," Jenny said wryly. "I looked. We definitely would need two more roommates to afford it. Besides, when you had the car to drive JoJo everywhere, I got used to the downtime on the train and the Marguerite."

"This way we'll stay closer to JoJo too."

"I know." The sisters shared a look. Lissie had told Jenny ninety percent of the story about losing JoJo in Seattle—a deathly secret to be kept from Auntie Rhoda—because only her sister would understand the fear and guilt Lissie had experienced. Well, Preston too, Lissie supposed. Not that he cared. It had been thirteen days since he'd dropped them back at the Hampton Inn. Thirteen days of nothing.

"I'm so, so glad he was there," said Jenny when Lissie finished her sanitized narrative. "Though I do wonder how he knew about the Edgewater." Lissie could only shrug. "Well, however he managed it, I am so thankful since you weren't having any luck hunting her down. I always told you, Lissie, that he wasn't as bad as you thought."

"Yeah, it's true, you did tell me that."

By six o'clock, the restaurant was loosely full, or as full as it ever got post-Preston-Lin. Not that she was thinking about him. Even the benches by the entrance had a couple walk-ins, and Lissie could see her aunt's satisfaction clear across the room. She knew Rhoda Liang was telling herself, *If we've recovered this much, just wait till we're on TV!* Truth be told, Lissie shared that feeling. Because they had indeed survived, and she had played a part in it. Yeah, sure, she had been the one to bring disaster upon them in the first place, but she had also helped repair and rebuild. With Darren's unsolicited, miraculous efforts, surely they might prosper again.

"So good to have you back, Lissie," old Mrs. Fong beamed. "The other servers were nice, but we missed you."

"I've been back for a few weeks now," Lissie told her, "but Auntie hid me on less busy days, just in case."

"I liked it emptier," grumbled Mr. Fong. "You should poison another person."

His wife clicked her tongue at him in reproof and patted Lissie's hand. "It's the good kind of crowded," she said. Her eyes brightened as they focused past her. "Ooh! Look at the ones who just came in, Lissie. Too bad your aunt will give them to Jenny."

Grinning, Lissie turned to check out the new party, only to receive what felt like a kick to the gut. Because it was Preston Lin and the Bings and a few other people she didn't recognize. Not that she tried to—because something weird was happening. Her vision contracted to a tunnel centered on Preston Preston Preston; her legs locked; the restaurant sounds faded to a hum; her belly felt warm; and her mouth went dry. What were they doing here? Lissie hadn't seen them on the reservation list. Not Preston, nor Charles.

Preston was looking around. She had a wild urge to duck under the table or flee to the back, but she was like concrete poured in a posthole. Jenny appeared suddenly in the vision tunnel, blocking Lissie's view of Preston. "What are they doing here?" she hissed, flustered.

"How should I know?" said Lissie. Or she mouthed it, because no sound emerged.

"They are *not* going in my section," Jenny insisted. "Auntie wouldn't dare. But I'm going to hide in the back for a minute, just in case.

Twelve is in the window—can you drop it for me?"

Lissie's tongue came unstuck. "No!" But Jenny was already gone.

When Lissie didn't move, it was Mr. Fong who gave her a push. "Go on. Help your sister." Like a sleepwalker, Lissie lay the service napkin across her arm and loaded up the three plates. From the corner of her eye, she spied Auntie Rhoda leading the Preston party on an intercept course to Jenny's section—her sister would be so mad!—but she didn't dare look.

With a fixed smile, Lissie set the plates on table twelve. They were directly behind her now, the Preston party. She heard her aunt say, "We are so pleased to welcome you back, and thank you for trying us again. Jenny will be with you shortly, and may I offer you complimentary cocktails?"

Don't. Look. Back.

With a twitch, Lissie walked away. She was sweating profusely under her arms. One of her customers beckoned her with a half-raised hand, but she stalked blindly past.

Jenny was sitting in the walk-in fridge. "Where did she put them?"

"Your section. Eleven. Auntie offered them complimentary cocktails." The cold air felt good on Lissie's bare arms.

"That's nice. Tell Jeremy."

"Jenny, you can't hide from all your tables."

"Sure I can. I'll swap with Jeremy. He won't mind."

He didn't, accepting his new marching orders with a shrug while Jenny emerged to take over his upstairs tables. Lissie's section bordered Jenny's, however, and she could not escape so easily. Even if she were to swap with David, the only other server, he bordered Jenny on the opposite flank, besides having all the hardcore Chinese speakers.

Her uncle Mason pushed through the swinging door, having carried out one of his how-is-everything-tonight circuits. "Lissie, what are you doing? Sixteen wants to cash out. Let's turn that table."

Ugh. This was going to call for an Oscar-winning performance. She was going to have to suck it up and do it. She rose, smoothed her dress and hair, and headed back into the dining room. Keeping her gaze on her handheld point-of-sale machine, she made a beeline for sixteen and slapped their bill on the table. "Anything else I can get you tonight?"

The matriarch of the table put on her readers with the clear intention of poring over the itemized list before handing over a credit card. Lissie shifted from foot to foot, debating if she should go and return later. But then she would have to walk past Preston's table a second time, when now she safely had her back to it.

"Excuse me, Miss. Can we get more water, please?"

"Of course." Lissie looked up, and it was Charles Bing grinning at her uncertainly. "Hey, Lissie. How are you? This place is going to the dogs because I asked your aunt to seat us in Jenny's section, and instead, we got some guy."

"Oh, hi, Charles." Lissie felt her back prickle, and she knew, just *knew*, Preston was looking at her.

"Is she still here? Preston told me she crushed the MCAT."

Lissie hesitated. *Jenny would kill her*, she thought. But what was the point of lying? They'd likely seen both sisters the moment they entered, just as the girls had seen them.

"We never got this second bowl of rice," protested the matriarch at sixteen, jabbing the bill with her finger, "but you charged us for it."

She snatched the slip from the old woman. All she needed was someone whining about her crappy waitressing within earshot of Preston Lin. "I'm so sorry about that, let me delete it. So glad you checked!" And then, taking in Charles's laughing and pleading eyes, she made a snap decision. "She's working the upstairs tables," she murmured. "If you park yourself at the top of the steps, she'll have to go past you at some point."

The feeling that she was being watched grew stronger, like a summer sun climbing the sky to beat down on her head. Lissie tried to concentrate on the incorrect bill, accidentally adding three more rice bowls before she managed to go back and delete the original offender, the whole time wondering, *Whose idea was it to come, Charles's or Preston's?*

She printed the check again and held it out. The matriarch put her readers back on for a second perusal. Whoever's idea it had been, Preston didn't have to come, Lissie told herself. Which meant he was here because he wanted to be here. Would he try to talk to her, as Charles was trying to talk to Jenny? Or was he just here as moral support for his best friend?

There was a tap on Lissie's arm. "Excuse me."

Again she turned. It was a stocky, milk-pale, redheaded guy wearing a baseball cap. They blinked in mutual recognition.

"It's Lissie, the shrimp-paste killer!" he exclaimed. "Good to see you again."

"Hi, Jay. How are you?"

"Gracing this establishment with my presence again, as you see. I'm definitely a fan."

"Uh . . . thank you."

He tapped her again when it looked like she was going to turn back and lowered his voice conspiratorially. "I know you're not our server, but I wanted to let you know it's Lin's birthday. He didn't want to say anything about it." He pointed across the round table, and Lissie inevitably, reluctantly raised her eyes. "So . . . do you guys do a song or ice cream or anything? The more embarrassing, the better."

"This isn't Applebee's, and it's not his birthday," blurted Lissie, alarmed by the tunnel-vision thing happening again. But this time, handsomer-than-ever Preston was staring back from his end of the tunnel, and it felt like all the oxygen was being sucked from the room.

Her graceless remark fell at one of those rare moments when every conversation in the room paused, when every other person present was either chewing or taking a breath or thinking or checking their phone or reading the menu or just about anything other than talking.

Which meant everyone heard her. Heads turned. Lissie went scarlet. Into this yawning gap, Preston said, "Who says it isn't my birthday?"

"Y-your mother," gulped Lissie. "She said it was . . . your birthday was . . . when you were in Seattle."

"You never heard of a belated celebration?" bellowed Jay.

"You did say, the last time I was here, that you knew all kinds of songs to go with the house-special lychee pudding," Preston said quietly.

A Lissie Cheng in the movies would have smiled coyly, lowered her lashes, and shot back, "I'm afraid the pudding is only for my very favoritest customers," but real-life Lissie Cheng stood there like a block of wood. No ready, flirty response rose to her lips, and the opportunity passed. Jeremy spun up with the tray of complimentary cocktails, and the old lady at sixteen poked Lissie with the edge of her credit card and hollered, "I said, I'm ready to pay now!"

As much as she had not wanted to face Preston's table a few minutes earlier, Lissie now hated to turn her back on it again, and she ran the woman's card with ill-disguised impatience. Especially when she heard a teasing toast being made to the birthday boy and when Charles slipped back to his seat, throwing Lissie a wink that could only mean he had seen Jenny and things had gone the way he'd hoped.

But resuming her budding interchange with Preston was not to be. Sixteen had to deliver a grousing monologue on the preset tip options. Fourteen wanted to-go boxes. Mr. Fong thought he forgot his wallet, but it had fallen beneath the table. The little boy at nineteen knocked over his glass of water and started wailing. And, and, and.

Through it all, Lissie promised herself, *He won't leave without saying something. He'll take me aside. Or, if he doesn't, Jenny and Charles are going to go out again, so I'll see him soon, if I have to invite myself along, everywhere they go. But I can't wait that long! He'll say something tonight. I know he will. He has to.*

When Jeremy cashed the party out, however, and the laughing, bantering group rose to go, Preston only threw a vague glance in Lissie's direction, stuffed his hands in his pockets, and followed. She snapped a fresh tablecloth over eighteen, fighting an urge to cry and hurl a plastic soup spoon after him.

It was Jay Goldsmith who circled back. "Hey, Lissie," he accosted her. "Tell your aunt and uncle that was another great meal."

"I will. Thanks again for coming." Why was Preston being so mysterious? What exactly was up?

Jay shifted his weight, throat working, and then suddenly blurted, "I just wanted to say I heard the good news about *Check, Please!* I know it's not announced but, just to throw it out there, when they come film, if you guys want lots of friends and happy customers, my girlfriend Katie and I would love to help out."

She straightened, her eyes wide. "Darren told you about it?" Jay Goldsmith was his roommate and everything, but she was still surprised. He didn't tell Mel or his parents, but he told loud-mouthed Jay?

"Told me about what?"

"About *Check, Please! Bay Area* selecting us," she said impatiently.

"Oh! Well, I mean, it's not a total secret anymore because you guys know, right?"

"It's not a secret anymore," Lissie agreed, "though we haven't announced it yet. But why did he tell you?"

"Oh, uh, who knows where I heard it. Talk around the water cooler or whatever." He cleared his throat. "So, anyways, just remember, Katie and I are totally down. I'm in the Stanford directory, Microbiology and Immunology, same department as Lin. Or ask Darren. Deal?"

"Okay. Thanks. I'll let you know."

He almost fled, leaving Lissie to wonder at his guilty response. Had Darren sworn him to the same ridiculous secrecy?

CHAPTER 26

D arren had not.

As the restaurant was getting ready to close, Lissie's phone pinged, and she read, all in lowercase and unpunctuated, as if he were too tired after Big Sur or too demoralized after Mel to deal with such things: *awesome about check please but it wasn't me have to admit i totally forgot to follow up sorry.*

Lissie sank onto the cement step behind the restaurant, where she had come to dump the trash. She was in her street clothes again, like Cinderella after midnight. Jeans, SJSU sweatshirt with unraveling neck, scuffed shoes. But like Cinderella keeping one glass shoe as a souvenir, Lissie's hair was still in its elaborate Four Treasures coil, pierced with an enamel chopstick.

Darren had not applied to *Check, Please! Bay Area*? Here they had been praising him to the skies—Uncle Mason even teased her and Jenny about reconsidering him, and Auntie Rhoda told Mrs. Liu what a wonderful son she had—and it had not been him at all! But if it wasn't Darren to whom her family owed its impending good fortune, there was only one other person it could be, the only other person connected to both Darren and Jay.

Preston Lin.

It had to be him, or how would Jay have known about it before it was announced? "Talk around the water cooler," he had said. Of course.

He lived with Darren, but it was Preston he worked with. Preston was the one trying to restore the Liangs' livelihood.

So why hadn't he said anything?

The door banged open again, and Ray flung out another bag of trash, nearly taking Lissie's head off. "*Elisabeth!* What are you doing sitting there?"

"Sorry, sorry." But he had already gone back inside. Lissie rose, dragging two black garbage bags to the dumpster. She threw back the lid with a crash and squatted, centering her weight to heave up the first load, only to have it inexplicably go light as air and fly in by itself.

Before she could make sense of this, the second bag followed, and she jumped in astonishment, colliding with a barrier that swiftly made all things clear.

"What are you doing here?" she squealed, whipping around to face Preston and finding her face only inches from his.

"Helping. Waiting."

"Do you always wait around in the dark by dumpsters?"

"This is my first time. And I was actually out front, but I heard your voice."

"Oh." He was tantalizingly close. When he spoke, she almost, almost felt his breath brush her. Her heart was pounding like mad. What would happen if she just closed her eyes and—

He stepped back, frowning at the bin. "Man. That thing is fragrant."

"It's just doing its job," she groused, disappointed. "It's a trash can." But she slammed down the lid and moved back toward the step, cleaning her hands furtively on the washrag in her belt loop.

"I like your hair," he said.

The simple remark felt crazily like the most romantic thing she'd ever heard, and she pressed her lips together so she wouldn't say something dumb like, "You do?"

"I was waiting for a chance to talk to you," said Preston. "You were busy earlier."

"Yes." *Lissie, get a hold of yourself!* She followed her internal instruction literally, pulling her sweatshirt sleeves down to cover her hands and wrapping her arms around her middle. "What did you want to say?"

He hesitated, giving the step an idle kick. "How's JoJo? And things at Mission Valley?"

"JoJo's fine. Mission Valley's fine. Coach Wayman quit and . . . the Yehs left. JoJo didn't have Emma's new number, so she DMed her a million times, until Emma finally said they were moving and her parents were getting a divorce."

"Oh."

"Preston, how did you know where to find Wayman Wang and Mrs. Yeh and the girls that night?"

He looked back at the dumpster, his jaw hard. "I thought I might know where he was, if it was somewhere near the Pike Place Market."

"But how?"

A long breath. Then he looked at her again. "I didn't. I just thought it was worth a try. Because years ago, when my mom went missing— like I told you, they tracked her by her cell phone. She was at the Edgewater in Seattle, near where we were."

"Preston," Lissie addressed him abruptly. "I know that, left to your-self, you would never have talked to Wayman Wang again as long as you lived. And I totally get that. I am just so thankful you did. So grateful for all your help that night. I hated to involve you because of your history with him, so I am so appreciative. I don't know what I would have done without you. I would never have been able to find Mrs. Yeh or put everyone back together like that on my own. JoJo and Jenny and I, we are deeply thankful to you. And my aunt and uncle would be if they knew what had happened—"

"Lissie," he interrupted, "this is all kind of you to say, and I do like your family, but I don't deserve their gratitude. Because honestly, the only thing going through my mind that night . . . was how I could help *you*."

Every drop of blood in her body felt like it was rushing toward her head, her face. It was hot. Dizzying. "I know I said in my letter that I wouldn't ever ask you out again," Preston went on, "that the sooner that was all forgotten, the better. But—"

"But," she whispered.

"But I have to try just one more time," he said, hardly louder. "Even if you still think I'm a smug, self-righteous, superior, bullying ass—"

"Stop!" cried Lissie, her hand flying to his lips. "Don't repeat that. I was horrible. I didn't know then the reasons for some of the things you did. And I don't think that anymore about you. Any of it. I didn't know then how kind you could be. How generous. I . . . I think exactly the opposite of you now."

She felt his incredulous smile spread beneath her fingertips, and she should have pulled her hand away then, but it stayed there of its own accord as his own rose to cover it. To press it between his mouth and his own fingers in a kiss.

"You mean you've changed your mind about me?" he murmured against her palm.

Lissie nodded, swaying. Oh, heavens. The feel of his lips on her skin. She was going to collapse like one of those inflatable stick people when you pulled the plug. But she didn't collapse—or maybe she did, but his arms were around her. The firm, comforting arms which had held her when she cried in Federal Way. And her hand slipped from his mouth to steal behind his head, to bury her fingers in his thick, dark hair as he pulled her closer. Closer, his mouth descending to cover her own. Lissie shut her eyes, her breath issuing in a sigh and mingling with his.

He was delicious.

He was wonderful.

She found herself crushed against the chest she had long admired, her arms half strangling him as they kissed, gently at first and then with increasing urgency, his grip on her tightening. Only when they were completely breathless did he pull back, but even then his mouth moved to her cheek and temple, her ear and hair, murmuring her name.

The restaurant door flung open again, and this time a bag of dirty table linens hit Lissie square in the back.

"Lissie?" thundered her uncle. "What are you doing there? Who is that with you?"

"It's Preston Lin," she gasped, the two of them flying apart guiltily as if they had been caught trying to hide a body.

"Hello, Mr. Liang, it's me," Preston spoke up, raising a hand. "I dined at the restaurant tonight."

Despite her uncle's face, Lissie couldn't help laughing at this, as if eating at the restaurant were reason enough to be found out back by the dumpster, kissing the proprietor's niece. Or maybe she laughed because suddenly everything was perfect and she could have burst with happiness.

"He's not just a customer, Uncle Mason," she explained, taking hold of Preston's hand again and pulling him forward. "He's Jenny's friend Charles Bing's friend. And it turns out Preston is the one who nominated us for *Check, Please! Bay Area*, not Darren Liu."

Preston made a surprised sound, and she turned to him eagerly. "Because it *was* you, wasn't it? You did it? We all thought it was Darren because he said he was going to, months ago, but he texted me tonight and said he had totally forgotten about it. So it had to be you! Jay Goldsmith from your department asked tonight if he could be in the restaurant when they come film, but how could he know about it if not through you?"

"Wow. Jay." He made a rueful face. "That guy has got one big mouth. But yeah. It was me. All I did was fill out the application online and answer some questions, though. They would never pick the Four Treasures if it weren't a great restaurant."

Look at him, buttering up Uncle Mason! Lissie stifled another laugh. And what nonsense! "All I did was fill out the application"—as if anyone would believe his own sparkling credentials and telegenic qualities had nothing to do with it.

"Then I thank you, young man," Mason Liang said, coming down the step to shake his hand. "We can't tell you how much we appreciate it. My wife, Rhoda, and I were reading online that other restaurants got a boost from being on the show, so we're pretty excited about it."

"Sir, then I should probably also say, if your business has . . . slowed down in recent months, most likely I had a hand in that too. I don't know if Lissie told you, but after the shellfish incident with Charles's sister, Hazel, I wrote an article in the school paper, the *Stanford Daily*, about food allergies, and I mentioned the restaurant by name. I realize now it was ill-advised and unnecessary to call the Four Treasures out specifically—"

"Well, there wouldn't have been anything to write about if I hadn't been careless," Lissie broke in, defending him.

"Ah." Her uncle smiled. "I see. Maybe we can split the difference and blame both of you. We can talk more about this later. It's late. Are you coming, Lissie, or should I tell Jenny you have a ride home?"

"I'll take her," said Preston. "If that's okay with you, Lissie."

Grinning, she looked down at his hand, which was still clutched in hers. "Okay by me."

"Why didn't you come sooner? Or text me, or anything?" she demanded. "It's been almost two weeks since Seattle!" They were crammed together on the same side of a table at twenty-four-hour Happy Donuts, sharing an apple fritter and a chocolate cronut, her leg slung over his. Lissie bought the pastries as a belated birthday present.

He grinned. "You blame me for hesitating? Like you didn't tell me in January that there was no universe in which I was going to ask you out and you were going to say yes?"

Lissie groaned and covered her eyes. "I cannot believe all the mean things I said to you! But how could you still think that after the Rising Stars Meet? I'm pretty sure I gave you clear indications I'd changed my mind."

"Not to belabor it, but when someone is that brutal, the usual clear indications might not do the trick. At least not for me, they didn't. I just hoped you might want to be friends to start with. And then, maybe a few months or weeks or days or hours later, when your guard was down, I was totally going to spring my nefarious romantic intentions on you again."

"Ooh! Same! That was my plan for you," she confessed, marveling. "Lure you with casual friendship into forgetting my past abuse, and then try to appear as alluring and adorable as humanly possible."

"Well done. I'd say it worked. I was ready to take whatever you were willing to offer."

"Then why didn't you come until today? Did I traumatize you too badly, making you contact Wayman Wang?"

"That was pretty bad," he sighed. He broke a chunk off the cronut and then licked the icing from his fingers. "It dredged up a lot of things. When I got back, I went home and had a talk with my dad, which was a huge deal in itself since we had all been pretending for years that nothing had happened. But it was a good talk. Good to work through some of it."

"Did you . . . talk to your mom too?"

His face darkened, and she was sorry she asked. "Not yet," he muttered. "One day. My dad says I have to try to forgive her. I asked him what made him stick around back then, and he said he did it for me. He didn't want me to lose everything all at once: Mom, Dad, swimming. And then, after a while, it got easier. She was sorry, and he forgave her. And he said what makes it hard for me to be around her is that I haven't."

Lissie wasn't able to repress a shiver. In her book, what made Mrs. Lin hard to be around was that she was terrifying. But would she be so scary about her son if she didn't think she'd already lost him?

Thinking she was cold, he put an arm around her shoulders, and Lissie didn't object. "She did stay," she said reluctantly. "Your mom. Mrs. Yeh didn't stay in the marriage and keep the family together. But your mother did."

He ran a hand through his hair. "Or maybe Mr. Yeh was less

willing to try to get past it than my dad was."

Lissie didn't know why she couldn't keep her mouth shut or why she should try to defend Mrs. Lin who hated her, but the words came anyhow. "Yes, but you can forgive a person and it still won't make them stay."

That did it. He removed his arm from around her and was silent for a while, watching the donut guy clean the glass display case, only to head back behind the counter when a group of loud students entered, joking and shoving each other.

"It wasn't like my parents had the perfect marriage," she said, under cover of their noise. "But with them both gone, the thought of having not one, but two who love you sounds like . . . luxury." The students were flirting drunkenly, playfighting over what should be included in the dozen. *I should be fun,* she chided herself. *Not a drag who goes on and on about his mom.*

Finally, Preston said, "I'm sorry about your folks, Lissie. I really am. And I'll think about it." Fair enough. She really, truly did want Preston and his mom to reconcile, for his sake, but that would do for now. "We do have my mother to thank for one thing," he resumed more cheerfully. "After she went by the restaurant to see you—oh, yeah, I know about that, trust me—she was so mad that she showed up at my lab to tell me what she thought of you. Thank God Bronklin wasn't there. I had to smuggle her out to the parking lot so she could get everything off her chest. I won't bore you with the particulars. Judging from the play-by-play she gave me, you probably remember them pretty well without my help. But she ended by saying you admitted to sleeping with me and that you outright refused to swear you would never marry me."

Lissie sat up so suddenly her head almost knocked him in the chin. "I did *not* say I slept with you!"

"But you didn't say you didn't." He was laughing again, to her relief. "Easy, killer. I'm just saying, what I *didn't* hear in her tirade was anything I'd heard before. She said nothing about you doing any name-calling. No I-wouldn't-consider-him-if-he-was-the-last-man-on-the-planet-and-the-perpetuation-of-the-species-depended-on-us, that kind of thing."

She snorted ruefully. "Meaning, it didn't sound up to my usual level of rudeness."

"Exactly," he agreed. "Knowing my mother certainly must have come at you pretty hard, you would have had no reason to hold back. If you still hated me, I figured you would have told her so, straight up. With glee. But you didn't. And because you didn't, I thought maybe, just maybe, there really was a chance."

"So then you booked your belated birthday dinner," finished Lissie. "And nominated us for *Check, Please!* I can't believe they turned that around so fast."

"I didn't send in the application this week," he laughed. "I applied for it back in January. After you told me off. I wanted to try to help your aunt and uncle get back on their feet."

"In January? You didn't say anything."

"Why would I? You and I weren't talking, and I didn't want to get anyone's hopes up in case the application went nowhere."

The loud group of students paid for their box of donuts and made it as far as the parking lot before ripping it open. Someone dropped one, to a chorus of screams, and then suddenly, they were all pelting each other with fritters and plain-glazed and cronuts and maple bars. Lissie and Preston didn't even notice.

"Was it my letter that helped change your mind?" he asked. "Once I learned what you really thought of me, I felt like the world's biggest, most deluded ass, but I thought, if I could get you on the show, I could at least make up for tanking your family's business and exonerate myself in your eyes from having wrecked an innocent swim club and Wayman Wang's life."

"Oh, Preston. I was so amazed and flattered that you would trust me with that secret. Of course your letter changed my mind. You were barely older than JoJo when it happened. And once I sympathized with you about that, it was easy for me to see your perspective on everything, including the shellfish incident."

"No, I wasn't right about that," he said with a frown. "It wasn't your fault that I had my own run-in with Hazel's allergies when I was a kid, and it wasn't your fault I have a scary, litigious mother. Neither thing justified me laying into you like that."

"Maybe not, but it was a snap decision, and one made for good reasons," Lissie insisted, "even if I could never have guessed them. And you were totally right about me being defensive and dismissive—"

"Later, when I thought about those words, I regretted putting it like that. You apologized; you accepted responsibility. You were even, so far as I knew, fired—"

"Except I wasn't fired, as you know," she pointed out. "It was a lie."

"But you did stop working there for who knows how long. You lost income, and it hurt the Liangs' business. I did it all so thoughtlessly, Lissie. It was all about me being right and making sure everyone knew it. I'm so sorry."

She pointed a finger at him. "I refuse to let you hog all the blame. My uncle thought there was enough to go around, so we don't have to be greedy about it, or we'll have our first fight."

"Okay, okay." He took her finger and kissed the tip of it. "Go back to my letter. Does that mean you liked me better already when you came to Hazel's open house?"

"Oh my gosh," Lissie groaned. "You must have thought I was stalking you, showing up like that. But I swear I had no idea it was your condo. I really, really was looking at places for my cousin Jeremy—it's still a secret that he was looking, so don't go telling anyone."

"I won't, but why is looking for his own place such a big deal? He looks old enough to live on his own."

"Says the rich kid who already has his own million-dollar place," Lissie said, rolling her eyes.

"I don't have it anymore. I sold it, remember? But I'm not the only guy my age in the Bay Area with real estate, so why the mystery?"

"Ugh, listen to you! You can take the boy out of Los Altos Hills, but you can't take the Los Altos Hills out of the boy. Trust me on this one. Normal people our age cannot afford real estate in the Bay Area. If you stuck your head out of your bubble more often, you'd know. Jeremy didn't want to have to answer questions until it was a done deal because he earned a lot of the down payment in high school and college doing something not strictly aboveboard. Something about Chinese workers and gold farming and *World of Warcraft*. I have no idea what that's about, but if Jeremy is swearing me to secrecy, it means not just his parents, but probably the IRS and maybe the Chinese government might also have problems with it. That's why I was weird about it when I talked to you."

"Not because you were crazy about me, then?"

She tapped the back of his hand. "Well, maybe that too. And don't look so pleased with yourself."

"I can't help it. I *am* pleased with myself. The most wonderful girl I've ever met likes me back. It was an uphill battle. Many lives were lost, but the good guys won in the end."

Lissie blinked at him, an embarrassing lump clogging her throat. She must be dreaming. What if she woke up the next day, on her top bunk, staring at the stained, asbestos-laden ceiling of Château Cardboard, and discovered none of this had happened?

If none of this is real, I'll text him tomorrow. I'll take a chance. I'll tell him I love him. No, no, that will freak him out. I'll tell him I want to talk to him.

"Why are you pinching yourself, Lissie?"

"Because I'm afraid I'm asleep and dreaming."

He glanced at his watch. "I'm surprised you aren't. It's almost one in the morning, and I still have some work to do and a Masters workout at seven. I'd better take you home."

This was reassuring. People in dreams didn't say such practical things. Surely Cinderella's prince never mentioned her chores or his own fencing lessons before the clock struck midnight.

"You've gone quiet," he said, when they pulled up outside her ratty apartment complex. She shifted, and the leather upholstery of his BMW squeaked beneath her. The navigation screen still read "Lissie," where he had programmed in Unit 114. And, most unbelievable of all, there he sat beside her, enormous in the dim cabin light. The air of unreality was only increasing as her brain and body got more tired. She had worked a full shift, after all, though it felt like years ago.

But if none of this was real, then there was no harm in being totally honest, because nothing would stick.

"I'm afraid I'll wake up tomorrow, and none of this will have happened," she murmured. "Not *Check, Please! Bay Area*, not you coming to the restaurant, not us talking, not you kissing me."

"You mean we might have dreamed it all?"

"Yeah."

"That'd be too bad," he said. "Because it's a really good dream."

"What would you do?"

"Well, first I would cry a lot," he grinned. "But then I would man up and text you, to say I needed to talk to you, and it was urgent. And then by day's end, we'd get back to this point because I'd know it could be done. And I wouldn't stop until we got here."

Her own smile returned. "Oh, good. Because same here."

"So, nightmare scenario avoided. But, if this is all a dream, tomorrow morning would be Step Two."

"What would Step One be, then?"

"Step One, Elisabeth Cheng, would be to make the most of the time we have." Reaching for her, he pulled her gently to him and proceeded to do just that.

She woke the next morning, exactly as she had imagined, in her top bunk, staring up at the Madagascar-shaped water stain, her pillow folded up on either side of her head to muffle the thumping from upstairs and the blower in the street and the voices of Mel and Nelson in the kitchen, before rolling onto her side the next instant and drawing her phone up by its charging cord, like a bucket from the bottom of a well.

The tenderness of her mouth as she smiled ear to ear in relief would have been evidence enough, but there was his text from two hours earlier.

ICYMI, I need to talk to you, and it's urgent. But I'm really hoping you didn't miss it.

Lissie threw off the covers and sat up at just the right angle to avoid banging her head. Hopping down, she stretched luxuriously and grinned at her still-sleeping sister. She was fighting a delirious urge to twirl in circles and sing and shout and clang cymbals like a drum major in a one-woman marching band. Because this morning she could do anything! She could leap over tall buildings in a single bound. She could write ten Pulitzer Prize–winning plays. She could PR the City of San Jose till it outshone Paris.

Because it was a new day and a new world.

A world with Preston Lin in it.

She reached for her phone.

THIRD STATE BOOKS is the first and only general-interest publishing house that focuses solely on bringing AAPI voices, perspectives, and issues to audiences who cherish them. Through fiction and nonfiction, for adults and children, we strive to publish stories that fully represent the total Asian American experience.

Our name, "Third State," refers to the unique experience of being a bridge between cultures as Asian Americans. We proudly occupy a distinctive space and identity all our own.

Visit us at www.thirdstatebooks.com
to see our current and future titles.

And follow us on ⓞ Instagram, f Facebook, and 𝕏:
@thirdstatebooks.

We look forward to hearing from you!

THIRD
STATE
BOOKS